The volume gives an account of the origins of troubadour music and the development of European secular music.

It focuses on the Spanish cantiga manuscript and the troubadour manuscript group. A significant part of the book deals with the Arab thesis modifying the theory by asserting that Arabic poetry was but one of the mediterranean influences on the troubadours. In an important chapter the author examines with musical orientation the social history of the 13th century period of Alphonse the Wise. A special chapter is devoted to the clarification of the role of the heretic movements. The stylistical analysis of all the extant melodies of Peire Vidal and Gaucelm Faidit brings out the interesting discovery that troubadour music has archaic features that may be close to European folk music.

Z. Falvy's book has a completely new approach to troubadour music demonstrating that court music adapted to court poetry has a structure independent of the poem.

ZOLTÁN FALVY

MEDITERRANEAN CULTURE AND TROUBADOUR MUSIC

STUDIES IN CENTRAL AND EASTERN EUROPEAN MUSIC 1

Edited by

Zoltán Falvy

ZOLTÁN FALVY

MEDITERRANEAN CULTURE AND TROUBADOUR MUSIC

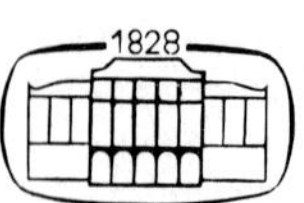

AKADÉMIAI KIADÓ · BUDAPEST 1986

ZOLTÁN FALVY

MEDITERRANEAN CULTURE AND TROUBADOUR MUSIC

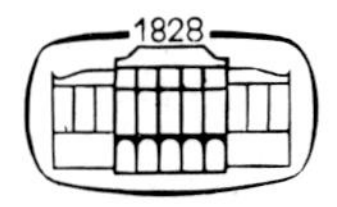

AKADÉMIAI KIADÓ · BUDAPEST 1986

TRANSLATED BY MÁRIA STEINER

TRANSLATION REVISED BY BRIAN McLEAN

Distributors for the U. S. and the British Commonwealth:

Pendragon Press
R.R.-1 Box 159
Stuyvesant, N. Y. 12173-9720 U.S.A.

Distributors for all remaining countries:

Kultúra Hungarian Foreign Trading Company
P.O. Box 149
H-1389 Budapest 62 Hungary

ISBN 963 05 4062 2

Printed in Hungary

CONTENTS

INTRODUCTION

Music played an equally important part in the development of the social history of Europe as any other field of cultural history. As a component of social history, the history of music helped mould the thinking of mankind in every age.

This book is about a period in the cultural history of Europe when music fulfilled an important function, for secular monody, both with and without instrumental accompaniment, featured in the life of every sector of non-clerical society—peasantry, urban craftsmen, landowners, provincial princes, traders, or noblemen of any rank in the ruling hierarchy from king to ordinary knight.

Secular monody had begun to develop in the 10th century. Even though there were scarcely any real climaxes in its history before the end of the 13th century, the colourful and variegated forms it assumed during the early centuries of its development indicated that it had been born as an expression of new social demands. Within its own terms, music responded in those centuries to poetic trends which had been centuries in the ripening, by creating musical forms analogous to it. These forms took shape in the Mediterranean basin and became the formal bases for European music in the centuries to come. Music and poetry, or text and melody, did not arise from one another: as society developed, they mutually affected each other, although that mutuality was not an influence but an identity of development, where one could serve as a pattern for the other, but never as a compulsory model. For the developing medieval world, in which human existence and the contours of human life were much sharper, this alliance, dialectical unity and balance between music and poetry created a new inventory of forms. One can say with Huizinga that the distance between suffering and joy, misfortune and fortune, seems to be greater. In every experience there throbbed an excessive and unconditional tension. There were fewer 'soothing balms' for destitution and physical suffering. The dividing line between sickness and health was much clearer and the cold and the gloom of winter a more tangible peril. Conversely, the pleasures of rank and riches were enjoyed more eagerly and this contrasted far more sharply with the plaintive sufferings of the poor than today. Every fact of life was proudly or ruthlessly displayed in public. Lepers swung their rattles as they walked in procession, beggars moaned before the churches and displayed their deformities. Every class in society, every order and rank, every occupation could be told by its dress. Great noblemen would never leave their homes without a retinue of armed followers and servants; fear and envy beset them on all sides. Attention was drawn with songs and processions to executions and other forms of dispensing justice, to trading, to weddings and to funerals.

If one draws the lines that intersect in the musical history of the 11th and 12th centuries, the following picture emerges: before and around the time of the Great Schism between Rome and Byzantium in 1054, the body of church music was still comparatively unified, and in character the music of both fed on Mediterranean musical sources. Taking this into account, on the one hand there is Gregorian in which (influenced by Near Eastern poetic forms) the sequence and trope were born, from the appearance of Notker at the beginning of the 10th century to Adam of St. Victor at the end of the 12th. Monophonic church music had developed into polyphony by the first half of the 12th century; the earliest organum was that of St. Martial of Limoges (1140), almost contemporary is the Spanish Compostela type, where some scholars have already identified an influence of folk-dance music, and finally there is the Parisian Notre Dame period, whose great composer-conductors are known by name.

On the other hand, there is secular monody, whose first collections are of Troubadour songs and Hispanic *cantigas*; the method of notation was still the same as for Gregorian, but it is vital for an interpretation of secular music that the presence of an instrumental culture should be recognized. During these centuries the instrumental consort was undoubtedly of Near Eastern origin, and the instruments must have influenced the musical genres they accompanied. Just as church music became polyphonic through the *organum*, so secular music became so through 'instrumental music', which in medieval practice mainly meant dance music (the *lai, virelai, rondeau* and *ballade*), in which the musical refrain form first appeared.

The scenes are the same for both: the south of France, which maintained a relationship with the Mediterranean region, as in the Hispanic lands of the Iberian Peninsula, which directly transmitted that relationship.

Let us anticipate a single example for the initiating effect of music in the relationship of music and poetry: the case of melisma. From the 10th century onwards, texts began to be written for the rich melodies so often found left without words in medieval manuscripts. From these texts developed poetical genres which represented something new and 'secular' in liturgical practice, for example the sequences. Melisma itself is a Near Eastern phenomenon transmitted by the Arabs. The earliest European manuscripts still preserved the heritage of melodies lacking a text, but this music was also capable of spawning new poetical forms which later became divorced from the original melody and developed into independent musical and poetic forms. If these new forms were in some ways analogous to Arabic and Hebrew metrical forms, these in turn were not far removed from the whole realm of Mediterranean culture.

Our task is to examine the other side: secular monody. Even though it has been preserved in the same notation as the relics of church music, and even though many see an analysis of medieval music in its entirety as the natural point of departure, since church and secular music form two sides of the same musical coin, we shall make a different approach principally because the two had different functions. The function of secular monody was to serve and entertain the court and the people living at court, as well as the burgesses and some other urban layers of society. Moreover we shall pick out two great music groups we consider fundamental: the *cantigas* of Alfonso the Wise and the music of the troubadours. We shall shed light on the latter through the musical styles of two important figures, Gaucelm Faidit and Peire Vidal, whose activities we choose to centre on also because both went to Hungary and one way or another lived for some years with Hungarian court musicians. They thus became acquainted with each other's music and each other's style of musical performance. From the stylistic traits of these two the present treatment arrives at general conclusions which are also valid for other troubadour musicians and even have a certain relevance to the method of musical construction in 12th century Europe. Although the material treated here does not allow a discussion of European folk music, trends in melodic construction at that time must nonetheless have been very close both to folk music and to art music.

The manner of playing music, that is, interpretation, cannot be adequately examined in this book, but we firmly believe that the only way to justify any theory concerning the Middle Ages is through living musical practice. In this context a key role is played by instruments which may in the Middle Ages have been used for art music, but today survive only in folk music, and whose method of sounding has remained unchanged down the ages. An important starting point for scholarship on this question is iconography, which along with ethnomusicology has proved a reliable basis for all further reconstruction. Only by following this path can the music that has survived in medieval notation be turned once again into a living music—an aim this study wishes to further.

MEDITERRANEAN CULTURE AND TROUBADOUR MUSIC

"Comparative musicology, the history of instruments, and the examination of cross-national melodies increasingly require the assistance of geographical categories, alongside those of ethnology, anthropology and history. Clearly it is no coincidence that in the last two or three decades a growing number of writings on music have appeared which rely both in their material and in their points of view on the findings of modern geography,"[1] wrote Bence Szabolcsi, and in his own discussion of pentatonic styles he established certain geographical categories: "Different pentatonic styles are born from the melodic preferences of different regions... Among these dialects one of Central Asia, one of Asia Minor, and perhaps one of the Mediterranean can be clearly differentiated."[2] On his map of musical geography, the pentatonic style marked II spread from the Near East through North Africa right up to the Iberian Peninsula. Assuming one accepts the theory of 'riparian' and 'litoral' cultures that coincide with early trade routes, the major determining influence on European music must have been the Mediterranean region. However, several awkward questions arise out of that supposition. Was the culture uniform? Did there actually exist a Mediterranean culture that exerted its effect independent of society, nations, and emerging and vanishing ethnic groups? To put it another way, if there existed a primitive pentatony appearing, for example, in a declamatory, recitative manner of interpretation, did it cover the entire Mediterranean region? If there existed in the eastern Mediterranean basin a markedly melismatic performing art that later appeared in the western part, was it a musical style, was it a formal principle, was it a type of folk expression or, to use a geographical term, was it a kind of 'Mediterranean music'? Whatever the case, great cultures developed along the shores of the Mediterranean. Discounting still earlier instrument finds, in the initial stage of our musical tradition the Ancient Hebrew, Moorish, Hellenistic Greek and Latin cultures brought forth fundamental musical phenomena which were still to be found in medieval written records. Alongside the theories propounded by P. Wagner, Lach E. Werner and W. Wiora, the musical development of the region has been charted and analysed by János Maróthy, who was the first to approach the problem with the methods of Marxist

[1] Szabolcsi (1957), p. 333. Szabolcsi wrote this chapter ('A zenei földrajz alapvonalai'—The Outlines of Musical Geography) in 1938 and lists the relevant literature in Note 1 (p. 355): works by Hornbostel, Lack, Sachs, Bartók, etc.

[2] Szabolcsi (1957), p. 35.

musicology. A characteristic example of social transformation at the end of antiquity and the related development of musical forms is the several-hundred-year history of psalmody.[3]

At the time the scene is still set in North Africa and the vehicle of musical culture is still the colonist of the Latin provinces, whose peasant song form laid the foundations of a new art-music. The new musical culture was to reach its height only in the musical forms of the Middle Ages; before that, it would be exposed to several major influences on both the northern and southern shores of the Mediterranean. On the southern shore there was a typical 'litoral' culture, on a territory more suited for transmission than for the formation of great independent centres. The territory in the period from the 7th century onwards is usually included in the Arab-Islamic cultural sphere, so providing the basis for the 'Arab theory' that is emanated through the Iberian Peninsula into Europe, a theory also applied to the early period of Troubadour music. In our opinion this view covers only one element in the matter, perhaps one of several. That its role was a dominant one is argued in an abundance of literature on the subject. But there are reasonable grounds for supposing that the culture of the North African Maghrib region, and, through the constant give-and-take with the Omayyads who conquered the Iberian peninsula (*Al-Andalus* in Arabic) the culture of the parts of Europe that bordered on the caliphate, were influenced not by an 'Arab' culture but by a Near Eastern one that developed in several layers out of the cultures of several peoples and ethnic groups. European musical history owes much to Arab musicians who arrived in Europe with the spread of Islam. Their musical interpretation and their transmission of the Ancient Greek works on the theory of music greatly influenced the revival, and indeed the very existence of European musical life. All this went hand in hand with the transmission from the one to the other of certain social conventions, primarily in courtly culture.

By Arab influence we mean not the oriental influence of a certain ethnic entity, but the *transmission* to the West of a very ancient culture, using the Mediterranean basin as the route. We place the emphasis on transmission because the culture that arrived in Europe also contained the tradition of the Latin colonists and the social norms of the Near East as laid down in the Jewish scriptures, which were incorporated in various ways, or modified, by Christianity and Islam.

When examining the social historical background of European secular monody, one must survey all the possible factors which may have been in contact with this music, the first to be noted down on paper, or which may have exerted a strong and perhaps decisive effect on the two large corpora of music to be examined: troubadour music and the *cantigas* of Alfonso the Wise.

The theories propounded at the beginning of this century primarily concern poetry, and within poetry, primarily form. In a narrower sense research into musical history is concerned to know whether there are any traces of poetic

[3] Maróthy (1960). See in particular Chap. III: 'Az énekformák átalakulása a "latin világban". A jobbágy-paraszti dal első csírái' (The Transformation of Song Forms in the 'Latin World'. The First Germs of the Serf-Peasant Song), pp. 256–366.

forms in the musical forms, i.e. to know the extent to which the two share identical means of formal development, and in a broader sense, it is concerned to know whether music and poetry shared processes of cultural history in the development of their social historical background, and to discover a theoretical basis for the florescence of secular monody in the 11th and 12th centuries.

The simplest way of examining this is to make a comparison, to match the final, mature and accomplished *musical forms* with *poetic forms*. This method runs up against terminological problems, *since musical forms cannot be labelled with the names of poetic forms*. The basis for comparison is also upset in that prosodic analysis relies upon syllable counts, final sounds of lines and their rhyme schemes, whereas musical analysis always examines the melodic line (i.e. each element in a line of melody), the structural relations of the melodic phrases, and the connection between the whole musical idea and the *final,* the last note. However, end-rhyme of prosody rarely correlates with the musical final, which as a phenomenon closing the line or a full section began to be a determining part of a musical idea in those very centuries (the 11th and 12th). Those were the centuries when deliberate musical construction began, based on Greek works of musical theory translated into European languages (mainly through Arabic).

The basis for musical and prosodic analysis can be:

1) *Grouping of notes, or one note, corresponding to a syllable*;
2) Correlation of *rhyme* and *final*;
3) *The internal construction* of poem and melody.

However, certain phenomena will appear in an identical form in both halves. Identical features can be observed in the way the structure is built up. Musically, a major constructional device, especially in the earliest records of secular monody, is repetition (line repetition) and the *refrain,* which is a higher development of the repetition principle.

Of the medieval musical forms, the following can be classed as line-repeating, refrain types:

1. *Lai* — *a*,b,c,d,e,*a* or *a,b*,c,d,*a,b* or a,a,b,b,c
2. *Estampie* — *a+b*, a, *a,b*
3. *Strophic lai* (reduced) — *a,b,c,* d; *a,b,c*
   a,b,c

   Together with three more *lai* segments, all are mentioned in musical histories dealing with the Middle Ages among the sequence types;

4. *Kanzone* (canso) — *a,b, a,b*,c,d,e,f

5. *Rund-kanzone* (Gennrich's term) *a,b, a,b,* c,d, *e,*b_2

The above two belong to the group of hymns. (The so-called *Oda continua* type, which makes up a large percentage of troubadour songs, also belongs here, although it contains neither line repetition nor refrain.)

6. *Virelai* *a,b,*c,c,*a,b,a,b,* or *a,*b,b,a,*a*
(the melody of the *Abgesang* equals the refrain)

7. *Ballad* *AB,* cd, cd, e a(B), *AB*
(2 *Stollen, Abgesang* and refrain)

Both these belong to the family of rondel types and were popular in the performance of pieces of an instrumental character.

8. *Laisse* a,a,a,a,a,a, . . . b

9. *Rotrouenge* a,a,a,b,b

These last two are the simplest line-repeating musical forms, usually classified among the litany types.

These medieval musical forms with line repetition and refrain were not only the frames for music in general in the 11th and 12th centuries but also the genres in which the earliest texts for secular monody have been put to music. (That applies equally to troubadour songs and *cantigas.*)

One cannot conceive that these final forms appeared all of a sudden among European musical forms without any forebears, or that these forms, recorded in the Middle Ages and referred to in church music as having developed under 'secular' influence (for example, the sequence type), originated in Europe. Medieval Europe merely constituted a last stage where these genres were first written down in musical notes.

However difficult it may be to compare poetic forms with musical forms and genres, the lack of musical written records means that the only way to illustrate the path of development is to use literary texts in such a manner that lessons for music can be drawn from them. To illustrate our point, we shall present excerpts from a few cultural and scientific records, without aiming at completeness. Completeness in this case would surpass the length of a chapter; the material is intended as an attention pointer.

One important source for European cultural history is the Bible, where the Song of Solomon appears between Ecclesiastes and the Prophets. The Song of Solomon is thought to originate from a time after the Captivity, around the 5th century B.C. In the Hebrew scriptures it heads the five Torah scrolls and is read at Passover. This collection of love songs is a dialogue of responses between Solomon and the Shulamite, as bridegroom and bride, and the chorus. Jewish scholars maintain it has an allegorical meaning, in that it identifies the relationship between Yahweh and Israel with the love bond between people. It consists of an introduction, five songs and a conclusion. That structure contains what may be the first appearance of the idea of a refrain: both Solomon and the Shulamite turn to the Daughters of Jerusalem for protection and care, or merely to tell them of their sorrows. This provides the frame for the first song:

Shulamite (at the beginning of the first song):

"I am black, but comely,
O ye daughters of Jerusalem,
as the tents of Kedar, as the curtains of Solomon."

(in the middle of the second song):

"I charge you, O ye daughters of Jerusalem,
by the roes, and by the hinds of the field,
that ye stir not up, nor awake my love,
till he please."

Solomon (in the middle of the third song):

"I charge you, O ye daughters of Jerusalem,
by the roes, and by the hinds of the field,
that ye stir not up, nor awake my love,
till he please."

Shulamite (in the fifth song):

"I charge you, O daughters of Jerusalem,
if ye find my beloved..."

Shulamite (at the end of the fifth song):

"His mouth is most sweet: yea, he is altogether lovely.
This is my beloved, and this is my friend,
O daughters of Jerusalem."

Shulamite (at the beginning of the eighth song):

"I charge you, O daughters of Jerusalem,
that ye stir not up, nor awake my love,
until he please."

To go beyond matters of form and formal framework, the Song of Solomon covers all aspects of the fundamental human relationship between man and woman; several hundred years later the same subject matter was to have a determining role in troubadour poetry. There is no evidence from which one can deduce whether or not the Song of Solomon was really sung or performed to a musical accompaniment, unless the words in Song 6, said by Solomon, are taken to refer to wedding dance:

> "What will ye see in the Shulamite?
> As it were the company of two armies."

The music of the North African coastline at the turn of the 6th and 7th centuries must certainly have figured large in the material collected by Pope Gregory well before the Great Schism, to create a musical frame for the Catholic liturgy of the Christian church. The corpus of plainsong (or Gregorian chant) consisted of music of the Mediterranean area. In part 'popular' and in any case generally *known,* this Mediterranean music provided the basis of the sung material for the Latin liturgy and offices, which became the first corpus of European music, to be noted down from the 8th century. Its notation system, which was one of several in use (Byzantine, Armenian, Mozarabic, etc.), soon became the sole system employed in Europe. Its signs and neums record many points of interpretation over which scholars have debated to the present day; many seek a solution to them in Mediterranean musical practice. As an example let us take Mozarabic notation, the first examples of which occur in the 10th century and the last in the 11th. Within the notation family it bears a closer relation to the ancient Byzantine and Armenian systems than to the Latin, and may have formed a link between the eastern and western systems until the end of the 11th century when the introduction of the Roman liturgy brought an end to the Mozarabic rite and its song, although some elements of it were incorporated into Roman liturgical practice.

An almost exact contemporary of Pope Gregory was the illiterate Prophet Mohammed (571–632), who founded the monotheistic religion of Islam after the Judaeo-Christian pattern and summarized in the 114 surahs of the Koran the public and civil law, the moral and ethical precepts of Near Eastern society. He took into account Jewish religious ideas to the extent of naming Jerusalem as the direction in which to pray.[4] Only later was the direction changed to Mecca in order to foster Arab nationalism. The 19th surah of the Koran contains (in 38 sections) the Prophet's instructions for the veneration of Mary, who thus came to constitute the feminine ideal for the believers in Islam.

Islam spread rapidly along North Africa and reached the Iberian Peninsula in 711, bringing the culture and social background of the Near East to Europe as early as the 8th century. By that time sporadic communication through seafarers and mercantile travellers was dwarfed by the influence of the cultural centres of the caliphate of the Omayyads in Cordoba and of the other southern Hispanic towns, which maintained constant reciprocal relations with the territories of the Maghrib in North Africa and of Provençal Occitania in southern Europe.

Before we turn to some questions that concern the Arabic poetry which reached Europe through the medium of Islam, we would like to call attention to two Occitanian architectural remains in southern France, in which Near Eastern Arab influence has been preserved to the present day. One is Toulouse and the other Moissac; both are splendid examples of Romanesque architecture and sculpture. Toulouse was one of the three main places of pilgrimage.

[4] Germanus (1962), p. 44.

Construction of the basilica with a nave, two aisles and a single transept began in 1082; major work was again done on it in 1118. The capitals are decorated with clearly Arabesque motifs. Examples are the floral patterns in the centre of each capital, surrounded by animal figures and surmounted by a narrow line of positive and negative cubes, the motifs of flowers whose heads end in small pompons, and the large pompons heading floral tracery patterns. An important development is the appearance of human figures: Daniel with lions' heads, and Lazarus, the symbol of poverty, whose depiction was associated with the reform movements and who made his first appearance here in French Romanesque sculpture.[5] The Abbey of Moissac can be traced back to the 7th century, and the double colonnade of its cloisters shows, if possible, a still clearer Arabesque influence. From the keystones over the slim double columns only a single arch begins. The Corinthian-like capitals are decorated with floral Arabesque tracery and clusters of grapes; some capitals entirely consist of small round patterns, while on others the heads of animals, mainly lions, appear in the middle of the rings. Among the abundant ornamentation human figures also appear (e.g. Gog and Magog), as does a large composition showing the scene of the wedding feast at Cana, when the water was turned into wine. Moissac was built partly of marble and partly of a kind of sandstone. It is on the softer, more easily worked stone that the Near Eastern, Arabesque motifs are to be found. Moissac also has significance for the history of musical instruments: the apocalyptic Elders on the tympanum of the main entrance (c. 1100) hold a pear-shaped violin, the originally Arab rebec or rebab in their hands.[6]

Having briefly introduced the artistic influence that spread northwards, let us now return to the relations the Cordoba Caliphate had with the lands to its south and to the constant cultural and social interactions that grew up between Andalusia and the Maghrib territories and stabilized for several centuries.

The matter will be treated from two aspects

1)

poetry and poetic forms, and

2)

aspects of social history.

The emphasis will be upon phenomena that may have directly or indirectly borne upon troubadour poetry and the social position of the troubadours. We shall also be referring to ancient Greek works of philosophy and musical theory transmitted by the Arabs, without which medieval music in Europe might well have taken an utterly different course, even though they cannot be connected directly to troubadour music.

[5] Durliat (1967), pp. 195–202.

[6] Lafargue (1938), pp. 135–216; Schapiro (1931), pp. 249–351 and 464–531; Durliat (1965), pp. 155–77.

POETRY AND POETIC FORMS

Arabic poetry constituted a much stronger bond in tribal life before Islam than after. In that early period the poet embodied the consciousness of the community, and was indeed a sorcerer: he prophesied, healed, cast spells and killed.[7] The poet and the reciter were not always the same person. Often a poet's work would be declaimed by professional reciters; a reciter might perform the works of several poets, and himself render different dialects into a uniform language. This poetry had developed in an essentially desert, tribal environment. Its unstructured, unending sequence of lines, recitative manner of performance and rhyming of identical vowels or consonants actually became the literary language of Arabic, to which the Koran gave its authority when Islam was founded. After the religion had been founded, the poems were collected from memory and 'pagan' Arabic poetry was first written down. The poetry can be divided into three main groups: panegyrics, elegies and satirical songs. Unlike the prose literature which was meant for solitary reading, the long *qasidas* were performed at evening gatherings (*samars*), with female singers present, so that poetry became the common intellectual pursuit and entertainment of a larger or smaller community. Written records of Arabic poetry, then, began in the 7th and 8th centuries, when Islam spread westwards along the North African coast and so reached Europe.

A few decades later, around 822, Ziryab, perhaps the earliest Arabic poet and singer known by name, arrived in Andalusia from Baghdad. There he trained a whole dynasty of musicians, including several members of his own family. It is related that he knew 10,000 songs by heart, and his knowledge of musical theory was compared with Ptolemy's. Ziryab is also accredited with having added the fifth string to the four-string lute used in Europe.[8]

So the early poetic forms lived on in the Arab areas of Europe, but in Andalusia one can trace the *strophic form* from the 10th century onwards, both following and existing side by side with the endless *qasidas* as a 'newer', synthetic form of Arabic poetry divided into strophes, with rhyme schemes and returning lines.

Of the two basic strophic forms, let us take first the *muwashshah,* because its three types were performed to a music accompaniment (or sung, or performed as a song with instrumental accompaniment), and still more because from the 10th century it became an extremely popular form; in fact popular *muwashshah* poems were still being published in the 20th century. It became popularized without becoming a folk form, although folk poetry was unavoidably influenced by it. The *muwashshahs* can be divided into three types which differed in their subject matter but shared a common social background of the court:

[7] Germanus (1962), p. 29.

[8] Gayangos (1840), Vol. I, pp. 410–11 and Vol. II, pp. 116–20; Hoenerbach (1970), p. 86; Hickmann (1970), p. 49.

a) the *ghazal* (song with a love theme);
b) the *madih* (eulogistic song);
c) the *khamriyya* (drinking song).

The *madih* or *panegyricus* would be recited in the audience chamber during audiences, often by the author himself. The *khamriyya* was sung at court entertainments, and so was the love song, the *ghazal,* but by girl singers.[9]

A counterpart to the *muwashshah* was the *zajal,* to which most studies that propound the 'Arab thesis' attribute the greater influence (on European troubadour poetry). Both the *muwashshah* and the *zajal* have a *refrain*, the only difference being that in the *muwashshah* the whole rhyme scheme is repeated in the refrain, whereas the *zajal* repeats only half the rhyme scheme. The refrain of the *zajal* developed from a four-line stanza where the first three lines had monorhyme with a refrain, while the fourth line rhymed with the previous refrain; indeed the same rhyme was repeated throughout the poem in the fourth line of every stanza. One *zajal* formula was: stanza—A A A B, refrain—B'B'.

The formula may vary, but its essence is the invariable relationship of the rhyme of the last line with the refrain. (Of the musical forms it is most closely related to the *virelai.*)

In the *muwashshah* a two-line introduction (prelude) is added to the structure, which closely resembles the *zajal.* This prelude is repeated after each stanza. Placing the rhyme schemes of the two refrained, stanzaic verse types side by side yields the following:

muwashshah	A A b b a a A A
zajal	A A A B B'B'

The *muwashshah* type is already known in the 10th century, when it was used by the poet al-Muqaddam al-Qabri, who lived in Cabra,[10] and it proliferated from the 11th century onwards, while the *zajal* appeared in the late 11th and early 12th centuries. The first great poet and singer to use it was Ibn Quzman (died c. 1160). He was of Moorish-Spanish extraction and mixed Spanish words into the poems he wrote in vulgar Arabic.

Rhyme, and in some cases repetition of the whole stanza, was certainly not unknown in early European Latin hymns. Around 550 this European phenomenon was used by poets such as Caesarius and Aurelianus,[10a] the 9th century *Freisinger Petrus-Lied* (Freising Song of St. Peter) also has rhymes, while important relics have also been preserved in Mozarabic hymns, and medieval poetry from Germany and the British Isles.[10b]

[9] Stern (1974), p. 44. This scholar of Hungarian extraction, who died prematurely, was one of the most eminent experts on the subject. The work quoted here was posthumously published.

[10] Stern (1974), p. 209.

[10a] Szövérffy, J.: Die *Annalen der Lateinischen Hymnendichtung, Ein Handbuch,* I. *Die lateinischen Hymnen bis zum Ende des 11. Jahrhunderts,* Berlin, 1964, p. 118.

[10b] Véber, Gy.: 'Überlegungen zum Ursprung der Zagal-Struktur' in *Studia Musicologica,* Budapest, 1979, Vol. XXI, pp. 267–76.

In discussing poetic forms, we have already mentioned that the stanzaic, refrained form traceable back to the European territories of Islam in the Middle Ages, was primarily the poetry of the courts. Even though it exerted an influence on folk poetry both in North Africa and in Andalusia, it did not itself become folk poetry. In the earliest times its link with ritual or entertainment in Islamic courts of varying rank precluded popular participation, but involved all those in the social hierarchy of the time who in any capacity took part in the life of the court. Not all the poets were Arabs. Specifically in that early, initial period one can find *muwashshahs* of Jewish inspiration and even Jewish poets who showed a preference for this refrained form. In Cairo there is a pre-10th century Geniza fragment in which the *muwashshah* can be recognized. Here are the names of some Jewish poets who lived among the Hispanic Arabs: Moshe ben Ezra wrote in Granada in Hebrew and Arabic between 1060 and 1140. Judah Ha-Levi was a most important figure, born in 1075, and active in Tudela, Toledo, Granada, Cordoba and Seville; in the mid-12th century he was living in Egypt and Jerusalem. His contemporaries included Yosef ben Saddic in Cordoba, and Abraham ben Ezra in Toledo (1092–1167). Abraham ben Ezra lived after 1136 in France, Italy and London, but his *muwashshah* poems and Andalusian songs may originate from before 1136 (all his poems were accompanied by melodies).[11]

The medieval *muwashshah,* whose constantly recurring refrain and the monotony of its refrains was reminiscent of the line-repeating form of the old *qasidas,* did not die out. It lived on in North Africa, where more poets who used it were born: Ibn Khalaf, Ibn Khazar, and Ibn al Khalluf, who was active around 1600, and whose *diwan* includes a number of *muwashshahs.* In North Africa the form was also adopted by the town musicians, and by the 18th century it had turned into a form of popular urban song. Every musician knew the music traditionally attached to it, and so there was no need for that to be written down. Only the texts were collected in manuals for the musicians. Around 1700, Al-Ha'ik compiled a collection that included many *muwashshahs,* and also touched on their interpretation: he described the musical modes (*tab*^{c}) of the Maghrib territory, each of which consisted of five parts, making up a 'concert' (*nauba*). Al-Ha'ik's manuscript inspired several similar works, the last published in 1903 in Algiers, edited by Nathan Edmond Yafil (himself a musician), under the title *Majmu*^{c} *al-aghami wa-l-alhan min kalam al-Andalus.* From the seven collections made in modern times, Miklós Stern lists the titles of 10 *muwashshahs* of medieval Andalusian origin.[12] Stern considers the collections to have preserved a still living tradition handed down from generation to generation.

Both poetic forms clearly played an important role in the development of European stanzaic poetry, and social history has shown that these types, born in a court environment, and the quasi-ritual customs that accompanied the performance of the poems spread northwards and southwards from the

[11] Menéndez Pidal (1968), pp. 84–5.
[12] Stern (1974), p. 71.

southern Hispanic centres. They spread so far that stanzaic forms with a refrain similar to the *zajal*'s can be detected in northern Spain, southern France, England and Italy, while kindred manifestations occur in troubadour poetry and the collection of *cantigas* made by Alfonso the Wise. It was partly this spread and partly the periodic strengthening of certain social strata (e.g. the role assigned to and played by the Jewish population in both the Arab and Christian parts of Spain) that led ever broader social strata to adopt the types as their own, and they may even have developed into a vernacular, a form of expression that exerted an influence on folk expression, regardless of its origin and components. Traces of it can be found in the southern Spanish flamenco, which is both a folksong type and a manner of performance (an 8-syllable, 4-line technique with virtuoso, improvised variations on the same theme at the recurring sections). A major type is the *Cante jondo,* to which the *Soleá* dance belongs. Even today its music mingles Hebrew-Arab elements into the later, flexible music of the Spanish gypsies.

In examining the aspects of social history, attention must also be paid to the philosophical works that arose out of western Arab society or shaped its social awareness. The basis of this social awareness was Islam. European Arab philosophers sought to provide believers in Islam with commentaries on the works of the Greek philosophers so as to reconcile these to the teachings of the Koran. That incorporation of Greek philosophy into the thought of the Arabs as they expanded westwards was the completion of Mediterranean culture, and thus Islamic civilization was able to draw the whole of western Europe under its influence, and from the 9th to 12th centuries Islam played an important role in shaping European social awareness, particularly at the time when the nation-states were emerging.

The first European renaissance of Greek philosophy occurred through the translations made by the Arab philosophers, who particularly concerned themselves with the works of Aristotle and Plato. They adopted from the Greeks their natural philosophy, formal logic, dialectics, rhetoric, political philosophy, biology, astronomy, psychology, magic and so on, but above all the philosophy of the Arabs became imbued with Neoplatonism,[13] which went on to affect Islamic theology and provide the foundations for Muslim mysticism (e.g. Sufism, which dissociated the absolute soul from the body). One radical Neoplatonist was the philosopher al-Kindi (d. 873), who was of Arab descent and lived under the ᶜAbbasid Caliphate.[14] Al-Kindi's works have preserved the natural philosophy of the Greeks for posterity. He accepted the philosophy of Aristotle in its entirety,[15] combined it with the Islamic mysticism of Kalam, and was the first to debate the doctrine of resurrection. In his approach to the Koran, 1. he was a rationalist on the matter of belief in one god, and 2. he managed to combine natural philosophy with the philosophy of deism. He also wrote a work of musical theory concerning the lute.[16]

[13] Walzer (1957), pp. 201–26.

[14] Guidi, M. and Ritter, H.: *Studi su Al-Kindi,* Vols I–II, Rome, 1938–40.

[15] Walzer, M. R.: *Greek into Arabic, Essays on Islam Philosophy*, Cambridge, Mass., 1962.

[16] Shiloah, A.: *Un ancien traité sur le 'ud d'Abu Yusuf al Kindi*, Tel Aviv, 1974.

Al-Farabi (died c. 950) was of Turkish extraction; he became acquainted with Aristotle at second hand through Neoplatonism. He saw both Aristotle and the Koran as embodiments of truth. In his three-chapter work *Ehvan as-Safa* he argued that society must be organized on a national basis,[17] a thoroughly modern idea for the first half of the Middle Ages. Al-Farabi criticized materialism, while his own concept of the world was irrational, visionary and metaphysical at the same time; he professed the divine triple unity of the world. His work is important to the history of music because his studies on the theory of music were translated into Latin and used in many places in the syllabus of the *quadrivium* of the seven liberal arts. Whereas al-Kindi had confined himself to making use of Greek writings on the theory of music (he translated Aristotle's *De anima* and works with a bearing on music by Aristoxenos, Euclid, Nicomachos and Ptolemy), al-Farabi compiled an original work entitled *Kitab al-musiqi al-kabir* (Great Book on Music). According to Farmer, "al-Faraby was probably the greatest writer on the theory of music during the Middle Ages."[18] Other theoretical works of al-Farabi include *Kalam fi'l-musiqi* (Conversations on Music), *Kitab fi ihsa' al-iqa*ᶜ (Book on the Classification of Rhythm) and his great compendium *Ihsa' al-ᶜulum* (The Classification of Knowledge), an encyclopaedia of all the sciences of al-Farabi's age, including music. It had an extremely wide circulation in the Middle Ages, and was translated into Latin as *De scientiis* in the 12th century by Johannes de Sevilla and Gerardus de Cremona (who actually lived in Toledo). Moses ibn Ezra (fl. 1140) also knew the work and from his time onwards it was taught in Jewish schools. In the 14th century it was even translated into Hebrew by Qalonymos ben Qalonymos. In Arabic one 13th century and three 14th century copies have survived. In al-Farabi's classification system music is placed after grammar and logic, among mathematical sciences like arithmetic, geometry, optics, astrology, statics and mechanics. Farmer (in the study mentioned earlier) publishes one of the Arabic versions and compares the texts of all extant Latin translations: here is Farmer's list of sources for al-Farabi's music section in Latin translation:

- A Gerard of Cremona: *De scientiis* (Bibl. Nat. Paris, No. 9335. 148–148_v—13th century)
- B John of Seville: *De divisione omnium scientiarum* (British Mus. London, Cotton MS. Vesp. B.X.—13th century)
- C John of Seville: *De scientiis* (In Camerarius, Alpharabii vetustissimi Aristotelis interpretis..., Paris 1683, pp. 23–5)
- D Vincent of Beauvais: *Speculum doctrinale* (Venice 1494. Lib. XVII. Cap. XV.)
- E Jerome of Moravia: *Tractatus de musica* (Coussemaker, Scriptorum de musica medii aevi... Paris 1864–76. Tome I., Lib. I.)
- F Gundissalinus: *Compendium scientiarum* (British Mus. London, Sloane 2461, fol. 26–27_v—13th century)

[17] Walzer (ms.).
[18] Farmer (1934), p. 4.

G Gundissalinus: *De divisione philosophiae* (British Mus. London, Sloane 2946, fol. 214–214_v—13th century)
H Pseudo-Aristotle (Coussemaker, Scriptorum de musica medii aevi . . . Tome I., Lib. VI.)
J Pseudo-Bede: *De musica quadrata* (Bede, Opera . . . omnia, Cologne 1612.)
K Simon of Tunstede: *Quatuor principalia musicae* (Coussemaker, Scriptorum . . . Tome IV., Lib. II.)

So there exist in fact two 12th century Latin translations of the 10th century Arabic source. Here are a few lines from the manuscript of Gerard of Cremona (Farmer's Source A), which shows the unity of theory and practice, and the use of instruments (for al-Farabi was not only a theorist but a practising musician):

> Scientia vero musicae, comprehendit in summa, cognitionem specierum armoniarum, et illud ex quo componuntur, et illud ad quod componuntur, et qualiter componuntur, et quibus modis oportet ut sine donec faciant operationem suam penetrabiliorem, et magis ultimam. Et illud quidem quod hoc nomine cognoscitur, est due scientiae. Quam una est scientia musicae activa, et secunda scientia musicae speculativa. Musica quidem activa, est illa cuius proprietas est ut inveniat species armoniarum sensativarum in instrumentis que preparata sunt eis aut per naturam aut per artem. Instrumenta quidem naturalia, sunt epiglotis et uvula et que sunt in eis deinde nasus. Et artificialia sunt sicut fistule et cithare [in Sources B, D and F "corde"], et alia. Et opifex quidem musice activa, non format neumas et armonias, et omnia accidentia eorum, nisi secundum quod sunt in instrumentis quorum acceptio consueta est in eis . . . etc.[19]

The excerpt includes the names of two instruments: the *fistula* and the *cithara*. Curiously enough, the same two instruments (plus the military bugle) are mentioned in the *Gesta* of Anonymus of Hungary in his description of the Hungarian conquest of their new homeland in the Carpathian Basin. Anonymus studied abroad (in Paris), where he may have become acquainted with this text in the *Quadrivium*. The *fistula* has been translated into Hungarian as *síp* (pipe) and the *cithara* as *koboz* (a type of lute). This is not the occasion for discussing matters of translation into Hungarian, even from the point of view of music, but the basic lesson is that the *fistula* was clearly a woodwind instrument and the *cithara* either bowed or plucked, but in any case a stringed instrument.

To return to Hispanic literature on the theory of music (which sheds a concurrent and interesting light on other matters of concern to social history), several authors mention the names of instruments in use; these recur as iconographical survivals in the manuscript of Alfonso the Wise and spread throughout Europe in the 12th and 13th centuries. Another writer to describe instruments was Ibrāhīm aš-Salālū, whose *Kitab al-imtāᶜ wa'l-intifā' fī mas'alat*

[19] Farmer (1934), pp. 20–1.

sam^c al-sam^c[20] has been translated and commented on by Farmer.[21] Elsewhere we shall go into the question of instruments in detail (see The Spanish Centre of Secular Monody: The Court of Alfonso the Wise).

What remains to be done here is to assess the extent and nature of the Arab influence.

Burdach[22] and Ribera[23] have taken a passionate stand in favour of the 'Arab Thesis', and turned up a quantity of phenomena and documentation; as a result they have committed themselves to tracing the medieval manifestations of European music, particularly the origins of troubadour music, from the presence of the Arabs in Europe, and to attributing the development of troubadour music to the influence of Arabic poetry and Arab music. Around the poetry major debates have raged, but these have scarcely touched the music, which has been conceived of as an organic part of the poetry. Scholars have contented themselves with noting the overall correspondence of mensural notation or modal rhythm with poetic forms. Only a few have realized that it is this musical interpretation that rules the 'Arab Thesis' out of troubadour music.

In our opinion the matter cannot be decided by questions of chronology, since it is not certain that the whole sphere of a type was influenced by a phenomenon of which earlier records or documents bear witness. In the line of thought taken so far we have sought to show how Arab culture bore with it, as it spread into western Europe, all that had played a decisive role in the development of the Mediterranean world, how it transmitted to the western Mediterranean the cultures which had evolved in the eastern region, and then passed them over to the countries of western Europe. At the same time we seek to show how that cultural expansion was temporal as well as spatial, in that it lasted from Antiquity into the Middle Ages and its vehicles were not only the Islamic Arabs but also the Hispanic strata of society living under either the Arab caliphate or the northern courts of Castile, Leon and Aragon.

Though the significance of the *transmission* cannot be underrated, one must also note that the *social vernacular* might equally have developed without copying anything (either social customs or poetic forms). Something similar might have arisen for the simple reason that society was making similar demands, that certain phenomena were producing a social demand.

From that point of view significance must be attached to the formative (and thus determining) role of musical geography. At any time social demand may differ from social stratum to social stratum, but to take an example, the depiction of instruments in the *cantigas* bears out that folk instruments were being used as much by court society as by the peasantry, and *vice versa*: the *cantigas* that emerged from the court fulfilled more than the court's social demands; judging from their subject matter, they were intended for wider use—

[20] Perkuhn (1973), p. 134.
[21] Farmer (1925).
[22] Burdach (1925).
[23] Ribera (1923–5); Ribera (1929).

for simpler people taking part in pilgrimages. Some melodies may also have fulfilled the role of a medieval 'song of the masses'.

What determined the function of troubadour poetry were the demands of Occitanian society. Poetry and music were required by the environment of a court. The social background of the troubadours is so motley because their career was a means by which anyone might succeed. Yet no troubadour was obliged to copy the metrical forms popular in the Arab caliphate merely because the social demands of the court were the same in both places. If the refrain form appeared in both, it meant that after long centuries of development the type was maturing at the juncture into a vernacular. The rising demand for music caused by the poetic refrain types can be considered as a natural stage in the development, for the two arts had always been closely connected, even though comparing them poses problems. It is a historical fact that the types of instruments originated in the Near East and were in part transmitted to Europe by the Arabs. It is equally a fact that a considerable number of those instruments had been in constant use in European art music since the earliest times, when they had been used to accompany monody. They were also used on processional occasions at court, and they were available for entertainment; in examining relationships or influence one must not only discover the route by which they spread from Spain, one must realize also (particularly in the initial period) that the structures of the instruments remained unchanged wherever they appeared. The structure of an instrument determines the way it is sounded; moreover, it delimits the *potential for interpretation.* To overstate the question raised by the Arab Thesis, one might say that the matter of instruments is the only 'tangible' component in the question of Arab influence, since one can compare depictions of instruments used at that time as well as specimens still used by folk musicians today. When a troubadour musician became acquainted with a three-stringed rebec (al-Farabi's *cithara* type, in the interpretation of the Latin translation), he also learnt the performing style of the rebec. That style cannot be separated from the medium of transfer. The way that style developed further is another matter; for example the Arab 'violin' was held *vertically* and bowed horizontally, while violin-type instruments in Europe were placed on the *shoulder,* and only some centuries later did some bowed types (like the *gamba* family) return to a vertical playing position (which can no longer be attributed to Arab influence, of course).

As far as instruments are concerned, one can see a direct and undiminished Arab influence on troubadour musicians up to the end of the 12th century, and that, too, links the whole question to the geographical area of Mediterranean culture. To go on from there one can only discuss the part played by the troubadours at court, their service, and their poetic and musical satisfaction of the court's social and political requirements as a component in a major social phenomenon in which the troubadours' part did not differ from that of the entertaining stratum at any feudal court. The seat of a caliphate and a feudal princely household may not be strictly comparable, but in any case a court in

Aragon or Toulouse bore a resemblance to an Arab court in southern Spain not because it wished to imitate it but because both had to perform the same functions. Among these functions music and poetry invariably featured, and through them a broad section of society was brought close to sovereignty—political as well as cultural purposes were served. "Their songs in many instances reflect conditions and events in the social and political world of the time."[24]

In troubadour poetry there was a special genre for political subjects and opinions: the *sirventés* (Provençal *sirven* 'servant'), or in its shorter form, the *cobla*. However, political subjects might be treated in other forms as well. The *tenso* served for dialogues between poets, and poetic contests, but if troubadours wanted to conduct their dialogues in a form other than alternating stanzas and display their style in full poems, they might use the *partimen* or the *joc-parti*. There was also a genre called the *planh* (plaint) written at the death of a friend, an esteemed patron or a lady. For love themes, homage to a woman, the liege lady, or womankind as a whole there were the *canso*, the *pastourelle* (knight and shepherdess theme) and the *alba*. (The dawn-song type was also found in Arabic poetry, but without the vigil-keeper element; and with a different conceptual content than was given to it by the troubadours, it can be detected as early as in the Song of Solomon.) Virtuosity and ingenuity as exhibited in diplomatic political poetry and in the elaborate language of the love theme, were two applications of the same skill, the *ars bene dicendi*.

To play his part at court and to observe the system of requirements of *curtoisie*, a poet needed certain 'virtues' and 'qualities': he had to be capable of expressing his art well and appropriately, so that it accorded with the delights of elevated conversation (*bels digz plarens* and *solatz*); a troubadour had to be temperate in all things (possess *mezura* and *cauzimen*); there was also a need for generosity (*largueza*), for that was the main foundation of the troubadour's way of life, although it was a dangerous virtue for the feudal economy; the supreme virtue (*valor*) was the veneration of women, but that is a simplistic description, since it developed into such a cult that poetry without the ideal of women became inconceivable. The dominant factor was *aesthetic morality*,[25] for according to the poetry women came to play a major part in the society of the age. Thus the veneration of women by society grew to a peak by a process that had begun far back in history. The veneration of women by medieval secular culture had no new features compared to early tribal matriarchy and the subsequent Marian trend in the theology of the monotheistic religions. It also accorded with the traditional practice of Mediterranean culture, whilst it came about under different social conditions on the soil of feudalism.

Unlike the exponents of the secular genres developed within ecclesiastical literature, the troubadour consciously professed his poetic personality, and by doing so furthered the development of literate medieval society. A troubadour needed a great store of knowledge and also a good memory, if one remembers

[24] Reese, G.: *Music in the Middle Ages*, London, 1941, p. 205.
[25] Jeanroy (1934–5), Vol. I, p. 97.

that he could be called upon to perform, for instance, the long series of *lais* that made up a heroic song. Not all were capable of doing so, whence there arose the need for *writing*, and another person had to be involved in the interest of *good performance*.

Writing. Of the troubadour manuscripts those marked *D* and *V* show individual manners of writing. In some cases a *Vida* will also record that a troubadour wrote down his poems.[26] In the 12th century Arnaut de Tintignac wrote in one of his poems (Pill. 34.2): "Here is my poem, successfully completed. Now all it needs is a talented singer. O Clerk, dear in God, pray write this down!" To a *trobar clus* poem (Pill. 174. 8.) Gavaudan added the following dedication: "This poem is good, if someone will write it down well."

Knowledge of the texts could not be neglected (nor could knowledge of textual rhythm, rhyme or music), otherwise so many *contrafacta* could never have been made, since to make a *contrafactum* the melody had to be known as well. Melodies were constructed on the principle that the notes and note-groups of a melody were determined by the syllables of the text. Without the melody a poem was only determined by the number of syllables, rhyme and rhyme scheme of the stanzas, which was insufficient. The melody determined the length of the poem, even where from a textual point of view there was no rhythmic determinant in the melody and the finals of the musical lines did not influence the rhyme scheme of the lines of text. When an imitator chose himself a model formula for producing a new poem, he did so in the knowledge that the model of the first stanza would commit him to expressing his theme in a similar form throughout the whole poem; the scheme as it appeared in the first stanza would run through the whole poem, and for a counterfeiter to express his new message in one single formula throughout was no easy task. Frank has argued that the troubadours took writing far more seriously than is generally supposed.[27] There is an important lesson in the practice of counterfeiting: the originals were respected and the form considered the property of the original author, even though free use was made of it.

Performance. This forms a major and fundamental concern for historical research into both poetry and music. From a musical point of view, what we initially have in mind is not the field of interpretation, but that of written sources, terminological matters and iconographical records that may clarify the sphere of activity partly of the troubadour and partly of the *jongleur*. In the art of the troubadour, poetry and music are twin components of equal rank. One cannot be conceived of without the other. While a single person may have sufficed for performance, few troubadours possessed all the abilities required for the 'full' presentation of a poem. The term *jongleur* occurs frequently in connection with matters of performance; P. Beck writes the following:

[26] Frank (1967), p. 490.
[27] Frank (1967), p. 491.

> Ces . . . terms (jongleurs et troubadours) en effet ne sont pas synonymes. Si les Biographies désignent parfois le même personnage indifféremment par l'un ou l'autre mot, c'est par suite d'une confusion que certains troubadours se sont plu à entretenir, mais que la plupart d'entre eux, plus soucieux de leur dignité, ont bien vite cherché à faire disparaître.[28]

So the two terms did not mean the same thing. In the chapter on Alfonso the Wise we shall describe in detail a classification proposed by the last 'great' troubadour, G. Riquier, who refers to the practice developed in the 13th century asking the king to intervene and ensure that due respect is accorded to the "dignity" of the troubadour, and to sustain that "lawful" respect by means of a decree.

When considering the sense or value attached to these two terms by contemporaries, one must take into account that the troubadour devised or invented (*trouve, troba*) his subject and created (*crée*) his work in a musical and poetical sense, whereas the *jongleur* (Occitanian *joglar,* Old French *jogler*) derived from the Latin *joculator*, was a joking jester who in a narrower sense performed feats of strength and sleight of hand at fairs. In the 12th and 13th centuries the *jongleur* followed the troubadour's example and began to sing poems (i.e. do the job of a troubadour) in order to climb a rung of the social ladder. But even though a *jongleur* would perform a troubadour song and so exercise his ability to interpret poetry and music, he created nothing new.

At this point it is worth recalling the tribal practices of the pagan Arabs in the Near East. Though no direct relationship or actual continuity need be posited for the two phenomena, among the Arabs the poet expressed the intellectual life of the community. Each tribe had its own poet, whereas the reciter (*ráwi*) was merely an interpreter of the poet's works. Later it was the *ráwis* who adjusted to a linguistic standard the poems written in different dialects.

There is also a Hungarian angle on the *jongleur* (*joculator*) which should not be neglected. Anonymous in his *Gesta* at the end of the 12th century has obviously followed the French example in using the term *joculator* for the interpreter. He knew no other expression for performers of folk poetry as a vehicle of historical tradition than *joculator,* the common Latin term used in France. When he added that "false tales" had been performed by *our* joculators, he gave a credit to the *Hungarian jongleurs* who *performed but did not create.* (This subject is dealt with in more detail in the chapter on the Hungarian court.)

If one is seeking the relationship between court culture and folk poetry, the activity of the *jongleur* is one of the major questions in the social history of music in the Middle Ages. Every researcher has stressed that troubadour poetry is not folk poetry and troubadour music is not folk music. But having been convinced of that, one still cannot ignore the question of how wide or how narrow were the strata of society familiar with the creations of that poetry and that music. The troubadours themselves came from an extremely broad spectrum of society and

[28] Bec (1970), p. 13.

from a great variety of different regions and towns. Wherever they went and whatever new or higher social strata they entered, they brought with them a cultural foundation—a social background. They had left their original environment behind, and they would not have remained in the service of the court if they had not been able to adapt themselves to its demands, but by their assimilation they became successful 'self-made men' whose consciousness of their own talents and creativity prevented them from considering their patrons as their absolute masters. No troubadour would hesitate to change his patron if it became expedient. His subordination lasted only so long as he was free to express his thoughts, and his very talents ensured him that full independence. But the troubadour's scope for movement and independence were confined within a single sphere: the environment of the court, whereas the *jongleur* could earn his living anywhere; if necessary he might enter the service of a troubadour, but without one he would not starve. Left with no troubadour, a *jongleur* would perform the poems and songs he had learned wherever people would listen to him: at other castles, in other towns, in other regions, or amid the hurly-burly of the fair. In this way a high proportion of troubadour songs were able to reach the common people; though they might not become folk music, the *jongleurs* made them known to far wider circles than merely the participants or potential participants in the social life of a court. The *jongleur* was the only man who could convey the latest poetry and music from the castles and manor houses to the common people, to the market-place; at the same time he was the man who could acquaint the troubadours, divorced from their original environment, with the songs and stories popular among the people, i.e. he was the vehicle of transmission.

In the closing section of my book I shall analyse the full musical material of two troubadours. During the work I encountered a number of typically archaic manners of melodic construction, for example the descending melodic line, which has also survived in many folksongs classed as archaic. However, that does not imply a direct link between troubadour music and the older layer of folk music, although it shows that from a musical point of view troubadour music was not so far removed from medieval European music in 'current use' (e.g. the great medieval instrumental forms: the *lai,* the *virelai* and the *ballade*) as a type of art music category might be from folk music. Another important distinction from art music is the 'floating' melody and tonal uncertainty of troubadour music (which is frequent in the repertoires of the two troubadours analysed in this book). In essence the melody hovers between modality and tonality: the tonality is also stressed by the sounding of the leading note before the final. (In this context it is still difficult to describe the final as a tonic.) However, such uncertainty is not characteristic of Europe; it points outward to the musical phenomena of Mediterranean culture.

Summary

In the course of the development of troubadour music and medieval secular monody, we have not sought a *single* point of departure among the precedents and patterns, nor have we examined the influence of a single metrical form or social practice. The intention has been to demonstrate that medieval European music, particularly the refrain type, became a final stage that determined the direction of further development and Mediterranean culture. Troubadour music arose after several centuries as a slowly developing product *common* to several strata of society. These results stemmed from music, then from the interaction of poetical and musical forms, and from the joint poetical and musical activities of those social strata. The road had led from the Near East along the northern coast of Africa to Spain. There it had mingled with the culture of Europe to produce the 'new' forms which conquered the countries of western Europe. Those forms permeated every domain of music, not leaving the Gregorian repertoire unaffected. But their greatest effect was upon secular music, both instrumental music and the most remarkable body of vocal monody: the music of the troubadours.

THE SPANISH CENTRE OF SECULAR MONODY: THE COURT OF ALFONSO THE WISE

(TROUBADOURS, MOORS, JEWS AND ARABS)

The court of the House of Aragon became a major centre of troubadour art as early as the mid-12th century. In fact it was more than a centre, it was a home and a refuge for the troubadours from the campaigns against the Albigensians. King Alfonso II (1162–1196), himself a troubadour, was an eminent troubadour patron; poets and musicians were likewise welcomed by his successor, Pedro II (whose sister, Constanza, was sent to Hungary). But all branches of the arts came to flourish fully at the court of Alfonso X of Castille (called the Wise, whose wife Jolanta was the granddaughter of the Hungarian King András II). The name of Alfonso the Wise is linked with the mid-13th century Cantiga Manuscript, which contains more than 400 melodies and important illustrations of contemporary musical instruments. Since it reflects the literary and musical practice of a still earlier period, the melodies and instrumental depictions to be found in the codex provide an interesting account of the complexities of cultural history in the Iberian Peninsula, and it constitutes one of the major sources for the links between Mediterranean culture and certain aspects of troubadour music, and between the instrumental culture of the Mediterranean countries and the development of European instrument types.

István Frank (an eminent Hungarian researcher into troubadour and *trouvère* literature, who worked in France) found in Spanish literary sources the names of 50 Provençal troubadours who lived for longer or shorter periods on the Iberian Peninsula, along with those of 15 Catalan troubadours who wrote in the Provençal language.[1] But these figures decrease if one only considers the number of troubadours whose melodies have survived. At the court of Aragon the troubadours found a favourable climate and another reason for their concentration was the dispersal caused by the historical situation which developed north of the Pyrenees. The war against the heretical Albigensians scattered the troubadours in three directions: towards northern France, northern Italy and the Iberian Peninsula. It is worth mentioning that in the first half of this century students of European social history attributed the Near Eastern and Arab influence to the crusades. But of the 450 troubadours whose names are on record, only ten actually went to the East and one of them only took part in the 4th, or Balkan, Crusade, which brought the Latin Empire of Constantinople into being. He was Raimbaut de Vaqueiras (1180–1207), who

[1] Frank (1967), p. 494; Frank (1950), pp. 63–81.

set his poems to a great variety of different musical types. One should add that the crusade song represents a separate genre only from the textual, not the musical point of view. In terms of the latter, crusade songs normally belong to the hymn or litany types.

It was necessary to say all this as this chapter aims to refuse the old romantic views. For here in close proximity to troubadour poetry there flourished a Near Eastern culture which had spread in all its variety along the Mediterranean to Aragon and Castille. So the culture and courts of the Iberian Peninsula were more than just a refuge and source of patronage for the troubadours; during their travels in Spain they encountered new cultural horizons which left marks upon their poetry, music and musical performance, and strongly influenced the way they worked.

In the mid-12th century none of the early troubadours visited Spanish soil—neither Guillaume IX, nor Marcabru, nor Jaufre Rudel, Bernart de Ventadorn, nor even Beatriz de Dia. The first to do so was Bertran de Born, just as the first campaigns against the Albigensians were beginning (around 1180). In the next couple of years he was followed by Giraut de Borneill, Floquet de Marseilla, the singer and friar Montando, and somewhat later, though still in the reign of Alfonso II, by Peire Vidal and Gaucelm Faidit. Thereafter came Aimaric de Peguillan, Pistoleta and Romain de Miraval (perhaps even after the 1200s). The largest group left Provence around 1230.

It is difficult to set exact time limits, because the *vidas* only allow the periods of active creativity to be determined. They rarely record other dates in a troubadour's life. In the 1230s the Inquisition operated throughout the Albigensian areas and persecution of Catharist sympathizers became increasingly cruel. One can be sure that most of the troubadours sought refuge in Aragon or Castille in this final period, including Perdigo, Gui d'Uisel, Guillem Magret, Cadenet, Peire Cardenal, Aimeric de Belenoi, Albertet de Sestaro, Pons d'Ortafas and the highly prolific Guirat Riquier, who wrote almost 50 melodies.

Of the troubadours who travelled in Spain, the poems and biographical details of Cadenet and Riquier prove a conclusive connection with the court of Alfonso the Wise and all the cultural and intellectual currents that characterized it. Of Cadenet's work only a single poem with melody has survived.[2] The melody has been published by Gennrich, but in an 'interpreted' transcription, corrected in certain places.[3] The song begins "S'anc fu belha ni prezada" (Pill. 106.14); in form it can be classified among the *Oda continua* group of hymn types, but the repetition of its first melodic line means it is not far removed from the *Kanzone* either. In the Cantiga Manuscript of Alfonso the Wise it features as No. 340, under the title "Virgen, madre groriosa". Apart from Gennrich, H. Anglès has also analysed it in detail.[4] In the fascimile edition of the Cantiga Manuscript

[2] Appel (1920), p. 80 of text edition.

[3] Gennrich (1958), p. 173.

[4] Anglès (1964), pp. 351–2.

there appears before Song No. 340 an instrumental picture showing two peasant musicians blowing straight flutes. The poor quality of the publication precludes a precise description of the two instruments, but their type can be clearly seen. Although *cantigas* are not normally associated with instruments, the question arises as to whether the placing of an instrumental picture at a certain point in the codex was delibrate. In the case of Cantiga No. 340, which can be identified with an interesting troubadour melody, some remarkable ligature-conjunction solutions are found. From that the connection between instrument and melody might be self-evident, but the earlier transcriptions in modal rhythm, or in a different rhythm, blur the character of the music. The 'neutral' reading of the melody here used brings the note picture nearer to the possible folk interpretation implied by the illustration. Here the interpretation of Gennrich,[5] the transcription by Anglès[6] and the solution we suggest are compared:

[5] Gennrich (1960), p. 91.
[6] Anglès (1943).

ANG.
san - ta no - - bre pre - ci - o - - sa
GEN.
Quen te lo - ar sa - be - ri - a
ANG.
quen te lo - ar sa - be - ri - a
GEN.
Ou po - di - - - a
ANG.
ou po - di - - - a
GEN.
Ca Deus, que e lũa et di - a
ANG.
Ca Deus que é lũ - a et di - a

Anglès published the *cantiga* in 1934, and he transcribed the allegedly mensural notation into the 2nd type of modal rhythms: *Modus Jambus,* with an iambic opening. He realized that the basically triple time was insufficient and substituted a twofold definition: 4(3). In this way he was able to do everything but force the ligatures, primarily the compound ligatures, into an exact metre.

These places he bridged over with subjective intuition. Gennrich opted for a different method: he tried his hand at the 5th mode, the *Modus Spondeus,* thus developing a rhythmic picture quite differing from Anglès', and his interpretation (at several points crudely contrasting from the latter's) maintained the same melodic line but resulted in a totally new melody which was quite mistaken as to its note picture. One only has to look at Bar 3 of Line 8, where the original note picture of a *virga* and a *climacus* (ending with a distrophic formula that closes with a *plica*) corresponds to two syllables; Gennrich devised a most complicated rhythm:

At the same place Anglès made a division into two bars:

Neither conveys the ease of movement that the manuscript shows is so clear and simple. This matter has been touched upon only because the imposition of 'theory' resulted in reconstructing one and the same melody in two conflicting manners.

For comparison with Cadenet's troubadour song, we shall use a 'neutral' transcription. Let us first give the two melodies, followed by the two texts.

al - - ba

Cadenet	Cantiga 340.
S'an fui belha ni presada	Virgen, madre groriosa
Qu'a un vilain sui donada,	De Deus, filla et esposa,
Tot per sa gran manentia:	Santa, nobre, preciosa,
E murria,	Quen te loar saberia
S'ieu fin amic non avia,	Ou podia?
Cuy disses mon marrimen;	Ca Deus, que é lun'e dia,
E, guaita plazen,	Segund' a nossa natura
Que mi fas son d'ALBA?	Non viramos sa figura
	Se non por ti, que fust'ALVA

In Cadenet's text we meet one of the early *Albas.*[7] The texts and the links between them have been analysed by Spanke.[8] Although according to biographical information on Cadenet he was in Spain before the *cantigas* were collected, the *cantiga* melody antedates the first record of the Cadenet song as such (which occurs in Provençal Manuscript *R* in the Bibl. Nat. franç., Paris: 22.543). The relationship between the two melodies is absolutely clear, and their structure is identical: A A B C D E C F G. The *cantiga* only differs insofar as its first five lines would be repeated after every stanza, so that the troubadour *Oda continua* has been altered by Alfonso the Wise into a *rondel* type.

Cadenet's sole surviving melody indicates the significance of the Cantiga Manuscript for the mid-13th century, even for troubadour music. In Cadenet's case music formed the connecting link between the literature of the troubadours and the cultural history of the Iberian Peninsula.

Guiraut Riquier, on the other hand, actually spent the decade from 1269 to 1279 at the court of Alfonso the Wise. He was the last of the 'great' troubadours, and 47 of his poems have survived, with their melodies. Characteristically all his melodies are found in a single codex, the Provençal Manuscript *R* (Bibl. Nat. franç., Paris: 22.543). This is all the more interesting as the collecting of troubadour songs already began during his lifetime with the compilation of the mid-13th century Lotharingian Manuscript X. (see the chapter on the methods of troubadour song notation). However, *X* contains no songs at all by Riquier, which would lead one to suppose they were not known in those northern parts.

The literature on troubadour music has ascribed no special significance to the interpretational practice of the day. Mention is generally made of the troubadour being accompanied by a *jongleur,* who was either an instrumental musician, or a singer, or perhaps both. Certainly not all troubadours were musicians, nor did they have to be, as their primary task was to exhibit their

[7] Schmidt (1881), p. 331; Stengel (1886), pp. 407–12; Scudieri (1943), pp. 191–202.
[8] Spanke (1958), pp. 217–18.

talents through their poetry. To be able to perform their poems, or compose melodies for them, counted as an additional virtue. Since most types of troubadour poetry (e.g. the *kanzone, alba, pastourelle,* and *sirventes*) could not be conceived of without music, the poet had to provide the conditions for their performance. There certainly must have been misunderstandings over the remuneration of the participants, who claimed similar rights to those of the troubadours who brought forth the poems. (This primarily concerned donations.) The confusion must have been great, for Riquier came forward at the court of Alfonso the Wise with an appeal for a decree to regulate the categories of troubadour, and that may have implied differences in payment as well. His epistle of 1274, beginning "Pos Deus ni a dat saber", seeks to distinguish four groups, which in ascending order of status were

1)

jongleurs, whom he described as fair showmen, tightrope-walkers and animal-tamers;

2)

menestrels (minstrels), whom he called singers and propagators of songs, with a knowledge of poetry;

3)

troubadours, who devised and composed the songs; and

4)

doctor troubadours (*doctores de trobar*), who were the most respected and outstanding of the authors.[9]

Riquier must certainly have based his classification on his own experience, and there is no reason to doubt that he took the examples from actual life at the court of Alfonso the Wise. Yet, as far as the *jongleur* was concerned, Riquier's description can hardly have accorded with the truth. A medieval *jongleur* was not merely a fair showman, tightrope-walker or animal-tamer. Guiraud de Calanson, a contemporary and for a period a close acquaintance of Riquier's, described the things a *jongleur* had to know and the instruments he had to play:

> Sache bien trouver et bien rimer, bien parler, bien proposer un jeu-parti. Sache jouer du tambour et des cliquettes et faire retentir la symphonic. Jongleur, sache jouer de la citale ou sistole et de la mandole, manier la manicarde et la guitare qu'on entend volontiers; garnir la roue avec sept cordes jouer de la harpe et bien accorder la guigue pour égayer l'air du psaltérion.[10]

[9] Gennrich (1965), p. 80; Stäblein (1975), p. 81.
[10] Cordes (1975), p. 75.

That was a huge scope of knowledge and range of instruments, and included nearly all the requirements for the first three of Riquier's categories. By transferring this whole group of questions to the person of Alfonso the Wise, and through him to his court, one can discern within them a flourishing cultural centre of equal poetic and musical importance.

Alfonso X, the Wise, is considered one of the major kings in Spanish history. He led several campaigns against the Moors, he commissioned a history of the country and an attempt was made at his court to compile a universal history as well; he had the Bible translated, he was well versed in chemistry and philosophy, and he founded at Salamanca a university with a famous school of music (to whose organist he paid 50 *maravedis* a year). In addition to all that, Alfonso was a poet who wrote in several Galician dialects. No traces remain of his abilities as a composer, but his musical discrimination is all the clearer from the Cantiga Manuscript, one of the largest and most famous collections of songs in medieval social history, containing in all more than 400 pieces. That manuscript is the richest storehouse of European secular monody.

He was crowned as King Alfonso X of Castille and Leon in 1252, at the age of 31. The power of the Moslem Arabs on the peninsula had almost been eliminated; the last Almohads had been driven out of Spain in 1225 and forced to settle in North Africa. The small states they had founded in southern Spain (such as Cordoba, Valencia, Seville and Cadiz) surrendered one by one to Spanish rule. Moorish power prevailed only in Granada and its surrounings, where it had been established in 1231 by Muhammed al Ahmer I, who maintained his independence only by recognizing the kings of Castille as overlords, which also entailed a permanent cultural and political relationship. The construction of the Alhambra in Granada was also started in the 13th century, and although Cordoba, the seat of the caliphate, fell to the Spaniards in 1236, Arab mystics, writers and singers continued to be active. Indeed, Alfonso the Wise himself seemed to consider that the sole way to achieve cultural development was to collect all who pursued the arts at his own court. The great Cantiga Manuscript and several other phenomena witness that he surrounded himself with scholars, writers and musicians from various social strata, men who had played similar important roles in the Caliphate. The whole realm of Arab and Mediterranean art could be found in the Caliphate of Cordoba, and similarly, Alfonso's court included, besides the troubadours, a number of Moorish, Jewish and Arab writers and musicians whose arts enriched the culture of the Iberian Peninsula and was transmitted by it to Europe. In the arts are included works of theory, forms of literature and poetry, types of instruments, occasions for music making, and interpretational techniques, in short all the phenomena that could be called a common 'musical vernacular' of Mediterranean culture. At the court of Alfonso the Wise, every kind of music and poetry was free to exist, although Alfonso subordinated their manifestations to his own ideology, and content and form so complemented each other that many issues of the social history of the 13th century found their place there. For musical history his greatest achievement is the Cantiga Manuscript[11] mentioned before. Its more than 400 songs and 40 instrumental miniatures were compiled under the king's supervision, and he even took part personally in constructing the texts and melodies of the songs, as can be concluded from the tone of the prologue, which, freely translated, declares: "For someone to sing well considerable expertise is needed; even if I do not possess this to the extent desirable, I hope I can express at least part of what I wish; my sole desire is that Mary should accept me as her troubadour." Here the Arab reverence of women and the Marian ideal of the Christian Middle Ages are combined with the fashionable secular musical practice of the period: only a troubadour in medieval society could speak in that manner. Interwoven in the contents of the songs lie the difficult social problems and everyday cares of medieval man: pagan symbols of idolatry, concerns of welfare, impoverished knights, the desire for food and plenty of hungry masses on pilgrimages. Most of the songs have a pilgrimage setting. Compostela was a famous medieval place of pilgrimage which attracted thousands of people from France and other parts of Europe. In the 12th century European polyphonic music developed there, as it did in Paris and at St Martial (Limoges). Along the pilgrim routes towns grew up and trade boomed.

Let us examine the content of some of the songs: Cantiga No. 1118 tells of a woman of Zaragoza who has had several stillborn children. After her third child has been born dead she offers a wax doll to Mary, but the fourth child also dies after birth. The woman pleads with Mary to restore her fourth child to life. The miniature that introduces this series of ten *cantigas* (110–119) depicts two musicians, each with a rebec in his hands. Cantiga 79 deals with what is presumably also a social concern: it tells of a young courtesan "of easy virtue", Musa by name. She dreams that Mary calls on her to lead a serious life and abandon her bad habits. As a reward she will be placed among the heavenly women in 30 days. Musa changes for the better, but after 30 days she dies. Song 58 belongs to the same theme. A nun is tempted to become the lover of a knight. They have already arranged the time for her escape and the meeting place when the nun dreams of a deep abyss into which 'evil' souls like hers are thrown. She awakes and asks the knight who is waiting to go without her.

Several songs feature the rich man who has lost his fortune. In Song 216 he offers his own wife to the devil in order to regain his riches. Several ailments occur in the songs (a whole range of Arabic medical books were translated or written in the territories of the European caliphate[12]): paralysis occurs in Song 166, and a lame woman in 179. Interestingly, both those illnesses are cured in the town and monastery of Salas (near Ovideo). A large place in the subject-matter of the songs is taken by pilgrimages, but it is never the destination that is important, only the events that take place on the way: of nine portions of meat, one is stolen while it is being cooked (Song 159); a pilgrim steals his companion's

[11] Anglès (1943, 1958, 1964).

[12] The 25-volume medical work of Rhazes (Al Razi, 864–926), and the *Canon* of Avicenna (Ibn Sina, 980–1037) formed the foundation of European medicine until the 16th century.

money (302). Money, or rather money lending, is also the subject of Song 25, during the course of which we learn how the Jew who has lent the money becomes a Christian.

These are all questions that concern society, that shape the society of medieval Spain, and poetry and music as important a role here as the troubadour songs in Provençal culture. The music of the *cantigas* can hardly be understood without a knowledge of the social background, of which examples have been given. To expand the matter further, the realm of the *cantigas* is indispensable to an understanding of troubadour music. The two great 'corpora' of medieval secular music complement each other, and by doing so throw light on major topical questions concerning medieval society. The question of an Arab origin for the music of the *cantigas* has often been raised (as it has in connection with troubadour music). Without giving an account of the set schools, contrasting views and their debates with one another, it is worth pointing out the potential solutions that lie in further study (beyond the partial results already obtained) of the more than 400 melodies contained in the manuscript and the depictions of more than 80 different instruments in the initials.

In this examination we apply the methods of musical iconology, which has gained ground in recent years and consists of a comparative study of illumination, musical paleography and the sporadic hints as to interpretation. We also discuss in broad outline the relationships between the *cantigas* and troubadour music, primarily from the point of view of musical construction and melodic formation.

The texts of the *cantigas*, which were written in the Galician (*gallego*) language, consist in general of 4-line stanzas, with a couplet as refrain repeated before and after each stanza. According to their musical structure they can be ranged into 3 types: *virelai*, *rondeau* and *kanzone* (*cancon*). The *cantigas* have strong links with the Latin *conducti*. Each musical type characteristically appears in some kind of refrained form, similarly to the character of the text. Spanke has made an exhaustive analysis of the forms of the songs.[13] Here are a few examples of the musical types:

of the 2-section strophes a b // a' (260);

of the 4-section strophes that appear in almost 80 varieties a b // a' a' / a b (299, 61, 114, 74, 86, etc.), or a a' //b b/a a' (123, 226, 307, etc.), as well as a b/ /b' b' a' b (21, 63, 131, 186, 275), a b/ /c c/a b (83, 373, 24, 68, 92, 17, 44, 58, 118, 126, 339, 317, 145, 265, 78, 93);

the forms employing 8 musical sections appear in 135 varieties, always with a refrain, e.g.: a b a c // a c a c/a b a c (293), or: a b c d //a e a e/a b c d (196, 323, 325), as well as a b a'c // a c a c/a b a' c (194, 297, 335, 355);

also frequent is a b a' b' // c b c b' / a b a b' (152, 199, 301, 303, 304, 338, 347), or a b c d // c d c d / a b c d (177, 235, 238, 245, 291, 295, 313, 324, 337, 351, 382, 388). The musical lines with refrain are expanded up to 12 phrases. Altogether a mere 10 *cantigas* were written without refrain (here only musical refrains are

[13] Spanke (1958).

considered). We attribute very great significance to the refrained form in the manuscripts we have examined, not because it was a discovery that began to conquer European music in precisely those decades and centuries, but because it was the common idea that connected, through the poetic and musical types, the new European types with Mediterranean culture. In this respect, too, the Cantiga Manuscript maintains a relationship with the corresponding types of troubadour music, and even certain principles of melodic construction are similar: for example the *psalmodic* character can be registered in several *cantigas* (Nos 6, 43, 60, 62, 68, 83, 121, 125, 213, 231, 232, 234, 236, 255, 320, 322, 328, 335, 344, 347, 351, 354, 371, 385, 391); besides the traditional Mediterranean, Near Eastern type of psalmody there appears a *recitative* manner of performance, without any part being played by the psalmodic *initium* (Nos 1, 26, 33, 40, 63, 81, 91, 119, 120, 149, 157, 162, 166, 313); nor are *descending* melody openings rare (Nos 20, 24, 27, 87, 88, 96, 103, 113, 114, 115, 117, 122, 133, 137, 142, 155, 156, 171, 182, 202, 204, 233, 263, 272, 334, 338, 349, 350, 352, 387) and, indeed, as the figures bear out, they form a major structural element in the *cantigas*. Beyond the above criteria, many of the manuscript's melodies are syllabic, almost a third of the songs being written without ligatures or ornament signs.

In analysing the links between the troubadours and Alfonso the Wise in the first section of the chapter, we have referred to a song of Cadenet's. But the musical idiom of the *cantigas* is linked by many other threads to the music of the Provençal troubadours. The melodies of Peire Vidal, whom we shall introduce in detail, include several motifs which were also used by *cantiga* music, a fact we mention not because there was any direct relationship, adoption or mutual influencing, but because we assume the existence of a motivic treasury generally available and made use of in both places. The motifs of Vidal's 1st song (*Anc no mori per amor*) are encountered in Cantigas 224 and 307, the dance-inspired motifs of the 2nd song (*Baro, de mon don covit*) could be found in Cantigas 1, 8, 159, 341 and 360, parts of the 3rd song (*Bem pac d'ivern*) are contained in Cantiga 133, motifs of the 4th (*Ges pel temps*) in Cantiga 333, the tune of the 6th (*Nulhs hom no pot d'amor*) in Cantiga 382, that of the 11th (*S'eu fos en cort*) in Cantigas 39 and 48, and finally that of the 12th (*Tart mi veiran*) in Cantiga 41.

The series of miniatures form one of the most valuable parts of the Cantiga Manuscript; they have a bearing beyond the scope of musical history as a source material for social history as well. The depiction of more than 80 instruments in the 40 miniatures is the earliest presentation of the inventory of instruments in European musical history, even though some depictions in statues and codex miniatures about 100 to 150 years earlier are also known. The instruments of the *cantigas* have preserved a period before *trecento* art, but whereas in fine arts (e.g. in Giotto) instruments scarcely serve as more than decoration, in the Cantiga Manuscript they have a functional significance; they are shown along with their performers and that combination of instrument and performer is what throws a 'photographic' light on the court circle of Alfonso the Wise and fills out the picture formed so far of its social historical background. Moreover, one can form a picture not only of the court, but of the whole of contemporary society, since peasant musicians are frequently to be found alongside their court counterparts; these are placed in a rural, non-courtly environment. Chase writes in his book on Spanish music: "Another miniature shows how the *Cantigas* were performed by the people, for whom they were written." And later, "One curious circumstance is that no one is visibly singing in this picture. Have we to do, then, with a purely instrumental performance?"[14]

When we have analysed the instruments and instrumental groups we shall return to this question of Chase's. A closer discussion of the instruments is called for because works that deal with them have always limited their coverage to the particular instruments with which they were concerned. Bachmann's excellent treatise on the history of the violin is an example. He gave a minute description of the stringed instruments in the manuscript, but dealt with no other instruments shown.[15]

So a coherent discussion of the instrumental depictions in the manuscript is overdue, as is a comprehensive analysis of the functions of those instruments.

The manuscript is carefully constructed, which one can see from the appearance of an instrumental depiction before every tenth *cantiga*. With the exception of six pictures, which each contain a single figure and instrument, every picture shows two musicians who sometimes play the same and sometimes different instruments. The first miniature, before the prologue, is an initial that stretches over the whole width of the text, showing the interior of a building with five arches, the king being seated in the middle arch. To the right and left of the king are two groups of scribes (perhaps troubadours), who are writing down what the king dictates. The instrumental musicians are to be found in the two outside arches: to the left are two fiddle-players, one with and the other without a bow, while to the right there are two persons playing guitars (of the *guitarra latina* type), one with a plectrum in his hand.

There are several criteria for grouping the miniatures (e.g. those showing a single instrument, as against those with two instruments or performers). We have chosen to group them according to the types of instruments. The instrumental miniatures of the manuscript can be divided into two large groups:

the *first half* of the codex (up to and including Cantiga 210) i.e. mainly shows stringed instruments (bowed and plucked), while the *second half* (from Cantiga 220) shows mainly *wind* instruments (with one exception they are woodwind instruments).

[14] Chase (1959), p. 27.
[15] Bachmann, W.: *The Origins of Bowing*, London, 1969.

1) The stringed instruments

1

2 39^{v}

3 46^{v}

4 54^{v}

5 71^{v}

6 89^{v}

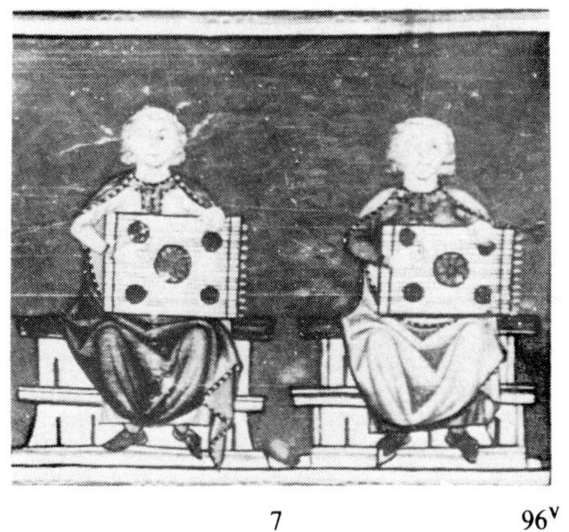

7 96^{v}

8 118^{v}

8a 125^{v}

9 133^{v}

10 140^{v}

11 147^{v}

12 162^{v}

2) Instruments other than strings in the first group

13 193^v

14 79^v

15 154^v

16 169^v

17 176^v

18 185^v

Among the stringed instruments one can find the ancient European and Near Eastern as well as the Arab types of the violin (*vielle*, rebec), varieties of guitar and lute (*guitarra latina*, *guitarra morisca*, the common lute, long-necked lute, pandora), and various forms of the psaltery (*shantur*) family (trapezoid psaltery, square psaltery, *canun*). Non-stringed instruments in the first group include the hurdy-gurdy, also called the *organistrum* (Illumination 15), of which two are shown as elongated, oblong boxes (whereas in other sculptural depictions, for example, it has the form of a flat-lying number '8' and two musicians play the one instrument), two instruments next to each other in one picture. Other pictures of non-stringed instruments show a *carillon* consisting of three small bells sounded by a single musician with a hammer (Illumination 16), a small pair of double *cymbals* (Illumination 17) and a *portative* organ (Illumination 18).

3) The wind instruments

19 201ᵛ

20 209

21 218ᵛ

22 227

23 235v

24 243v

25 251v

26 268v

27 276v

28 286

29 295^{v}

30 304^{v}

31 313^{v}

32 323^{v}

33 333^{v}

4) Instruments other than winds in the second group

34 260

35 341

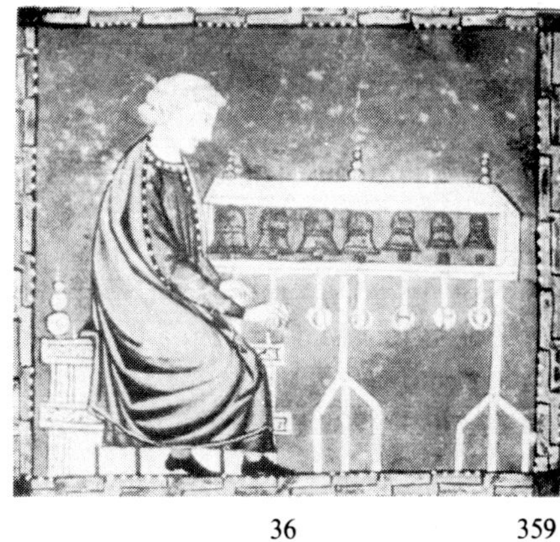

36 359

The large group of wind instruments also presents a most colourful picture in the second half of the manuscript. Besides the transverse flute (Illumination 21) all the major types can be found from the small flageolet (shepherd's pipe) through the double flute to the *launedda* consisting of three pipes (this is the last among the stringed instruments in Illumination 14). There are also depictions of the crumhorn and several bagpipes (three, of different types, in Illuminations 23, 25 and 31). Among the wind instruments are a pipe and tabor and a flute with castanets. There appears only one brass instruments, a straight trumpet (Illumination 28).

On two occasions a stringed instrument appears among the winds: a *canun* (in Illumination 34) and a harp (in Illumination 35); in the final illumination (36) there appears another carillon, which is noteworthy for its seven bells, on whose clappers are written the names of the notes they sound—[a b] c d e f g—the first two note names being covered by the hand of the musician. We shall refrain from a mechanical listing of the whole range of instruments, which can be found in earlier publications, above all in J. Ribera's strongly Arab-oriented, but fundamental book.[16]

Some observations can be made from the instrumental depictions, and some social historical lessons drawn from them.

Illustrated histories of instruments and other iconographical publications have not always considered that the miniatures of the *cantigas* (apart from six) always contain two musicians. Often they are playing different instruments, and perhaps for this reason it has been thought justifiable to treat just the instrument the work is concerned with i.e. to describe only *half* an illumination. So the opportunity is lost of presenting the illumination and the instruments it depicts in the function intended by the illuminator, that is, *in the course of performance*. In almost every case it is possible to observe the performance or the interpretation, since a large majority of the musicians are *looking at each other and watching each other* as they play.

The background in the illuminations and the apparel of the musicians are also worth analysing, since they provide considerable help in pursuing the points of social history raised by the miniatures and complementing the musical information they give.

In many cases the illuminations have a coffered background evoking Arab carpet patterns or architectural interiors; others have architectural formations of a different type, while yet others show simple rural landscapes. In each case there is a frame that corresponds with the subject, the instrument, the apparel, and the musician. For example, the first instrumental picture, at Cantiga 10, has two standing musicians watching each other, against a coffered background: one holds a (4-stringed) fiddle placed on his shoulder and plays with a bow, while the other has a Moorish guitar in his hand, which he plucks with a plectrum. Their clothes show no peculiarities; they might perhaps be simple court musicians, but even with this first illumination it can be seen that the musicians are not put there

[16] Ribera (1970), pp. 231–3.

randomly (Ill. 2). By their active interpretation, they are participants in the performance of the *cantiga* above which they were depicted (and maybe of the other nine *cantigas* before the next illumination).

The musicians playing together provide opportunities to make several interesting observations of detail. Along with the many Moorish and Christian court musicians, a significant part in the medieval society of the Iberian Peninsula was played by Jewish musicians, as typical depictions in both the first and second half of the manuscript bear out: at Cantiga 70 (Ill. 6) and Cantiga 380 (Ill. 35). The composition of these miniatures is striking in that they are not framed by a Moorish–Arab coffered environment, but by a different background, in part plain and in part connected with the structure of the picture. Illumination 35 is particularly remarkable. It shows the interior of a building with a vaulted ceiling; where the ribs of the vaulting meet a lamp is suspended, similarly to illustrations in some Haggadah manuscripts.[17] Above the vaulting that frames the illumination there is the only townscape to appear in the codex. The clothes of the musicians are also typical: both pictures show characteristic high caps and hats of types which could be identified in the illuminations of several medieval Hebrew manuscripts.[18] The instruments the musicians play are unequivocally Biblical instruments, used in medieval miniatures as the attributes of David. The illumination at Cantiga 70 shows two trapezoid *psalteries*, the most frequent of the many psaltery forms. The Jewish musicians are holding the instrument on their knees with their left hands, while with their right hands they play the instrument (with the help of a plectrum). The trapezoid psaltery only appears with Jewish musicians. Moorish and European court musicians in other miniatures are shown playing other forms of the instrument (square, arched, etc.). The medieval *harp* is another instrument shown throughout the manuscript only in the hands of Jewish musicians; the illumination before Cantiga 380 has two Jewish harpists, whose hand positions show they are actually playing. The instrument is recognizably portrayed with the sound box and string-tension pegs clearly visible.[19]

Rustic figures and peasant musicians never feature against an 'oriental' coffered background. They are surrounded either by a blank field or some kind of landscape. At Cantiga 60 (Ill. 14), in the first half of the manuscript, they are shown blowing a 3-piped launedda (a folk instrument still employed in Corsica today); in the second half, at Cantiga 340 (Ill. 30), they each play a short flageolet, while at Cantiga 370 (Ill. 33), there is a pipe and tabor held in a playing posture particularly common among medieval European entertainers: pipe in the left hand and tabor played with the right.

At Cantiga 130 a western Moor and an eastern Arab (who can be distinguished by their dress) together play long-necked guitars, which the Arab

[17] Scheiber (1959), p. 1.
[18] Blumenkranz (1965), pp. 35, 44, 47, 49, 62–3, 65, 67 and 77; Rubens (1957), pp. 124–5.
[19] Falvy (1978).

plucks with a plectrum. They too appear to watch each other while playing. At Cantiga 140 (Ill. 10) the illumination shows a Moorish and a Christian court musician playing the tambur together, each using a plectrum to pluck the strings. At Cantiga 300 (Ill. 26) a Moor is blowing a conical flageolet (būq zamrī) while a female figure next to him holds a *darbuka* on her shoulder and beats time.

The last mentioned three instrumental combinations were typically of Arab origin in Europe; only the tambur (also called the pandora) perhaps pointed to a more distant source—Persia. The instrument, and variants of it, was not exclusively introduced into Europe through the Iberian Peninsula, since it occurs in a Caucasian sculpture relic from as early as the 10th century,[20] and records of it survive from the 12th century in Hungary, where it was called the *koboz*. The instrument's pear-shaped resonator can be compared with surviving instrumental depictions in the Byzantine sphere, and Hungarian scholars suppose it may have reached Europe directly from the east in the age of the great migration.[21] The role Byzantium played in passing Arab instruments on to Europe, particularly to the Balkans, has not been fully clarified, but the rebec, for example, reached Europe through the Balkans as well as through Spain. Indeed, among the Balkan peoples it was taken over by folk music and remains as a folk instrument to this day. In the Cantiga Manuscript the rebec makes several appearances: at Cantiga 170 (Ill. 12) it is shown in company with an Arab lute that has an enlarged resonator, while at Cantiga 100 it features alone in a short-necked form held *vertically* on the knee (as elsewhere in the manuscript) and bowed horizontally. In the Middle Ages this was the *eastern playing technique* as opposed to the *European,* in which the instrument was held on the *shoulder*. The European performing style scarcely appears in the manuscript: single musicians are shown using it at Cantiga 10 (Ill. 2) and in the large introductory initial depicting the environment of Alfonso the Wise.[22]

Other clues besides the bowed instruments help establish the extent of Near Eastern–Arab influence versus European influence. Looking at the range of instruments depicted, the two carillons (at Cantigas 180 (Ill. 16) and 400 (Ill. 36) are instruments which were almost unknown to Near Eastern musical performers. The second offers a particularly striking example, since its seven bells may correspond to the diatonic stock of notes, and as has been mentioned, the note names appear on the clappers of the bells. The bagpipes with several drones, shown at Cantiga 350 (Ill. 31), can also be considered European. Bagpipes feature in other illuminations (at Cantigas 260 (Ill. 23) and 280 (Ill. 25) but these only show blowing pipes and the instruments could have been used anywhere along the Mediterranean coast, for the multiple drones were the European development. Another European phenomenon appears at Cantiga 200 (Ill. 18): a primitive portative organ in which the player is working the bellows with his left hand and playing with the right, or rather his right hand is

[20] Bachmann: *op. cit.*, Ill. 9.

[21] Gábry, Gy.: *Fejezetek a magyar hangszeres kultúra történetéből* (Chapters from the History of Hungarian Instrumental Culture), manuscript.

[22] Jullian, M.–Le Vot, G.: (1984).

resting on the manual. Very little is known about the course of the organ's development between Antiquity and the Middle Ages, and one is tempted to assume that this is one of the very earliest medieval European depictions of a portative organ.

So a very high proportion of the almost 80 instruments that appear in the 40 miniatures are from Near Eastern–Arabic musical practice, regardless of the social stratum to which the performer belongs. It is beyond the scope of this study to examine either the spread of instruments from the Iberian Peninsula through Europe or the development of Europe's inventory of instruments, but it is certain that the (mainly oriental) instruments listed here accompany a collection of European secular monody that cannot be interpreted without taking the instrumental depictions into account. The question posed by Gilbert Chase (see Note 14), as to whether the *cantigas* were perhaps for purely instrumental performance, we can answer the following:

1) The instrumental depictions in the codex indicate a manner of performance in which the instrument actively joins in the vocal performance and no separate musical material is provided for the instrument. That is the case with folk performance in North Africa today, where the instrument and the voice perform the same melody, together or alternately, using the same ornamentation.

2) A high proportion of the instruments found in medieval depictions have survived to this day, some in European and some in North African and Near Eastern instrumental folk music. Here musical iconography can play a most significant role, since the evaluation of old miniatures allows comparison with today's folk instruments. In an extended sense, musical iconology, with the help of ethnomusicology, can reconstruct the practice of medieval art music and create the framework for authentic interpretation.

MEDIEVAL HERESIES AND THE TROUBADOURS

As the Middle Ages reached their zenith, or perhaps as decline set in, a large-scale movement against the Roman Catholic Church developed in society, hardly a century after the Great Schism that had sent Byzantium and Rome on their separate ways, each seeking separately to exert their political influence on the peoples of Europe. The resistance flared up in the southern regions of Europe that bordered on the Mediterranean and was seemingly about dogmatic differences, but the underlying cause was resentment against the doctrinal, political and social control asserted by the Roman Catholic Church. From the Occitanian province of Albi, the centre of the Cathars, the 'pure', the 'good Christians', Catharism spread through southern France to extensive areas of northern Italy and the Balkans. There is evidence of close links between the troubadours and this heretical movement, both indirect links via those aristocrats who were themselves Cathars, and direct links through the ideals of the troubadours, as shown in their biographical details and poems. A long epic poem about the Albigensian Crusade in the 13th century was written by the Spanish troubadour Guillaume Tudèle, of Navarre, who begins with a reference to music:

"Senhors, esta canso es faita d'aital guia
com sela d'Atiocha et ayssi's versifia
E s'a tot aital so, qui diire lo sabia"[1]

(Lords, this chanson has been modelled upon the *Chanson d'Antioche*, both upon its stanzas and its melodies, which were recited and declaimed.) The *Chanson d'Antioche* was written in Provençal at the end of the 12th century, and has survived only in a fragmentary form.[2] Martin-Chabot[3] declares that Tudèle's poem was accompanied on a bowed instrument. It was written between 1210 and 1213, and mentions the Battle of Zadar in 1204, where the crusaders were led by Simon de Montfort.[4] At the time of the battle, Zadar (Zára in Hungarian) was under the authority of the Hungarian King Imre, who did not interfere in the fighting. In fact there are several indications that King Imre was

[1] Martin-Chabot (1931), pp. 8–9, and Martin-Chabot, E.: *La Chanson de la croisade albigeoise. Tom. III: Le poème de l'auteur anonyme*, Paris, 1961.

[2] 'Fragment d'une chanson d'Antioche en provençal, published and translated by Paul Meyer in *Archives de l'Orient latin. Tom. II*, Paris, 1884.

[3] Martin-Chabot (1931), p. xiv.

[4] Martin-Chabot (1931), p. 87.

no sworn opponent of the heretical movement; although he maintained his relations with the Pope of Rome, he did not interfere during his reign with the spread of Byzantine Orthodox Christianity in the regions of Hungary east of the river Tisza. One cannot be certain whether troubadour guests of King Imre went to Buda only because of the presence of the Aragonese princess[5] or because it also offered an opportunity to get in touch with the 'secret society' of those who espoused the ideas of Catharism in Hungary's Balkan dominions: the Bogumils. In connection with King Imre we shall be returning to this group of questions at the end of the chapter.

We have already mentioned that the troubadours identified themselves both with the Albigensians as a social movement and also with their heretical doctrines. The identification was so strong that when Pope Innocent III declared war upon them and ordered the destruction of their castles, including their chief stronghold at Bézier (where 20,000 Cathars were killed), the troubadours fled from southern France, to seek refuge in northern Italy, the Iberian Peninsula and the north. That, one might say, marked the end of the Golden Age of troubadour poetry, for

the success of the Albigensian Crusade meant the end of troubadour poetry and the dispersal of the troubadours.

The relationship of the heretical movement and troubadour poetry has yet to be defined, although passing comments have been made on certain aspects. Stäblein's latest book, which discusses the types of medieval music through the development of musical notation, mentions only that many of the troubadours left Occitania after the war against the Albigensians.[6] The question has many sides; before expounding its relationship with the troubadours, let us outline first a few of the fundamental tenets of Catharism. The kernel of Catharist belief was the duality of *good* and *evil*: not only the distinction between them but the conjunction of the two. This doctrine has been summarized by René Nelli, the scholar best qualified to do so:

> il y a deux seigneurs, sans commencement ni fin, l'un profondément bon et l'autre profondément mauvais. . . . il y a deux natures, l'une bonne, céleste et incorporelle, créée par le Dieu bon, l'autre mauvaise, créée par la Dieu mauvais, à laquelle appartiennent les choses animales et terrestres.[7]

Any man or woman could be a Cathar; the Perfect of the Order fasted, did manual work and practised celibacy. Their chief rite was the *consolamentum* (the laying-on of hands and the touching of the Gospel), in which only the Elect and those on their deathbed could take part.[8] Sociologically the movement was highly complex in composition; its membership included noblemen, rich and

[5] Faidit, for instance, was reputed to be a heretic. Réan (1959), I. 46: "Les biens des faidits, c'est-à-dire des proscrits pour cause d'hérésie furent confisqués."

[6] Stäblein (1975), pp. 77 and 79.

[7] Nelli (1968).

[8] Dupuy (1972), p. 199.

poor burgesses, tradesmen, and even members of the urban and village proletariat (*du proletariat urbain et rural*[9]). This very broad social spectrum and particularly the struggle for the development of the towns in the south were certainly big factors in the rapid spread of the movement and the antagonism it aroused in the established church. The striving for emancipation of the towns provided a congenial background for the heretical movements, written evidence of which can be found in the 12th century history of Arles.[10] At the beginning of the 12th century that town already had significant links with the heretical movement, made more intensive by the residence there of Cathar merchants.[11] The town's *Confratria* became increasingly closely tied to Catharism for the additional reason that their emancipation was opposed by Church circles:

> Seit dem frühen. Mittelalter hat sich die Theologie immer wieder gegen die conspirative, durch Eid verbundene Confratria gewendet. Das mußte diesen Verband folgerichtig in innere Konflikte mit der herrschenden Kirchenlehre bringen.[12]

The urban attempts to gain independence were frequently condemned in resolutions of Synods and in peace treaties. As urban development progressed, the communes growing up in the south of France sympathized with Catharism because, while demanding the purification of the Church, it was also loyal to the gilds and urged secularization, which was precisely what the new urban citizenry were demanding as well.

From these southern French Occitanian towns came the troubadours, many from families of urban artisans (Peire Vidal, for example, was of a furrier family, as was Guilhem Figueira, while Aimeric de Peguilhan was from a family of cloth merchants) and many from very poor urban families (like the 'great' Bernart de Ventadorn, whose *Vida* describes him as an "ome de paura generacion"[13] and Guiraut de Borneill, who "era ome de bas afar"[14]). We shall later return to the subject of their social position, but in this context it is worth considering whether the lure of the 'new' religion might not have been rooted in their backgrounds; there is also the possibility that it may have arisen from their position of subordination, which in many instances must have been identical with the position from which they had earlier broken away. Many or most of the noblemen to whom they became attached were ardent followers of Catharism. One nobleman, who was both a troubadour himself and a Cathar, was Raimon Jordan, whose *Vida* relates that he was a member of "l'ordre des hérétiques".[15] Raimon Jordan was Viscount of St Antonin (Tarn et Garonne) in the final decades of the 12th century and his biography declares that he paid court to

[9] Dupuy (1972).
[10] Engelmann (1959).
[11] Bru (1952), p. 48.
[12] Engelmann (1959), p. 134; on the same subject see Cornaert (1942) and Sidorowa (1953), p. 74.
[13] Cordes (1975), pp. 56–7.
[14] Cordes (1975), pp. 96–7.
[15] Cordes (1975), pp. 82–5.

women of Albigensian families, becoming a 'perfect' only after receiving a mortal injury in battle. Two of his poems have survived with their melodies. Mir Bernat belonged to a noble family all of whose members were Cathars. He was an active troubadour and attended his brother's *consolamentum* around 1232. The troubadour Raimon de Miraval of Cabardes was a poor knight. The melodies of 22 of his poems have survived, which in terms of troubadour music is a very high figure (exceeded only by Riquier). His family lived in Hautpoul and Puylaurens (Tarn), and like him were determined Cathars from the beginning of the 13th century onwards. During the Albigensian war he lost his castle and fled to Raymon VI in Toulouse, with whom he suffered another defeat at the Battle of Muret in 1213, after which he sought refuge in Aragon. The *Vida* of Almeric de Peguilhan, who came from a family of Toulouse cloth manufacturers, relates that he died a heretic: "en eretgia segon com ditz".[16] His death occurred in Lombardy, and according to a highly uncertain source, he had returned to northern Italy from Hungary. Among the few poems of his which have survived with their melodies is a fine *descort*. Guilhem Figueira came from Toulouse, where both he and his family were tailors. After the Albigensian war he fled to Lombardy, where he "se fit bien accueillir des truands, des putains, des hôteliers et des taverniers".[17] Against Rome he wrote a revengeful *chanson* which was found by the Inquisition.[18] Peire Cardenal is placed among the heretics because of a satire he wrote against the clergy, "Clerges si fan pastor", although there is no biographical corroboration that he was a Cathar. However, his *chanson* was widespread among the Cathars.[19]

The *vidas* rarely state openly the degree to which a troubadour was associated with the great heretical movements that were shaping society, but the poems are no less significant as source materials, since in part *directly*, and in part *indirectly* through certain expressions, they make it clear whether a troubadour was living among Cathars or was himself a Cathar. Among the direct poetic evidence is a *tenso* from the 1240s entitled "Débat entre Sicart de Figueiras at Izarn", about a conversation in which the Cathar bishop of the Albigensians is forced to take part. Many personal names and a precise description of Cathar doctrines are included.[20]

The sense of belonging and the secret anticlericism of the Cathars, which remained despite all persecution, were indirectly conveyed by certain expressions in the poems. One significant expression was *tot be* (*omne bonum*), which was the usual greeting between Cathar 'perfects' since being a Cathar meant one possessed the ability to "hear good" (*entendensa de be*).[21] A response

[16] Boutier and Schütz (1950), p. 4.

[17] Boutier and Schütz (1950), p. 173.

[18] Anglade, J.: *Anthologie des troubadours*, Paris, 1953, p. 149.

[19] Lavaud (1957), p. 170.

[20] Douais (1881), p. 118. The book contains the chronicle of Guilhem Pelhisson, which features *Izarn*, the priest of Denat (Tarn), whose name crops up several times in the Inquisition.

[21] Duvernoy (1976), p. 274.

to this greeting would primarily be elicited from initiates, but at certain periods from everyone else as well. If a troubadour attributed the expression to someone in a poem it followed that the person was, as the believers put it, *one of us*. Thus Sordel at one point wrote that Guida de Rodez "appreza de tot be", meaning that he was a Cathar believer. Aimeric de Peguilhan, in his poem that begins "Qui soffrir", sings in a similar sense to a lady:

Una on crois e nais
Bes, plus c'om no'n pot dir[22]

(One can say not better or more of someone than that he was born under the cross.)

Another expression can be found in Peire Raimon de Toloza:

Bona dona, on totz bes
Vezem granar e florir[23]

(Fair lady, in all good I see you bloom and grow [reach perfection].)

Granar e florir was the second topic to occupy a major place in Cathar conversion. The two expressions *totz bes* and *granar e florir* feature side by side in Jean Maury's supplication;[24] the occurrence of one or the other in a poem would almost certainly be a Cathar mark of recognition to the audience.

The latter also appears in the famous romance *Flamenca*:

Aisso es de merce sos fruitz,
Et es florida e granada
Et em bona razis fe(r)mada
Car ab si mena caritat
Per cui tot ben son coronat[25]

After Guillaume IX the term *granar e florir* appears frequently in troubadour poems and becomes a standard Provençal poetic formula. It could be that the Cathars took it over from the troubadours and began using it in a ritual sense, in which case it would be less 'compromising'. Besides the term *granar e florir*, Jean Maury's supplication took over from Peire Cardenal the attribute *dreiturier* (applied to God) and the phrase, *Datz mi podar qu'eu am so que amatz*[26] (Give me the power to love and be loved).

[22] Duvernoy (1976), p. 275.
[23] Anglade: *op. cit.*, p. 129.
[24] Anglade: *op. cit.*, p. 189.
[25] Lavaud, R. and Nelli, R.: *Les Troubadours*, Paris, 1960, p. 882.
[26] Lavaud (1957), pp. 254–6.

But one cannot ignore King Imre and the heretical movements in the Balkans. In Imre's case it is tempting to assume that he was not averse to the heretical movements against the Roman Church. From the mid-12th century there existed in Dalmatia and Slavonia, which were dominions of his, a church independent of Rome, as Nicetas reported to the Council of St. Felix in 1167. In fact some towns of Lombardic heretics were affiliated to Slavonia, since some decades after the Council of St. Felix, Mantua, for example, sent representatives to Slavonia to obtain confirmation of their bishop. The school of Bagnolo was a major centre of the northern Italian movement. Some interesting references to the Balkan movement are contained in a letter from Pope Innocent III to King Imre II. The letter is partly a threat and partly a proposal for steps against the heretics:

> It has come to our notice that scarcely had our venerable brother Archbishop of Spalato expelled a certain number of heretics (Patarins) from Spalato and Trau, than the noble Kulin, Governor of Bosnia, extended them safe resort and open protection, surrendering his land and person to their depravity, esteeming them as if they were Catholics, and what is more, incorrectly calling them Christians.[27]

We do not know what Imre replied or what steps he took against Kulin. Soon after, Innocent III sent Casamare to Hungary to settle the matter of the Patarins. The legation was successful: the legate was presented in the name of the rebellious families with a set of rules they undertook to abide by, and these were also accepted by Rome. The agreement was signed at Bilino Polje, near Zenice, Kulin being among the signatories. It was approved by King Imre on April 30, 1203.[28] Despite these measures, the papal legate, Cardinal Conrad of Porto, still reported to the Council of Sens in 1223 that in Croatia and Dalmatia an anti-pope existed, to whom the Albigensians adhered and whose seat was close to the Hungarian people.[29]

Without analysing the relations of Hungary with the Balkan heretical movements, it is clear that the matter was certainly of moment to the Hungarian court as well. King Imre was obviously not and could never have been an Albigensian, but one must not forget that he had found a wife for himself from Aragon, the place to which the Albigensians had fled before the crusaders and at which they had received shelter. Historians will decide whether Imre just happened to marry Constanza or whether he intended by this gesture to keep Rome's power in check and to reach right across Europe, as it were. Certainly for the beleaguered troubadours it meant refuge to accompany Constanza to Hungary in the last decades of the 12th century.

[27] The letter is given in French translation in Duvernoy (1976), p. 348.
[28] Arch. Secr. Vatican. Reg. Vat. 5, f° 103 v°.
[29] Martene-Durand: *Thesaurus*, Paris, 1717, *Tom. I*, p. 902.

The first crusade against the Albigensians was launched in 1180, Lavour capitulated in 1181, and in 1198 the Inquisition began. After the first Inquisition a considerable proportion of the troubadours lapsed into silence. The table that follows lists the main stages in the four crusades against the Albigensians, and marks alongside them the troubadours by whom melodies have also survived, or whose period of activity has been ascertained by troubadour scholarship. There is a surprising parallel between the period after the first crusade and the period at the end of the fourth, when the troubadours who were still active in the 13th century, were silenced for ever or fled to other areas (Lombardy, Aragon). After the massacres and burnings of the first half of the 13th century no suitable social background remained in southern France.

To sum up, the war against the Albigensians put an end to the social position of the troubadours and dug the grave of troubadour culture. Regardless of where the lyrical art of secular monody might flower again in Europe, its golden age had ended.*

The wars against the Albigensians	*Authors of troubadour songs*	
1180 First Albigensian Crusade	Bernart de Ventadorn	1150–1180
1181 The fall of Lavour	Peire d'Alvergne	1158–1180
1198 Establishment of the Inquisition	Raimbaut d'Aurenga	1147–1173
	Bertran de Born	1180–1194
1208 Assassination of the Papal Legate Pierre de Castelnau	Berenguier de Palazol	after 1160
	Jordan Bonel	1160–1200
	Arnaut de Maroill	2nd half of 12th c.
	Peire Raimon de Toloza	1170–1210
	Guiraut de Borneill	1165–1200
	Peire Vidal	1180–1206
	Pons de Capdoil	1180–1190
	Arnaut Daniel	1180–1200
	Guillem de Saint Leidier	1165–1200
	Raimbaut de Vaqueiras	1120–1207
	Uc Brunec	c. 1185
	Raimon Jordan	1190–1200
	Daude de Pradas	c. 1190
	Guillem Ademar	c. 1200
	Guillem Magret	c. 1200
	Richart de Berbezil	c. 1200

* Other related works that may interest the reader are: Manselli (1953); Werner (1953); *Vaudois languedociens et pauvres catholiques*, Toulouse, 1967; Borst (1953); Manselli (1963); Thouzellier (1966); *Cathares en Languedoc*, Toulouse, 1968.

1209 Second Albigensian Crusade The fall of Béziers (July 22); the massacre of several thousand men, women, sick persons and children	Raimon de Miraval	1190–1213, 1220
1210 The fall of Minerve (July 22), 140 people burnt at the stake	Lo Monge de Montaudo	1180–1213
1211 Second fall of Lavour, 400 people burnt at the stake		
1212 Simon de Montfort regulates the political and legal position of the vanquished		
1213 The fall of the castle of Muret (Sept. 12)		
1215 Third Albigensian Crusade; King Philip Augustus of France ordered Simon de Montfort to take command		
1216 Victory of the Cathars at Beaucaire		
1218 Simon de Montfort, Earl of Leicester, killed during the siege of Toulouse (June 25)		
1219 Fourth Albigensian Crusade	Floquet de Marseilla	1180–1231
1226 The excommunication of Raymond VII	Pistoleta Gaucelm Faidit	c. 1230 1185–1220
1229 The signing of the treaty of Meaux; establishment of the Inquisition in Toulouse	Peirol Perdigo Uc de Saint Circ	1180–1225 1195–1220 1217–1253
1233 Gregory IX gives definitive sanction to the Inquisition	Aimeric de Peguilhan Cadenet	1195–1230 1208–1239
1242 The Avignonnet massacre	Guillem Augier Novella	1209–1235
1243 The siege of Montségur commences (May 13)	Peire Cardenal Aimeric de Belenoi	1180–1278 1210–1241
1244 Montségur capitulates (March 14) Montségur is set to fire (March 16)	Albertet de Sestaro Blacasset Guiraut Riquier	1210–1221 till 1279 1254–1282
1255 The fall of Quéribus		

THE TROUBADOURS IN HUNGARY

(HISTORICAL LINKS)

HUNGARIAN ANTECEDENTS: THE SOCIAL POSITION OF ENTERTAINERS IN THE MEDIEVAL HUNGARIAN COURT

The cultivation of music at Hungary's royal and aristocratic courts partly resembled medieval musical customs at other European courts and partly differed from them. It resembled them, inevitably, insofar as the kings of the House of Árpád had established dynastic links with the other reigning houses in Europe (partly by marriage), thereby bringing to Hungary groups of foreigners with their own customs and cultures. A new queen would be accompanied by a complete royal household including knights, gentlemen-in-waiting, and also musicians and entertainers, and as a result the Hungarian court might often provide a home for French, Italian, Walloon or Byzantine *conditionarii.* Yet other elements were also fostered at the Hungarian court. While willing to accept cultural customs from abroad, the Hungarian kings always set great store by the Hungarian musicians among their servants, who would express in Hungarian verse the warlike deeds of their monarch and his forebears, using, either for an epic or a lyrical song, the language the king himself spoke.

One must suppose that Hungarian music was kept alive by the court musicians, who at the same time interspersed it with topical new elements. Through their activity, and sometimes through their mere existence, knowledge can be gained of Hungarian music one thought lost. In the first century or two after the Hungarian state had been founded, one can presume that court music still bore a very close resemblance to folk music, the music of the people, and no essential distinction had yet arisen between 'folk music' and 'art music'.

With the spread of literacy there is more material that assists in discovering the musical activity of the Middle Ages, including information on musicians, performers and instruments. This passive source material is of great importance to research into the history of music since no notated melodies from the early centuries of court music have survived.

Before turning to the written sources, mention should be made of the ancient Hungarian folk custom of *regölés* (ballad recitation), both as a folk custom and a folk-music phenomenon. The texts include many references to a pre-Christian, pagan, shamanistic body of beliefs. King Stephen I (St. Stephen of Hungary), the founder of the Hungarian state, persecuted *regös* singers, but also features in *regös* songs, as do elements of the legend of the origin of the Hungarians, etc. *Regölés* is a repository of a great antiquity and a frequent subject for research by both ethnographers and historians. The musical of the *regös* songs does not belong to the typical ancient layer, but to European tradition. A passage recurs like a refrain: *Rőt ökör, régi törvény—hej regő rejtem.* Today this has already become unintelligible; it represents a vestigial remembrance that forms an organic part of today's *regös* song, but bears no conceptual relationship to the text sung by the *regös* singers. The constant repetition of it is reminiscent of the continuity of an incantation and of falling into a trance, which partly corresponds to its current function (of bringing young couples together by *regölés,* of casting a love spell, wishing abundance in the New Year, and later soliciting donations) and partly conserves a memory of its former function.

Persecution in the Middle Ages diverted *regölés* into two paths. On the one hand *regös* singers disguised themselves behind various forms, accepting Christian, western elements (thereby managing to preserve something of the old set of beliefs, too) and adjusted themselves to the international folk custom of mummery; on the other hand they entered court service as professional minstrels.

A whole range of analyses have been published on the historical development of *regölés* into a folk custom and of the *regös*-shaman parallel, and so here we shall confine ourselves to making use of some surviving manuscript records in order to highlight the means by which the pagan legacy and the new Christian tradition of the Middle Ages came to appear as a joint manifestation that led new connotations to begin attaching themselves to certain elements of it.

Regölés was linked to the traditional feast of the winter solstice, which became amalgamated in the Middle Ages with Christmas. Nowadays *regölés* begins on December 26, the feast of the proto martyr St. Stephen, who gave his name to the Hungarian King Stephen I. This coincidence led to some confusion of ideas and mixing of practices. The oldest surviving Hungarian manuscript to contain musical notation, the Codex Albensis (compiled in the first half of the 12th century, some decades after King Stephen had been canonized)[1] contains a series of pen-and-ink drawings that begins exactly below the Office of St. Stephen the Proto Martyr with a picture of a galloping, saddled, riderless horse; later there is an antlered stag being chased by a hunter who is lifting his axe above his head, and also a few animal pictures, as a sitting dog, or a braying ass whose open mouth emits the word 'Allelujah'. Particularly in relation to this cycle of feasts it may well represent some recollections of *regölés.* In certain variants of the folk custom the *regös* singers began their song by declaring themselves servants of King Stephen, and therefore immune from persecution. The series of pen-and-ink drawings recalls the version of the *regös* song found in Dozmat (Vas County):

Noha kimennél, uram, Szent István
király vadászni, madarászni,
De ha nem találnál sem vadat, sem
madarat,
Hanem csak találnál csodafiúszarvast,
Hej, regülejtem, regülejtem.[2]

[1] Falvy and Mezey (1963).
[2] Sebestyén (1902), pp. 42–8.

(Though my lord, saint and king Stephen, your were
to go forth to hunt or to fowl,
You would find no game, nor fowl,
You would only find a magic boy-stag,
Hej, etc.)

Gyula Sebestyén claims there are historical reasons why Hungarian *regös* singers name the pursuing hunter King Stephen. In the west and south of Transdanubia there were particularly hard struggles with 'pagan' *regös* singers, which would become still more acute during the *regös* week after Christmas. Against shamanism (in which *regölés* was included) the official Church set up its own set of beliefs, primarily through the figures of Jesus and Mary. The hunts on horseback recalling pagan times gained legendary qualities by the inclusion of a stag that was no ordinary game but the magic boy-stag of the *regös* singers. The 14th century Illuminated Chronicle expands the story still further: "non cervus, sed Angelus Dei", not a stag but a messenger of God, with altar candles burning on his antlers. The Illuminated Chronicle relates that the knights began shooting arrows at the stag and giving chase, but at first he would not move, and then suddenly disappeared. A church had to be built on the site of his disappearance. Even in the Codex Albensis we can think of the magic stag of the Illuminated Chronicle, since one of the knights jumps off his horse to strike the stag down with his axe, and his untethered horse bolts. Between the bolting horse and the figure of the stag about to disappear, there is the figure of Mary in a floating triangle. The melody written later in the margin of the other half of the page on which the drawing appears (28) may also refer to Mary: "Salve nobilis virgo jesse, salve flos campi Maria" (in a 13th century hand).

So a new mediating and helping figure had now emerged in place of the pagan shaman. Many churches were built and dedicated to Mary, a fact obviously connected with King Stephen's idea (derived from Byzantium) of Mary's patronage. Corroboration of this is the juxtaposition of the magic boy-stag with Mary and not with Jesus. The last drawing of the series, the sitting ass who sings Allelujah (88) must be a caricature on those who resisted conversion: they sang their gregorians without really believing.

Many different elements are mingled in this series of drawings: *regölés* started on the feast of St. Stephen the Proto Martyr, but the reference was to the Hungarian King Saint Stephen; they were chasing the legendary magic boy-stag but linked it with the symbol of Mary; the Antiphonal was designed for church singing, but the pen-and-ink drawings in the margin poked fun at the chants or the singers.

As entertainers at the royal court, the *regös* singers played an important part alongside the minstrels and *joculatores* (jesters). In fact the three terms used to describe entertainers at the medieval Hungarian court (*joculator*, *regös*, *igric*) can scarcely have expressed any major distinctions. The three terms are more a reflection of the parlance of characters and other documents, of the local usage of the scribes or, perhaps, of topographical factors. All three, with slightly different shades of meaning, expressed a single scope of duties: entertainers had to create a good atmosphere at court, they had to transmit the latest news, and remember the great deeds of ancestors and forebears, presumably with the help of music.

Not much is known about the court *regös* singers or their society, or about the origin of the folk custom of *regölés*. The identity of the terms may possibly refer to some ancient historical connexion, but this can no longer be ascertained.

Of the terms used for the entertainers, the word *joculator* (jester) is first found in the *Gesta Hungarorum* of Anonymus, dating from the end of the 12th century. The *Gesta* also sheds light on the musical practice of the Hungarian court, not indeed about the time of the Magyar conquest of the Carpathian Basin, which the work is concerned with, but about the musical practice of the time when it was written—precisely the period when foreign troubadours were arriving in Hungary and the first, early or pre-Renaissance of Hungary was occurring through contact with Europe as a whole, after the death of King Béla III.

Anonymus's references to music have been published several times. Using the latest facsimile edition[3] as a basis, if one interprets the texts from the point of view of court music, an interesting picture emerges that concerns in part the minstrels, and in part the instruments in use at the end of the 12th century. As early as the introductory section, Anonymous refers to the custom that *joculatores* performed heroic songs at the Hungarian court:

> If... from the false tales of peasants or the garrulous songs of jesters the Hungarian nation should hear, as if in a dream, of its earliest origins and certain of its heroic deeds...

(in Latin [1^v]: ...*ex falsis fabulis rusticorum vel a garrulo cantu ioculatorum quasi sompniando audieret*...)

As we have already mentioned in the chapter on Mediterranean culture and troubadour music, Anonymus, on the basis of his studies or experiences in Paris, described the role and songs of the *joculator* in the same terms as the *jongleur* functioned in relation to a troubadour. A *jongleur* (or *joculator* in the *Gesta*) was a performer who performed songs he had learnt somewhere from some other person. Dezső Pais considered that *regös* was the best Hungarian synonym for *joculator*, but in our opinion the term *regös* does not exactly correspond with the Franco-Latin *joculator*, because the task of the *regös* among Hungarian court entertainers (*conditionarii*) may well have been greater and different from that of a mere passive performing musician. It more closely approximated to the function of a troubadour than to that of a *jongleur*. The two terms of *joculator* and *regös* existed side by side in 12th and 13th century Hungary.

The next musical reference in the *Gesta* is to an instrument: a horn. (Here it is worth mentioning that coeval with *Gesta* is the 'Horn of Lehel' found at

[3] Anonymus: *Gesta Hungarorum. Béla király jegyzőjének könyve a magyarok cselekedeteiről* (The Book by King Béla's Clerk on the Deeds of the Hungarians), transl. Dezső Pais, introduction by György Györffy, Budapest, 1975.

Jászberény, which is technically speaking an oliphant.) Here is an excerpt from Chapter 8 (5^r):

> The warriors of Chief Álmos... blew their battle horns (*statim que sonuerunt tubas bellicas*)... the two opposing forces joined battle...

In the foreword Anonymus expresses reservations about the historical value of the songs of the *joculatores,* but in Chapter 25 he still makes use of them at "Tétény's cleverness" (11^v), and even quotes one of them, maybe word for word:

> As our jesters relate, they acquired a place for them all and earned themselves a good name. (*Ut dicunt nostri ioculatores, omnes loca sibi aquirebant et nomen bonum accipiebant.*)

The last two lines of the Latin are rhyming lines of 10 syllables. Anonymus's "nostri ioculatores" expressly refers to *court joculatores*, who belonged to the same circle as he did himself.

Chapters 39, 41 and 44 again feature (battle) horns:

> 39: Lél, the son of Tas, blew his horn (*tuba*).
> 41: Bulcsú, the son of Bogát, sounded the battle horns (*tubas bellicas*).
> 44: ... then the Hungarians blew the battle horns (*tubas bellicas*).

In Chapter 42 (17^v) Anonymus refers to the songs performed by the joculatores as verification of his own story:

> If concerning their wars and bold deeds you will not credit the letters written on this page, then believe the songs of the jesters and the false tales of the peasants, who to this day have not allowed the Hungarians' wars and bold deeds to sink into oblivion. (*Eorum etiam bella et fortia queque facta sunt si scriptis presentis pagine non vultis, credite garrulis cantibus ioculatorum, et falsis fabulis rusticorum, qui fortia facta et bella hungarorum usque in hodiernum diem oblivioni non tradunt.*)

Here the conception has changed, since Anonymus distinguishes the song of the *joculator* from the peasant folk tale, but in both cases recognizes the significance of the attempt to honour, maintain, and indeed consciously foster tradition.

The last musical reference, in Chapter 46 (19^v) mentions, alongside *joculator* song, two further instruments as well:

> There [at Buda] all the lutes and pipes sounded sweetly together with all the songs of the jesters (*Et omnes simphonias atque dulces sonos cythararum et fistularum cum omnibus cantibus ioculatorum habebant ante se.*)

The Hungarian translation of these lines calls for some explanation from a musical point of view, as it does not fully correspond with the terminology of the 12th century. It has already been mentioned in the first chapter that the medieval Latin translations of al-Farabi's original Arabic text called two instruments *cythara* and *fistula*. Anonymus must have been familiar with this or similar theoretical works when he put these particular two instruments into the hands of the Hungarians. The *fistula* is unequivocally a *pipe*, i.e. a woodwind instrument, perhaps some early variety of today's pipe. *Cythara*, however, is a collective term that may refer to several types of stringed instruments, either plucked or bowed. Several forms of body are known: it could be shaped like a bisected pear or be a slightly curved oval. Dezső Pais's translation of it as a *koboz* (kobsa or lute) refers to the pear-shaped, plucked variety, but the term itself featured in several documents in Anonymus's time, so that he ought to have been familiar with the instrument from its Hungarian use. Something else was also meant by *Et omnes simphonias*: not harmony, consonance or euphony, but simply *musicians playing an instrument*.

Let us append some names of persons and places taken from references to court minstrels in medieval charters:

A charter of King Andrew (Endre) II in 1219 describes the Transylvanian estate of Wynchy (Felvinc, in the former county of Aranyos-Torda) as being presented to the Chapter of Esztergom along with 36 courtiers including one by the name of Regus.

The most important documentary reference to the minstrels and their role at court is a rather late one from the reign of King Lajos (Louis) the Great in 1347. The king sanctioned Senechal Pál's letter of judgement from Visegrád dated 1346, which affirmed the *comes* Loránd, a gold assayer and juror of Buda, in possession of the Regtelek estate in Pest County. The village of Regtelek received its name from its long extinct owners, *regös* singers who had once been royal *conditionarii* or *combibatores*. The passage of the charter referring to them reads: "...*Combibatorum Regalium condicionariorum wlgariter Regus dictorum*..."[4]

This document on the giving away of the Pest settlement of the royal *conditionarii*, who had left no descendants is the most that is known about the group of court *regös* singers. By the mid-14th century there were no more royal *combibatores*, usually called *Regus*, and they left no offspring. Their estate at Regtelek lay in the north-east of today's Budapest, where, like other servants of the court, they had a separate dwelling place. The word *combibator* means a 'drinker-together'. It was coined in Hungarian Latin, but its acquired meaning and function are obscure, and it does not appear in Du Cange's dictionary. Dezső Pais, in his discussion of the etymology of the Hungarian word *részeg* (drunk) connects it with the verbs *révül* (fall into a trance) and *rejt* (conceal) or with the substantives *reg* and *regös*, and says that it signified the shaman priest's descent into a religious trance. As shaman ideas were expunged from the culture

[4] Szabó (1881), pp. 553–68.

of medieval Hungarians, the word came to denote other states of trance and unconsciousness as well.[5]

> As for the meaning of *combibator*, a close equivalent is *Regus* (pronounce *regüs*), since at that time the latter word denoted participants at the royal symposia presumably called *reg*; thus a major connotation is the notion of 'a partaker in heavy drinking and carousing'... The royal or... court minstrels also acted as court jesters, at least at a certain period, which is how they came to be drinkers-together at the royal *reg* and indeed had to drink in company with noble society; it enabled them to perform their task of entertaining better, as the wine would loosen their tongues... The main factor in the effectiveness of their role as jesters would certainly be the awkwardness that arose from the difference of social rank. But their *regölés* also had its practical uses; it could provide the opportunity of conveying to the 'right ears' many things that would otherwise have been hushed by etiquette or by the silence of piety or cowardice.
>
> Having once been applied only in the context of 'sorcery', then acquiring the meaning of 'incantation', the word *reg*... could come to mean 'song' outside any sorcery context, so that a name applied to the 'sorcerers' or 'enchanters' of former times might thus be applied to 'singers'.[6]

In the later, 15th and 16th century documents *regös* appears on several occasions as a personal name: as the name of a bondsman in Baranya County, and as the name of a taxpayer of Pest, for example.

The documentary evidence, then, points to the existence of a group of court servants called *regös*, of whom there is no mention after the 13th century. No one knows what happened to them, whether they dispersed or were dissolved. However, the Mongol invasion swept through the country at that time, to be followed by a strong influx of western musicians into Hungary. One can surmise that the *regös* singers employed at court had their origins way back in pagan times. In the early centuries of Hungarian Christianity they underwent a number of changes and eventually survived only in one or two names.

It is generally agreed that the Slav loan-word *igric* was another name for the old Hungarian minstrel. In Old Russian and Old Czech the Slav *igruc* was equivalent to *Spielmann*, in Slovak to *Spieler* and musician, and in Ukrainian it meant actor. A closer source for the Hungarian word cannot be established.[7]

Identification of the term with Hungarian minstrels may have arisen from the fact that several dwelling-places and sometimes villages that were inhabited by *joculatores* were called Igric or Igrici. This may have led to the practice of replacing the Latin term *joculator*, found in documents only, with the Hungarian

[5] Pais (1951), p. 138.

[6] Pais (1958), pp. 181–96; Pais, D.: *A magyar ősvallás nyelvi emlékeiből* (Some Linguistic Records of Hungarian Prehistoric Religion), Budapest, 1975, pp. 109–42.

[7] Kniezsa (1955), Vol. I, p. 221.

vernacular term *igric*. (It should be noted that the term *joculator* never appears as a place-name.)

In the 14th century, and perhaps even from the mid-13th century, the concept of *joculator* underwent a double transformation: from denoting the function of an epic *joculator*, it appears in contexts that unambiguously suit the meaning of entertainer, which is very close to the concept of *igric* (*Spielmann*) in the Slav languages.

The first historical reference to the *igric* ("*Igrech villam ioculatorum*"[8]) dates from 1244, the period when mentions of epic *joculatores* were slowly dying out. Later occurrences are extremely varied: in 1377 it appears as the name of a field in a deed dividing up an estate: "... *quas transeundo, ad plagam septemtrionalem vergendo, venit ad quendam campum Igrischtya vocatum, quem per medium dividendo*..."[9]. Around 1400 the Hungarian Vocabulary of Schlägl translates the Latin *palpominus* as *igric*.[10] In 1449 an inhabitant of Eger is called Blasius Igrecz de Agria.[11] The pre-1466 'Munich Codex' translates *tibicen* as *igric*: "vidisset tibicines—he would have seen *igric*'s there".[12] Around 1466 it occurs in the 'Vienna Codex' in the sense of an instrument. The Nagyszombat Codex of 1512 (p. 356) mentions "*igrich-beszéd*" (igrich speech), while the scribe of the early 16th century Nádor Codex lists it among the 24 sins of speech and language:

Hazugság, Ruth bezed
Hyzelkodes, Igrecseegh...[13]

(Deceit, lewd talk, cajolery, 'minstrelsy').

These occurrences give a very scattered picture, and the use of the single expression of *igric* well demonstrates the huge change that had taken place in the ranks of Hungarian minstrels and entertainers as the expressions *regös* and epic *joculator*, who had fostered real traditions, were becoming scarcer in documents.

The semantic content of the word *joculator*, which initially had belonged to the concept of 'serious' interpretation, was shifted towards light performance, amusement and entertainment, so that the *joculator* became a figure in 'frivolous' carousing. Bertalan Korompay thinks that the Hungarian epic *joculatores* became absorbed into the *jongleurs* from other nations that they encountered.[14] We subscribe to the view of Bence Szabolcsi that the concept of the *joculator* underwent a double transformation in the 14th century Hungary: in part his role as an entertainer came to be dominant and in part the *joculatores* became instrumental performers. This also means that after the 14th century

[8] Szamota and Zolnai (1902–6).

[9] Sebestyén (1891: 'Anjoukori nyomok...'), pp. 413–22.

[10] Szamota (1894).

[11] Szabolcsi (1928); reprinted in *Magyar Zenetudomány*, I. ed. F. Bónis, Budapest, 1959, p. 31.

[12] *Nyelvemléktár* I. p. 208.

[13] The original of the Nádor Codex is to be found in the Budapest University Library, Cod. Hung. XVI, Nr. 1, p. 691.

[14] Korompay (1956), p. 61.

they would feature in written records and parlance not as *joculatores* but as pipers, or later as lutenists and fiddlers.[15]

Anonymus had a low opinion of the *joculatores* whom he quoted at several places and of the songs they performed. Another factor that may have contributed to this opinion was that the troubadours were already arriving in Hungary at the end of the 12th century, when he wrote his *Gesta*. Understandably a complete contrast to the serious *joculator* songs about grave battles and wars was offered by the light troubadour music brought from Occitania, by the carefree music of the lovely Provençal poetry, which aimed solely to express all the niceties of 'courtoisie' in the most sophisticated way. But this sophisticated form of expression was based on a social climate utterly different from that which could taken root at the Hungarian Court of the early Árpád kings.[16]

THE BIOGRAPHICAL EVIDENCE ON PEIRE VIDAL AND GAUCELM FAIDIT AND THEIR LINKS WITH HUNGARY; THE TRAVELS IN HUNGARY OF AIMERIC DE PEGUILHAN

Hungary's literary historians have been aware of the sojourn of Peire Vidal in Hungary since the final decade of the 19th century, mainly as a result of a communication by Gyula Sebestyén.[1] Included in one of the first studies was an excerpt from a poem beginning "Ben viu a gran dolor", which Vidal is supposed to have written while in Hungary.[2] The beginning of the same poem has also been published in facsimile.[3] The most recent study of relevance is by Sándor Eckhardt, who dealt with Gaucelm Faidit as well as Peire Vidal. He reinterpreted the poem Sebestyén had earlier analysed (in a translation by Mór Herzl). He also published Gaucelm Faidit's 'Lament to Richard' along with its music.[4] In describing Vidal, Eckhardt relied not only on biographical evidence but on his detailed knowledge of Vidal's poetry.[5] For example, he writes as follows:

> On more than one occasion Peire Vidal struck an individual and frequently debonaire tone in his poems which would make him easily understood by the half-educated clerical *joculatores* of Hungary, who may well have used the same style. . .[6] By and large he liked to show off; he had such a high regard for

[15] Szabolcsi; op. cit., pp. 33–4.

[16] Falvy (1977).

[1] Sebestyén (1891: 'Imre király. . .'), p. 503; Sebestyén (1891: 'Adalékok. . .').

[2] Diez (1965); the work refers in detail to his stay at the Hungarian court: p. 143.

[3] Békefi, R.: *III. Béla magyar király emlékezete*. . . (In Memory of the Hungarian King Béla III), ed. Gy. Forster, Budapest, 1900, p. 143.

[4] Eckhardt (1961), pp. 129–37.

[5] Anglade (1923) is the source of Eckhardt's quotations from Vidal's poems. The Roman numerals assigned by Eckhardt refer to Anglade's numbering, e.g. "Ben viu a gran dolor" is XXVIII, on pp. 118–22 of the book; Eckhardt based his information about Gaucelm Faidit on Hoepffner (1955).

[6] Pais (1952).

his own poems as to rank himself among the highest Maecenases... To a degree one can consider Peire Vidal as the forefather of Villon. Under his troubadour coat he retained and passed on the tone and customs of the Goliardic entertainers.[7]

At this point we can cite the 6th stanza of the melody he published as No. 2 (Pill. 364.7—Provençal Manuscript *R*, p. 65[a]):

So es En Peire Vidal Cel qui mante domnei e drudaria E fa que pros per amor de s'amia Et ama mais betalhas e torneis Que monges patz, e semblal malaveis Trop so jornar et estar en un loc.	This is Peire Vidal Who honours politeness and gallantry And acts like a noble in his love of his loved ones And loves battles and tourneys more Than a monk loves peace, and for whom it seems like Sickness to stay too long in one place.

Gennrich describes Vidal as a rare mixture of a wise man and a fool; to himself he appeared so important and so unique that only the heroes of legend could compete with him.[8] His *Vida* has much to say about his personality and social background, and about the course of his life and travels.[9] Although the *vidas* of neither Vidal nor Faidit make any mention of a journey to Hungary, the main evidence about their lives must be added to our description of them and of their musical style, particularly since the lives of Vidal and Faidit have never been dealt with in detail in any Hungarian published work.

Vidal was the son of a Toulouse furrier, which means he stemmed from the artisan stratum of the rising medieval urban citizenry. When Vidal left his home, Toulouse was an important centre of the Albigensian movement. He first entered the service of *Raimund V*, Count of Toulouse; later he went to Marseille, to *Barral de Baux*, whom he mentions in six poems under the code name (= *senhal*) Rainier. Barral's wife's name was Azalaïs, and Vidal must have been particularly attracted to her, since she appears in 14 of his poems under the pseudonym Na Vierna. The *vidas* next mention *King Alfonso II* of Aragon, who reigned from 1162 until 1196, and from whose court King Béla III himself brought Constanza to Hungary as his daughter-in-law, to establish a dynastic link between the Hungarian House of Árpád and the kings of Aragon through her marriage with his son Imre. It is not known whether Vidal came to Buda at that time or later. There is biographical evidence only that he went to Toulouse and around Carcasson on several occasions while he lived at the Aragonese court.

[7] Eckhardt (1961), pp. 130–1.

[8] Gennrich (1965), p. 65.

[9] The *vidas* have survived in several manuscripts, which show minor divergences. We have used two of the original manuscripts: 1. Paris, Bibliothèque Nationale Française (hereafter PBNF) 854 (33 recto—Gaucelm Faidit, 39 recto—Peire Vidal); 2. PBNF 12.473 (22 recto—Gaucelm Faidit, 27 recto—Peire Vidal).

From Aragon he returned to Marseille, where his relationship with Barral de Baux's wife brought him into conflict with the viscount (and it is said that Vidal had his tongue cut out). In any case he had to leave. He went first to Lombardy and then to the island of Cyprus, where he joined the entourage of *Richard Cœur-de-Lion*. It might have been here that he married a Greek woman and in his exaggerated dreams imagined himself heir apparent to the throne of Constantinople. Not long after, he was in Montferrat with *Boniface I*; in one of his poems (Pill. 364.8 "Baro, Jesus, qu'en...") he campaigns for the 4th Crusade, which Boniface has undertaken to lead, and in the same poem he manages to say hard words about King Philippe Augustus of France. Soon after Vidal turns up in Malta (Pill. 364.30), and in his last years he may have been connected with the troubadour Balacasset (Blacatz, Pill. 364.32), who also was a good patron. Vidal's last known poem dates from 1205 (Pill. 364.38). Dates are difficult to ascertain from the *vidas,* but some help is offered by references in the poems to historical persons and events. Barral de Baux died in 1192, so Vidal must have been at his court before that date. Raimond V died in 1194; Alfonso II lived until 1196, and he was succeeded on the Aragonese throne by Constanza's brother Pedro II, who was himself a troubadour. Constanza married King Imre in 1198 at Buda; the 4th Crusade began in 1202, when the army set out towards the Balkans. Richard Cœur-de-Lion died in 1199, and if Vidal was in Cyprus with him, it could only have been during the 3rd Crusade, which ended in 1192. Vidal must have set out for Buda before the death of Alfonso II (and according to Anglade he was in Hungary after the death of Henry IV in 1197[10]), but in 1202 he was back in Montferrat. Important evidence that he came to Hungary is contained in the poem "Ben viu e gran dolor", which has been discussed in great detail in the sources already mentioned,[11] from the point of view of interpreting the poem itself and its political content. None of the sources, unfortunately, gives the melody, although most of the manuscripts have staves over the first stanza, from which one can presume that it had one. The following sources for the poem are missing from the Hungarian studies (they are to be found under No. 364.13 in Pillet's bibliography):

Rome — Bibl. Vat. 5232 (100–284)
Paris — Bibl. Nat. fr. 856 (33)
Modena — Bibl. Estense a,R,4,4, (24–83)
Paris — Bibl. Nat. fr. 1749 (30, MG 41)
Rome — Bibl. Vat. 3207 (25–76)
Paris — Bibl. Nat. fr. 12.473 (31)
Paris — Bibl. Nat. fr. 12.474 (59, MG 922)
Florence — Bibl. Riccardiana 2909 (71, 184 p. 137)
Paris — Bibl. Nat. fr. 22.543 (17, -140)

[10] Anglade (1923), p. 270: "Le séjour du poète en Hongrie se place peu après la mort d'Henri VI (11 Sept, 1197)."

[11] Eckhardt (1961), pp. 131–3.

In the last manuscript listed (Provençal *R*) many melodies by Vidal have survived—9 out of the 13—but the staves over the text of "Ben viu" are empty.

As this work is primarily intended to present *troubadour music*, we can touch on poems that survive without their melodies only insofar as they contain biographical information. An extensive body of work on Vidal has appeared abroad, but none of the studies analyse his musical activities. We have chosen to deal with Vidal not merely because of his link with Hungary. Through him (and through the composing done by Faidit) a valuable cross-section of troubadour music can be obtained. His was the art of a man who began life as the son of a Toulouse furrier, got close to obtaining the throne of Constantinople, and who did not miss the opportunity at the royal court of Hungary to paint, in his poem "Ben viu e gran dolor", a panorama of the European political situation, to brief the Hungarian king, as it were, on which European rulers were worth co-operating with and which were to abhor. Several manuscripts depict Peire Vidal, usually with a large hat and without an instrument.[12]

The other troubadour visitor to Hungary whose musical style we analyse in detail is Gaucelm Faidit. Jeanroy, who has done eminent research into troubadour poetry, gives the following brief summary of him:

> Quelques-uns peut-être suivirent en Hongrie Marguerite de France, veuve du Jeune Roi, qui épouse Béla III. en 1185; deux au moins, Peire Vidal et Gaucelm Faidit y accompagnèrent sûrement Constance, fille d'Alfonse II d'Aragon, qui fut, de 1198 à 1204, femme du roi Émeric.[13]

The quotation mentions both Vidal and Faidit. Again, the latter's stay in Hungary is unconfirmed by his biographical sources, but made clear in his poem "Anc nom parti de solatz ni de chan" (Pill. 167.6), which Eckhardt discusses in detail.[14] The music has not survived, and only one line refers to Faidit's having been to Hungary and having paid homage to Constanza:

> Et ai estat en Ongri' ez en Fransa et si-m dones Damisella Constanssa, totz mos volers no-m passera-l talen q'ieu ai de lieis, cui am tan finemen.
> (But I was in Hungary and in France, and should you grant me Damsel Constanssa my desire for joy will be fulfilled, so faithfully do I love her.)

Gaucelm Faidit's *Vida* has survived in every manuscript that contains the life of Vidal. The codices depict Faidit in the company of a woman,[15] and the biographical sources say he married a former nun by the name of Guillelmá. Faidit was born into a family of burgesses in Uzerche (Vézère, the province of

[12] Pictures of Vidal can be found in PBNF 854 = 39 recto; PBNF 12.473 = 27 recto; the latter was published in Keresztury, Vécsey and Falvy (1960).

[13] Jeanroy (1934–5), Vol. I, pp. 269–70: "Séjour de quelques troubadours à la cour de Hongrie." The section quoted can be found on p. 270.

[14] Eckhardt (1961), pp. 134–5.

[15] PBNF, 854 = 33 verso; PBNF, 12.473 = 22 recto.

Corrèze), presumably in the mid-12th century since in one of Montaudon's *sirventes* (written between 1191 and 1194) some biographical details of him already feature. Accordingly, his initial sphere of activity ranged from Uzerche to Agen on the Garonne. Most of the songs he wrote at that time were dedicated to *Marie de Turenne*, the wife of Viscount *Eble V* (Ventadorn). During his life he may have come into close contact with *Richard Cœur-de-Lion*, who was then also Duke of Aquitaine. Richard died in 1199, after suffering much persecution, and Faidit wrote a lament (*plank*) for him beginning: "Fortz causa es que tot lo major dan". (This we shall discuss in detail in the chapter of musical analysis). The same relationship is referred to in a crusader song of his, "Ara nos sia guitz" (Pill. 167.9, of which the melody has not survived). In the 4th stanza he (like Vidal) abuses Richard's adversary, King Philippe Augustus of France. Sándor Eckhardt declares that the *plank* was written in Hungary, a supposition that is not contradicted by the biographical chronology. Unfortunately no real proof can be gained either from the text or the music. After 1200, Faidit's patron was at first *Raimon d'Agout* (lord of Apt and Saut), but by the time of the 4th Crusade he was in Montferrat, in the entourage of *Boniface I*, like Vidal. He may have set out with the crusaders, but in 1204 he was back in Provence. From some of his *tensos* we know that he had contacts with Peirol (1180–1225), Aimeric de Peguilhan (1195–1230), Perdigo (1195–1220), Albertet de Sestaro (1210–1241), and Raimbaut de Vagueiras (1180–1207). The dates in parentheses denote the periods of literary activity, so that the seemingly late friendship with Sestaro could have begun earlier, before any poems of Sestaro can be accurately dated. Faidit died around 1220.

Jean Mouzat says that Faidit wrote a political play about the heresy of the priests, entitled *L'Eretgia dels prèires*, and that it was performed in Toulouse. The manuscript has been lost.[16] This would confirm Sándor Eckhardt's supposition that "his emigration from his own country and also his journey to Hungary may conceivably have taken place to shake off orthodox persecution."[17]

The journeys of both troubadours to Hungary were linked with the marriage of Constanza of Aragon in 1198. Bergert, who wrote about the female characters mentioned by the troubadours, believes that after Constanza's marriage with King Imre she went on to marry Frederic of Sicily, as early as in 1209, and that she died in 1222.[18]

In the course of our research it became apparent that a third troubadour also came to Hungary, a few decades after Vidal and Faidit. This third troubadour was Aimeric de Peguilhan, who was in the service of the Italian family of Este at the time the Hungarian King Andrew (Endre) II married Beatrix. The evidence for Peguilhan's stay in Hungary is indirect, and we discovered it in a poem by a fellow troubadour, Guillem Raimon. The poem, which begins "N'Aimeric,

[16] Mouzat (1963–4).

[17] Eckhardt (1961), p. 134.

[18] Bergert (1913), p. 25; he writes her name as Costanza von Aragon.

digatz qu.us par d'aquest marques" (Pill. 229.2), has survived in a Provençal manuscript preserved in Rome.[19]

The relevant stanza on Aimeric de Peguilhan's link with Hungary reads:

> Nobs de biguli se plaing. tant es iratz e dolenz. a deu e pois a las genz . del rei car chantan vol dir. gue ges bon partir . no fai dos priuatz . et es tan se notz . n obs qe locs no sai en chanz. a sofert plus c'us rolanz . sofrir no poria . c'ab sen enqeria. gerras trebailbz et affanz . e per sen zom dis bertrans . cazet d'un aut solar ios. no dis pas q'en peiz en fos. *[Q]ant eu uing d'ongaria. n'aicelis rizia.* car per saluz e per manz . er en fobz mas si l'enchanz . q'eu sai d'autre color fos . e seria per un dos . plus ras de mi e plus tos . setot s'en feing salamos.[20]

The poem alludes clearly to Aimeric de Peguilhan's return to Ferrara from Hungary, which Jeanroy dates at around 1215.[21] This date fails to correspond with the dynastic links between Hungary and the Este family. Our starting-point is that six of Peguilhan's poems laud a certain Beatrix. At the beginning of the 13th century three members of the Este family bore the name Beatrix.[22] The one who married King András in 1234, was only born in 1215, the daughter of Aldobrandino. She had an aunt called Beatrix (the daughter of Azzo VI: 1191–1226), but this aunt had no Hungarian connections. One would presume that Aimeric de Peguilhan came to Hungary for the wedding, but it is also possible that he visited the Hungarian court quite independently of that event. It is quite unclear which Beatrix he celebrated, although biographical evidence would lead to the assumption that it could only have been the first, who became a nun in 1218, the poems being addressed to her before she took the veil. Their first lines are as follows:

Ades vol de l'aondanse (Pill. 10.2)
Albert, cauzetz al vostre sen (Pill. 10.3)
Cel que s'irais ni guerrej' ab amor (Pill. 10.15)
with music: G 36
Chanter voill—per que?—jam platz (Pill. 10.16)
Per solatz d'autrui chan soven (Pill. 10.41)
with music: G 37
Qui la vi, en ditz (Descort) (Pill. 10.45)
with music: W 165–186
R 49–50

All these poems mention Beatrix by name, but none contain any reference to Hungary. Peguilhan is considered to have been active between 1135 to 1230,

[19] The manuscript is in Rome, Biblioteca Vaticana 3207.

[20] Gauchat and Kehrli (1891), pp. 341–67. The poem is given on p. 537, No. 233.

[21] Jeanroy (1934–5), p. 248.

[22] Bergert (1913), pp. 81–2.

which in itself does not preclude him travelling to Hungary in 1234. The stay could not have lasted longer than a year, since King András II died in 1235. Even though no other allusions than the line quoted can be discovered, it is worth taking a brief look at Peguilhan's biography, since his patrons were almost the same as those who favoured Vidal and Faidit. He was the son of a Toulouse cloth merchant and began his career as a troubadour at the court of Raimond V. By 1196 he was in Aragon at the court of Alfonso's son Pedro II, just as the king's sister, Constanza was about to leave, or perhaps already en route to the Hungarian court. From 1207 Peguilhan's home was in Montferrat, then ruled by William IV. Later he lived under the Viscount of Malaspina. He spent a final long period of his life at the Ferraran court, first under Azzo d'Este VI, and after his death in 1212, under his successors.

The number of Peguilhan's melodies to have come down to us is too small for any exact account of his musical style: for four of six surviving melodies he used the *Oda continua,* in one the *kanzone* form and in one of his works addressed to Beatrix: ("Qui la vie..." Pill. 10.45) the very rare *descort* (a long form belonging to the family of *sequentia* types, with many similar melodic phrases). In his lyrics he favoured refrain solutions, and he was generally held to be a master of poetry. He was one of the most important troubadours,[23] whom Gennrich describes in the following terms:

> Aimeric de Peguilhan ist ein Meister der Sprache, für den es keine Reimschwierigkeiten gibt, der seine Kunst nicht nur in den Dienst der Minne, sondern ebenso in den der Politik stellt.[24]

[23] Shephard and Chambers (1950); Torraca (1901).

[24] Gennrich (1951); MGG Vol. 13, column 832.

THE MUSIC OF PEIRE VIDAL AND GAUCELM FAIDIT

METHODOLOGICAL PROBLEMS: THE METHOD OF TROUBADOUR SONG NOTATION

Scholars in the 20th century have had two basic methods of editing medieval secular monody to choose between. One of them was based on 19th century tradition; it assigned mensural values to the notes, paying most attention to the medieval modal notation; but it could not represent modal notation with full precision, so that new rhythmic patterns had to be determined within certain value limits. To deal with the history of this matter would require a study in itself, but it should be mentioned that Gennrich, from the 1920s up to his most recent publications, has never deviated from this 'rhythmicized' method of editing that he himself created. Our research has been to a large extent founded upon Gennrich's considerable published work—almost 30 studies, mainly concerned with clarifying matters of form. Gennrich's whole work rests principally on theoretical bases. He follows a single system for representing the medieval note picture right from his *Grundriß einer Formenlehre des mittelalterlichen Liedes*[1] to his volumes in the series *Summa Musicae Medii Aevi*[2]. Initially (in *Grundriß*) he followed Beck's method[3] and identified himself with the modal rhythm. But the extent and variety of Gennrich's activity later led him to publish troubadour songs in his own rhythmicized system, which he employed in *Der musikalische Nachlaß der Troubadours*. But the material he published departs in several respects from the musical text of the original melodies and even from a diplomatic printing of the original texts. As we have said, he made arbitrary changes to the rhythmic pattern, as well as creating an independent rhythmic form of his own. Unfortunately his analyses in the *Kommentar* volume of *Nachlaß* (see Note 2) are imprecise both as to text and melody. In our own analyses we invariably draw attention to these differences where they appear, and with a knowledge of the contemporary notation of the original manuscripts one can scarcely say that Bruno Stäblein exaggerates in commenting on Gennrich's latest publishing method as follows:

> Mit Fleiß hat der Autor aus allen möglichen Bereichen das Material zusammengetragen. Allerdings ist es im Hinblick auf seine Darstellung ausgewählt und täuscht so eine nach außen hin tadellose Systematik vor. Ja, er hat diese, ein bedauerlicher und vielfach bedauerter methodischer Fehler,

[1] Gennrich (1932).
[2] Gennrich (1958), Sum. III; Gennrich (1960), Sum. IV; Gennrich (1965), Sum. XV. Coll. III.
[3] Beck (1908, 1910).

mit angeblichen entwicklungsgeschichtlichen Vorgängen verknüpft. Daß er hierbei willkürliche Veränderungen an den Melodien vornahm, um sie seiner Systematik gefügig zu machen, auch angebliche Zwischenglieder konstruierte, muß das Vertrauen in den Wahrheitsgehalt seiner Darstellung noch mehr erschüttern.[4]

In the printing without time values employed here we have sought to avoid the pitfall of distorting the medieval melodic picture in any way by the use of a 20th century theoretical basis. We feel that printing without time values provides a clear distinction between the single notes sung to one syllable and the larger and smaller melisma groups, likewise sung to one syllable. This method more closely corresponds with the text and note picture as it appears in the manuscripts, since wherever they originate from they uniformly adhere to the principle of *one syllable to one musical value*. A musical value, sung to a single syllable, consisted of one or of more notes (up to nine). In this respect the manuscripts show no variation: the notational technique for troubadour music was uniform in every territory.

In Hungarian publications today troubadour songs still appear in a rhythmicized form, presumably because the editors were reared in the old school. It is high time Hungary subscribed to the method developed internationally by musicologists, who have come out firmly in favour of value-free printing. The method was adopted as early as 1958 in Zingerle's *Tonalität und Melodieführung*,[5] in Hendrik van der Werf's volume of 1972[6], and more recently in Stäblein's *Schriftbild*... of 1965 (see Note 4) and Gülke's *Mönche, Bürger, Minnesänger*.[7]

Besides publishing the melodies without time values, we have transposed them all to a g^1 *final*, borrowing a method from comparative ethnomusicology that makes comparison easier. It allows particularly interesting observations to be made on the differences and similarities of the melodic lines of poems which survive in several manuscripts. In the manuscripts themselves most melodies end with a final c^1 or d^1, while g^1 finals make up scarcely 1–2% of the total.

Where several melodies have survived for the same poem, only the *notes that differ* have been written out, unless the note differences exceed 10%, in which case *the whole melody* has been written out. So two kinds of comparative notation can be found in this book: the chance merely to record the differences between variants occurred more often with Gaucelm Faidit. In Vidal's case almost every variant had to be written out in full.

The melodic material by the two troubadours has been taken from *four manuscripts*. We have collected all of them ourselves, by on-the-spot research. In troubadour literature the manuscripts have the distinguishing marks, *R*, *G*, *W*

[4] Stäblein (1975), p. 84.
[5] Zingerle (1958).
[6] Van der Werf (1972).
[7] Gülke (1975).

and *X*, *R* and *G* being Provençal manuscripts, *W* and *X* French. *X* is the oldest of them, dating from the mid-13th century; *W* is from the end of the 13th century, *R* and *G* from the beginning of the 14th.

Description of the manuscripts

R Repository: Paris, Bibliothèque Nationale, franç. 22.543. A parchment manuscript from the Provençal linguistic area, dating from c. 1300 or after. Size 435 × 305 mm. The text is in two columns per page, with the melody recorded above the first stanza of every poem on 4–5 staves (on red stave lines) in the F and C clefs. It is in early quadrat notation, not yet in mensural, but at the ligatures use is often made of one of the most important ornamental neums of early quadrat notation, the *plica*, particularly the *plica descendens*. Around the 1300s this mark may have referred to earlier interpretational practice, principally to indicate *glissando portamenti* accompanying the ligatures, which could not be expressed in the diatonic whole and half-note intervals of the melody as set out in the staves. Most of all, the use of the *plica* makes it more likely that there was Mediterranean influence. In our transcription we have refrained from resolving the mark, since its precise tonal relation cannot be determined for the above reasons.

G Repository: Milan, Biblioteca Ambrosiana, R 71 sup. A parchment manuscript from the territory of northern Italy, dating from the early 1300s. Size: 290 × 190 mm. The text is in two columns per page. Each melody is written out in full only for the first stanza; the first line of the melody is repeated adjacent to the first line of the 2nd stanza, so that the melodic continuity is indicated. It uses 5–6 stave lines, and the F and C clefs according to the range of the melody. Early quadrat notation is employed. The original intention was to record many more melodies than have actually come down to us: of the 169 poems with staves, the melodies of only 81 are written in.[8]

W Repository: Paris, Bibliothèque Nationale, franç. 844. This codex is the famous *Manuscrit du Roi*, which mainly contains *trouvère* songs from northern France, but also includes a number of Provençal poems, i.e. troubadour songs. It is a parchment manuscript from the second half of the 13th century. Size: 318 × 218 mm. The text is laid out in two columns, but many of the leaves with miniatures have been cut out. There is also a later part, from the 14th century. The main, earlier body of the codex, which includes troubadour songs, was taken down in square notation using four red stave lines and the clefs of F, C and G. The *plica descendens*, discussed under *R*, frequently appears, and raises the same problem of performance. Again it has not been indicated in our transcriptions. A complete fascimile edition of the manuscript has been published.[9]

[8] Sesini (1939), XIII–XV.
[9] Beck (1970).

X Repository: Paris, Bibliothèque Nationale, franç. 20.050. The manuscript is known as *Chansonnier de Saint-Germain des Prés* and was written in Lorraine in the mid-13th century, i.e. in the final period of troubadour activity. It is a small parchment manuscript, 180 × 120 mm in size. It might easily have been a performing copy which the troubadours carried about with them. In 1732 it was presented by its then owner, the Bishop of Metz, to the Abbey of Saint-Germain des Prés in Paris. The script and notation are the oldest of all the troubadour manuscripts. It was written on red four-line staves in the delicate *Metz* notation, using the F and C clefs.

The manuscript contains no indications of *glissando portamenti*, but of all the manuscripts used for this study this codex presents the greatest number of uncertainties about key, and several cases of floating tonality. A facsimile edition was published in the last century.[10]

In our transcriptions, melodies which have survived in several manuscripts are arranged with the southern (*R*, *G*) variants above, and the northern (*W*, *X*) variants below. This practice has been departed from only rarely.

In the comparative analysis and for every troubadour song printed in the book we have given the Pill. number, without which the songs and poems can no longer be identified. The numbering was the work of Alfred Pillet and Henry Carstens in their *Bibliographie der Troubadours*, Halle (Saale), 1933. The book appeared in three parts, the second of which gives an alphabetical list of each troubadour's work along with its sources. The first part of each compound number refers to the troubadour (e.g. Vidal's number is 364), and the second to the particular poem (Vidal's poem beginning "Anc no morir" is numbered '4' among Vidal's works, so that its full number is 364.4). The Pillet-Carstens bibliography also includes a complete register of rhymes.

The order of the melodies

In the case of both Peire Vidal and Gaucelm Faidit, we have taken the alphabetical order of the texts as a basis for arrangement. The Pill. numbers are not always consecutive as some poems lack melodies. Pillet and Carstens numbered all the works of each author alphabetically by text, whereas we have examined only the poems of which the melody survives.

Formal questions

In the analyses we have several times referred to the second of Gennrich's three volumes on troubadours—the *Kommentar* (See Note 2), usually marking it in parentheses (Gennrich *Komm.*) with the page number for reference. In Gennrich's analyses the melodic sections are marked by Greek letters, the text syllables by numerals and the rhymes by Roman letters. We have contracted the minor melodic lines, whenever the musical phrase so required, and marked the musical form by Roman capitals, the metrical form with a combination of

[10] Meyer and Raynaud (1892).

Roman lower case and figures, the melodic groups (whether individual notes or melismas) by numbers, and finally the line cadences by indicating the degrees of the scale in relation to the keynote. We have always indicated new conclusions and points of difference with Gennrich.

In the analyses we have also used the term *Oda continua* for the song form which contains a new musical element in every line. The expression comes from Dante, who used it in his work *De Vulgari Eloquentia.* The sentence from which students of troubadour music have borrowed the term runs as follows: "*sub una oda continua usque ad ultimum progressive, hoc est sine iteratione modulationis cuiusquam et sine diesi.*"[11] Most of the poems employed this song form; 84 troubadour songs were written in it, led by Floquet de Marseilla (1180–1231), 12 of whose 13 songs are of the *Oda continua* type. He is followed by Raimon de Miraval (1190–1220), who used the form for 11 of his 22 songs. Earlier Ventadorn had had a liking for it; he wrote 6 songs of the *Oda continua* type. In the later period the form was frequently employed by Guiraut de Riquier (on 9 occasions).

ANALYSES OF VIDAL'S SONGS

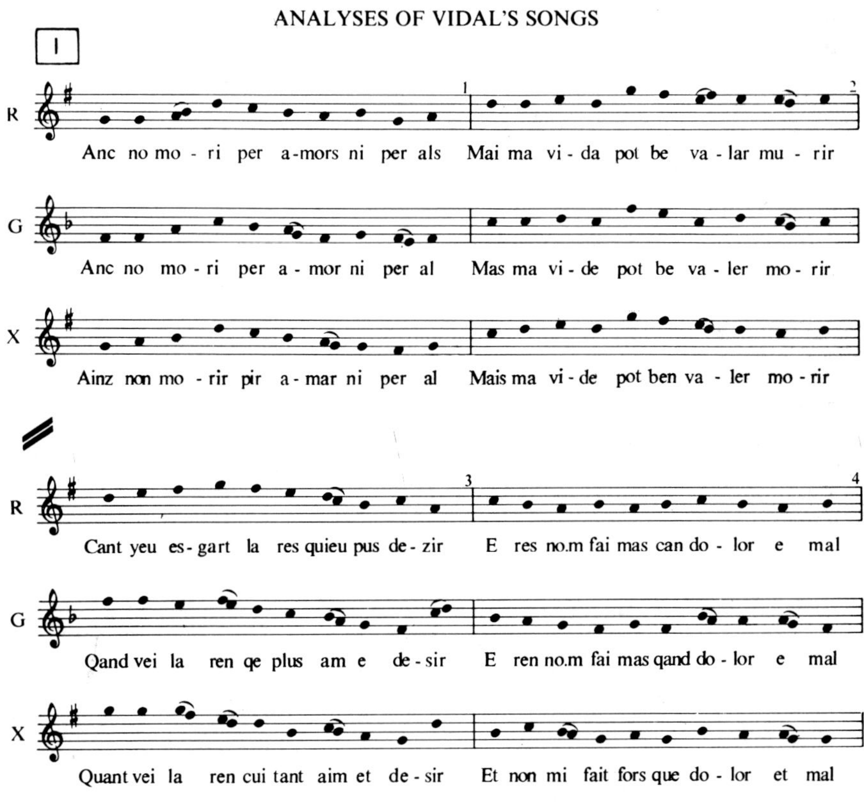

[11] Dante (1577), II. 10. 2.

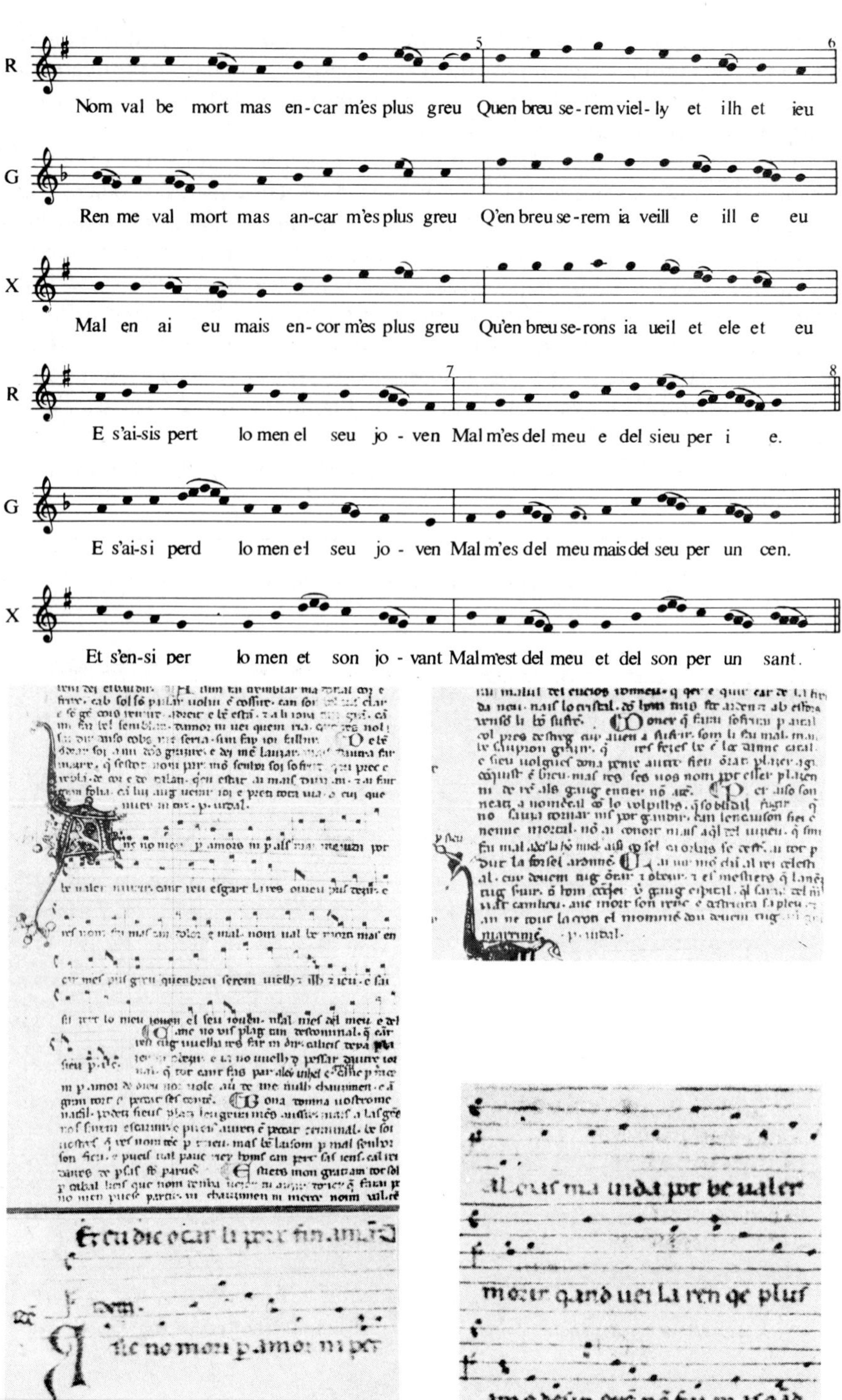
R
Nom val be mort mas en-car m'es plus greu Quen breu se-rem viel-ly et ilh et ieu
G
Ren me val mort mas an-car m'es plus greu Q'en breu se-rem ia veill e ill e eu
X
Mal en ai eu mais en-cor m'es plus greu Qu'en breu se-rons ia ueil et ele et eu
R
E s'ai-sis pert lo men el seu jo-ven Mal m'es del meu e del sieu per i e.
G
E s'ai-si perd lo men el seu jo-ven Mal m'es del meu mais del seu per un cen.
X
Et s'en-si per lo men et son jo-vant Mal m'est del meu et del son per un sant.

dolor e mal. fe me mal mort out

ancar me plus greu qe breu

seron ta uell ta ill e eu e tant

p[er] lo seu. el me iouen mal del

del meu mans del seu pun an.

Ar e mal n ui plais tant del
comunal

a ell son tan desliat camiuen.
l an tolt son reg e destrut e plus
e e siurt an la co s ei monum
dond deuenrut un grid espauc.
Comps d prieu d rex mueil abu
e de us am[er] pa qel es couc
e ambdos laier tuus mor mals
menz.
luis de la croc eun d mo a rren.

ç e qan eu po nulla re for mudar
e lei deguer plaiser m tesli
q mus no por sur nul uit uenir
e rot qi sais parlle uil eten.
çe p mer ni p amor de deu.
no pose trobar. lei nul ckuitors.
Tot idem eperlat ses coten.
Esteri mo gurr am ror sol perbu.
leis qi no dergni ueier ni aurir.
Ar de farar pois non pre peur.
Ai chiusun ni mcei nom ual.
Teniar malus dei enoior romeu.
qu qer eqer qe dla frida neu.
plus lo cristal dond hom trail for
arden.
Ep effor uemon ti tv so fren.
Bona dona uostr me n ituiel.
podes suis plir lengram. mar.
eriui al igen uer fares eskarnur.
Et aures en gran pechir eminal.
uostrom suite cur ges no teng
per meu.
eus be lursom amul segnos so fou
fiual be paue ries hor qd po sa ger
ce daurel rei dels plit fu puen.
Pero me sui getar am om cal.
com lo uni pri qi soblidat fugir.
qi no siuia tornar ni por gaidir.
qi un crazom sei enemie mortal.
No su conort mais aqei del ludeu
qe sim far mal far ades lo seu.
Aisi cor cel q oclui se defen.
Ji tor pedur la fora el ardun.
Lu uir mo chu al rei celestial
sui deuen tuir honra roberur.
Et es be dreir qe lui ansur
crogeir Laiudi spriteil.

Hinz non mozu pir qmour ni per al. mais ma uide por
ben ualer morir qe qanc uei la ren cui rant aim y deslit
y non mi fai te fora que dolor y mal. mal en ai eu. mais encor
mes plus greu qen breu serons ta uel y ele y eu. y sensi per

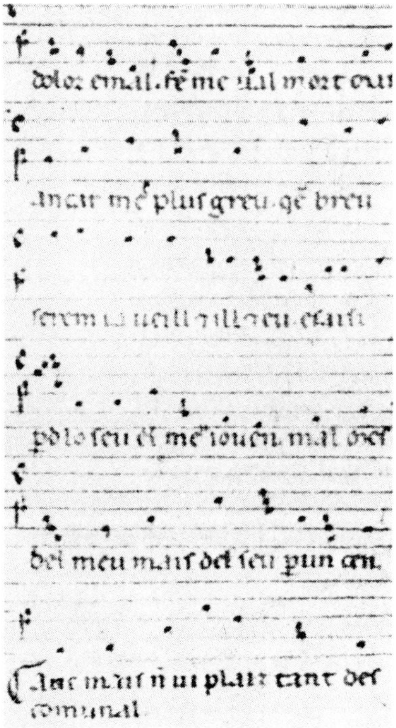

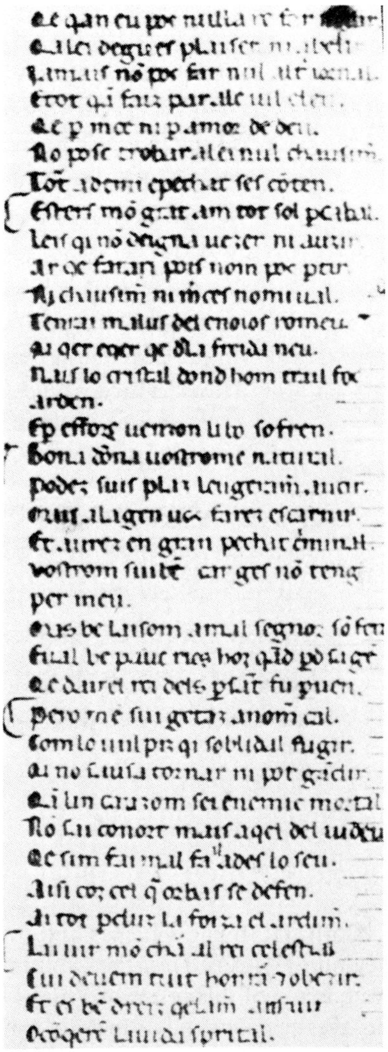

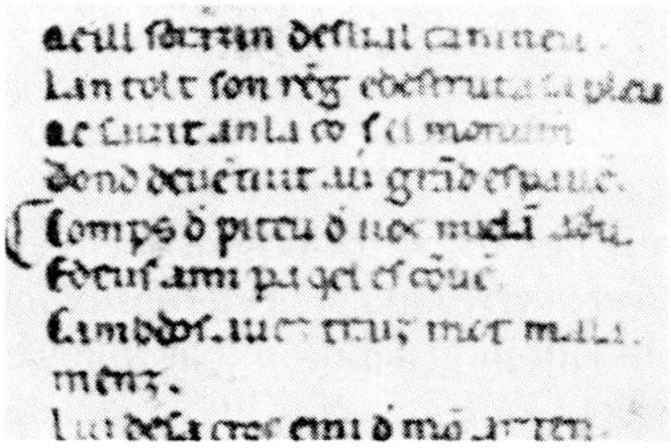

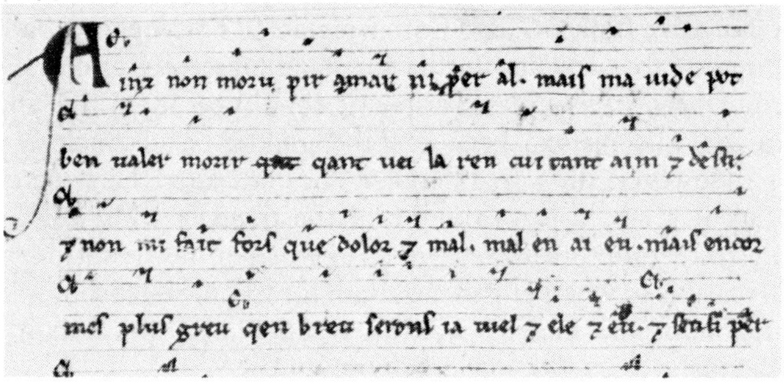

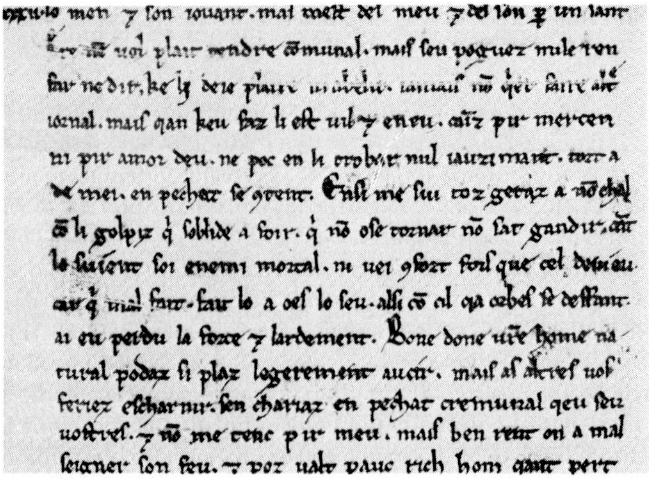

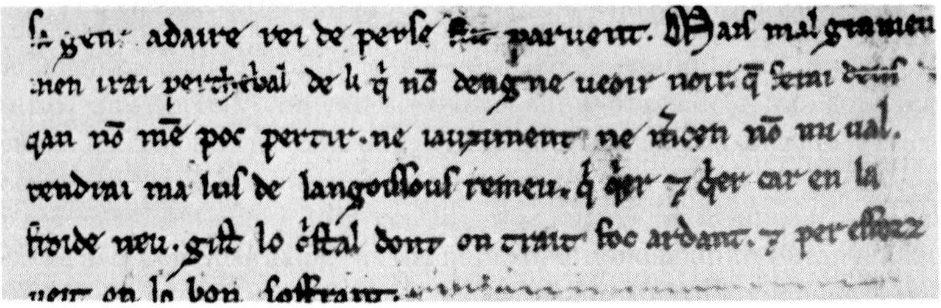

Pill. 364.4 Mss. *R*, *G*, *X*

Both the rhyme schemes and the frequently employed melody of the poem beginning "Anc no mori per amor ni per al" were very popular. Ten *contrafacta* were made of this poem of Vidal's by the troubadour generation that followed his. So the poem and its melody can be considered a major work, and one of the starting points of troubadour literature from several points of view.

The melody appears with Vidal's name and poem in three manuscripts: Provençal *R*, northern Italian *G*, and Lotharingian *X*. This highly syllabic song is in the major in the Provençal and Lotharingian manuscripts, and in the Dorian mode in the northern Italian manuscript. (It should be noted that the final g^1 may well be a copyist's mistake, because if the final were f^1 the melody would be in the major.) However, the key difference does not alter the structure of the melody, in fact it serves as an example of the *freedom* with which key was interpreted in troubadour music, regardless of whether the alteration in key had geographical reasons or whether it came about for technical reasons of notation. The construction of the melody was of greater importance than identical solution of details.

The melody of the first and second sections of "Anc no mori" contains a very important structural principle: the second section provides a *response at a fifth*, i.e. the first section is repeated five notes higher. This occurs consistently in all three manuscripts. Manuscript *X* may contain a notational error, in that the first section contains one note more than the other two, which makes it a melodic line of 11 notes. This looks like an error as the extra note is the lower major seventh (F sharp^1), without the keynote following in this or even in the next section. The melody leaps from f sharp^1 to c^2, a diminished fifth, as against the fourth of Manuscript *R* and the fifth of Manuscript *G*. However, the direction of the melodic movement is the same in each manuscript: a step of a second upward. A discrepancy can be found in the last section of the 3rd section: the northern Italian and the Lotharingian variants close the strophe with an upward interval of a fifth at the end of the descending melodic line, while the Provençal manuscript uses a downward interval of a minor third at the end of an arched structure. Yet in all three variants a descending tendency is prevalent. Gennrich listed the melody (*Komm.* p. 51) as of the *Oda continua* type. In the case of Manuscripts *G* and *X* no line repetition or recurring musical idea can be found apart from the first two sections which are A and A^{5v}; it is an 8-line melody, set throughout, which can be divided into four main musical groups. However, the Provençal Manuscript *R* repeats Musical Line B (= Text Line 2.b) in Section 6 and, a fourth lower, in Section 7, too.

To sum up, Variant *R* (or the Basic Type) is composed of the following musical sections:

$$A\ A^{5v}\ B\ CD\ B^{v}\ B_4\ E.$$

The repeat of the first melodic section a fifth higher may be an isolated phenomenon, although the popularity of the melody (10 occurrences) almost raises it into a type, and one is strongly reminded of the similar basic construction principle of the "new" Hungarian folksong style. Without seeking any link, it should be noted that this melodic structure was present in troubadour music, that is, in medieval secular monody, as early as the 12th century.

R

SONG TYPE	A	A^{5v}	B	C	D	B^{v}	B$_4$	E
METRIC FORM	10a	10b	10b	10a	10c	10c	10d	10d
NOTE GROUPS	10	10	10	10	10	9	10	10
CADENCE	second	sixth	second	third	fifth	second	lower seventh	keynote

G

SONG TYPE	A	A^{5v}	B	C	D	E	F	G
METRIC FORM	10a	10b	10b	10a	10c	10c	10d	10d
NOTE GROUPS	10	10	10	10	10	10	10	10
CADENCE	lower seventh	fourth	fifth	lower seventh	fourth	third	lower second	keynote

X

SONG TYPE	A	A^{5v}	B	C	D	E	F	G
METRIC FORM	10a	10b	10b	10a	10c	10c	10d	10d
NOTE GROUPS	10	10	10	10	10	10	10	11
CADENCE	lower seventh	fifth	fifth	keynote	fifth	third	second	keynote

2

Ba - ros de mon dan co - vit Fals lau - zen - giers des - li - als

Car en tal don' ai chau - zit On es beu - tatz na - tu - rals

E tot a quo que ta-nha cor-te - zi - a Be soi as-truey sol que mos cors lai si'a

Car sa va - lors e son fin pretz pla - zens De - nan to - tas c'ac d'a-mors nos feis

Per que soi ricx s'il - ha·m de - nha dir d'oc

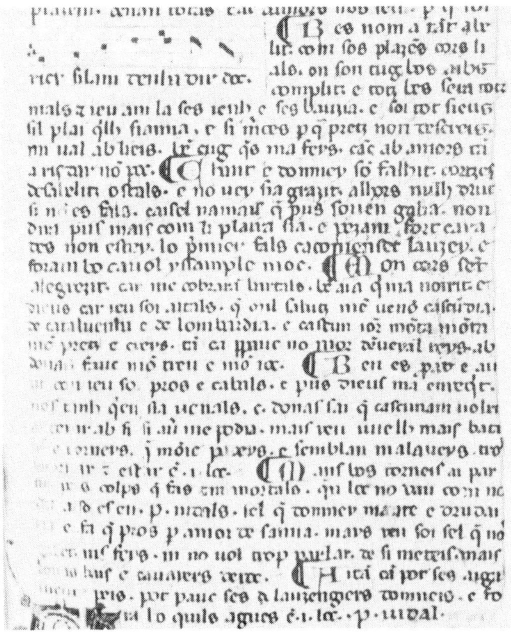

Pill. 364.7 Ms. *R*

Musically the poem beginning "Baros de mon dan covit" is a *lai*, a popular form in the Middle Ages. It resembles a dance, with the musical phrase alternating every second line. In accordance with the practice at that time, the *lai* is both a poetical and a musical form, but whereas the poetical form is determined only by the number of syllables and the rhymes at the line-ends, in the music the whole melodic phrase (and within it all the notes that form the phrase) have to be identical in every two lines. In Vidal's melody three identical notes open each melodic section. In the first four groups, each of seven syllables, the *dance* character is determined by these three notes, together with the descending second that follows them. Sections 5 and 6 expand to ten syllables, and the dance character appears twice within each section, the second responding to the first a fifth lower. Strophes 7 and 8 remain in this lower range, reaching down to the lower fourth. The musical structure is very varied, perhaps even sophisticated, and seems more closely allied to dancing than to singing. Every pair of sections is a *unity* because the first section ends with a question (a third), and the second with the response (a second). In the longer section the question returns to the upper fourth, and the response steps down to the keynote. The repetition of the three stamping or leaping notes appears once again in the second half of Section 7. Section 9 must be considered a half-line, a kind of a closing section to the dance after the four double sections. A note each may be missing from Sections 6 and 8 (there are only nine groups of notes), but since both form the second component of a pair of sections, one can perhaps see a conscious musical construction in them. The text offers little help in establishing the required count of ten syllables, as in both cases of note-group loss there are clusters of vowels (*zi-a, sia* or *zens, feis*). The piece is remarkable from the point of view of key in that the augmented fourth is only resolved or flattened in the very last half-line of the Hypolydian melody.

SONG TYPE	A	A^{v}	A	A^{v}	B	B^{v}	C	C^{v}	D
METRIC FORM	7a	7b	7a	7b	10c	10c	10d	10d	10e
NOTE GROUPS	7	7	7	7	11	10	10	9	10
CADENCE	third	sec-ond	third	sec-ond	fourth	key-note	sec-ond	lower fourth	key-note

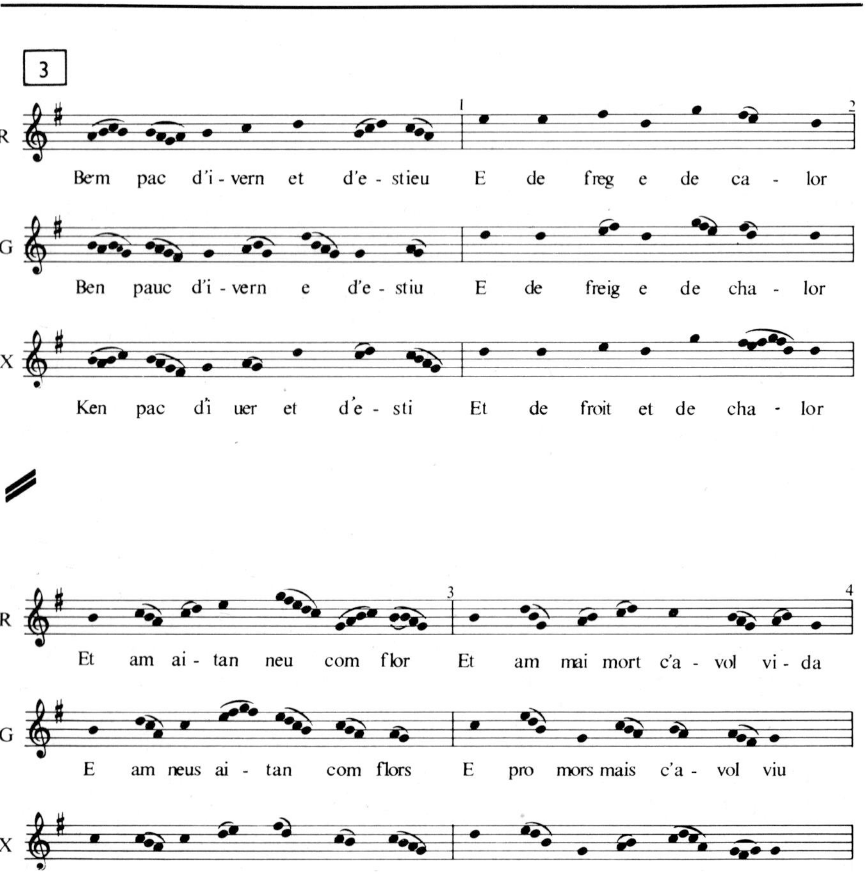

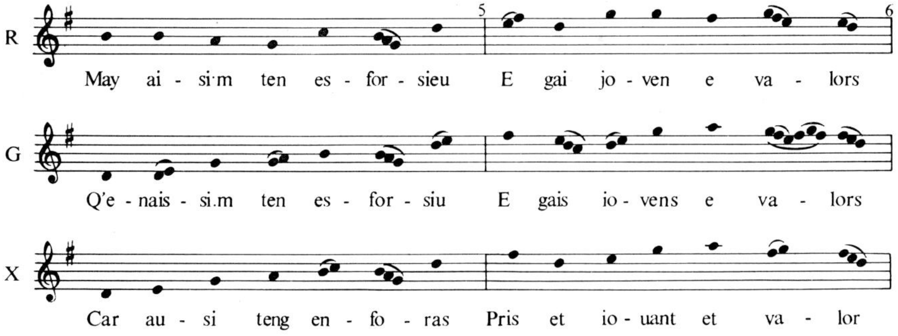
R
May ai - si·m ten es - for - sieu E gai jo - ven e va - lors
G
Q'e - nais - si.m ten es - for - siu E gais io - vens e va - lors
X
Car au - si teng en - fo - ras Pris et io - uant et va - lor

R
E car am do - na no - ve - la So - bra - vi - nen e plus be - la
G
Car am don- na no - vel - la So - bra - vi - nen e plus bel - la
X
Et car aim do - ne no - ve - le Sobr' a - vi - nant et plus be - le

R
Sem-blan ro-za en - tre iel E clar tems a tre - bol sel.
G
Pa - ro.m ro-sas in - tre gel E clar temps a tre - bol cel.
X
Pa - rans ros'es en - tre - giel Et clar tens en tro - blous ciel.

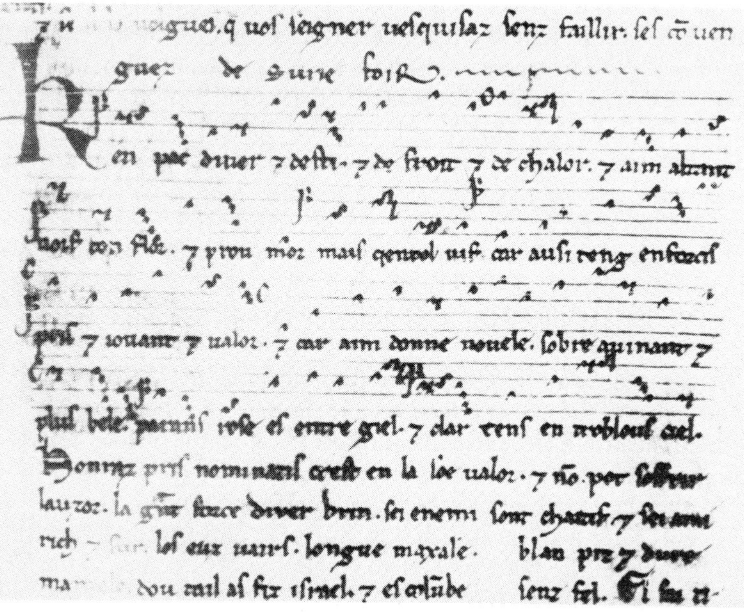

The melody to the poem that begins "Bem pac d'ivern et d'estieu" has survived in three sources. Its rich colouring sets it above all Vidal's other works as one of the loveliest pieces of troubadour music. In addition it has the large compass of a *decima quarta*. Either Vidal had an extraordinary voice or somebody around him was able to sing over such a large compass, or else the melody have been played on a (bowed) instrument while the text was recited. The supposition that it was vocally performed is favoured by the general correspondence between the syllable count of the text and the note groups of the melody. The text has a syllable count of seven, while the melody has seven and sometimes eight groups of notes. This melody also demonstrates the important principle of *terraced* construction which we have also seen in the first two Vidal songs: here the first musical idea is repeated in the second section a fourth higher. The unusually broad vocal range has already been mentioned: the highest point in the compass, where the melody appears high, appears again in Section 3 and in accordance with general practice plays a decisive role in the song's formal construction. As regards the formal devices employed, one can endorse Gennrich's categorization of it as an *Oda continua*: each section carries a different musical content. However, beyond the musical sections that correspond with the lines of the poem, the musical phrasing has longer melodic lines that embrace several lines of text and shows that the beautiful melody to the poem "Bem pac d'ivern" is also in the four-strophe 'grand' form: after the terraced structure of the first two sections and the line of Sections 3 and 4, which move around the fifth and then descend to the keynote, the melody arrives at a grandiose peak through four sections (5, 6, 7, 8), from the fourth below the keynote (d^1) to the fourth above the upper octave (c^3)—this is the third large melodic group. After that, the fourth part returns to move around the fifth, and arrives at the final of the piece with an abundance of ornaments. So the 'grand' form has linked the poem together in 2-2-4-2 lines. There are some minor differences between the three manuscripts, but the melody is identical; in this case the key is also the same: each version is in the major. The Provençal Manuscript *R* resolves the major seventh in the final cadence (Line 9 of the poem—f^2 instead of f sharp^2), which is unusual both in this piece and elsewhere. This one resolution, however, reinforces the major sevenths of the first eight lines, which would suggest it was delibrate.

A melodic similarity: in the 2nd line of the poem Manuscript *X* builds the melody out of the same notes as Section 2 of the Provençal *R* variant of the first Vidal work, "Anc no mori". Besides this melodic similarity, we find at the end of Line 5 of this poem the same upward leap of a fifth as at the end of Line 3 of the poem "Anc no mori". The melody has no precedents in troubadour literature, nor was it used as a model by others.

R

	A		B		C				D	
SONG TYPE	A	B	C	D	E	F	G	H	I	J
METRIC FORM	7a	7b	7b	7a	7a	7b	7c	7c	7d	7d
NOTE GROUPS	7	7	7	8	7	7	8	8	7	7
CADENCE	second	fifth	keynote	keynote	fifth	fifth	octave	third	fifth	keynote

G

SONG TYPE	A	B	C	D	E	F	G	H	I	J
METRIC FORM	7a	7b	7b	7a	7a	7b	7c	7c	7d	7d
NOTE GROUPS	7	7	7	7	7	7	7	8	7	8
CADENCE	keynote	fifth	keynote	keynote	sixth	fifth	octave	third	fifth	keynote

X

SONG TYPE	A	B	C	D	E	F	G	H	I	J
METRIC FORM	7a	7b	7b	7a	7c	7b	7d	7d	7e	7e
NOTE GROUPS	7	7	7	7	7	8	8	8	8	7
CADENCE	keynote	fifth	keynote	keynote	fifth	fifth	octave	third	fifth	keynote

Because of its interesting implications for social history, we give a full English translation of the poem:

Peire Vidal: *Bem pac*

1. I like winter and summer and the cold and the heat, and I love snow as much as flowers, and I prefer the brave dead to the base living, and so they keep me in excitement, because youth and esteem (valour) so arouse me: since I love a new lady, most gracious and fair, I see roses among the ice and fair weather in the cloudy sky.
2. My lady's worth alone is before a million warriors, because she holds Montesquieu against the evil hypocrites, so the slanderers cannot harm her great power, for she is led by honour and sense and when she responds or questions, her words exude honey, and give her a resemblance to St. Gabriel.
3. She arouses greater fear in the common suppliants than a gryphon, and converses gracefully with the consummate lovers, who leaving her all swear and assert that she is of the very best; that is why she attracts me, and tears my heart from its place, she to whom I am sincere and faithful and truer than Abel to God.
4. Her worth is so much enhanced by her priceless and great merits that no praise could bear the weight of her true worth, her enemies are wretched, and her friends mighty and cultured; her brow, her eyes, her nose, her lips, her chin, her full white bosom, her waist, her height, all are like those of the sons of Israel; she is a real dove (without bile).
5. My heart is dull and pensive since I have been apart, but joy will come to supplant grief when I approach her graceful, lovely body. As if I had a fever, I

am now warm, now cold; because she is a noble and pure maiden, free of every sin, I swear by Saint Raphael I love her better than Jacob loved Rachel.

6. In France and in Barry, in Poitiers and in Tours, our Lord seeks help against the Turks who have banished Him, since they have taken from Him the vales and the brooks where He cleansed the sinners, and whoever does not rise up against this base breed, cannot resemble Saint Daniel, who killed Bel the dragon.
7. Poem, go to Montlieu, and tell those three sisters that I like their love so much I shall engrave it on my heart; I shall bow down to all three of them, I shall make them my mistresses and masters. I would rather have a Castilian colt than a thousand camels laden with gold, along with Manuel's whole empire.

Pill. 364.24 Ms.*R*

A melody for the poem beginning "Ges pel temps" has only come down to us in the Provençal Manuscript *R*. The mainly syllabic melody begins with a descent. Our transcription only partly follows a sectional melodic arrangement dictated by the lines of the poem, as we have merged the short, 6-syllable lines into 12-syllable ones for two reasons: firstly, the last two lines of the poem are anyway of 10 syllables, or 11 counting the terminal vowel, so that the poem itself suggested a major unit; secondly, the musical units seldom correspond with the 6-syllable structure. In the middle of the poem there are three units of 6 note groups each, closed with cadence formations, corresponding to the 6-syllable structure of the poem; but before and after this there are larger musical sections that accord with a syllable count of 12. Thus the melodic structure falls into six sections, as opposed to the 10 lines of the poem. The three short melodic 'half-lines' are in sections 3 and 4; this constitutes the second phase in the 'grand' form of the melody which moves low, and is followed by an ascending third part and a closing fourth part. The fragmentation of the melody into half-lines (covering lines 5, 6 and 7 of the poem; rhymes: *b b c*) is a new phenomenon in Vidal's songs. So far we have not encountered such a close fitting of the music to the text. The musical form of the melody is *Oda continua,* with no indication that any section of the melody is to be repeated. The key is Mixolydian, the melody progresses calmly, with no intervals greater than a third. It has no Provençal antecedents and no other texts were written to it.

R

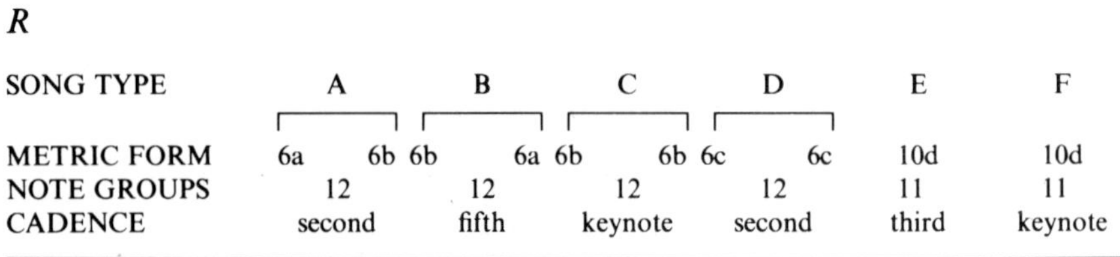

SONG TYPE	A	B	C	D	E	F
METRIC FORM	6a 6b	6b 6a	6b 6b	6c 6c	10d	10d
NOTE GROUPS	12	12	12	12	11	11
CADENCE	second	fifth	keynote	second	third	keynote

Pill. 364.30 Ms. *R*

The poem beginning "Neus ni glatz" has survived complete with melody in the Provençal Manuscript *R*. The syllable counts of the poem correspond exactly with the note groups of the melody (8 syllables), and the melodic phrases show no major interrelationship. The variety in the calm progression of this mainly syllabic melody stems from the step of a fifth plus a third in Section 3. The step also opens a new melodic section that recalls the terraced character, but the structure does not develop, because once it has reached the upper sixth the melody descends again to the lower third. Stronger melismatic coloration only appears in the first and last sections. The key seems to be Hypophrygian, the only Phrygian melody known in Vidal's work. But it still does not give the feeling of the Phrygian mode because the minor second characteristic of the key appears only four times altogether in the whole melody, and only twice at accentuated points. The *tuba* does not help in defining the key either, because the determinant note occurs very rarely in the piece. If some other (extra-European) tonality does not play a role here, the correct key interpretation would be Aeolian, although this is somewhat rare at so early a period in Europe. This melody has no Provençal predecessors either, and no use has been made of it for later poems. In musical form it belongs to the *Oda continua* group.

R

SONG TYPE	A	B	C	D	E	F	G	H
METRIC FORM	8a	8b	8b	8a	8c	8c	8d	8d
NOTE GROUPS	8	8	8	8	8	8	8	8
CADENCE	lower third	keynote	third	lower second	fourth	fourth	second	keynote

Pill. 364.31 Ms. *R*

Vidal's poem beginning "Nulhs hom no.s pot" is known from the Provençal Manuscript *R*, and has survived in no other source. In has no Provençal predecessors, and the melody was never set to other poems. The 8-syllable lines of the poem correspond with the note group arrangement of the melody, but in terms of musical form major textual units appear again. At the end of every second section (i.e. the end of every second line of the poem) the same cadence appears (f^1–g^1), and even the last line does not form the melody-closing final (or preparation for the final note) any differently. This consistency points to conscious composition. In general the melody is highly syllabic, and it shows another interesting feature: the first halves of the melodic sections (thinking of the sections in accordance with the lines of the poem) are always syllabic, and if an ornamental melisma appears at all, it is always in the second half of the section. This development form has already been described in the second Vidal piece, where it occurs with a dance character, less typical of "Nulhs hom". In this very simple melody the 'grand' form is again present as the division into four parts by the cadences, and within this structure there are several lesser motivic cross-references. The lesser motifs have a psalmodic character which determines the structure, even though there is no note-for-note tallying. The formal division is into linking sections, Lines 1–2, 3–4, 5–6 and 7–8. 1–2 and 3–4 each form a *psalmodia initium*, starting from f^1. 5–6 opens the same formula from b^1 (this being an augmented fourth as compared to the opening note), and finally the last section, 7–8, starts a scale progression from d^1 (which is the lower fourth as compared with the keynote). The sense of key has again become uncertain, because modal theory would term the piece Hypomixolydian, yet it is not the minor seventh that dominates, but the f–b, which points instead to the Lydian mode.

Because of its formula repeats, the melody cannot be unequivocally ranked among the *Oda continua* type, nor is it a typical *kanzone*; the best definition seems to be a construction *resembling a kanzone*.

In Section 5–6, and partly in 7, there is a reminder of Geoffroi de Breteuil's famous *Planctus* poem, which Bence Szabolcsi adapted to the Hungarian translation of the poem, the Old Hungarian Lament of the Virgin (*Argonauták*, 1937). It was from an Evreux manuscript (Evreux, Bibliothèque municipale 39, fol. 2r) that Gennrich published the melody, which also survived in a manuscript at Rouen in Metz notation (Rouen, Bibliothèque de la Ville 666—A 506—fol. 94v). The part of Vidal's song mentioned above recalls Lines 7 and 9 of this Evreux manuscript. The section of the *Planctus* quoted above runs: "*Fili, dulcor unicae, Singulare gaudium, Matrem flentem respice, Conferens solatium*".[1] Even if the melodic fragment cannot be considered a direct link, it needs stressing that medieval secular monody may have had typical melodic turns which lived on as a musical vernacular in the everyday practice of medieval society. (Geoffroi de Breteuil died in 1196.)

R

SONG TYPE	A		A_vB		C		D	
METRIC FORM	8a	8b	8b	8a	8c	8c	8d	8d
NOTE GROUPS	8	8	8	8	8	8	8	8
CADENCE	keynote		keynote		keynote		keynote	

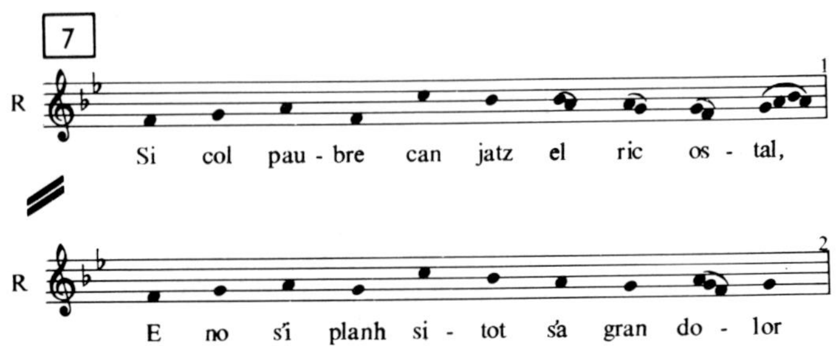

[1] Gennrich (1932), p. 143.

R
3
Tan tem que torn ad e - nueg al se - nhor
R
4
No m'aus pla - nher de ma do lor mor tal
R
5
Bem dey do - ler, pus e - la·m mostr' er - guelh
R
6
La res del mon qu'ieu pus de zir e vuelh
R
7
Que si - val re non l'aus cla - mar mer - ce
R
8
Tal pa - or ay que se e - nueg de me

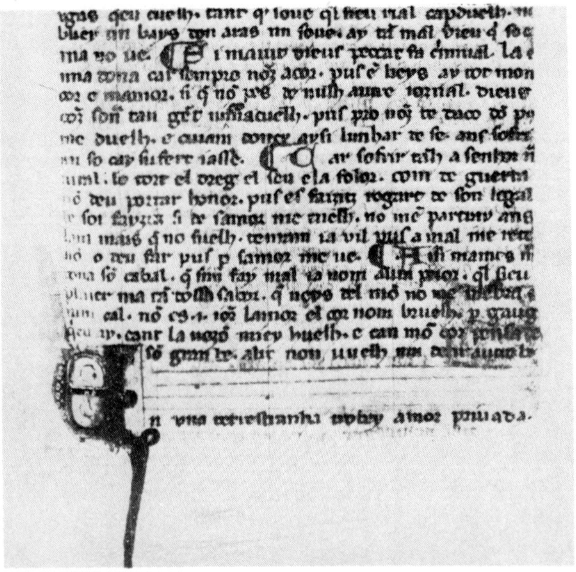

Pill. 364.36 Ms. *R*

Vidal's poem beginning "Plus que.1 paubres" (according to the Provençal Manuscript *R*, *si col paubre*) has survived complete with melody only in one manuscript. In form it belongs to the *kanzone* type, where the first musical line is repeated in the second. Compared with the opening note of f^1, Section 3 continues the melody on c^2, i.e. on the fifth, so that a terraced construction appears again in this song. Like the previous poem, "Nulhs hom", each pair of lines of the poem belong together musically. In accordance with Vidal's composing technique there is a fifth at the end of every second line, and at the end of the 8th and last line the keynote predictably appears—achieved in this work by a 6-note melismatic scoop. Apart from the terraced construction, the attempt at recitation appears again, with the repetition of a note in the beginning of Lines 5 and 6. The cadence shows an interesting picture: stepping from the lower seventh (f^1), to the octave by way of a fourth and two leaps of a third, it gradually approaches the keynote. The end of Line 6 brings a rare step: the line closes with an upward interval of a sixth. This upward leap which closes the line has already featured in Versions *G* and *X* of Song 1, and in Versions *R*, *G*, and *X* of Song 3; the practice presumably formed part of Vidal's melodic construction. The piece is in the Aeolian mode; this time there is no uncertainty.

R

SONG TYPE	A	A_v	B	C	D	E	F	G
METRIC FORM	10a	10b	10b	10a	10c	10c	10d	10d
NOTE GROUPS	10	10	10	10	10	10	10	10
CADENCE	keynote		keynote		fifth		keynote	

8
G
Pois tor - naz sui en Pro - en - sa Et a ma do - na sa bo
Ben dei fa ga - ia can - zon Si - vals per re - co - nois - cen - za
Qu'ab ser - vir et ab hon - rar Con - qer om de bon se - gnor
Dons et ben - faiz et ho - nor Qi'l ben sap te - nir en car
Per q'eu m'en voill es - for - zar

Pill. 364.37 Ms. *G*

Vidal might have written the poem "Pois tornaz sui en Proensa" on the occasion of a return to Provence after a fairly long absence, something which might have occurred several times during his adventurous life. He may have written it after his Eastern trip (to Cyprus) and before he came to Hungary; scholarship considers it to have been written around 1189. The ornate melody with its animated melismas can be compared with "Bem pac d'ivern" (Pill. 364.11; here No. 3) chiefly in its quantity of coloration; but its formal structure is different. The work, consisting of 9 lines of poem and melody, falls into two greater parts (Lines 1 to 4 and 5 to 8) plus a 'cadence' (the 9th and last line). Within these parts the melody may be further divided, but the linear construction of the music closes first in Line 4 and again in Line 8, after which comes the cadence line. The melody descends through an octave; in Line 2 it becomes extraordinarily playful, with a melody above the syllables consisting of one, respectively two notes. By Line 3 it reaches its first peak (a tenth). As an interesting structural phenomenon, the melody reaches the same peak for a second time at the analogous place of the section we called the second greater part (Line 7). Also typical of the melody is the step of a third that predominates in its structure: not merely a single third, but usually a series of steps of a third. The do-mi-so-la series features frequently, something which often occurs in other types of medieval European music, e.g. Gregorian. The many leaps of a third lend an agitated, animated character to the melody, emphasizing the major key, which at that time was still rare in European music, although Glarean in 1547 did include it at the end of his list of medieval modes as the *Ionic* (*Dodekachordon*). In Gennrich's classification (*Komm.* p. 53) the melody is an *Oda continua.* We also consider it as such, but mark the major units, which the details mentioned above may justify from the point of view of the musical structure. It should be noted that this gives a different grouping to the rhymes of the lines of the text: *a b b a* in Part 1 and *c d d c* in Part 2, while the half-line as *c*.

G

	A				B				C
SONG TYPE	A	B	C	D	E	F	G	H	I
METRIC FORM	8a	7b	7b	8a	7c	7d	7d	7c	7c
NOTE-GROUPS	8	7	7	8	8	7	7	7	7
CADENCE	third	sixth	third	key-note	fifth	sixth	octave	third	key-note

There are two *contrafacta* of the poem and the melody: an anonymous Provençal song (Pill. 461.96) and a German song whose author is known: Rudolf von Fenis-Neuenburg set his song "Nun ist niht mêre..." to the version of Vidal's melody opening "Pois tornetz...".[2]

[2] On the German Minnesang see: Gennrich, Fr.: 'Sieben Melodien zu mittelhochdeutschen Minneliedern' in *Zeitschrift für Musikwissenschaft*, 7/1924, and Frank (1952).

R
7
8
E.ls tortz e.ls dreg e.ls dans e.ls pres Qu'ai-si m.o co-man-da ra-zos.
G
E.l torz e.l dreiz e.l danz e.l pros C'ai-si m.o co-man-da ra-zos.
W
Et torz et dreis et dans et prous Qu'en-si lou co-man-de rai-sons.

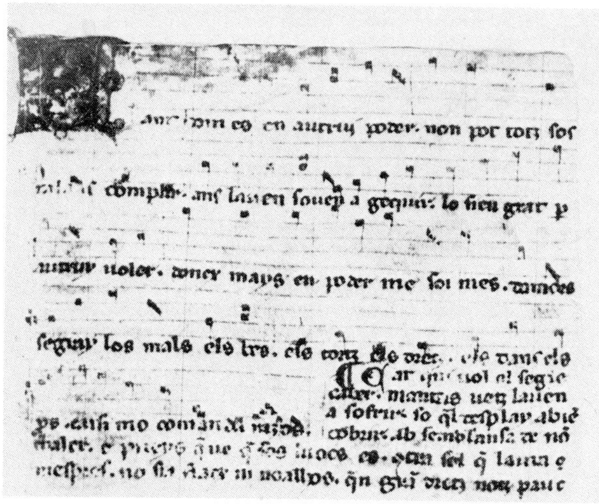

S'anc hom es in altrui poder.

Pope tot se talent complir.

Anc l'auen souen grepir. p.il

trui grlo seu uoler. done pre

el poder me sui mo' d'amor fe

gnai loc m.ils el bes. el tor z

el drecz el d.mt el prof. car fe

me comm.mt .hoc.

ar qu'eus ei egle griter.

om pas' ues l'auen d'ofiir.

Co q'eill desplaz. lb gen cobir.

p scembl.nza d'no chaler.

dond po q'm neq' ses locs es.

Con' fel qi .iuri' mesps.

No fui fiic ni meuillos.

C en gen dretz noz p.me tocr.nsor.

Bon.a don.a deu car z uoder.

Cilo ure gen cors remir.

Sp'is t.m uoz .im eus' d'fiir.

G r.is ben me deuria eschar-te

Cui m.a nostra .imor conort.

tuccrit el.n.ut eprer.

Cab tot lo segle qi me tr-

pre tenren pel buis sens tos.

Bon.a q.me nus u' ten.mer.

En.iuee de qes .ipetir.

T.m m.igreser on li sos pir.

Capr.nt nom.tue aerser.

h.a dolz.a don.a tricia res.

utill.un abuec des enees.

Kerenes mi em.is c.icoe.

Se tot pes .il co' tes gretor.

p' cio uen uoill m.itenir.

Hom.is don.is obeir.

Ea coerez.a gen suir.

Hon.u grand cuin d.uii.

Cuf po seu poder .iuger.

Ho es cops ni dur ni m.irqes

J.mi mei pl.iges messor.

Remeir se p.ig d.iuoc t.iroe.

Timt.n d sen ede saber.

Ac del tor lu mo m'etill.z euisir.

Fl.n conoiser egr.nir.

Cum c.iph'o iar ni c.ir tener.

Fong m.i luf del genoer.

Cab bel se'bl.int g.us eronel.

Hon .iloz .imiel .imoze.

Fr.il inimie e ozgoilles.

Sel qi pot enoiul u.iler.

Com ne ses forz.a del mou-

deu c.ir l.imor nol dgn.a .iuar.

p' far enoi eder pl.izer.

Et ef trop l.iud don.ir p.ig .ies.

C.ind renoil l.is r'd.ii el ber-

Cosf p'ite .ib eo u'menoe.

uu ses gr.iz d deu ede noz.

En p.nie dels genes rem.ing.

Fr.ii gr.id feu coqes. dond

On' teng hon.ir eprer.

Esui .imie del los loi oe.

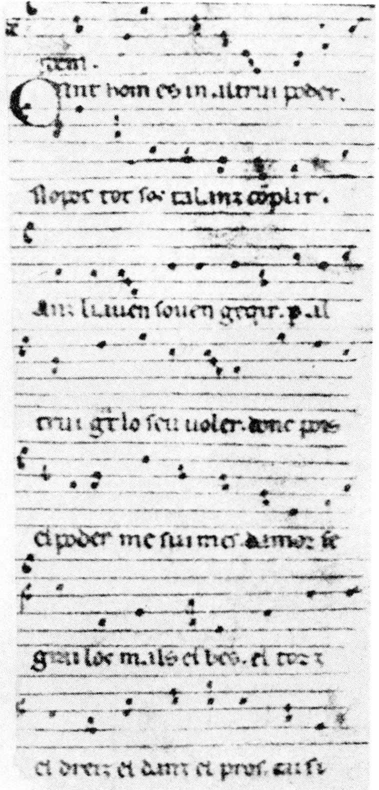

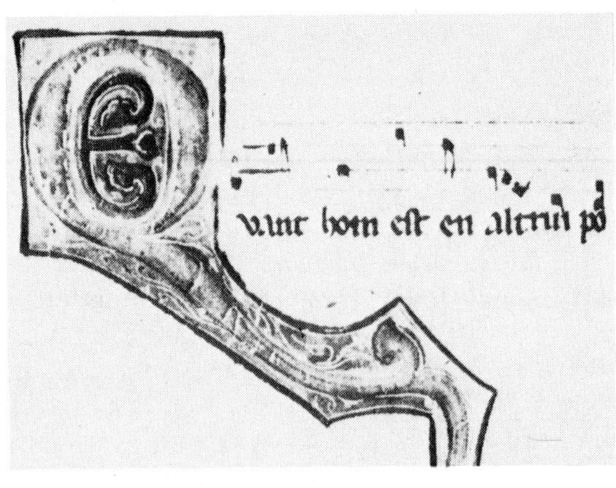
vant hom est en altrui po

der. non pos toz sous talanz çplir. anz
auen soliein aguerpir. per altre graz.
lou son voler. et pos en poder me sui mes.
damors sigrai et mans et bens. et tozher
dreis et dans et prous. quensi lou çman
de raisons.

Vidal's poem "Quant hom es" has survived in three manuscripts: the Provençal *R*, the northern Italian *G* and the so-called *Manuscrit du Roi*, *W*. The last mainly includes trouvère melodies, i.e. it is from late 13th century northern France, but it also includes some troubadour melodies. It is significant in that it bears out the troubadour-trouvère continuity, or rather, the way troubadour melodies survived along with trouvère melodies after the extinction of troubadour poetry, mainly in the 'fringe' areas. By fringe areas we mean all the regions that lay north, east or south of Occitania, and where, with a single exception, the manuscripts of troubadour songs were compiled. From this point of view the melody of "Quant hom es" has survived, through manuscripts *G* and *W*, in such areas, and it is perhaps not surprising, despite the geographical distance separating the two manuscripts, that it is the melodies in the two manuscripts which are perhaps related to each other, as opposed to the melody in Provençal *R*. The melodies provided for this text are far removed from one another, and scarcely any relationship can be found. The only common feature between the three is merely that each has a very *uncertain tonality*, at least according to the notation in the manuscripts. The accidentals may have been inscribed inconsistently, or, if they are consistent, it is hard to say unequivocally what key the melodies are in. In the Provençal variant (*R*) the melody opens in the major, and the seventh loses its sharpness only in the melisma group that precedes the final cadence; thus the piece ends in the Mixolydian. The north Italian *G* version is purely Mixolydian, and so is the northern French *W*, although in this last there are two triad-like leaps at accentuated points in the first three lines. (These are triad-*like* because between f and b there is a step of a second, although it does not change the character of the interval.) The key itself would not have been disrupted if the melody had not lost its sharpness in Line 6. The scribe gives a key signature only once at a passing melodic section, but presumably from there on it remained valid for every b note. The second half of the melody can therefore be considered Dorian. Looking over the keys of the three melodies one notices the Mixolydian appears in some one melodic section of all versions; and apart from the north Italian version, once at the beginning of the piece (*W*) and once at the end (*R*). If a statistical method could mean much in that age, all should be transcribed into the Mixolydian. Since that is out of the question, one has to accept the supposition that the basic melody might once have been on the *Mixolydian principle*, but by the time when the manuscripts were compiled, this had been revised to suit local tastes (perhaps influenced by the geographical surroundings). The question of *fluctuating tonality* should also be considered a possibility.

The loveliest and most interesting version of the *Oda continua* melody has been preserved in the Provençal Manuscript *R*. The descending melody set to the first two lines of the poem contains turns familiar in Hungarian folksongs too—*Fecském, fecském* (My swallow, my swallow), *Éva, szívem, Éva* (Éva, my heart, Éva) and *Cinege, cinege* (Titmouse, titmouse). The melody to Line 3 of the poem begins a reciting phrase which is repeated a fifth higher in Line 5, again giving a terraced structure, but the proportions observed earlier are changed in this melody: the peak does not occur in the third melodic section; instead the melody starts downwards from the peak, culminates in the middle section (Line 5 of the poem) and reappears before the closing cadence. It emerges three times during the piece, which makes the musical form extremely well proportioned and grandiose. The other two variants move within much more modest dimensions, although they are far more richly embellished. In the northern French Manuscript *W* there are several distrophic formulae, which point to an attempt at mensurality. The line cadences are identical in *G* and *W*, but differ in *R*.

R

	A		B		C		D	
SONG TYPE	A	B	C	D	E	F	G	H
METRIC FORM	8a	8b	8b	8a	8c	8c	8d	8d
NOTE GROUPS	8	8	8	8	8	8	8	8
CADENCE	sixth	key-note	fifth	fifth	seventh	sixth	ninth	keynote

G

	A		B		C		D	
SONG TYPE	A	B	C	D	E	F	G	H
METRIC FORM	8a	8b	8b	8a	8c	8c	8d	8d
NOTE GROUPS	8	7	7	8	8	8	7	8
CADENCE	third	key-note	sec-ond	fifth	fourth	lower seventh	fifth	keynote

W

	A		B		C		D	
SONG TYPE	A	B	C	D	E	F	G	H
METRIC FORM	8a	8b	8b	8a	8c	8c	8d	8d
NOTE GROUPS	8	8	8	8	8	8	8	8
CADENCE	third	key-note	sec-ond	fifth	fourth	lower seventh	fifth	keynote

The poem and the melody has a single *contrafactum*, an anonymous Provençal song (Pill. 461.222).

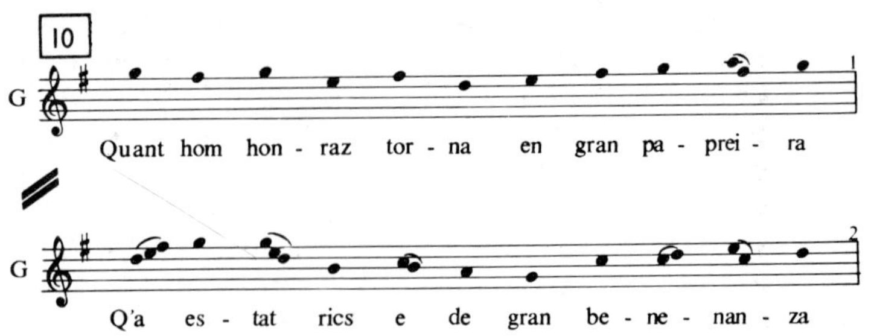

G
De ver - go - gna no sap re con se quei - ra
3
G
Anz a - ma mais co - brir sa ma - le - nom - za
4
G
Per q'es ma - ger mer - ces e plus franc dos
5
G
Quan hom fai ben al pa - bres ver - go - gnos
6
G
Q'a mainz d'al - tres q'an en que - rer fi - an - za
7

Pill. 364.40 Ms. *G*

The melody of Vidal's poem "Quant hom honraz" has survived only in the north Italian Manuscript *G*. In the opening line of the song one can recognize the first line of the popular medieval funeral sequence "Dies irae, dies illa". That might have been one reason why five *contrafacta* were made of Vidal's melody for poems by later troubadours. They include a poem by Peire Cardenal (Pill. 335.24) and two by Uc de Saint Circ (Pill. 457.5 and 457.22).

The formal structure of the song can be defined in two ways. One either interprets the melody line by line which makes the seven seemingly independent lines constitute an *Oda continua*, or one seeks major interrelationships by grouping the melody into two-line phrases. In that case it consists of 3 lines and a cadence of half a line. This solution still remains an *Oda continua*, but musical units of two lines express the relationships of the melodic ideas better. The first two-line unit opens with the melody segment of the above-mentioned sequence and shows a descending tendency; it comes from the upper octave down to the keynote. At the end, according to a construction principle already observed in Vidal, it closes on the fifth after a step of a fourth. The following 2-line unit continues to build the melody from this prepared fifth, and in its second half there appears the reciting or repetitive "Vidal formula" (= 9 G/3 or 9 W/3). The third 2-line unit forms the melody's broadly phrased peak, while the last half-line in its entirety constitutes the cadence. According to this musical arrangement, the rhyme scheme of the poem is as follows: *ab*, *ab*, *cc*, *b*. Lines 1–4 and 7 of the poem consist of 11 syllables (5–6 = 10), and the melodic groups, too, are, with the exception of two, all of 11 syllables. The melody assigns a separate group to every line-end vowel. Where the melody has 10 syllables, the line ends in a consonant (Line 5 = *dos*, Line 6 = *gnos*). There is no uncertainty regarding the key, which is noted down as a pure major.

G

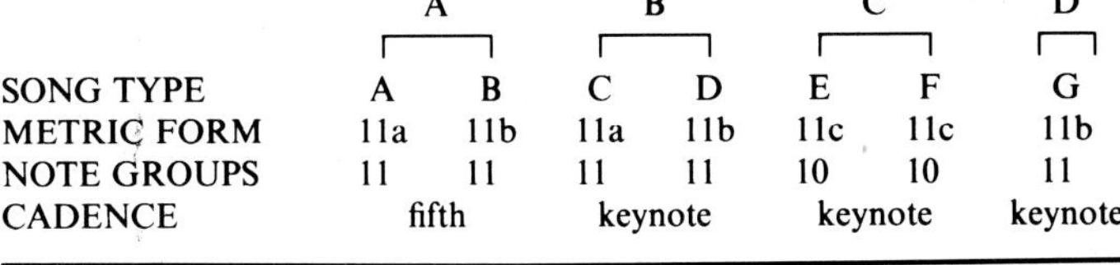

	A		B		C		D
SONG TYPE	A	B	C	D	E	F	G
METRIC FORM	11a	11b	11a	11b	11c	11c	11b
NOTE GROUPS	11	11	11	11	10	10	11
CADENCE	fifth		keynote		keynote		keynote

II

R S'ieu fos en cort que hom ten - gues dre - chu - ra 1

R De ma do - na si tot s'es bo - n'e be - la 2

R Mi cla - me - ra car tan gran tortz mi me - na 3

R Que no m'a - ten ple - vir ni co - vi - nen - sa 4

R E donc per que.m pro - met so que no.m do - na 5

R Non tem pec - cat ni sap que es ver - gon - ha 6

Pill. 364.42   Ms. *R*

The melody of the poem that begins "S'ieu fos en cort" has survived in the Provençal Manuscript *R*. No other variant is known, and it was not used for other poems. The syllables of the text-lines are given 11 musical syllables. Every line ends with the vowel *a*, which Gennrich, for example, classifies according to the preceding consonants as a rhyme scheme of *a,b,c,d,e,f* (*Komm.* p. 54). The melody is markedly syllabic, in the Hypomixolydian mode. In structure the song belongs to the *Oda continua* type; every line of the poem carries a new melody but, as in several earlier examples, one can think in major units. The 6-line melody can be divided into three groups of 2 musical lines, all three being major and independent components of the formal construction. The first two musical lines descend in a broad line from c^2 to c^1 (Lines 1 and 2 of the poem). The second musical phrase (Lines 3 and 4) is linked by frequent repetition of the keynote: after a psalmodic beginning it returns three times to g^1. The third musical phrase (Lines 5 and 6 of the poem) constitutes the peak, moving around a sixth above the keynote, from where it arrived at the *tonus finalis* in waves. The structure of the melody again shows terraced construction, but here not an upward but a downward one: the recitative on g^1 in Line 3 responds to the recitative movement on the opening c^2. A movement of 2 thirds downwards appears in Lines 1 and 3 of the poem, and upwards in Line 4.

R

	A		B		C	
SONG TYPE	A	B	C	D	E	F
METRIC FORM	11a	11b	11c	11d	11e	11f
NOTE GROUPS	11	11	11	11	11	11
CADENCE	lower fourth		keynote		keynote	

W
7
Quan mi mem - bre vos - tre cors a - vi - nenz
W
[♮]
8
El dolz re - gars et la bou - che ri - ens

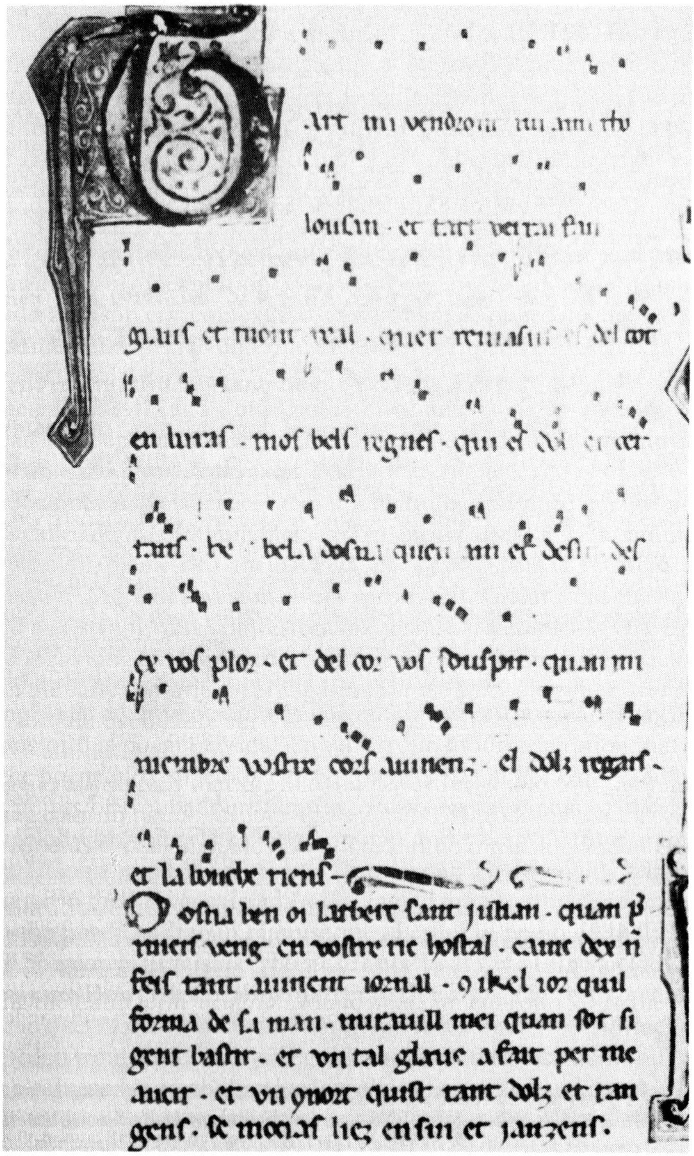

The melody of Vidal's poem "Tart mi veiran" has come down to us in the northern French Manuscript *W*, which mainly contains Trouvère pieces, but which also includes one other Vidal poem (Pill. 364.39—"Quant hom es") and one of uncertain origin which however is also attributed to Vidal (Pill. 461.197—"Pos vezem"). In form "Tart mi" is a *lai* fragment, belonging in type to the 2nd group of *lai* fragments, where the last two music lines duplicate or repeat an earlier section of the melody: that of Lines 3 and 4 of the poem. Unlike the syllabic melodies so frequent in Vidal, it is richly ornamented and contains a surprising number of distrophic formulae, which gives it a stronger than ever mensural tendency. The same phenomenon was observed in "Quant hom es", given here as No. 9, but there we had three variants to compare and distrophic formulae appeared only in Manuscript *W*. This seems to indicate that the mensurality does not come from Vidal, but from the scribe of the manuscript. There appears to be no system whatsoever in the placing of the distrophes within the melody: it does not correspond to the theory of modal rhythm, nor does it identify itself with the accents of the poem. It may therefore be considered arbitrary.

As to the question of key, it is difficult to give an unambiguous answer, since the seventh note of the originally major-key melody is sometimes flattened and sometimes not. Unfortunately, the scribe was not consistent in this either, and so he has left scholarship with the choice either of accepting the version given in the manuscript or correcting it. There is only one possibility for making a logical correction: in the melody of Line 8 of the poem; here the melodic section is analogous to that of Line 4 of the poem, where he spelt out the flat sign mollifying the seventh. In the melody of Lines 1, 2 and 6 of the poem not only are there no flat signs, but the seventh in question is even reinforced by distrophes. This situation is not a question of ti-ta fluctuation, or of an undecided tonality, where the tritone as a criterion is such an important factor, but of a faulty interpretation of the melody.

Nevertheless the basic melody may come from Vidal; certain principles of construction and melodic line are familiar, for example the intertwining of the lines of the poem (2 poem lines) into one melodic phrase, and the upward steps at line ends (here on three occasions at unaccentuated line ends); the peaks are so placed as to create not a domed structure but a concave arch, because of the low middle section; of the eight lines—since the melody opens with a descent and right at the beginning intones the highest note—it touches the a^2 in Lines 1 and 3 and at the end of Line 7.

W

	A		B		C		B	
SONG TYPE	A	B	C	D	E	F	C	D
METRIC FORM	10a	10b	10b	10a	10c	10c	10d	10d
NOTE GROUPS	10	10	10	10	10	10	10	10
CADENCE	fifth		keynote		fourth		keynote	

13
W
Poc ve zem que l'i - ver s'i - rais et part se del tanz a - mo - ros.
que non au - ges no - tes ni lais Des au - selz per ver - gers fuil - loz
per lou freit del brun tem - po rau non lei - sse - rai un vers a far.
et di - rai al ques mon ta - lant

The melody of the poem "Poc ve zem" is not unequivocally attributed to Vidal. Nor does Pillet count it among Vidal's pieces, but among the anonymous poems. This is also apparent from the first component of the index number, which is not 364 (Vidal) but 461. It has survived on recto 190 of the northern French Manuscript *W*, ascribed to Pieres Vidaus. It has no Provençal antecedents and the melody was not used for other poems. Gennrich (*Komm.* p. 54) definitely ascribes it to Vidal. On the strength of its *musical stylistic features* we also attribute this *kanzone*-type melody to Vidal. The most significant stylistic mark is the strongly recitative linear construction, in some lines with a psalmodic introduction; in the first half of the lines more than once with a syllabic movement, and in the second half with a melismatic movement; by contracting two lines of the poem into a single musical period results in a 'grand' structure of Sapphic form: three whole musical lines (one musical line per two lines of poem) and one half-line (one line of poem). Of the three whole musical lines, the second repeats the first.

The musical structure in part reminds one of the 'dance' character of the music to the poem "Baros, de mon", here No. 2. The key is Aeolian, although it is distinguished from the Dorian only by a melismatic group in the last musical half-line.

W

	A		A		B		C
SONG TYPE	A	B	A	B	C	D	E
METRIC FORM	8a	8b	8a	8b	8c	8d	8c
NOTE GROUPS	8	8	8	8	8	8	8
CADENCE	third		third		third		keynote

PEIRE VIDAL'S MUSICAL STYLE

From the 12 + 1 melodies analysed here (which with all the variants total 19 semi-independent works) we can arrive at the following description of Vidal's musical style:

1. *Terraced construction.* In some of the songs (1, 2, 3, 4, 5, 8, 9, 11) he builds upon the musical idea so as to repeat certain melodic sections a fourth or a fifth higher, usually using a melody that corresponds to several lines of the poem. That repetition is not necessarily note by note, although lines of that kind are not rare. This technique encompasses the possibility of an arched song-type.

The reverse of this, a concave melody, can also be found among his works (11), with an identical musical idea repeated a fourth lower, within the frames of the plagal key. A terraced construction does not always appear at the beginning of the songs; usually it occurs after the statement of the theme in the first half of the melody; more rarely it occurs in the last lines before the final cadence. This formal pair of elements is independent of the peaks or stresses of the melody which help to determine the whole grand form. The terraced structure forms only one ingredient of the broadly arched melodic form but its appearance or presence is certainly a factor that must influence how the arched structure unfolds.

2. *Descending melodic line.* A descending melodic contour is characteristic of the opening line of several Vidal songs. We have considered a line as descending only where the descent is over a range of at least a fifth; even an octave descent is not rare (4, 8, 9, 10, 11). The descending opening melody line is typical not only of Vidal. Of the 163 troubadour songs in the northern Italian Manuscript *G* (the codex which contains the largest number of troubadour songs), 62 begin with a descent. In Vidal's case it may be worth noting that he often places the main musical ideas in the opening lines, which in the case of descending melodic lines can lead to certain associations: e.g. "Quant hom es", given here as No. 9, with its downward step of a fourth and a later leading back of the melody reminds a Hungarian analyst of the folksongs of the type "Béreslegény jól megrakd a szekeret" (Farm lad, load the cart up full); in the opening of "Quant hom honraz" (No. 10) one can recognize the melody of "Dies irae dies illa", a hymn by Thomas of Celano that later spread as a funeral sequence and is today known to have been one of the most popular melodies in the Middle Ages. But Thomas of Celano was born only in 1190, and so he must have picked the melody known today by his name for his poem because it was a popular secular song in the Middle Ages, as Vidal's version and the five *contrafacta* that followed go to show. One would be bold to assume Vidal was the composer, but he certainly was one person to use it. In any case its great popularity in troubadour music throws an interesting light on the career of a church melody.

3. *Further characteristics of melodic construction*

a) There are many syllabic sections in the melodies. Since the melody is as closely matched to the syllables of the poem as possible, the relationship of music to text is clearly borne out. However the text is not an exclusive influence: it does not determine the musical fabric as such and the musical idea remains independent while still taking a clear expression of the text and interpretation of its contents into account. The syllabic passages are often in the first half of the lines of the poem, while the melismatic units of several notes are in the second half. In some of the poems this technique would indicate that *dance music* practice of the time has to be reckoned with in the musical pattern, i.e. certain sound formulae are consistently lined up and even in the absence of a mensural marking they point to a dance. A striking example of this is Melody No. 2, to the poem "Baros de mon". It is a sung dance melody which belongs in type to the *lai*. A similar phenomenon can be seen in the song given here as No. 13.

b) The recitative melodic sections are closely related to the idea of syllabic construction. The repetition of the same note in accordance with the syllables might be used to underline the message of the poem, but in most cases it is applied not where the text would demand it, but where it fits into the melodic structure (2 *R*, 6 *R*, 7 *R*, 9 *R*, 11 *R*, 13 *W*). On several occasions, the use of a few preparatory notes even recalls psalmody. Recitative in a given melody could also have served to reinforce the key, by making the repeated note sound as a *tuba*, but Vidal never uses recitative in that way.

c) Verse lines and melodic sections, in contradiction to the findings of earlier research, do not usually correspond exactly to each other. Vidal likes to employ larger melodic phrases that disregard the rhymes of the poem, and wherever possible he contracts the number of lines into groups of two or sometimes four text lines, through the use of an arched melodic line. In the case of odd-numbered lines this produces the form we term 'Sapphic' (in poems consisting of 7 or 9 lines). The term 'Sapphic' was introduced into the terminology of Hungarian musical history by Bence Szabolcsi as an explanation of certain peculiar forms.

On the other hand, Vidal's note groups reflect the text so faithfully that they can help resolve questions of the prosody and analysis of the poems, since in most cases an increase of note groups occurs through the vowel at the end of a word being counted as a separate syllable and sung as such. Often the note groups decide textual questions. The adjustment of text and music can be well studied in Lines 3 and 4 of No. 4, and in the 8-syllable poems (5, 6, 7).

d) Identical melodic sections and line-final fifths. Both the identical melodic sections and the upwards steps of a fifth at line ends are clear marks of Vidal as a composer. The repeated use of a certain musical idea in different poems, particularly in melodies occurring in different manuscripts, may mean that Vidal constructed the melodies himself. At the same time that underlines the local significance of differences in melodies by the same authors in different manuscripts, since in the life-time of the authors the troubadour songs were spread in oral not written form, and even the final recording was done on the basis of the oral tradition. So if one finds resemblances between melodies by the same author, as in Vidal's case, noted down in different geographical environments, those melodic sections reflect the author's original ideas; indeed, so strongly do they do so that even a time lapse of 100 or 150 years, or a marked difference in geographical environment was unable or unwilling to alter them. Besides the several identical melodic sections and musical phrases, a note by note correspondence can be found between the Lotharingian variant of "Bem pac d'ivern" (Line 2 of the poem) and the Provençal variant of "Anc no morir" (Line 2 of the poem), and also between the Provençal version of "Anc no morir" (Line 8 of the poem) and the Provençal notation of "Nulhs hom" (Line 7 of the poem). Major differences between variants of Vidal melodies in different manuscripts can only be found in the case of "Quant hom es" (No. 9), where both the keys and the melodic lines differ markedly.

One of Vidal's favourite intervals is an upward step of a fifth, which is highly characteristic in the northern Italian and the Lotharingian notations of "Anc no morir" (Line 3 of poem), the Provençal, the northern Italian and the Lotharingian versions of "Bem pac d'ivern" (Line 5) and in the Provençal notation of "Plus quel paubre" (Line 7). Instead of or alongside the fifth, a line-final upward step of a fourth often occurs. One can therefore say Vidal liked to use intervals of more than a third at the end of the lines of the poems, but it is difficult to tell whether these steps coincided with the ends of phrases in the function of the melody, or whether they served rather to lead the musical idea on at the end of a line of the poem. In the latter case one may speak, from a musical point of view, of 'unstressed' text line endings. There are examples of both.

4. *Keys and tonalities*. There is no unified tonality in Vidal's 13 melodies. The keys used are tabulated here in three groups:

Modal	Major	Fluctuating (transitional)
Hypolydian No. 2	Nos 3, 8, 10, 12	major-Dorian No. 1
Mixolydian No. 4		major-Mixolydian No. 9
Hypomixolydian No. 11		Hypophrygian-Aeolian No. 5
Aeolian Nos 7, 13		Hypomixolydian-Hypolydian No. 6

Disregarding the 3rd group of fluctuating tonality, it is surprising how rare the typically *modal* keys are. We have put the Aeolian in the modal group, as the other three keys in this series are also of a "minor" character. While the proportion of melodies which can be said to be purely major in key is striking, particularly if one bears in mind that most of the songs were created at the turn of the 12th and 13th centuries, or even earlier. In the *transitional* group we have placed the songs of uncertain tonality. Uncertainty may arise for a number of reasons, for example faulty notation or perhaps a lack of a sense of tonality. Today it can no longer be established what was felt to be 'false' in the Middle Ages. It cannot be ruled out that the notations were *correct*, although these 'mixed' tonalities cannot be pigeonholed according to any theoretical system and so are *fluctuating* tonalities. Certainly in the transitional group the keys that would today be called minor prevail. The final conclusion we can draw is that Vidal preferred the softer, minor-like keys, and their plagal variants.

Both with Vidal and Faidit the question arises of the definite appearance of major-minor tonality, and, due to the comparison with modal keys, the question of fluctuating tonality. Bence Szabolcsi dealt with the early appearance of the major in his *A melódia története* (The History of Melody): "In the Middle Ages there was a fear of intervals lesser than whole notes, particularly of the sharp stressing of a leading note: the use of semitone intervals and chromaticism was not their realm (much rather that of the Near East and subsequently of the late Renaissance). If at all possible, they avoid such instrumental and heathen-sounding *musica falsa*; they avoid it and also the leading note, at least, by calling its leading note status into question . . . It often seems as if the major emerged only gradually and with difficulty out of church modality and always bordered on the territory of the Lydian and the Mixolydian."[1]

[1] Szabolcsi (1957), pp. 58–9.

Szabolcsi also refers to Arabo Scholasticus, who mentions "rustica sonoritas" in connection with the major tetrachord, and to Guido of Arezzo, who uses the epithet "agricolae dictus" for the Lydian scale, since he, like many others saw folk, peasant, and also pagan characteristics in it. At the same time the determining role of the final also arises, in which connection János Maróthy noticed that the idea of the final might have been linked with the development of the European rhyme.[2]

5. *Musical types.* Of all the possible types of troubadour music, Vidal used a mere three: *Oda continua*, *kanzone* and the 2nd variant of the *lai* fragment. The first two types belong to the extensive family of hymns, and the third to the category of sequences. We do not know what else he was familiar with, but from his extant songs it is clear that he strove for simplicity: the *Oda continua* had no formal restrictions, the musical phrases could follow each other freely; the *kanzone* differed only insomuch as its first or first two lines were repeated. The *lai* fragment, which belongs among the group of sequences, does not seem to be a conscious exploration of form. This group includes much greater types, such as the basic form of the *lai* itself, or the *estample*, which Vidal did not use. Yet Vidal was one of the "great" troubadours: by the number of songs extant he takes sixth place (having composed 13 of the 302 troubadour melodies), and three of his works have survived in more than one manuscript. This is well worth of noting, as there are only five troubadours whose same poem, together with its melody, survives in three manuscripts. From this point of view Vidal ranks equal to Bernart de Ventadorn (1150–1180), and follows Floquet de Marselha (1180–1231).

6. *Contrafacta.* Vidal borrowed no melodies from any of his fellow troubadours, and used no other poem as his pattern. Vidal's works, however, were used on 17 occasions by troubadours of an older generation or those active at the same time as he was. "Anc no morir" (Pill. 364.4), here featuring as No. 1, was used by Aicart (Pill. 6a.1), Bartran Carbonel (Pill. 82.75 and 82.83), Duran sartor de Carpentras (Pill. 126.2), Peire Cardenal (Pill. 335.16), Raimon de Castelnou (Pill. 396.6), Reforsat de Tres (Pill. 419.1), Uc de l'Escure (Pill. 452.1), and it has also survived in a song by an anonymous author (Pill. 461.130).

The poem "Quant hom onraz" (Pill. 364.40), here No. 10, was used, along with its melody, by the following: Palais (Pill. 315.3), Peire Cardenal (Pill. 335.24), Peire Pelissier (Pill. 353.1), Uc de Saint Circ (Pill. 457.5 and 457.22).

"Pois tornaz" (Pill. 364.37), here No. 8, which was a Provençal song (whose origin is not known exactly, though Pillet dates it later than Vidal: Pill. 461.96), later appeared as a *Minnesang*, as the work of Rudolf von Fenis-Neuenburg: "Nun ist niht mêre nun gedinge" (for its literature see the analysis of No. 8).

The poem and melody of "Quant hom es" (Pill. 364.39) here No. 9, was used by an unknown author in the 13th century (Pill. 461.222).

"Tart mi veiran" (Pill. 364.49), here No. 12, served as a model for Reforsat de Forealquier (Pill. 418.1).

[2] Maróthy (1960), pp. 605 and 616.

VIDAL

1
Al sem-blan de rey tirs cant l'ac ven-cut l'em-pe-rai-re
e'l fes ti rar cant lac pres s' he-re-tat e son ar-mes
dom el chan-tan' al mal-tra-i-re ve-zen la ro-da vi-rar
el ser plo-rau' al ma-njar chant con plus ay ma-la-nan-sa
chant ca-zir en a-le-gran-sa mi pot mos mal-tratz tor-nar
en plor can vol jor nul bes als au-tres e mi so-ve
qu'ieu n'aic pro ar non ay-re.

Pill. 167.4 Ms. *R*

The poem beginning "Al semblan de rey tirs" has survived in the Provençal Manuscript *R*. The lines of the poem are each of seven syllables. The rhyme scheme differs from the cadences of the melodic lines. Taking only the melodic cadences into account a different structural picture of the poem would emerge. A musical idea is formed usually by two, and on one occasion by three, lines of the poem.

R

	A		A^{v}		B		C		D			D^{v}	
SONG TYPE	A	B	C	D	E	F	G	H	I	J	K	L	M
METRIC FORM	7a	7b	7a	7a	7b	7c	7c	7d	7d	7c	7e	7e	7e
NOTE GROUPS	6	8	7	8	9	7	7	8	8	7	7	7	7
CADENCE	fifth		fifth		fifth		keynote		keynote			keynote	

In song type the first two A lines are identical in character, moving in the upper octave and then descending by a fourth; the middle section has a melodic arch that rises by a third to its *peak*, after which the melody returns to the keynote with a downward step of a fifth followed by a fourth. Up to this point every melody line has closed on the fifth, but from here on the final note is always the keynote. Part C is followed by two lines of identical, domed melody, both beginning the form with third and fifth steps starting from the keynote, to reach the upper octave; the closing line prepares for the cadence with a downward step of the same thirds as the upward step at the opening of the last line of the melody, so that the arch is completed symmetrically.

Compared to the first part of the song, there is more melisma; apart from the last, which consists of five notes, these are triads and chords of four notes. The whole makes up an overall *descending* song form.

Gennrich sees no melodic interdependencies and thinks that each melody line corresponds to a 7-syllable line of the poem (*Komm.* p. 66). He describes the structure as *Oda continua* and declares that the song has no Provençal antecedents, nor were any *contrafacta* made of it. He also touches upon the deviations of the notes from the text: for example in Line 1 there is one note less than the syllable count, etc.

But by conjoining, a new form takes shape because—although as variant forms—certain lines are seen to bear resemblances to each other: A A_v B C D D_v. The *Oda continua* thus turns out to be a *lai* fragment (Lai-Group II).

2
R
1
2
Chant e de- port joi dom-ney e so - latz en- se-nha-mens lar- guez' e cor - te - zi - a
G
Chant e de -port joi domp-nei e so - laz en-sei-gnamen lar- gec' e cor - te - si - a
X
Chant e de - por joi don-noi et so - laz en-sen-gnalment lar- ge - te cor - tei - si - e

R
3
4
ho-nor e pretz e li - al dru - da - ri - a an si bai-sat en-gen e mal - ve - statz
G
ho-nor e preç e le - ial dru - da - ri - a an si baissat en-jan e mal - ve - statz
X
et prez et sen et le - ial dru - de - ri - e ont si ba - sat en-gens et mal - ve - statz
R
5
6
c'a pauc d'i - ra nom soi des - es - pe - rat car en - tre cen do - nas ni a - ma - dors
G
q'a pauc d'i - ra no sui des - es - pe - raz car en - tre cen don-nas ni pre-ja - dors
X
k'a por d'i - re non sui des - es - pe - raz car en - tre cent do - nes ni pre - ja - dors
R
7
8
no vey u - na ni un quen bes cap - te - nha en ben a - mar ni en be que nos fe - nha
G
non vei ni ne qi bes cap - te - gna en ben a - mar qa d'al- tra part noc fe - gna
X
ni a u - ne ne un k'au ben en - te - gne vers ben a - mar que d'au-tre part non fen - gne
R
9
10
quenz sap- cha dir qu'es de - ven- gud' A - mors gar-daz com es a - bai - sa - da Va - lors.
G
ni sap- chan dir q'es de - ven gut' A - mors gar-daz com es a - bai - sa - da va - lors.
X
ne qui sa - chent q'est de - ven - gud' A - mors gar-daz com es a - bas- sa - de va - lors.

semblansa. e vigats lum h almen feo vuptansa. q̃ mos comora
me rete fai tan gẽ. p q̃cu nestau q̃ nots uv puf fouẽ. G̃luct

hant e deport for e conincr e folar. enfen ames

Largueze corteziá. lonors e prez. e hal ozudaria. an si laisar

engan e maluestac̈ ca pauc vm̃ nom foi ctesepat. car ẽ

cherc̈. conap m amazos nõ uv vna m vhi quenbos up

tenha. en ben amar m en tre que nos feiula. qut̃ capeha vm̃

ques deuenguỹamors. gardiũ com et ba uf la ũ uaфлõ.
M af vrur m ẽ vonaf fm paifar. q̃ fentrum e vial ver
via. dih fon kaifa amo feo bauza. e puers eafeuf ef euvert̃
e fenbra. e michani fuv e lap vaf con lui. e lar vona t ve puf
an amazos. e maif cuiõ con a pren lor o cenhi. maif aical br
com coue lur ẽuenhi. q̃ a cafaif ef aure vfonoz. puf fofrẽ
vzun q̃ pueif vestev allova. A m̃ com es melf ẽ cõm̃f
leurrah. q̃ẽ acuihir z auineh cundia. e bio pailaro preu
e voffa paira. ai̇ vcu melhs gardar faf volũtati. q̃ ies no
val cor ve vaf meruati. m nõ ef fil puf p miria colova. cur̃
fola remova tih la vehvenh. nõ vie ies ca vmina nõ coue
nh̃. fom la entecvors. ni̇f gef nõ vu eu vos lur
fon cors C̃ fi plaguet dio brio plazers oman. q̃ rere re
ẽ hal fenixia. ca fumdftan puf en alo fomelia. q̃ pvoues
aifi fos afinati uaf lievs con laur cafina ẽ la fornar. e nõ
nagueo piuaries m vona. q̃ fe rem tol lo mal m far o ve
nhu. aifi femi aif feo kaifenareffen bi̇. cõ lo leo an golfiero ve
laf vora. cir lac eftort ve fos guervievo maiors. C̃ cafti
cor mia vonam fos promati. paffar agra la mar pair lom
baroia. maif nõ cug fur vaf uos h̃lme romania. fi nom e
ni vaf vos avecchmati. fol p uiб̃ vcuen uoler la pari. e car
nice co ẽuos er amoz. au maif elaufos q̃ re uõ la reteni.
piepar uos ar fumeamẽ̃ q̃uf fouenhi. ca gral cors vih fui
q̃e vefcora. e vieuf pvõ aif pronatora. aur com iuile
leruliment amiftan. fol legie too e fenev vitania. maif puf
amova vomer ẽ aichaviá. cõ veazua iouenf z amiftat. eicu
metrif puf iuielh lauer ucm. au vti apres ve faif vzun m
dutova. que nõ ef vier q̃u umiarf reuenhi. q̃ leif ẽ ioi
e prez e leurau renha. fi cõ m̃aev ni̇l fur fugev vel cora. ca

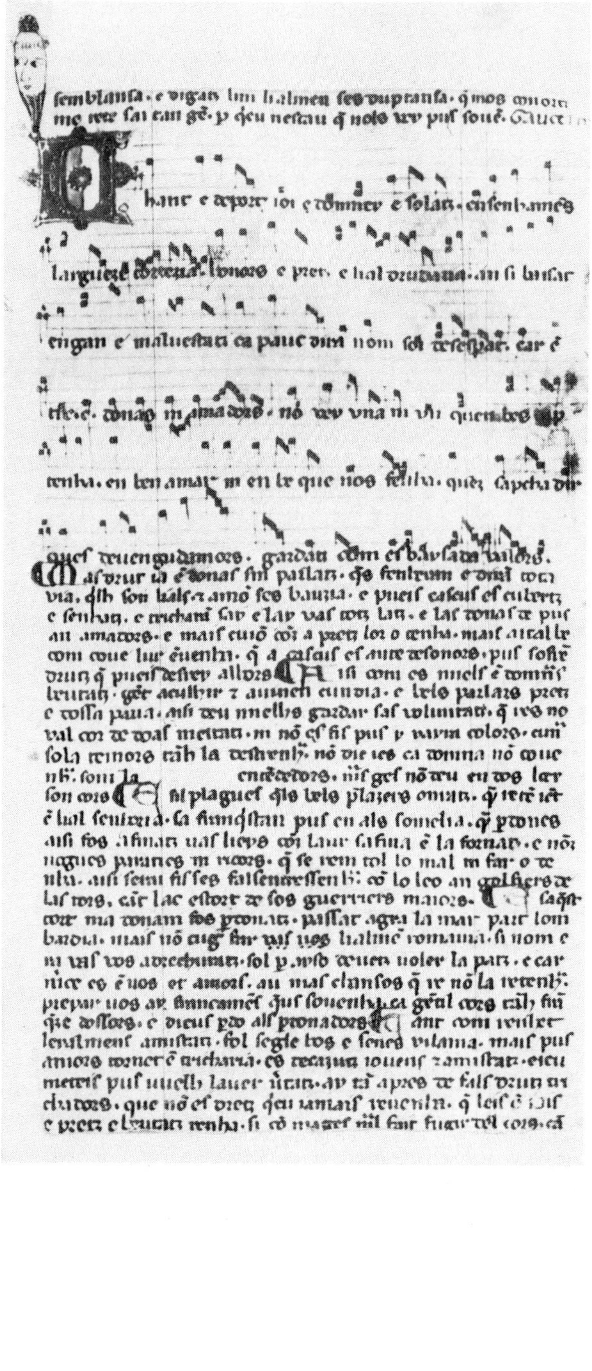

Pill. 167.15 Mss. *R*, *G*, *X*

This broadly phrased melody can be divided into three musical sections: after an initial descent it arrives at the upper octave after four bars (Part 1); in Bars 5–6 it does not range more than a fifth above the keynote (Part 2); from Bar 7 it once again rises to the upper octave (Part 3), and leads up to the cadence with a very rich melisma.

The range is an octave, which is sometimes extended to the lower seventh, upon which the line cadence occurs in one or two cases.

Twelve *contrafacta* are known of this melody, which is of the *Oda continua* type (Gennrich *Komm.* p. 66); its tonality is Aeolian or Dorian. A musical comparison of this 10-syllable, 10-line poem:

R

	A		A^{5v}		B		C		C^{v}	
SONG TYPE	A	B	C	D	E	F	G	H	I	J
METRIC FORM	10a	10b	10b	10a	10a	10c	10d	10d	10c	10c
NOTE GROUPS	10	10	10	10	10	10	11	11	10	10
CADENCE	keynote		third		lower seventh		third		keynote	

G

	A		A^{5v}		B		C		C^{v}	
SONG TYPE	A	B	C	D	E	F	G	H	I	J
METRIC FORM	10a	10b	10b	10a	10a	10c	10d	10d	10c	10c
NOTE GROUPS	10	10	10	10	10	10	8	11	10	10
CADENCE	keynote		third		keynote		third		keynote	

X

	A		A^{5v}		B		C		C^{v}	
SONG TYPE	A	B	C	D	E	F	G	H	I	J
METRIC FORM	10a	10b	10b	10a	10a	10c	10d	10d	10c	10c
NOTE GROUPS	10	10	12	10	10	10	11	11	10	11
CADENCE	keynote		third		keynote		third		keynote	

By contraction the formal analysis has again changed an *Oda continua* into a *lai* fragment (Lai-Group II)

Characteristically the melody reaches a melismatic resolution after three or four syllabic notes (III–, IIII–). By omitting the melisma and considering the initial notes to be the main ones, the first line, for example, becomes *pentatonic*.

The syllabic, melismatic alternation does not influence the rhythm of the text, but this characteristic formula of *dance* prompting does not always occur at the beginning of a verse line; it can occur at the 2nd, 4th or even the last syllable and continue into the next line of text; so the melody was probably not written for a 10-syllable poem.

Faidit's poem is dated to the 1200s. The following are some observations on the melody and the relationship between the three sources:

According to Manuscripts *R* and *G* the melody is Dorian, while Manuscript *X* inscribes a flat from Line 4 of the poem onwards, making it Aeolian from then on. This results in a certain fluctuation within the piece, exactly at the point where the musical Section A^{5v} ends and Section B starts (Lines 5–6 of the poem), which, compared to what has gone before, is lower in register, and does not include the diminished note. In Section C, however, this becomes a prevailing element.

Gennrich defined its rhythm according to the third mode (dactyl) and tried to carry this through every melodic line. This solution is contradicted by the frequent formula of dance prompting, as well as by a frequent formula in Manuscript *X*, where the two or three consecutive *clives* are aligned so that the two contiguous notes form a *pressus*, which in itself suggests mensurality:

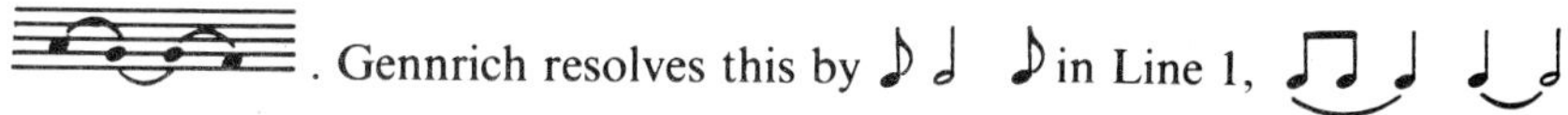

. Gennrich resolves this by in Line 1, and in Line 7. All three distort the weak appearance of the metre. Taking the whole melody into account, we take each note to have an identical value, so that the doubling means a double value: . Gennrich's solution of Line 1 came near to the correct solution, but with the meaningless quavers he changed the score picture dictated by the manuscript. The three sources, with their divergences from each other, still present an identical melody. In general *G* and *X* are the closest to each other, whenever there is some major melodic difference in comparison with *R*, then *G* and *X* choose similar solutions. The cadence of Line 5 is g in *R*, i.e. the keynote, and that of Line 6 a minor seventh f; in *G* and *X* these two line finals change places: Line 5 ends on a minor seventh and Line 6 on the keynote. In Manuscript *R* the melisma that leads up to g^2 in Line 8 continues the 3-note formula on c^1, while at the same place Manuscript *G* brings a step of a major sixth, which is practically impossible in the musical practice of the time (g^2–b flat^1). The mistake can be corrected with the help of Manuscript *X*; here a *torculus* mark at the relevant place (f^2–g^2–f^2) restores the equilibrium and develops the same step of a fifth as in *R*, only not with g^2–c^1, but with f^2–b flat^1.

In Line 7 Manuscript *G* is incomplete, giving three note groups less than the other two manuscripts, but the three relevant syllables are also missing from the text. This proves, in contradiction to previous arguments, that *the compiler of the manuscript did not treat the text as independent of the melody.*

In conclusion one can say, regardless of whether the melody was applied by Faidit to this poem or whether at the time of the compilation of the manuscripts the poem was known with this melody, that in the Provençal region (*R*) the *dance* character prevailed more strongly in the melody, whereas in the Lorraine (*X*) and in northern Italy (*G*), which are geographically distant from each other, the melodic line had richer melismatics. Furthermore, in Lorraine certain attempts were made to underline the accents (distrophic formulae), which is of great significance, even if these accents do not coincide with the contentual accents of the text.

G
5
6
mas tan m'au-ci ab dolz mar-ti-re q'eill per-don ma mort fran-cha-men
G
7
8
bel-la don' ab gai cors pla-zen per nos plaing e per vos sos-pi-re
G
9
10
e ren mas ma mort no a-ten pe-ro si con us plaz m'es gen.

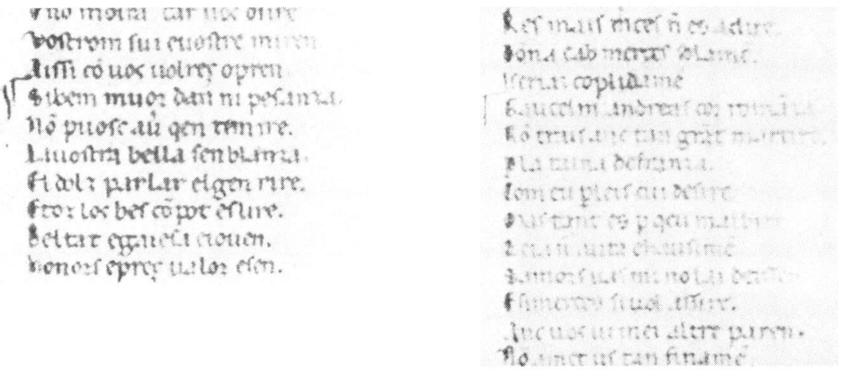

Pill. 167.17 Ms. *G*

The beginning of the melody has a similar formula to the first two Faidit pieces. The similar manner of construction is clearly recognizable further on as well: a descending opening (the first four lines are of a descending character, with two two-bar sections emerging within the four lines), a melody that keeps to the middle register close to the keynote or the fifth, and then in the last sections, a rise to the ninth, followed by a descent to the keynote. Here the peak comes in Section 7, after which the melody rises to the octave only in the penultimate Section 9 by gradual steps starting from the diminished seventh, syllable by syllable, to the fourth, from where there is a step down with a *clivis* to the base, and then with a step up of fifth to d^2; from that there is a turn of a second, and then again an upward step of a fourth. There are scarcely any precedents for such wild leaps in troubadour music. The last line again avails itself of a rare solution: from the upper diminished seventh (f^2) the melody comes down by thirds to the keynote, after which the 10-line song ends with a few melisma groups.

In Gennrich (*Komm.* p. 66) the musical form is *Oda continua,* set throughout, i.e. each line is different.

Comparison of the textual and musical forms:

G

	A		A^v		B		C		D	
SONG TYPE	A	B	C	D	E	F	G	H	I	J
METRIC FORM	8a	8b	8a	8b	8b	8c	8c	8b	8c	8c
NOTE GROUPS	8	8	8	8	9	8	8	9	8	8
CADENCE	fifth		keynote		fourth		keynote		keynote	

Through the varied repeat of the first two lines the *Oda continua* turns into a *kanzone*. In the second half of *C* it uses the second half of A^v ($C = c + A^{v2}$), and *D* uses the first half of *B* ($D = B^{Iv} + d$).

The rhyme *-ire* (b) frequently recurs: three times after the first line. The music (in five sections with two poem lines to one musical line) responds to this only twice: at the end of Lines 4 and 8 of the poem (i.e. in the second halves of musical Sections 2 and 4).

In conclusion, the poem and music have only a loose structural connection, although it is closer than in the first two Faidit works. The north Italian manuscript shows no independent musical construction. The same melody was also used by Floquet de Roman (Pill. 156.9).

W
4
M'a - ven a dir en chan - tan e re - trai - re
G
Co - vent o - ir en chan - tant et re - trai - re
X
Co - vent o - ir en chan - tant et re - trai - re
W
5
Qe cil q'e - ra de va - lors caps e pai - re
G
Qan cil q'es - toit de va - lor chief et pai - re
X
Qan cil q'es - toit de va - lor chief et pai - re
W
6
Lo ric va - len Ri - chart rei dels En - gles
G
Li rich va - lens Ri - chars reis des En - gleis
X
Li rich va - lens Ri - chars reis des En - gleis

7
W
Es morz a deus qal per - d'e qal dan es
G
Es morz he diex qals dous et qals per - te
X
Es morz he diex qals dous et qals per - te
8
W
Con es - traing mot con sa - lvage ad au - zir
G
Con es - treins moz sal - va - ges a o - ir
X
Con es - treins moz sal - va - ges a o - ir
9
W
Ben a dur cor toz hom qel pot so - frir
G
Molt a dur cor nus hom qel pot soff - rir
X
Molt a dur cor nus hom qel pot soff - rir

vn coup a tot le mieuz del mon preis. tote
lonor. tot lou ben tot lou mes. et quan
en vei q non li por guenchir. man en de
men redoutar amozir.

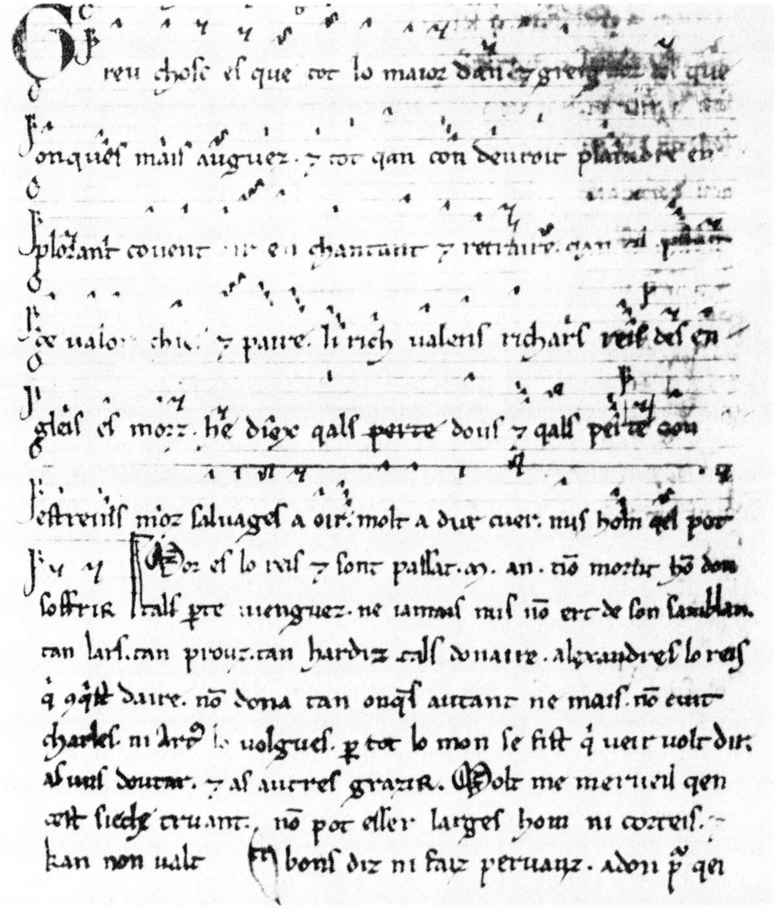

Pill. 167.22 Mss. *G*, *W*, *X*
Richard Lament

This poem, called the Richard Lament, is the most beautiful *plank* in troubadour poetry. Richard Cœur-de-Lion died in 1199, so that it would have been written in that or the following year. According to Sándor Eckhardt "Faidit may well have written his lament in Esztergom".[1] Eckhardt also posits a certain parallel with Hungarian laments, referring to a statement on that subject by Benjamin Rajeczky.[2] Based on the examination of the various melody sources, certain questions require clarification. Sándor Eckhard published the melody in J. Beck's transcription,[3] but it has been established that Beck

[1] Eckhardt (1961), p. 136.
[2] In *Deutsches Jahrbuch für Volkskunde*, Vol. III, 1957, p. 46.
[3] Beck (1910), p. 92.

compiled a version of his *own*, based on Manuscripts *X* and *W*. By so doing, he idealized the melody, as it were, and in accordance with the practice at the beginning of this century, he even gave it a rhythm, but in such a way as to make it difficult to rank the new melody into the types of modal notation. Even the text of Beck's publication did not tally with that of any of the manuscripts that include a score.

The versions of the melody, which we have transcribed from all the three manuscripts that include the music, generally resemble each other in their melodic line, so that we can assert at the outset that the Lament's musical variants may have had a *single* common source. Gennrich (*Komm.* p. 67) mentions no more than one anonymous *contrafactum* and an *Old French song*, entitled "E! servantois, arrier t'en revas".[4] So it appears the melody was set only to this *plank* of Faidit's, whose authorship is indicated by a typical opening formula that resembles those of the melodies hitherto discussed. The special lament character of the text seems to have had little influence on the melodic formulation. (Nor has the text any distinctive formal character.) But the relationship of the melody primarily to *this* text, can be well seen from Line 6:

W: "Richars reis des Engleis"
G: "Richart rei dels Engles"
X: "Richars reis des Engleis"

While these form the *textual peaks* of the lament, they also mark in all three manuscripts the *nadirs* of the melody, adequately representing the musical character. Though the manuscripts are not identical note for note or syllable for syllable, their musical solutions fall into line with each other more closely at this important point in the text than in the preceding and following lines: Manuscript *G* (northern Italy) is a second lower, and apart from a downward step of a fifth in the middle of the line, it proceeds in syllabic notes, and with scarcely touched passing (*liquescens*) notes offers particularly beautiful possibilities of performance. This variant closes at this point on the keynote. In Manuscripts *W* (Paris) and *X* (Lorraine), the tune is a second higher and closes a second away from the keynote. Variant *W* is syllabic, only once does it bridge a fifth with the help of a *pes*, while *X* uses more embellishment, and is thus closer to *G*. Even apart from Line 6, which we have just analysed, it can be established that the three melodic variants of the *plank* are variants of the same melody, and concern not so much the melodic line as its details. From this point of view, it is an extremely important example, thoroughly typical of troubadour music and of the scribes who recorded the music. A question that belongs in a more comprehensive treatment, but which cannot be ignored here, is the *extent to which the troubadours were concerned in the preservation of their music, and the role the compilers of the manuscripts played in modifying the melodies.*

Above all the keys of the three variants are striking. The same melody has a purely major character in the Paris variant. (In determining the tonalities I have

[4] Raynaud (1884), p. 381.

been governed by the score picture of the manuscripts, and referred the accidentals inscribed in them to the whole melody wherever it was musically justified.) The north Italian (*G*) variant would be Dorian, but by Bar 1 the sixth note of the scale has been diminished, turning it into Aeolian. The Lotharingian version (*X*) also raises an interesting tonal question: initially it would be major, like the Paris Manuscript, but there an accidental was inscribed in Bar 1—a diminishing of the seventh. Except in Bar 1, no accidentals occur anywhere else, but that one modification influences the development of the melody throughout, making the tonality oscillate between the major and the Mixolydian. That uncertain, virtually 'fluctuating' song picture is not unfamiliar in medieval monody (ti-ta alternation). It is one of the typical signs of the exploration and development of keys in European music. In this case the answer is that a common melody for the *plank* was known everywhere, but modified both in key and in ornamental indications according to local tastes. There is no reason to suppose that the melody was erroneously recorded in any of the manuscripts.

Comparison of textual and musical form

The poem has nine of the ten syllables in each stanza. Textually it has the form of a *plank*, while musically it is through-composed *Oda continua.*

W

	A		B		C		D		E
SONG TYPE	A	B	C	D	E	F	G	H	I
METRIC FORM	10a	10b	10a	10c	10c	10b	10b	10d	10d
NOTE GROUPS	9	10	10	11	11	10	10	10	10
CADENCE	third		third		second		second		keynote

G

	A		B		C		D		E
SONG TYPE	A	B	C	D	E	F	G	H	I
METRIC FORM	10a	10b	10a	10c	10c	10b	10b	10d	10d
NOTE GROUPS	10	10	10	11	10	10	10	10	10
CADENCE	second		second		keynote		keynote		keynote

X

	A		B		C		D		E
SONG TYPE	A	B	C	D	E	F	G	H	I
METRIC FORM	10a	10b	10a	10c	10c	10b	10b	10d	10d
NOTE GROUPS	9	10	10	11	11	10	10	10	10
CADENCE	third		third		second		second		keynote

In this melody Faidit used no cadences of a fifth for any of the lines. The cadences, which according to the song forms occur every second line, fall twice on the second, and three times on the keynote. Even within the two-line forms only the diminished seventh and the lower diminished sixth occur. This series of cadence formulae is a decisive one and in contrast to the other melodies, it points towards the music of folk laments. The descending melodic lines of Sections A, D and E also indicate a lament, and so do the augmentations of the diminished seconds in the first bars of the northern Italian (*G*) and Lotharingian (*X*) manuscripts.

The song form of four-and-a-half lines which we suggest is only one of several possibilities, which include the possibility of nine independent lines.

The real form of the melody could be confirmed by live interpretation. The downward glissandos of the Paris manuscript (*W*) are not indicated here; in general they extend to the first note from which the melody is continued lower, so that the possibility of a relationship with lament music seems even closer. A later task would be to seek possible relatives of the melody among the laments. The melody of the *Ómagyar Mária-siralom* (Old Hungarian Lament of Mary)—which is also a troubadour or trouvère melody—is certainly very distant, although it dates from around the same time. Though certain turns are reminiscent of the melody of the Old Hungarian Lament of Mary, it belongs, both its formal structure and musical character, to a different type sphere.

5
G
Ben fo - ra co - tra l'a - fan ge m'a dat d'u - na donn' a - mors
G
puos ab lei no truop mas dan qe.m fe - ces d'al - tra part so - cors
G
ab qe s'a - dol - ces mas do - lors qe·ill dir de non des - pla - cen
G
de lei on plus non a - ten m'an os - tat e vi - rat lo cor e·l sen
G
d'un greu fais per q'eu fais l'en - ten - de - men.

Among the melodies set to Faidit's poems or attributed to him, this song stands out as particularly beautiful. It may also be said to bear the closest relationship to Hungarian musical history of any examined so far. It opens with two descending lines, thus corresponding well with the Faidit type of beginning. Its tonality is Dorian, but steps of a semitone are so consequently avoided (and where used occur at unstressed points) that it gives a strongly pentatonic impression. After the melismatic, animated runs of the earlier pieces, the first two melodic lines here (i.e. the first four lines of the text) bring forceful intervals, with a downward and an upward step of fourth within one bar, and later, again within one bar, a downward step of a fifth and an upward step of a fourth. These so far unusual movements, as well as the cautious treatment of semitones all seem to relate the melody to a certain Hungarian folk-music tradition. This impression is reinforced by the inclusion of the melody in only one single manuscript, the northern Italian Manuscript *G*; nor was any *contrafactum* made of it. One old style Hungarian folksong, "Megvirágzott a diófa" (The Walnut Tree has Blossomed—Járdányi I. 37) is very similar to Faidit's melody: the folksong fits into the first two melody lines. Here the melody adjusts itself very interestingly to the poem: lines of seven and eight syllables keep alternating (resembling the so-called 'grand political' type of 15 syllables, generally used in the Middle Ages), but the poem closes with two ten-syllables lines; it thus has a delicate and interesting internal arrangement (3 + 3 + 4). Similar formulae can also be found in the Hungarian *Halotti beszéd* (Funeral Oration) and in the sequence from the Pray Codex which begins "Clemens et benigna". According to Gennrich's categorization Faidit's troubadour song is a *kanzone*.

	A		A^v		B	C		D			E	
SONG TYPE	A	B	A	B	C	D	E	F	G	H	I	J
METRIC FORM	7a	8b	7a	8b	8b	7c	7c	3d	3d	4c	3e	3e
NOTE GROUPS	7	8	7	8	8	7	7		10		10	
CADENCE	fifth		keynote		sec-ond	lower seventh			fifth		keynote	

We do not concur with Gennrich's suggested form, referring exclusively to the lines, whereby the first two lines of 7 + 8 syllables, identical or similar in character, are followed by independent musical units that correspond to the single lines of the text. According to our classification Section B is indeed incomplete, and yet its independence is obvious. Section C is a well-constructed domed melodic section, while the last two 10-syllable Sections D and E are, in spite of the internal division of each into three sub-sections, two independent musical sections, D having a cadence of a fifth, and E a final on the keynote.

By way of example, here is a rough translation of the whole poem:

G. Faidit: *Ben fora contra . . .*

1. How good it would be if Amor would help me revenge the sorrow a lady has caused me, and soothe my pain, for all I have had from her is insult; my true sorrow is lessened since those annoying refusals (of her whose love I desire no more) have taken a heavy weight off my heart and soul, and so I plead for her love no more.
2. Since I have pleaded with her in song my entreaties would be madness, from now on I shall save my pleas and my heart and my song for her in whom there is beauty and worth and all noble deeds, and if she willingly agrees and gives me full assurance, I shall never grieve or fear.
3. And yet, her lovely face, her charming attitude, the gentleness of her delicate young person, her beauty and fresh hue, which make her the flower of all flowers, urge me to love, but with such shyness that I have not yet dared reveal either my thoughts to her, by her leave, or that overwhelming desire that draws my joyful heart towards great daring.
4. I am drawn by far too great a daring, but I doubt if it would make a great noise; but I feared that the great favour this beauteous lady bestowed on me would attract attention; she saved me from a grave illness, when by her sweet permission I softly kissed her white neck, with great reverence and in secret, and that sweet kiss has broken my grief.
5. Her deeds are so perfect that all else seems to be vice, and ever since I have been before her, her attraction, her merits and charms have grown day by day, and her serence and gentle glance, with which she looks lovingly upon me, has dispelled my madness; so I throw myself before her feet, and that raises such joy in my heart as to preserve my rejoicing for ever.
6. I have never turned to her without an appeal, a message and persuasion; to her I bequeath my great fear, my heart and my song upon her, that I may paint her great values, chant her praise; she shows me kindliness, accords me her benevolence and affability, a dear donation, a lovely gift, in spite of the clamour of the evil ones, in secret.

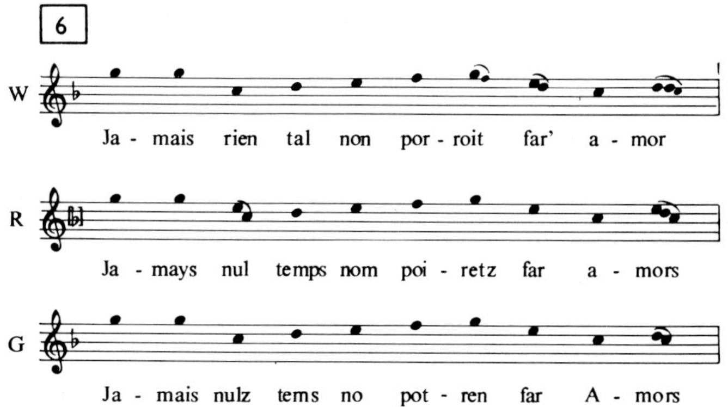

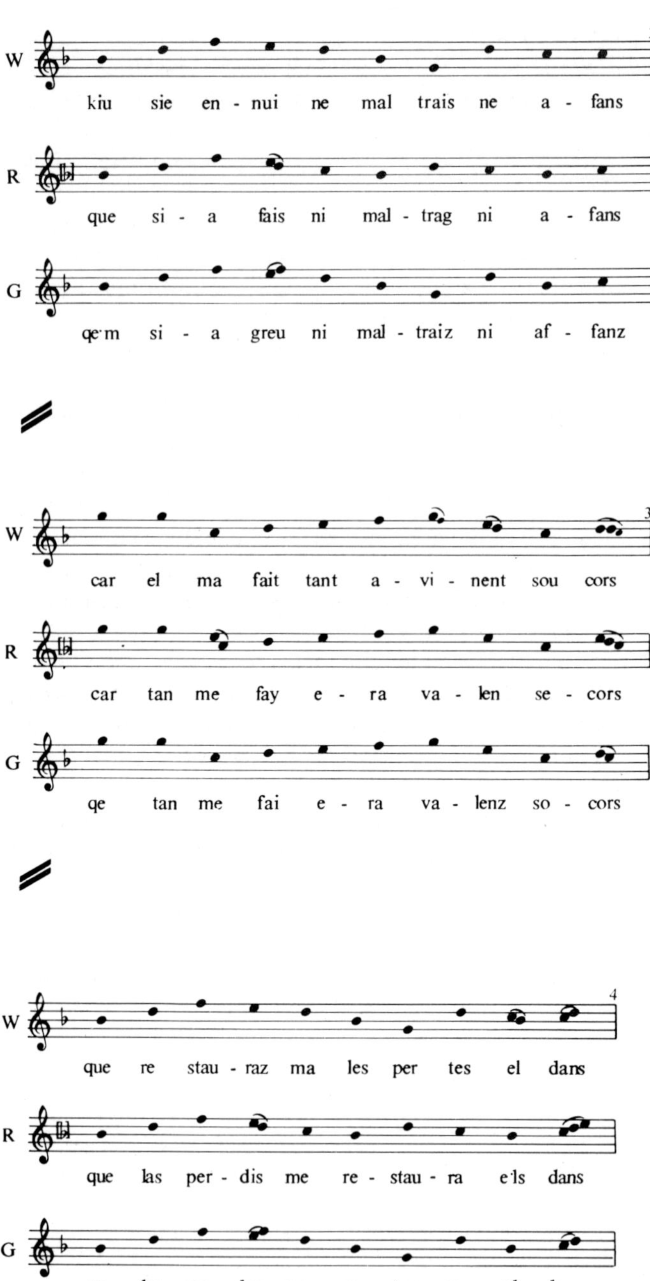
W
kiu sie en - nui ne mal trais ne a - fans
R
que si - a fais ni mal - trag ni a - fans
G
qe·m si - a greu ni mal - traiz ni af - fanz
3
W
car el ma fait tant a - vi - nent sou cors
R
car tan me fay e - ra va - len se - cors
G
qe tan me fai e - ra va - lenz so - cors
4
W
que re stau - raz ma les per tes el dans
R
que las per - dis me re - stau - ra e·ls dans
G
qe las per - das me re - stau - ra e·ls danz

5
W
quai - ve fes a dreit per mon so - la - ge
R
c'a - vi - a pres a dreg per so - lar - ge
G
c'a - vi - a pres a dreich per mon fo - lage
6
W
et si ainc jor de ren ma fet ma - ri
R
e si anc jor me fetz en re mar - rir
G
e si anc jorn mi feç de ren mar - rir
7
W
eu lou par - don lou de tric el da - ma - ge
R
e - ral per - do lo de - stric e·l dampnat - ge
G
er li per - don lo de - streich e·l dampna - ge

8
W
car tal dos - na fai mon preis a - cuei - llir
R
c'a tal do - na fa mos pre o - be - zir
G
q'a tal don - na fai moc percs a - mel - lir
9
W
qui ma - men - de tuit que ma fait suf - rir
R
don m'es - men - da tot cant m'a fag sof - rir
G
don m'es - men - dat tot qan m'a fait sof - rir

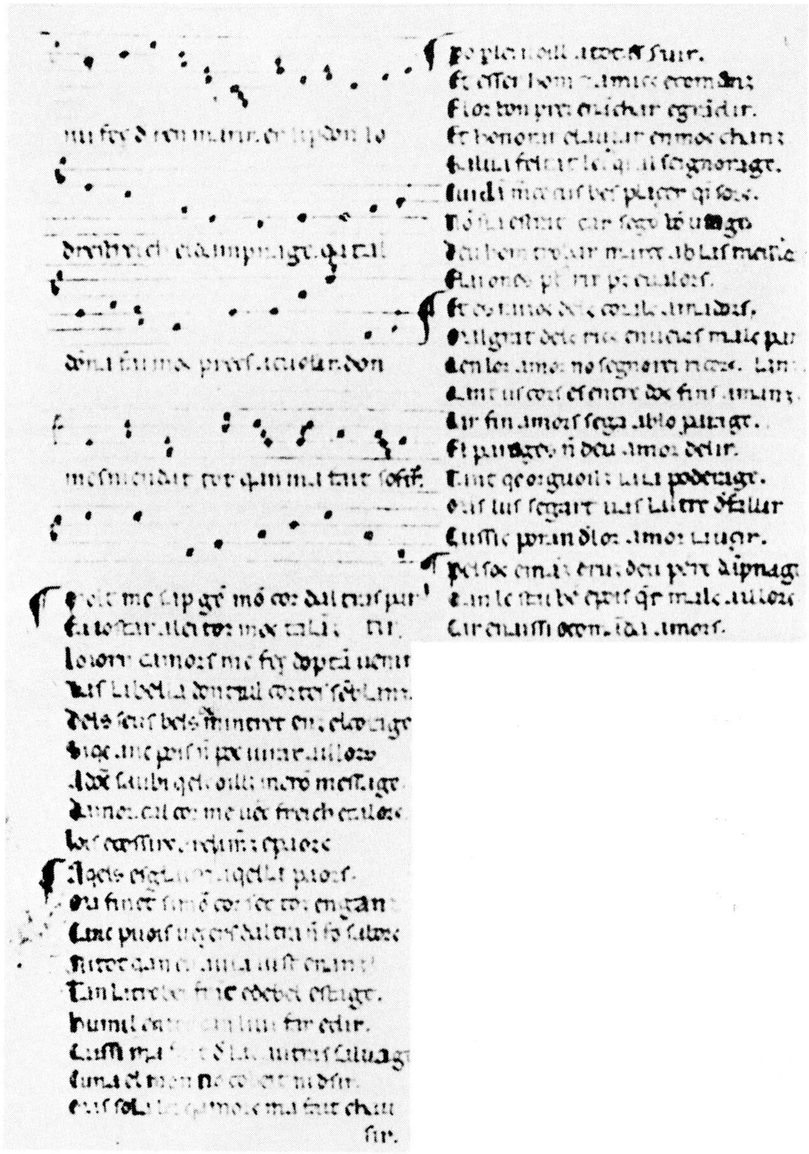

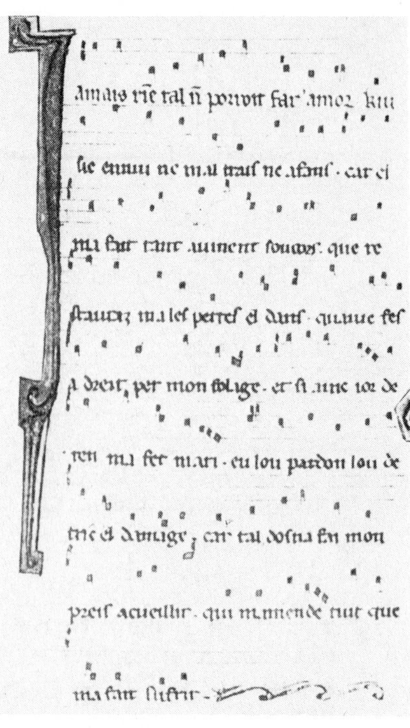

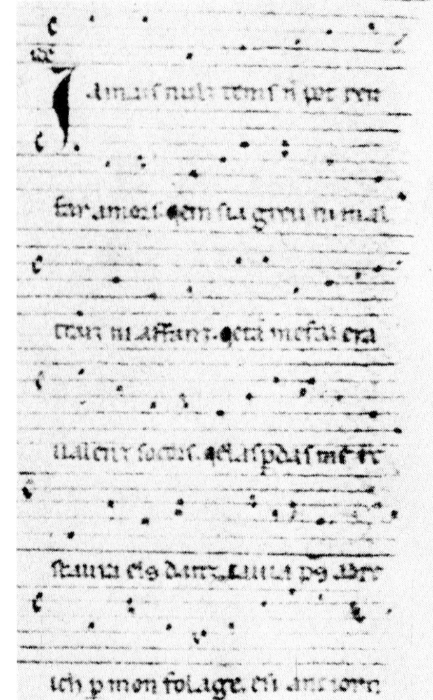

This is the first *syllabic* melody. It has a wide range, which is often encompassed by triads of thirds. Here again the ascending character is evident in the first two lines, which are repeated. Variant *R* deserves special consideration. The manuscript was compiled in the 1300s on Provençal territory. Compared with *W* and *G*, it closes the melody a fourth higher, on c^2 instead of g^1, forming a Mixolydian cadence in place of the Dorian finals of the other two variants. In transposing it I have allowed for this possibility, because the melodic line of the first two lines of music (four lines of text) remains the same. In Line 7 of the text we find a melodic variant of Lines 2 and 4 as opposed to the independent new melody line of *W*. Having said all that, one must add that Variant *R* does not change the character of the melody; in spite of the many differences one cannot speak of a new melody. Add to that the type of the poem—*coblas capcaudadas*—and one might surmise that the melody prepares for the new *cobla*. (In this type the rhyme of the last line of a stanza is repeated in the following stanza and the text is continued from there.) According to Gennrich (*Komm.* p. 67) the melody is a *lai fragment*, and he classifies it as Category III of the *sequentia* types. Here the lai formula—AA BB CC—can only be taken into consideration partially, as the stanzas, of nine 10-syllable lines, only tally with the first two formative lines (AA). If that were enough for a type definition, one might agree with Gennrich, but here there is a more complex melodic structure largely dominated by other components. Taking Variant *R* as a basis, the nine lines can be contracted into an A A B C form, where the second A is already a variant in its cadence (Line 4 of the text), the three lines of B (5, 6 and 7) have A-variant twice, once in Line 6 of the text (A_{1v}), and once in Line 7 of the text (A_{2v}). The last two text lines would constitute Part C. This arrangement is better suited to the melodic phrasing and keeps the broad melodic arches intact.

The melody was not used exclusively for this poem; two *contrafacta* are known: it was also applied to poems of Bertram Carbonel (Pill. 82.21) and Comtesse de Provence (Pill. 187.1). Compared with the Faidit melodies discussed so far it seems rather strange. The various possible ways of analysing the form raise questions of adaptation; in cases where it can no longer be established which was the basic melody one must think in terms of independent solutions having been arrived at by the compilers of the manuscripts. The closest to the poem's text is the five-line musical form of Variant *G*, but rather than a *lai* fragment it seems more of a *kanzone* type. This type classification applies equally to all three variants, as in each only the first two lines are repeats.

W

SONG TYPE	A	B	A	B	C	D	C^v	E	F
METRIC FORM	10a	10b	10a	10b	10c	10d	10c	10d	10d
NOTE GROUPS	10	10	10	10	11	10	10	10	10
CADENCE	fifth	fourth	fifth	fifth	fourth	key-note	key-note	oc-tave	key-note

R

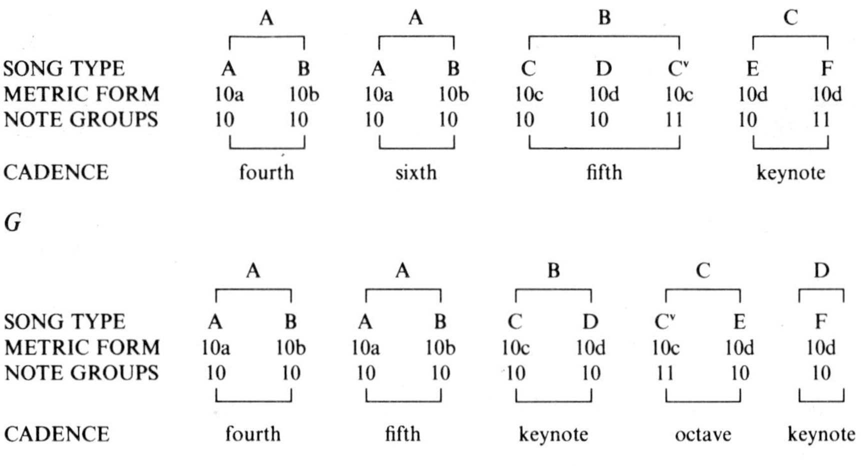

	A		A		B			C	
SONG TYPE	A	B	A	B	C	D	C^v	E	F
METRIC FORM	10a	10b	10a	10b	10c	10d	10c	10d	10d
NOTE GROUPS	10	10	10	10	10	10	11	10	11
CADENCE	fourth		sixth		fifth			keynote	

G

	A		A		B		C		D
SONG TYPE	A	B	A	B	C	D	C^v	E	F
METRIC FORM	10a	10b	10a	10b	10c	10d	10c	10d	10d
NOTE GROUPS	10	10	10	10	10	10	11	10	10
CADENCE	fourth		fifth		keynote		octave		keynote

R
on es pla - zen so - latz fran - quez hu - mi - li - tatz
3
G
on es plai - senz so - laz e franch' hu - mi - li - taz
X
ou naist plai - zanz so - laz et franch' hu - me - li - taz
R
de bel - la cap - te - nen - sa e gent pretz pre - zatz
4
G
e dol - za cap - te - nen - za e gais prez pre - jaz
X
et be - le cap - te - nan - ce et rich prez pre - jaz
R
me fay chan - tar so - ven ses so que non cos - sen
5
G
mi fai chan - tar so - ven ses cho qui non cos - sen
X
mi fait chan - tar so - vent senz ceu que non con - sent
R
qu'ieu jan si - a jau - zi - re d'a - ver joi pla - zen
6
G
q'eu jan si - a jau - zi - re d'a - ver joi pla - zen
X
kar eu si - e jau - zi - re d'a - voir joi plai - zant

7
R
ni d'al - lors non l'a - ten mais vel - ly lo de - zire
G
ni de - leis non a - ten mais l'en - vej' e·l de - si - re
X
ne de - li non a - tent fors l'e - nui gous de - si - re
8
R
c'ai del sieu cors jen que d'au - tral jau - zi - men.
G
c'ai de seu cors gen ses au - tre jau - ci - men.
X
k'ai de son cors gent senz au - tre jau - zi - ment.

Gancelm fauit

O ieu cois onan. comphr te grans leuicas.

a hev que plus magenca. eque mais me plag. on es

qi neu folan. frsse num leur. te leta capmue cale ger

pten precun. me fav dainter foueu. fen fo que non cof

feu. quieu ian fia tauine. nauer ioi plaieu. ni oillois

no laten. mmf melli lo reure en vel hieu coro ieu. q
er veil lm rē p far fo
mandame. e fil plin por mau
fire qeu no tm teften. po te es
puruen. catlas fat dadonne. fieu li fo fluiey foftuve e lu
fnamen. q fos sa uoluntera. ql plagues mamitan. en
cap will fufreufa. me fos iou uonan. ar q fos car copian
guaus fes fullenci. foral ros el gran p fen uobles uobln.
P neif auurau gqui fos camorau. te fina le uoleli. fi
en fos eu piq. mas pris ullis loran. trif fals puetados
fan. no non. e ment aricli. e mil coulpan. fels camoa
founeus. p qeu piec franeaime. mi uonf eur foi fuur ul
mar lulmeu. eauau galiame. e tamputarge. noz uue.
co dieg uagrune. er wit fi mal me pre. Daqft fullume
renlo ultuuaine. uonas p quem uapie. e lio repre. qo ui
adreg ualen. admeitume. e conoifse. car reguit ma maruiif
vf malf effentau. ab ge l tefconoifeufu. er feuli daiman.
qeu fir te folt malipn. mefte woei ualeu. e aur lor poare
e mamere e puira. amr eo pret baslur. qeu fora pue
nar. mauf p hers ar cemeuta. eui reue afteuaa. eui non
plag folaq. ni euts tefmeruaa. ni uiluauzecaretfa. ni auol
par. eaur uil qeui nefpaue. eic me prf mm albue. fo affe
eme fi mier nor oufieu. pro ai te q fofpire. que ala no ere
m ar lo coi mil fe. Gaucelm fauit

159

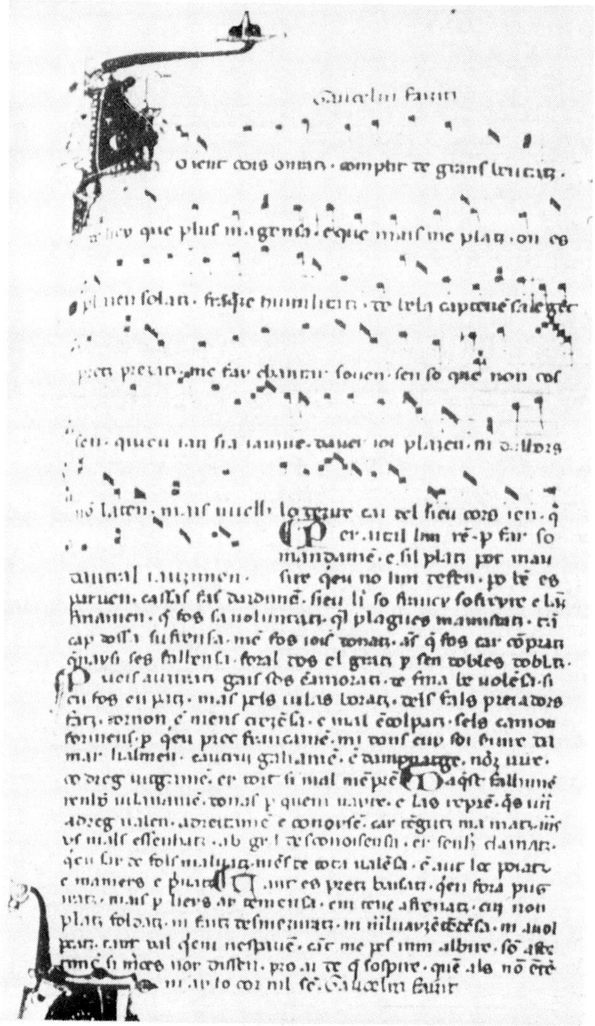

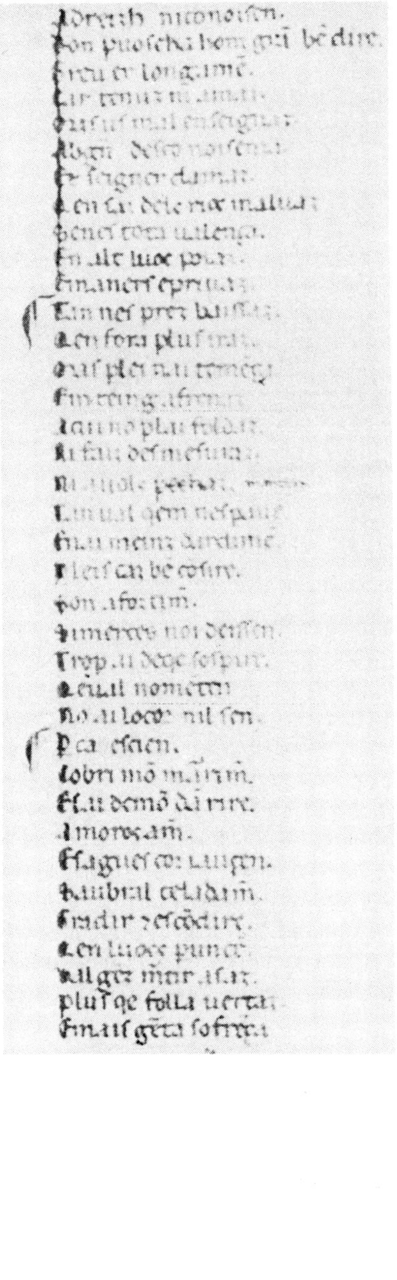

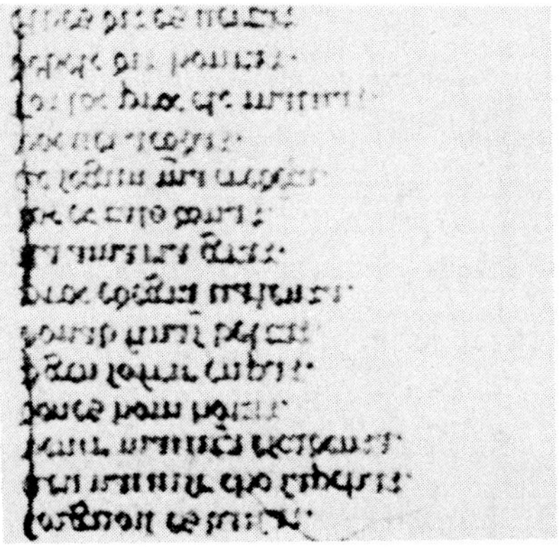

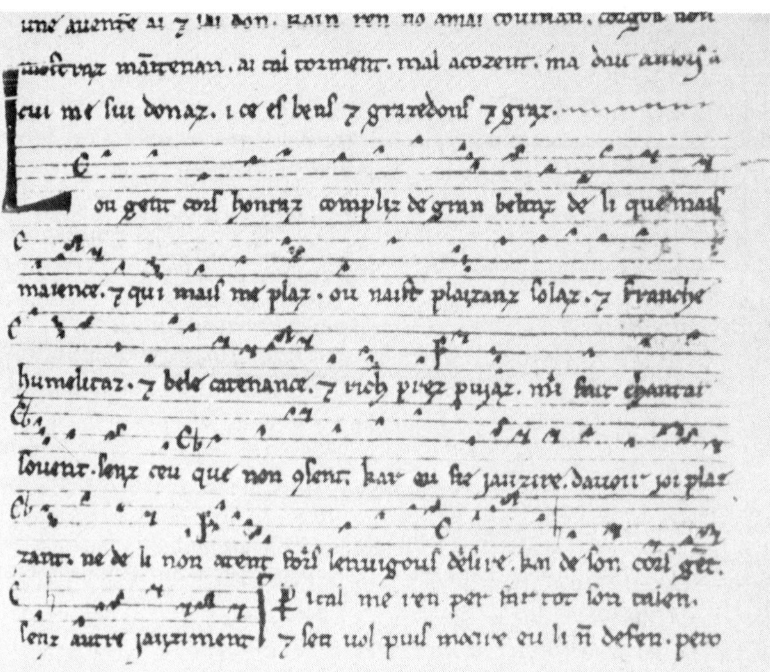

Pill. 167.22 Mss. *R*, *G*, *X*

The poem "Lo jent cors onratz" has a long form consisting of 16-line stanzas. It belongs to the *kanzone* type, with alternate lines of five and six syllables. The poem follows the structure of the *coblas capcaudadas*. In contrast to this structure of long stanzas with short lines, the melody consists of major arches that span several lines of text. Nor are the melodic arches proportionately divided over the lines. Compared with the songs analysed so far, this shift in proportion now for the first time divides the long stanza consisting of a great number of short lines.

The melody opens with a descent, but by the third syllable it steps up a fourth and remains high almost throughout the first line; after a step up of a fifth the second line gradually descends to approach the keynote: so every *two* lines of text together form *one* melodic line. This can be called Line A of the whole musical form, and it is right away repeated, so that from a musical point of view the first eight lines of text create an A A form. The two As might be further subdivided so that $A = A_1 A_2$ (with the second A_2 introducing a slight variant in its cadence). In Line 5 of the melody (equalling Lines 9 and 10 of the text) the arched melodic line brings a new formal element; starting from below it ends after a great domed structure in the middle of Line 7 of the melody (i.e. Line 13 of the text). Thereupon it starts again in the last one and a half melodic lines (Lines 14, 15 and 16 of the text) and is repeated in a diminished form. The extension concerns one line of text (Line 11) without which the two second melodic arches would be alike in proportions. The new melody that starts from Line 9 of the text will be marked B, or rather B ext for the sake of a correct definition; thus the complete form is A A_v B ext B.

Under A we have marked two melodies of differing character: A_1 and A_2. By substituting B for A_2, the formula can be refined as AB AB_v C ext D CD. That seeming musical symmetry matches the 16 lines of text only in part, as the short lines have no musical cadence formation, and each musical phrase usually consists of two or four short lines. But even this system allows no room for Line 11 of the text, and so one must assume that the first textual model for this melody was *not* Faidit's poem.

A single *contrafactum* is to be found in the corpus of troubadour music. It is by Peire Cardenal (Pill. 335.32), who was, however, younger than Faidit and who has no *new, independent* melody known. Though research so far has yielded no parallel or identity with any earlier poems, if Faidit's poem were the earliest sung to this melody, we still cannot believe that Faidit should have developed the melody in such a manner that its performance should push the text accents and the lines forming the stanzas into the background. Gennrich (*Komm.* pp. 67–8), when defining the musical form as a *kanzone*, did not notice the musical arches of the second part; he formed independent melodic lines out of each line of text except for the recapitulation of the first four text-lines, although even there he separated each element. By having 16 melodic lines corresponding to the 16 text-lines he broke up the melodic material so much that it became unsuitable for any kind of musical comparison and led to an erronous form definition. According to him the *kanzone* belonged to the category of hymn types. Our example, if correctly interpreted, fits better into the group of *sequentia* types (because of the repetition of every two lines): one of the *lai fragments*.

R

SONG TYPE	A	B	A	B_v	C	D	C_v	E
METRIC FORM	5a 6a	6b 5a	6a 6a	6b 5a	6c 6c	6d 5c	6c 6d	5c 6c
NOTE GROUPS	11	12	12	12	12	11	12	11
CADENCE	third	second	second	lower seventh	fifth	second	fourth	key-note

G

SONG TYPE	A	B	A	B_v	C	D	C_v	E
METRIC FORM	5a 6a	6b 5a	6a 6a	6b 5a	6c 6c	6d 5c	6c 6d	6c 6c
NOTE GROUPS	11	12	13	13	12	11	12	11
CADENCE	second	third	second	lower fourt	third	lower seventh	fifth	key-note

X

SONG TYPE	A	B	A	B_v	C	D	C_v	E
METRIC FORM	5a 6a	6b 5a	6a 6a	6b 5a	6c 6c	6d 5c	6c 6d	5c 6c
NOTE GROUPS	11	12	12	12	13	11	13	13
CADENCE	third	third	second	lower fourth	fifth	second	seventh	key-note

Apart from the Richard Lament, none of the Faidit melodies studied so far had so many cadences of seconds and so few of a fifth. What is more, the musical groups deviate from the poem-syllables in several places, although in the manuscripts they usually follow a very strict system.

One might make another interesting differentiation between the two main sections of the melody: the first two melodic lines (AB, AB) are syllabic in character, whilst the second two melodic lines (C ext D, CD) have a lot of melismatic movement. That is particularly true of the Provençal Manuscript *R*, whereas the Lotharingian Manuscript *X* shows a penchant for ornamentation even in the first two lines. The melody is identical in all three manuscripts.

oro seignoler siluage. a...

aurir q fes lui deu. p amor en

son lengage. efai me morir de

ueia. car fei eu desir. ñ uei nire

mir. en oluolgra ogan auzir

po pel dolz chancil elanuit fui

Esfog un pauc mon corage

fin nau conorta. oró coi ench

an ta. che qui ne augri far ogan

po nulz allegrage
tem dona tos qes eu ueia.
fear penennon folage.
ben er dreich eu ssim nesteia.
tan p fol cossir. ep fol albir.
Laissei mó tot auauisir.
fin anei tarçan. dot auira edan.
eronose en mon corage.
Qui estar u am ge ñ aie toi gran.
ñi ren qe uegues a talan.

efu tor plaig mon dipnage.
ero cort aclin. esopleia.
uus leu qi a seignoriage.
fin mi etalor oestor deia.

...e ñe põ pl euneia. uei aipar u
eur fi cõn ill in ebbir.
en dif sospein. adõ uos coman.
Lamor. ef feolan ppuie epleian.
flo m uez car nou fui deuin.
en dom qi tene mó corage.
preu fi eoet qi mirea.
se ñ uat en uolace.
ei fui laussigurs no enei.
deui mi fulbin geues a tram uir
se plung te enforpir.
tam fos eqñ eõs coi trian.
se ñ u ges tal ebage.
fo li fuls brur an qi tan golan.
r canters torn en fan.

chantes deu fui messtge.
fun adõ esplera.
Lu en toif a fon estage.
Amidons qi tan mi grea.
eper liz ti dir qeu muor de desir.
efol te digna euolir. a ui lirenebn
fro tã targil.lo sstes eloatge.
flamor tangra.dõ muor desiam.
car nola remir b usan.

165

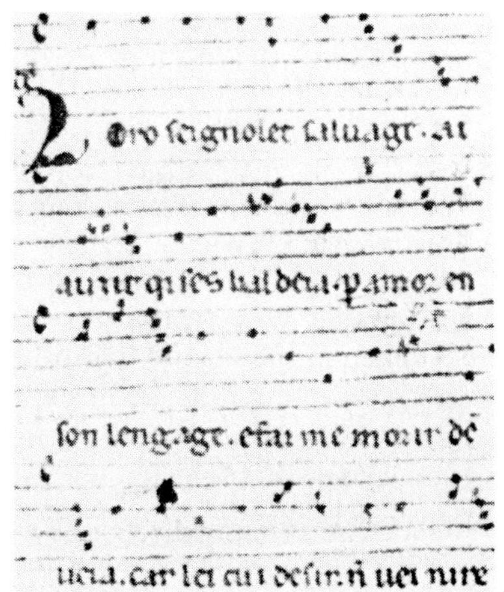

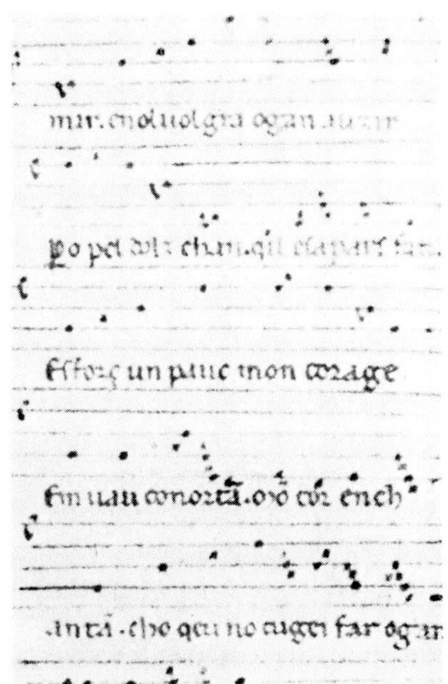

From the point of view of melodic kinship, Faidit's 'Nightingale Song' stands alone. It has no antecedents and was never used for any other poem. It is therefore possible that it is Faidit's own work, a melody he composed himself. Yet again, the lines, the rhymes and the caesuras of the poem do not exactly correspond to the melodic structure. Above the first two lines of text there is a connected melody which descends from the upper diminished seventh to the keynote, with the special delicacy that while descending at the beginning of the second line of text it anticipates the song's final. Then in the second half of the same line it embellishes, as it were, the end of the melodic arch with several melismatic turns, a *liquescentia*, a distrophe aspiring towards mensurality. Lines 3 and 4 of the text again bring a great descent, but instead of closing with the final, there is a step from the lower diminished seventh to the diminished third, a rare step of a fourth at the close of the melody. The two descending lines described above are followed by a 'middle section', where the melody lingers mostly on the diminished third; this would be the *tuba*. (According to the modal system that would be the characteristic reciting note of the Hypodorian, although the mode of this melody is authentic Dorian.) Text-lines 5 and 7 contain two lines of five syllables each. If considered from the point of view of the *melody*, the generally eight syllables here become expanded into 10. (A similar thing happens at Line 9 of the poem.) However, if one first considers the structure of the *text*, one can only speak of two 5-syllable lines and not of ten syllables. (In the manuscripts there is a full stop at the end of each line of text, even after the fives at the places mentioned.) Gennrich's (*Komm.* p. 68) terming the syllables of the lines of the poem (except the last line) as seven in number is incomprehensible. Both the series of note groups and the text of the (north Italian) Manuscripts *G* are definitely built of eight syllables. According to a melodic analysis, the melodies of the last two lines of text are very similar: Line 10 can be considered a variant of Line 9, although Line 9 is one of the lines expanded into ten syllables, as was mentioned earlier, while the last line consists of eight syllables. At this place one finds a clear example of text-melody interrelation: *identical melodic principle* but *different textual structure*. As regards the tonality, the modal system would call the melody Dorian, but the major sixth typical of the Dorian only appears a few times in the first part of the melody, and even then as a passing note (in Lines 1 and 3 of the text). The second half of the melody always avoids it, so that the b flat, which originally counts as a diminished third, gives a functional impression of subdominant, and with its frequent occurrence, transforms the character of the piece into F major.

The 13 lines of text fall into ten, partly independent, melodic lines; the melody of Line 6 is repeated above Line 8, and the consecutive lines of five syllables are contracted by the music into 10-syllable lines. With Gennrich the 13 text-lines are at the same time independent musical ideas, and as a consequence he ranks the Nightingale Song as one of the *Oda continua* family. That is reinforced by our examination, with the proviso that the melodic arches link several lines of text, and with the lesson that 'rhyming' music pieces of (identical variants) very rarely correspond with the rhyme formulae of the text-lines.

G

SONG TYPE	A	B	C	D	E	F	G	F_v	H	I
METRIC FORM	7a	7b	7a	7b	5c 5c	7c	7d 5d	7a	5d 5d	8d
NOTE GROUPS	8	8	8	8	10	8	10	8	10	8
CADENCE	fourth	key-note	fifth	third	key-note	fifth	key-note	third	key-note	key-note

R
l'a - mor qu'ieus ay don lan - guisc e sos - pi - re
5
X
l'a - mor q'eu trai don lan - guis et sos - pi - re
R
e pus l'a - mor no.us aus mos - trar ni dir
6
X
et poz l'a - mor non os mos - trar ne dir
R
ni.ls bes qu'ieus vuelh greu m'au - zeir e - nar - dir
7
X
ne ben qeu voi greu mes a e - nar - dir
R
qas vol - gues mal de mo mal cor a di - re
8
X
se vol - guez mais de mon mal cor a di - re

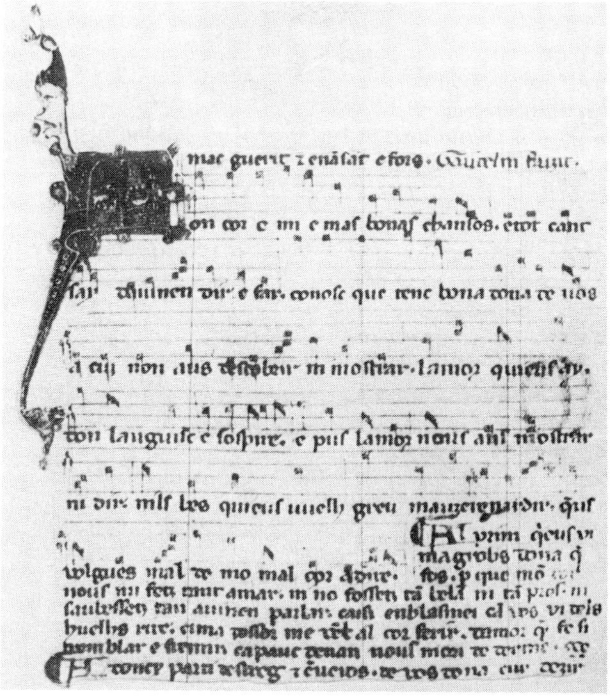

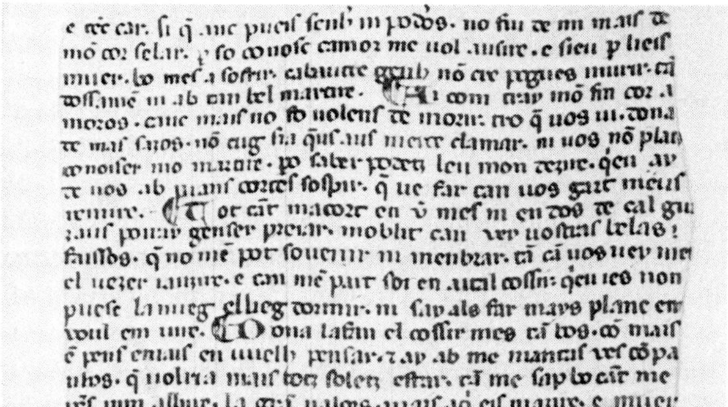

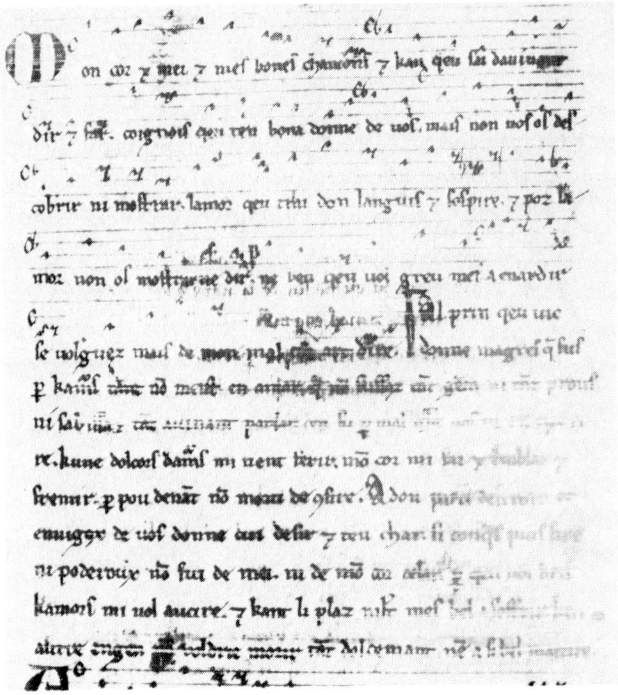

Pill. 167.37 Mss. *R*, *X*

The poem "Mo cor e mi" has survived with its melody in two manuscripts. Here, as in the previous songs, the melody opens with a descending character. Generally *one* text-line corresponds with one musical idea, which consists sometimes of two, and sometimes of more phrases. In the Provençal Manuscript *R* the third and fourth lines exactly correspond to the first and second lines, but in the Lotharingian Manuscript *X* the fourth line is only a variant of the second. Since the melody of one manuscript rarely agrees note by note with that of another, the question arises as to whether the poem lived on with the same melody, or as to when, in the case of troubadour music, one is justified in talking of a variant and when of another melody altogether. We find it justified to raise this question here because we think the two melodies, through their differing and identical peculiarities, serve as a good example.

The fact that the melody repeats its first musical idea puts it in the *kanzone* family. This can be found exactly in Variant *R*, as we have mentioned earlier, but Manuscript *X* shows such differences that both phases of the song section are variants: in Phase 1 (Line 1 of the text) it closes with a second, while the same final at the recapitulation (Line 3 of the text) becomes a diminished seventh; with Phase 2 (Line 2 of the text) the recapitulation goes down to the lower fourth (d^1), thereby making the scale plagal.

Despite all these differences the linear construction of the melody is the same. The melody to Line 5 of the text is also very similar: of the two variants, *R* avoids (with the exception of a single passing note) the characteristic augmented sixth of the scale, while *X* emphasizes it in several places. In Line 6 of the text Manuscript *R* brings in a new musical idea which virtually leads over to the next line. Manuscript *X* brings in no new melody here, but repeats the melody of Line 3 of the text (A). In Line 7 of the text there are several differences: while *R* arrives by repeated diminished thirds at the domed melisma that appears as the line's final (and remains on the fourth), *X* again dips down to the lower fourth (as in the former plagal situation). From there it steps up a fourth and then a fifth, to reach a point only a second removed from the accented augmented sixth. It then proceeds to the diminished third with a mirror inversion of the domed melisma of the other manuscript. So the only common feature in this line is that it has a 5-note melisma on the line final; in all other respects the variants differ. Line 8, which closes the song, is essentially identical in both manuscripts, but the traits of melodic formation discussed earlier apply here as well: Manuscript *R* arrives at the final with a lovely undulating, 'characterless' line, while Manuscript *X* reaches up to the diminished sixth in triads of thirds from the lower diminished seventh, then descends an octave, according to the plagal key, and from there ascends again to the final g^1.

All in all, an analysis of the two musical variants of the poem leads one to consider them essentially *identical*, with the rider that one (*R*) is a melody built on an authentic Dorian scale which by avoiding the characteristic diminished sixth where possible has rather a major character, while the other (*X*) is a plagal Dorian, a Hypodorian, in which a certain ti-ta fluctuation can be observed. There is no way of telling whether this fluctuating tonality is a copying error or a peculiarity in the melody. Taking the example of Provençal Manuscript *R* one would incline to say the former. So the answer to the question raised earlier should be that in this case we find a phenomenon in troubadour music where *different musical solutions of the details are built on an identical structure*.

The piece has no musical antecedents, nor were any *contrafacta* made of it.

R

SONG TYPE	A	B	A	B	C	D	E	F
METRIC FORM	10a	10b	10a	10b	11c	10d	10d	11c
NOTE GROUPS	10	10	10	10	11	10	10	11
CADENCE	keynote	keynote	keynote	keynote	fourth	second	fourth	keynote

X

SONG TYPE	A	B	A	B_v	C	D	E	F
METRIC FORM	10a	10b	10a	10b	11c	10d	10d	11c
NOTE GROUPS	10	10	10	10	11	10	10	11
CADENCE	second	keynote	lower seventh	keynote	fourth	lower seventh	third	keynote

Formally the song can be arranged in various ways. Our proposal coincides with the structure of the poem, which after the first two, repeated lines harks back only in the eighth and last line to Line 5, which is expanded into eleven syllables. In Gennrich's analysis (*Komm.* p. 68) the last four lines have the same rhyme: c c c c. He assumed the final 'e's were silent, although the note groups clearly bear out that they have a separate syllable value.

R
6
quem val - gues ab mi - dons pres ni mer - ces
G
qem vol - gues a mi - donz prec ni mer - ces
W
que vol - ghes a mi - dosn pres ni mer - ces
R
7
car nos tau - ghes qe per m'ilh si - a que - ritz
G
car noç tamg ges qu si - a qi - riz per - mi
W
car non ten - gues que per me si chau - sis
R
8
per - do frans li son fail - litz
G
per - dons tan li sui fal - liz
W
per - dons tal mi sui fail - lis

R
say sof - rir et ay sa - ber
7
G
sai gra - zir et ai sa - ber
X
sai so - ffrir et ai sa - ber
R
de far tot cant mi - dons pla - ia
8
G
de fair tot qan mi - donz pla - ia
X
de far tot q'a min don pla - ie
R
si que·l cor non puest mo - ver
9
G
si qe·l cor non pot mo - ver
X
si que cor non poc mo - ver

gem es vol malatia. tar se suffie ue. que mange mor
que lo senhor la sau... aces e far lr. el maluar no uol ir
ans cebn so q ce. Lia lu e car. co auer far te me. sil q
no a ab se. mas poter que techini. car cals m refr. re
sa perro sauara. q pus lr es sos pren plo preiar.
am qi co noni estrau. que promes en par. lo sieu coni
coes suuan. co chanr e nie solar. uener maysa
me lel tirzaui plan. te cui es mon sair. 6 rous e pres
sapnai. e sim so cariari. te leus ueier. nol
te preiar. q uuelh ochaison. ir. q la pioz mesglani. ni
rem son cors car. car no por te un. ir. halmen sea sup
tos. · Cucelin Snir.

om alegra dun m cui murelo mo tel cm

engres. m no tur q que ch mres. mmos dui me pres.

car le los pon a. sieu uini. quem ualgues. ab m

coni piger m meires. car nos amb gs. que per null
Doner p quer
mos chanf aunr.
sia querut pro suns h son salbui. pus nos amb q
pronen p que p so tei pgues ques uengues te mi. cu
arma un dia que triuia m no fes. m preiar muus.
plagues. rs q uolgues leus to amb q sia aumu. car
nul ar sos tos guate. uenaisi sorieu guerer se
lara sumlies. qn uequame nenreces. pus apres us
com sues dans me eluiias. sil plaua e car
ame si res qi pre. mes to mal pes. qirres ur mostres
complin. e p arso sor nar ce. car urengramim o
beurun mala nasqsme fes salbu. tl cures. me prar
sil que te mene nuuia. mes e dia te mon bes. sel u
gues moue cam me pres. e uor tos ciprels e quui pri
tos cors sort selies. D oney uoc fay el Zaroa. eu
mils mas uuntal cost. uar preia a sos pre. q conce
to q pron o mausia. lrm plauria maraues. mas un
no car qll stees res qeu no uolgues. qll sus q sieu
lo chansauen munt on us mariea. P ero non
sos pra renari. re jou m dia tl pres. quieu no sofu
e sebos. ini mostres so sen r la corrris. qm aiura
soure pres. sil seu luuul coes cones shiner qer a pra
te sen re pera quimi. qui te pondareu
Mceyhor cuy pe uiui ql pie quue.
sil rei m oza auge p ull oj yor ator.

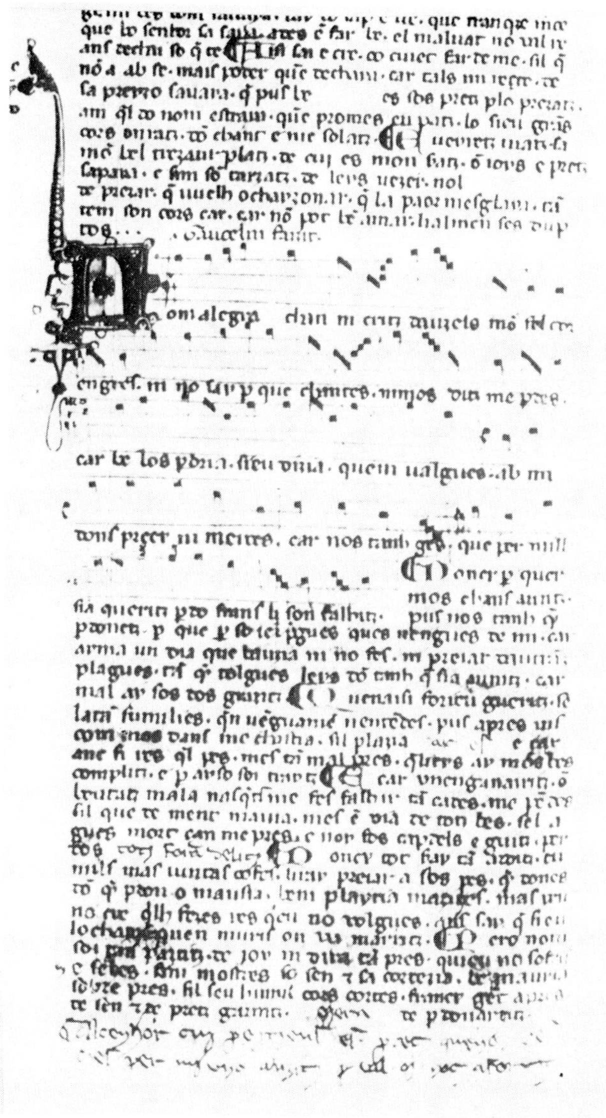

Don alegra chanm crnç datu

Sele mon fel cor engres. ni nota

pebe chantre. ni trobes. los moz

car be lespdru. ou rctal çem

u algibet au ndoru pe ni mernec.

Car noc ramer gres qil sia qitta.

Bini pdonf ti li sui falliz.

Donef pote er moz chanz augen.
ouus noc ranng qe pdoner.
poe ppo qel pgref qef uegres.
bemi car ane nd auer ora.
de baurta ni ofre.
inpcar dat tri plaguef.
Lan qi diref fodiu di efler aunz.
car mai li ef for dx grarit.
frengui beu p garir.
gi eua ran fumiliec.
len uenuam fenreder.
pois apdun comoc dir me chaftia
gu plaifu ausi ec.
lar ane firm qel pef.
lef tan mal pref.
len lei ai mait bef oplug.
p duç afat fon mat.
bar un enganairir.
pbeltaz mala ni fqof.
nafiir fallir ti quidef ni peder.

fel qi donen u mia
pos enua droz lef ja loro. er
a guer menf a ii mef pref.
le moi for capdels migui.
ferof qef fonn dear.
cas cor fon tan ardu.
euolf mans iuntas ofre.
luni puar. ffe. poide donef.
fer qi pdona matiria roudira.
e ama ef matern no fer qil frer.
et en qel uolguef.
An: fin qe feu le caufif.
quu uiuna roc finarir.
fo nofin tan parriz.
fer et ni dira tan pref.
c eu nofofin e qelof.
fenn moftret fo fen eu a corre fua.
fon mamria fo prepref.
fol fenf humilis coef coires.
friice etbe a pe. deior edamor noiz.
en for aur depdom aifi.

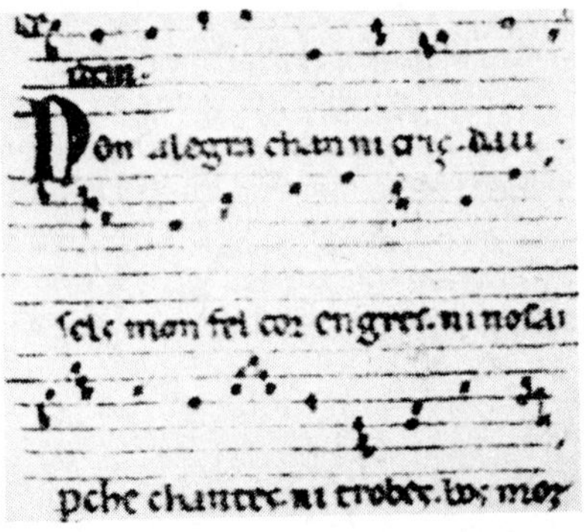

Pill. 167.43 Mss. *R*, *G*, *W*

The music of the poem "No m'alegra chan ni critz" has survived in three manuscripts. The poem can be analysed in several ways. It is built according to the principles of the *coblas capcaudadas*, but through its internal rhymes the seven or ten syllables also form smaller lines. Gennrich (*Komm.* p. 68) formed *eleven* lines according to the *text*, based on the following syllable-count and rhyme formula:

RHYME	is	eiz	ez	es	e	e	es	es	es	is	is
FORM	a	b	b	b	c	c	b	b	b	a	a
SYLLABLE	7	7	7	3	7	3	3	7	4	7	7

Though he does not say so, Gennrich presumably used Manuscript *W* for his analysis. But if one reaches back beyond the various published troubadour texts to the original manuscripts, one cannot help noticing that the scribe himself interpreted the lines of the text differently: although Gennrich's *rhyme* formula corresponds with that of the manuscripts, the numbers of syllables differ. Manuscript *G*, for example, composes the stanzas in eight lines, where the text appears not below the melody (i.e. in Stanzas 2, 3, 4, etc.) but after the melody. The eight-line variant is:

RHYME	ic	es	es	a	es	es	ic	iz
FORM	a	b	b	c	b	b	a	a
SYLLABLE	7	7	10	12	3	7	9	9

Since this is consistent with every stanza, for our part we have attempted to arrange the musical material accordingly, the more so as the melody of the poem has no antecedents in troubadour music, nor was it used for any later poems.

In his musical solution Gennrich kept the eleven-line text in mind, which in the case of five lines resulted in small music-groups of three or four syllables and broke up the melodic arches that connect larger relationships. Absolutely irrespective of the *eight*-line texts of the manuscripts, *eight* major phrases were likewise developed in the musical notation, in many places intersecting with the rhymes. We must emphasize that the marking off of musical phrases is highly *subjective*; in most cases the score picture of the manuscripts and the melisma-group placement of the notes in the manuscripts can serve as pointers. Matters are further complicated by the different keys in which the melody appears in the different manuscripts, and also by the different forms and structures.

Of all Faidit melodies the "No m'alegra" is the most difficult to solve. A true solution can be provided only by interpretational practice. Bearing these difficulties in mind we shall still attempt a musical analysis.

According to Gennrich (*Komm.* p. 68) the musical form is *Oda continua*, i.e. every musical line forms an independent musical formula unrelated to any other. Though this may generally be so, the assumption is contradicted by the Provençal Manuscript *R*. Here the first two melodic phrases are repeated exactly, which would rank the piece among the *kanzone* types (see the previous Faidit work, No. 9). The exact recapitulation structures and determines the musical form, but the text-rhyme separates the final of section 2, the last four note groups, and one note even lacks a syllable. Although the musical form may be perfect according to the text (A A, or A B A B), it still does not answer the requirements of the poem. The whole melody of Manuscript *R* is somewhat unique, since in its middle section it is almost completely syllabic and includes no large intervals. Its tonality is characteristically Mixolydian, and it never stretches beyond the compass of an octave. In contrast, the north Italian Manuscript *G* and the Paris Manuscript *W* are absolutely different. It is perhaps here that one first encounters the phenomenon of *two* different melodies having been used for *one* poem (only two, because the melodies of Manuscripts *G* and *W*, despite their different keys, are identical). The only kinship with Manuscript *R* is a resemblance at the beginning (in *W* this beginning is reverted to again), but in the two latter versions, independent melodic lines follow one another. Divergence from *R* is not only evident in the extremely rich ornamentation of *G* and *W*, but also in the very great intervals (once of an upward octave, later of an octave down) and in the plagal tonalities of both (in *W* reaching in the upper register to the tenth and in the lower to the fourth).

Also worth noting is that Manuscript *G* conforms quite well with the larger form of text division (into eight lines): in the middle section there are a few section shifts, but *five out of the eight lines* (the first three and the last two) *correspond with the text-lines of the stanzas as noted down in the manuscript.* The rhymes of the text are designated in the melody as printed here (by a broken line) wherever they differ from the melodic phrase determined by us. (Where they coincide no such marking has been given.) The key of Manuscript *G* is Hypolydian, and that of *W*, Aeolian. Both melodies can be easily transformed into characteristic Arab music by the addition of an accidental (b *rotundum*). This, however, is not indicated in the manuscripts, in which connection it should be added that all the notations are erratic in their use of accidentals.

R

SONG TYPE	A	B	A	B	C	D	E	F
METRIC FORM	7a	7b	7b 3b	3a	6c 4c	3b 7b	4b 7a	7a
NOTE GROUPS	7	7	7	6	10	10	11	7
CADENCE	fourth	keynote	fourth	keynote	second	third	fifth	keynote

G

SONG TYPE	A	B	C	D	E	F	G
METRIC FORM	7a	7b	7b 3b	8c 4c	3b 7b	9a	9a
NOTE GROUPS	7	7	10	12	10	9	9
CADENCE	fifth	third	fourth	keynote	lower fifth	fifth	keynote

W

SONG TYPE	A	B	A_v	C	D	E	F
METRIC FORM	7a	7b	7b 3b	8c 4c	3b 7b	4b 6a	7a
NOTE GROUPS	7	7	10	12	10	10	7
CADENCE	fifth	fifth	fifth	fourth	lower sixth	fifth	keynote

11
R
Si anc nulhs homs per a - ver fin co - rat - ge
1
G
Si anc nulz hom per a - ver fin co - ra - ge
X
Se anz nuls hom pir a - ver fin co - ra - ge
R
ni per a - mar le - yal - men ses fal - su - ra
2
G
ni per a - mar le - ial - men ses fal - tu - ra
X
ni pir a - mar le - ial - ment senz fein - tu - re
R
ni per suf - rir fran - ca - men son damp - nat - ge
3
G
ni per sof - rir fran - cha - men son damp - na - ge
X
ni pir sos - frir lon - gue - ment son dan - na - ge

4
R
ac si - dons null d'on - ra - da aven - tu - ra
G
ac de si - donz null hon - rad' a - ven - tu - ra
X
a de sin - don galc' on - rad' a - ven - tu - re

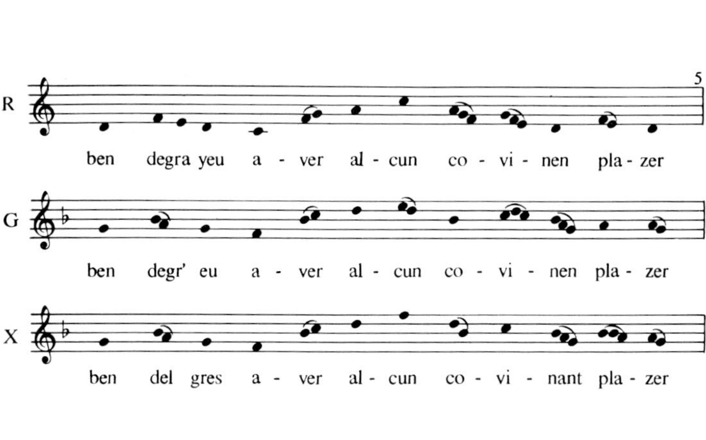
5
R
ben degra yeu a - ver al - cun co - vi - nen pla - zer
G
ben degr' eu a - ver al - cun co - vi - nen pla - zer
X
ben del gres a - ver al - cun co - vi - nant pla - zer

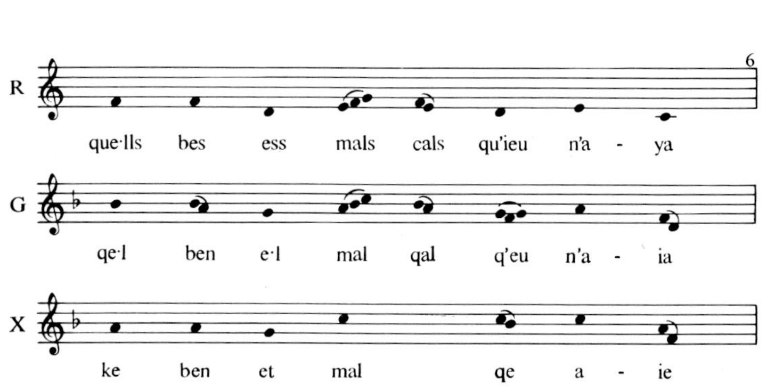
6
R
que·lls bes ess mals cals qu'ieu n'a - ya
G
qe·l ben e·l mal qal q'eu n'a - ia
X
ke ben et mal qe a - ie

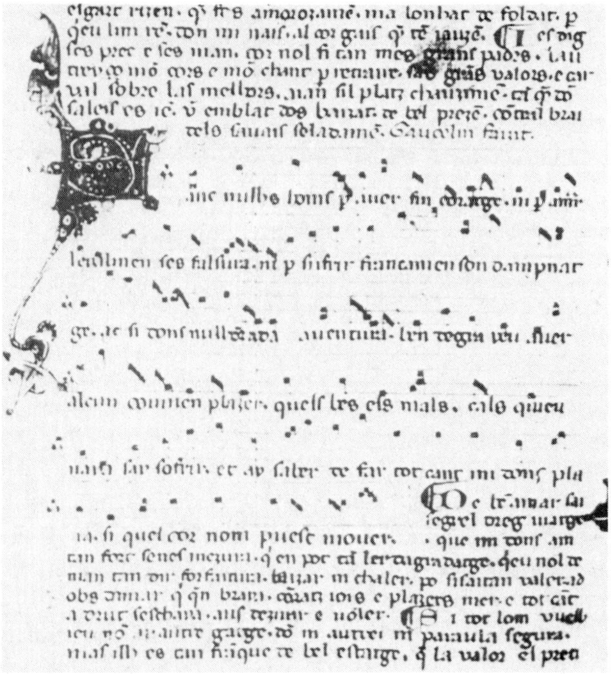

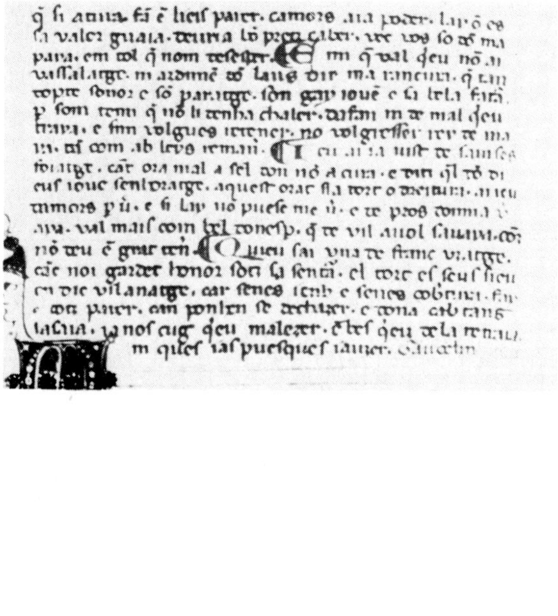

Si tuit mil hom p̃tut s fin co

rage in pamar leulm feu falfu

qui pofom̃ frunchim̃ feʒʒouʒ

gr̃ʒe defobʒ mill homʒʒu uein

men plauer qel bon et mal q̃llogu

ruiu lau grazir nan fuber de far

tot qm̃ midon plauɾ fuel cor

no̅ pɾt mouer.

Sein amoɾ fauf gr̃l dcir uaigeɾ
fuqe midon ain ta et ma mefina
fur pɾ dem̃ar tot qm̃ ior auguager
ʒeu noil dem̃a tm̃ tem̃ dir rouenʒa
luf ar in uigeɾ.

pe fi fau tan uuleɾ.
A doyſ darmar qi qem̃ plura.
confɾ iem̃ epl ʒeu fcr.
fcor eho qa drur fefebuua
Auf defir̃r euoleɾ.
Auꞇor lora uoil eno̅ iu uitre gare
Do̅ni aueren̄ m̃ pauuila fegum̃
Gra ſill oʒ tu frage ʒ bel eſtage
Par lauuilor ꞇ pry qua en laum̃
Ae pofau parr̃ cum̃ouf fuuia poʒuɾ
Ae la once uulor quua dur̃ meeɾ
uoſ uoſ tot ꞇo qm̃ uupua cab.
em̃ tot qem̃om̃ defefp.
Fouce qem̃ iuf qeu no̅ iu uaffulugu
A urdum̃e qeu iuf dur ma tauua
Ae tan do̅ pſonoꞇ efon pauuge.
Gon bel folaʒ ecu bella fauum̃.
Ouchein fou tem̃eꞇ qulei no̅ de
qem̃ eluiteɾ.
Gem̃ai iuauffau deu eauua.
Gem̃ deignoɾ rerenoꞇ uou ueil
groffeɾ reuſ ʒe ʒuu
Ean com̃ ublei uenuuueɾ
Au iaiꞇ ai dur ab fon uab foluge.
Aon om̃ iuiſ refiu ʒo fu auua
fcli qel bon dr̃ iouue fegnouuge.
Augeſt om̃ur fuu dr̃ueh om̃ fuueʒ
Aidaumeɾ puueulu no̅ defp.
ꞇ edepɾof do̅iu ueuua.
uil matif qem̃ me do̅ efp.
Auu do̅ duuel fauuua.
Ae deuu en do̅ rerener
Aen fuu iuuu qeq̃uu cu frue cou geɾ
Aine no garder honoɾ foꞇ eueuuu
Geuf eʒ fororꞇ feu euehe uuluu
Ae feneɾ gr̃iꞇ efenoꞇ coburuu gr̃
fauuuroꞇ uuegeɾ co̅ puuig au defchugoꞇ

Gem̃a cabtan fennu
Doeuꞇ ʒeu ma legeɾ.
ꞇ euu iu delei bon uennua.
Aouuuu qom̃ dru defchugeɾ.
Aomuuu do̅u geuu.
uoſ n̄ oʒ ʒe tau fuubeɾ.
Ae uen no fauu qe defpluuu.
uoꞇ pluu euꞇ edeu pluꞇeɾ.

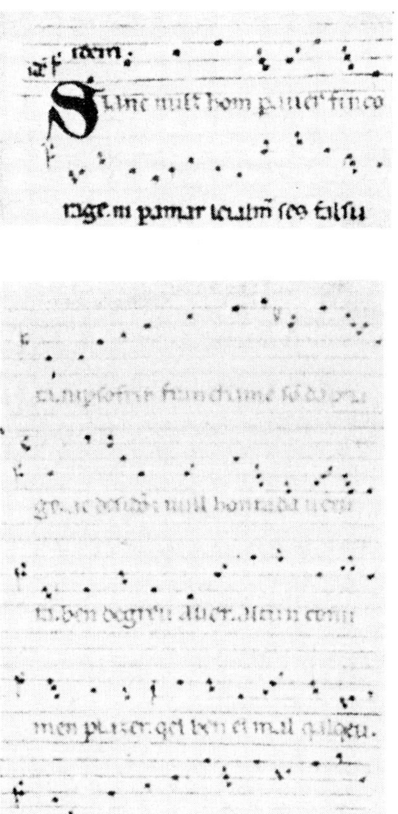

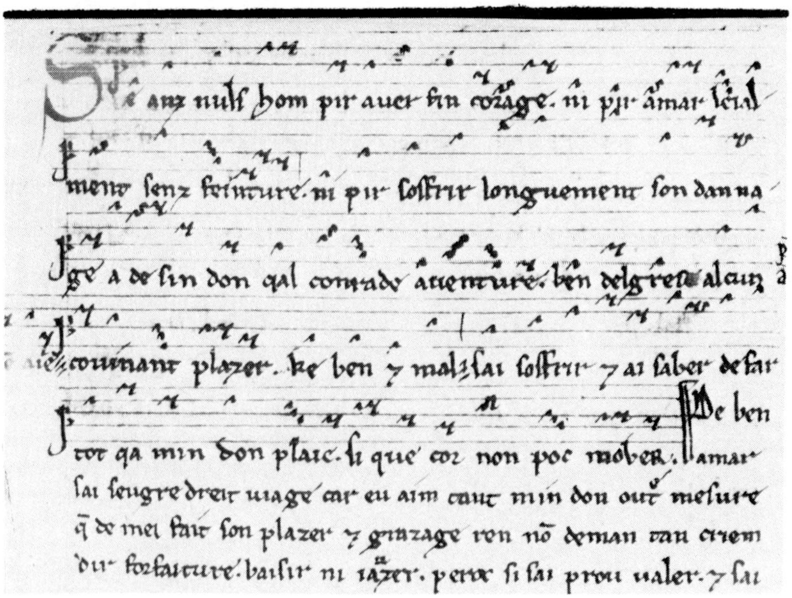

Pill. 167.52 Mss. *R*, *G*, *X*

The melody of the Faidit poem "Si anc nuls homs" has come down to us in three manuscripts in different keys. It is the only one which does not open with a descent, but already the first line intones a beautifully constructed double domed melody. This character runs through the whole melody, either with the two domes within one unit or with a major arched melody line stretching over two units. The melody can be divided into nine musical units which closely follow the rhymes of the poem. As a consequence, after the first five long lines (of ten and eleven syllables), the melody adjusts itself to the shorter seven and eight-syllable lines; thus the five long lines are followed by four shorter ones. Here the musical form is a true *Oda continua*: every line is independent, with no recapitulated musical idea anywhere. The three manuscripts give the same melody in different keys. The first, the Provençal Manuscript *R* is Hypomixolydian (if one disregards the flattening of b) and remains within the compass of a ninth. The second, the north Italian Manuscript *G* is in Hypodorian, where the lack of the second flat is highly dubious, especially in Units 3 and 5: in upward steps of seconds the flattening of note e is almost certain, which would make this version fluctuate between the Dorian and the Aeolian; the range is broader than in the first version: an eleventh. The third, the Lotharingian Manuscript *X*, is in Dorian; it does not reach down into the lower registers, but apart from that it is more closely related to *G*, particularly in smaller details and the use of melismatic groups. The most important difference between the first and the two following melodies appears in the last two sections, where the Provençal Manuscript gives a completely unornamented, evenly descending melody, tending towards recitative: Section 8 has a repetition of a^1 and Section 9 of g^1, the final, and a simple group of melismas only appears in the final. From that same point onwards the other two manuscripts progress from the upper octave (g^2), with frequent melismatic ornaments, towards the keynote, and close the piece with an extra cadencial melisma.

Since the manuscripts cannot be exactly dated and all three were compiled in a close chronological neighbourhood at the beginning of the 14th century, one must presume that the more or less identical Provençal melody with its differing cadence was an individual solution by the manuscript's scribe, or that the melody of the poem was known in the Provençal region (nearly 100 years after Faidit's death) in the form found in the manuscript. Even with the above minor difference it had not been used for any other poem, nor were any *contrafacta* made of it, and *so the musical adaptation of the poem must be ascribed to Faidit.*

The adaptation is presented by the following analysis:

R

SONG TYPE	A	B	C	D	E	F	G	H	I
METRIC FORM	11a	11b	11a	11b	5c 7c	7d	7c	7d	7c
NOTE GROUPS	11	11	11	11	12	8	7	8	8
CADENCE	lower fourth	lower fourth	lower seventh	lower fourth	lower fourth	lower fifth	fourth	lower seventh	key-note

G

SONG TYPE	A	B	C	D	E	F	G	H	I
METRIC FORM	11a	11b	11a	11b	5c 7c	7d	7c	7d	7c
NOTE GROUPS	11	12	13	11	12	8	7	8	7
CADENCE	second	key-note	third	lower seventh	key-note	lower fourth	major sixth	key-note	key-note

X

SONG TYPE	A	B	C	D	E	F	G	H	I
METRIC FORM	11a	11b	11a	11b	5c 7c	7d	7c	7d	7c
NOTE GROUPS	11	11	12	12	12	7	7	8	7
CADENCE	key-note	key-note	third	lower seventh	keynote	lower seventh	major sixth	key-note	key-note

12
R
Si tot ai tar- dat mon chant ni n'ay fayr trop long e - sta - ge
X
De tot ai tar - . zat mon chant et ai fait trop lonc e - sta - ge
R
e - ras n'ay cor e ta - lan qu'eu torn la perd' e·l damp-nat - ge
X
er mi pren coz et ta - lant que joi e fait grant so - la - ge
R
que l'a - men- dres el mar - ge e·m ditz qu'ieu mostr' en chan - tan
X
quant be - le en drec' el via - ge et volc que mostr' en chan - tant
R
lo joi e la va - lor gran que do - net e l'a - le - grat - ge
X
la joi e et la va - lor qe·m do - nat et l'a - li - gra - ge
R
lo jorn que·m re - tenc bai - zan
X
la jor que·l re - ten bai - sant

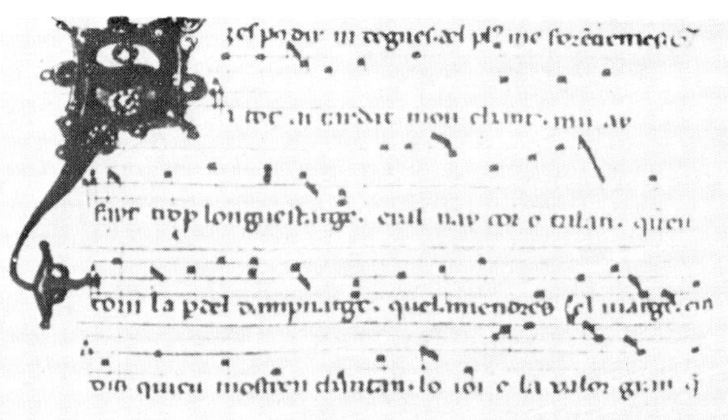

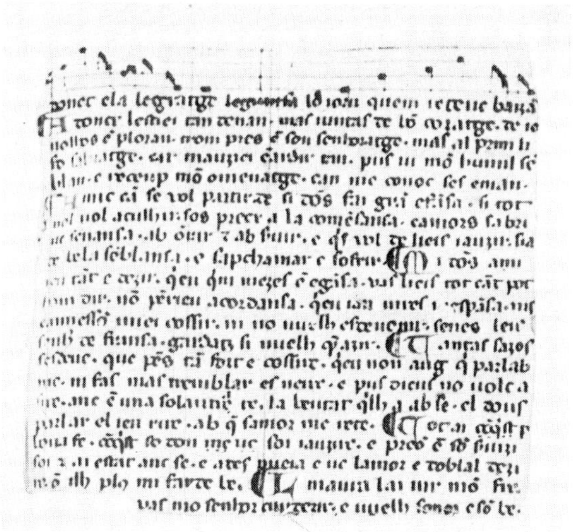

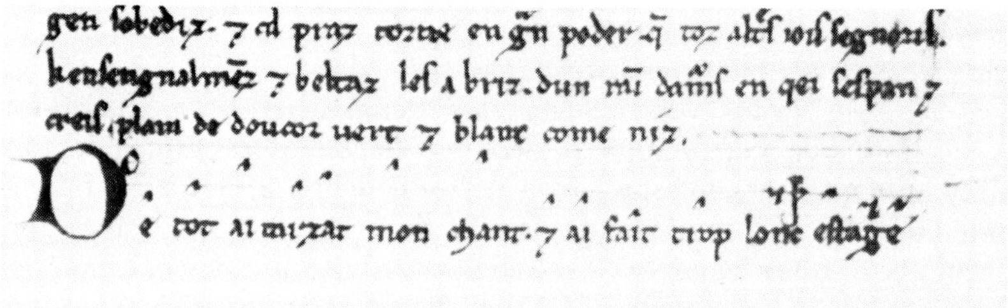

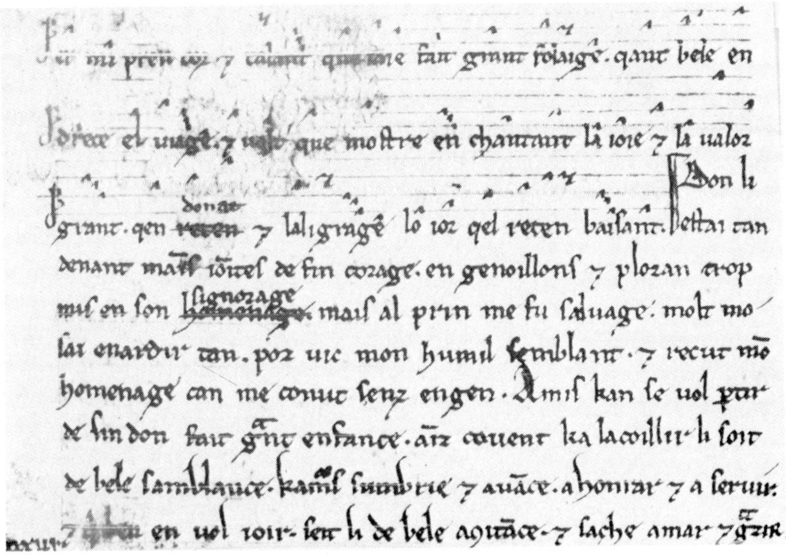

Pill. 167.53 Mss. *R*, *X*

The melody of the poem "Si tot ai tardat" has survived in the Provençal Manuscript *R* and the Lotharingian Manuscript *X*. As in so many other cases, we find two variants of identical musical material. In this case the keys are the same, both authentic Dorian. On the basis of the structure of the poem, nine melodic lines can be discerned. In some cases the cadences of the melodic lines do not agree with the rhymes of the lines of text. It seems both in *R* and *X* that the melody of Line 6, for example, forms a cadence only in the first half of Line 7, and begins a new musical idea in the middle of the line. A basic difference between the melodies as given in the two manuscripts lies in the formal solution of the first four lines: the Provençal manuscript repeats the first two lines, thereby making it a *kanzone* type, while the Lotharingian manuscript repeats nothing whatsoever, but produces a new musical idea for every line, so forming an *Oda continua*. The first version includes many characteristic, melody-forming steps of a fifth; the second adds to these two steps of a seventh, which might possibly raise questions of form, since where these appear in the Lotharingian variant a new melodic phrase might have started. (The two occurrences appear in the middle of Lines 3 and 7.) This seems particularly justified in Line 7, as we might count here the beginning of the final melodic phrase which arrives at the last cadence (stretching over two and a half lines). The Provençal variant also has a hint of this, but the same melody-opening peak is prepared more gradually.

It is difficult to prove an impression one gets that the popular liturgical sequence "Victimae paschali laudes" is present behind the melody of the poem. The question is not resolved, although influenced, by the fact that both variants include many syllabic lines in similar places to syllabic lines in the sequence. However, formally there are no resemblances to the *sequentia* type.

This troubadour melody has no Provençal model either, nor were any *contrafacta* made of it. It is worth noting that Gennrich (*Komm.* p. 69) analyses the poem's form on the basis of seven-syllable lines, although it is borne out precisely by the *musical groups* that the end 'e's are not silent but separate syllables. This raises the syllable count of several lines of the poem to eight, and in our view at every place where a final 'e' is to be found. In this poem *ge* is this particular rhyme, and it marks Line b (each b line having eight syllables).

R

SONG TYPE	A	B	A	B	C	D	E	F	G
METRIC FORM	7a	8b	7a	8b	7b	7a	7a	8b	7a
NOTE GROUPS	7	8	7	8	7	7	7	8	8
CADENCE	fourth	sixth	fourth	second	lower seventh	second	third	key-note	key-note

X

SONG TYPE	A	B	C	D	E	F	G	H	I
METRIC FORM	7a	8b	7a	8b	8b	7a	7a	8b	7a
NOTE GROUPS	7	8	7	8	8	7	7	8	7
CADENCE	octave	second	key-note	key-note	lower seventh	third	third	lower seventh	key-note

G
Car des las granz fol - daz qe son E de la ma - iors qi s'a - ten
X
Car de les granz fol - daz qui son Es de la ma - ior qui sen ten
G
Es son dan se - gre ad e - scien Car do - pla - men fai fa - li - men
X
De son dan seu - gre a e - scien Car dou - ble - ment fait fail - li - ment
G
Pe - ro greu er fins a - mics druc pri - uaç
X
Pe - ro non es fins a - manz drus pri - vaz
G
S'il bens e'l mals e'l jais e'l danc no.ill plac
X
Se bens et mals et jois et dols non plaz

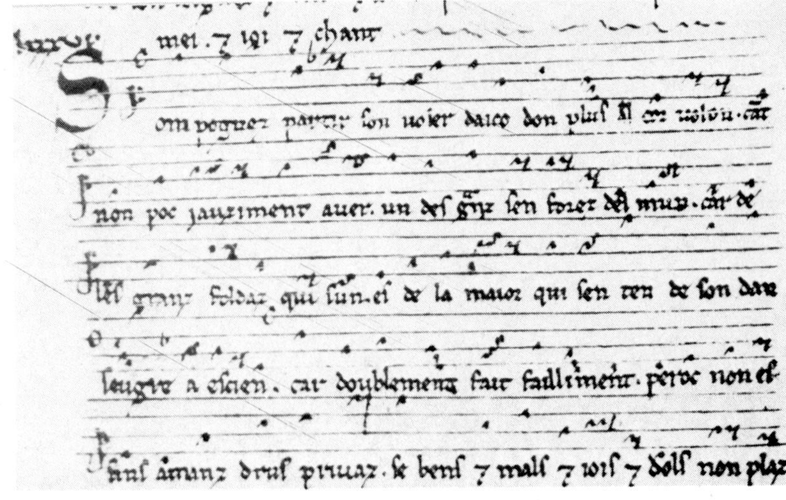
mei. 7 ici 7 chant
Som peguez partir son voler daico don plus ll en volon. car
non poc iauzimentz auer. un dels granz sen forez del mun. car de
les granz soldaz qui sun. es de la maior qui sen ten de son dan
leugiere a escien. car doublemenz fait faillimentz. per ce non es
nuls amanz druz priuaz. se bens 7 mals 7 ris 7 dols non plaz.

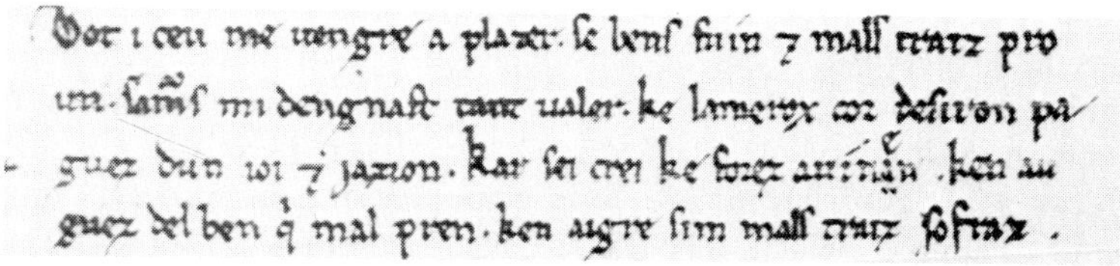

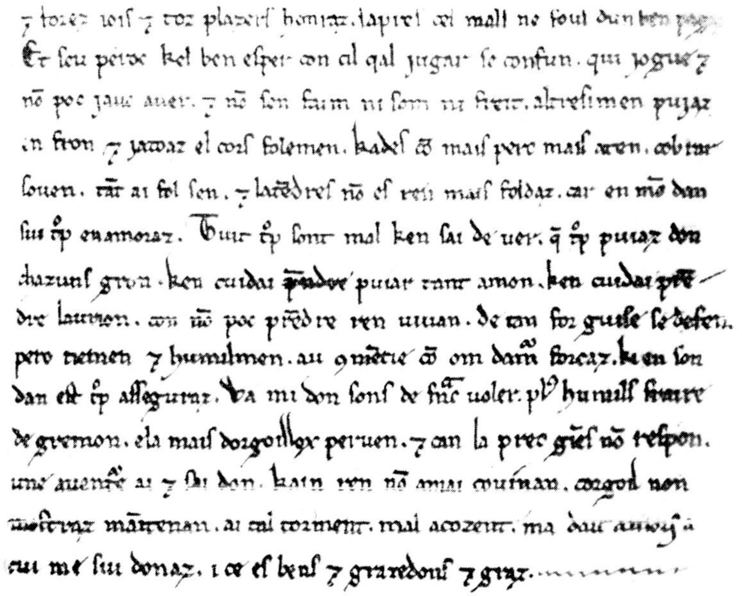

Pill. 167.56 Mss. *G*, *X*

The melody of "S'on pogues partir son voler" has not survived in the Provençal Manuscript, only in the northern Italian *G* and the Lotharingian *X*. The two melodies do not match note for note, yet one might speak of a musical material of identical structure, which on one occasion contracts two 4-syllable lines into 8-syllable lines. The first part of the poem consists of even 8-syllable lines, divided between a, b and c rhymes; only the last two lines are expanded into ten syllables, with d rhyme formula. The musical form generally follows the poem's formal solutions, especially in the number of syllables. However the rhyme formulae are not followed (although perhaps in the first four lines a and b can be equated with cadences on the *fifth* and the *keynote*). In general a new musical phrase occurs at every two lines. Syllabic lines are frequent, and it frequently occurs that syllabic passages in one manuscript are made more animated in the other by inflections, by ornamentations of them, as it were. One such place is in Section 3, where the repetition of c^2 in Manuscript *G* is adorned in Manuscript *X* with a distrophe and an inflection, which at the same time indicate an attempt at mensurality. (This distrophic formula features on four more occasions in the melody and can be considered characteristic of the *manuscript*.) There is also an example of the opposite—of an inflected, melismatic point where the other manuscript is syllabic: in Section 8 the syllabic melody of *X* is resolved by Manuscript *G*. Both places are good examples of how medieval monody ornamented a simple melody. The melody itself is again *descending* in the first two lines, reaching from the upper octave to the lower keynote. Sections 3, 4 and 5 of the melody move in the middle register, and from Section 6 onwards the melody again reaches the upper octave and starts twice towards the cadence before taking some significant steps of a fifth and then proceeding to the smooth final cadence. With regard to key, the northern Italian version of the melody is an authentic Dorian, and so would the Lotharingian version be, except that the manuscript sometimes marks the note e as flat, which lends an Aeolian colour to the piece. The flattening can be only a 'coloration', as it is not consistently used: it first appears in Section 1 and if it did not appear again in Section 7 one might have referred it to the whole tune. In our opinion such a reference would be to succumb to modern ideas of tonality. The melody raises one of the *most delicate* questions of medieval monody—especially if linked to a stringed or plucked instrumental accompaniment—because today it is very difficult for us to assimilate to a sound picture in which the key is left to '*float*' and there seems no desire to clarify the key. This *musical* phenomenon is not far removed, even in its philosophy, from one of the most important manifestations of troubadour *poetry*: the *trobar clus*—new 'ornate' lines of poems that remain firmly in obscurity, clearly intended to use symbols of uncertain meaning. The poem has seven known *contrafacta*, by Bertran Carbonel, Peire Cardenal, Uc de Saint Circ and several anonymous authors. The melody stands closest to the *Oda continua* type, but as shown by the analysis, in Manuscript *X* both Section 2 (B) and 3 (C) are repeated several times.

G

SONG TYPE	A	B	C	D	E	F	G	H	I	J
METRIC FORM	8a	8b	8a	8b	8b	8c	8c	4c 4c	10d	10d
NOTE GROUPS	8	8	8	8	8	8	8	8	10	10
CADENCE	fifth	key-note	fifth	key-note	key-note	seventh	key-note	second	third	key-note

X

SONG TYPE	A	B	C	D	E	C_v	F	B_v	G	B_v
METRIC FORM	8a	8b	8b	8b	8b	8c	8c	4c 4c	10d	10d
NOTE GROUPS	8	8	8	8	8	8	8	8	10	10
CADENCE	fifth	key-note	fifth	sec-ond	key-note	seventh	third	lower seventh	third	key-note

14
R Tant ai su - fert lon - gua - mens greu a - fan
G Tant ai so - fert lom - nia - men greu a - fan
R Que s'es - tes mais que no·m a - per - seu - pes
G Qe s'es - tes mais que no·m a - per - ce - bes
R Mo - rir po - gra tost e leu si·m vol - gues
G Mo - rir po - gra ni·l e leu se·m vol - gues
R C'a be - la no·m pre - ze - ra do - lors
G Qe la bel - la non pre - se - ra do - lors
R En cui ma - la fos beu - tatz e va - lors
G O ma - la fos bel - tat e va - lors

R
6
Don re - gar - dan part for - satz mon co - rat - ge
G
Dun re - gar - dan par forcha mon co - ra - ge
R
7
E plus nol platz se - gray au - tre vi - at - ge
G
E pois lei plaz se - grai au - tre vi - a - ge
R
8
C'a lieis non cal ni cre ques te - nha a dan
G
C'a lei non chal ni no s'o ten a dan
R
9
De per - dre mi ni'ls bels ditz de mon chan
G
De per - dre mi ni·l bel diz de mon chan

veu su eu moxs p̃ teller eechu · cauſſ ẙoo auſſur · ſin ſau
mo cõ eſpẽdir · q̃ ſa lauſẽquer tẽiu pſe · nõ ſabr̃ tõ pluſ
me ſoue ¶ D̃ omna mõ ſõie mõ plazer · mõ tear tõ ĩ noſ
parem tam eam uẽam vuellu valer · de uos eup am t̃ a
mauu eu com vicuau coſtemſe ia re nõil querrau dõ
uſtr̃ fin cors e maſ pẽec uos caſſ nõu auſ de
re q̃ a iatz anmem mercer de m̃ geuſ am p lõna t̃ẽ · t̃ al
loz̃ · ãimar nos ãu rener · q̃ puſ al amanſ nõ fozẽu lue
au ãnoe · e ſol ſer · p d̃eu nõm · deſeſperau · puſ cauſo ſu
auũ pẽec mõ neẽs · ea m̃eonſ la ſa de mõ xier · gẽazue · e
migas li caldois nos vur t̃ſueo m̃ on pla a mẽ · car eu
 d̃ bon pẽec en auſa e reue · Sauelm faziu

nur ai ſuferr longuameno giru a ami · que

ſeſtes m̃aiſ que nõm apſeupro · meau p̃gui roſt e leu

ſin volgueſ eu b̃ela nõm preteru roloz̃ · en eu m̃ala ſ̃os

lautueu e uuloz̃ con reguuaũ puſe ſoz̃luſt · mõ cȯ ȧgeu

e puſ uol plau ſeguiu auue vuã̃ge · ea heiſ nõn eui m̃ ãu

queſteuñ · a d̃m de pdee m̃ m̃le lrle dui de m̃on eham
eu eul uoſ de bonu vul q̃s prez̃ · e eal rẽ pẽec tõ ouſ q̃
eo b̃ pueſ q̃ pueiſ li eiu ſoſtacha meuſ de teſ · m̃iavo de m̃ tõſ
eſ tiſ g̃uiſ ſa uuloz̃ · q̃u re noſ re ſi pẽec m̃ niſalloz̃ t̃eꝛ ſiu
ueu t̃ omneuuar ſolauge · ear p̃eraſſieu m̃ amoee e mõ aũp
mauge · q̃ mo ſõl cõ q̃ ſ̃es vir e chameẽ · ſo dõ teguu q̃e ẽ cob̃u
mõ ealam · ¶ E puſ mõ cõe e meu ſuueſſ · nuue m̃an · e
m̃a maſſa wua · e m̃a bona ſeſ · ſi q̃ eaſeuſ m̃agu moꝛe ſi
peguue elamar mẽ rer com de m̃al buulãdoꝛs · e i uueẽ hu
euſ veader auudoꝛs · nõ erouu m̃aiſ m̃ fiãſa ſeſ gauꝯꝭ ear
ſel eſ ſoleſ q̃ ſar ſol vaſſalauge · e ſolſ q̃ uol a ſõ com̃m · cor
ſo que de plazem m̃ l̃eeſtum · ¶ E euuilli me puſ ab m̃
toſ eſtam · prerꝛ z uuloz̃ · ner ſ̃ib e diu eoꝛreſ com pꝛeſſ
q̃ noẙ ſa m̃er · em m̃auuſb de leiſ õ eſ onoꝛs · ſ̃eꝰ e leuuar
q̃ noẙ ſa amoeſ · em m̃auuſb re vona dius paiuꝛge · pꝛoſ egõ
alſ q̃o de m̃al ſeuuoʒauge · m̃ veu far conru eu uuloz̃ · eũ que
reſſm̃ẽeu ſõ fue huuul ſemblau ¶ E coꝛ auo au m̃auuſſõ
guu · e puſ li plaz̃ · q̃ no ſi eumeuu · noẙ reu m̃iꝛs che
nar ſo m̃al ſ̃os q̃aſ mẽ puꝛeſſu ꝛoe ſeſ veſnoꝛs er agũiʒ
obſ q̃ eul m̃al uuig ſ̃os · e puſ plau euſbu vur m̃õ eſ
eiuge · uõ ẽeõuueu uõ ſieuſ e lõ m̃iauge · em lauſ ꝛeban
doẙ a ſſeſ coꝛ muſ · eub m̃al ſeuuoʒ au eſtar · aq̃ſt̃ · m̃ · ¶ H b
roe aueul m̃al e beau e euuau uulguxeu eſtaꝛ ſ̃a m̃a coũ
plaqueſ · m̃aiſ eub auua que m̃aiſ de lrem ſ̃oeſ · e puſ
li plau aeul uoſ p̃ ſeeuuꝛ · rõ me reuõ al eoꝛ plazeuſ roſ
ſoꝛs · b̃l aſe pꝛoſ · e ãuuueẽ eſtiuge · e am m̃andar p̃ e
eoꝛreſ m̃eſiluge · eũ pauc auuel ſuſ mõ puuiſ q̃ noſ m̃i
 ·m̃ m̃aiſ q̃ ſeſ uua giua rolau · Sauelm faziu

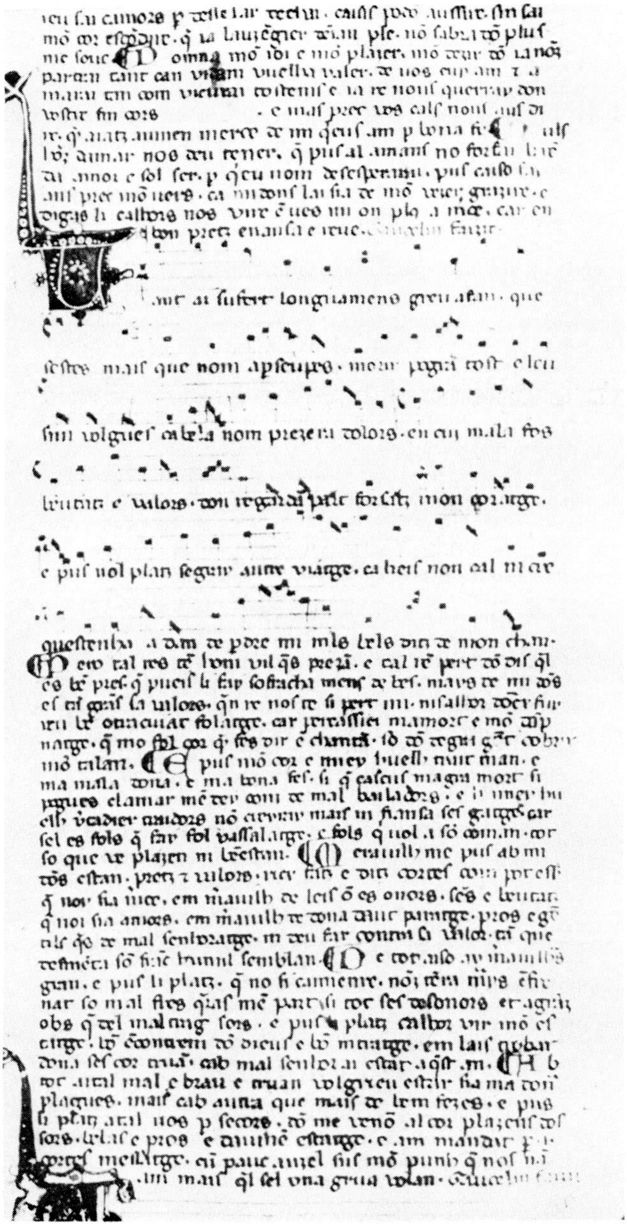

Tant ai sofert lonmain greu a
fan qes esser mals qeu no men per
esser menr pegra uil esur se uol
guer qe roeu la n pseu dolors .o.

mala fos bestat e ualors & dun regar
dun par forcta monce a gr. e bos
lei plus segra auer u uigr. caler
n eval ni noso ten aduin de per dir
mi ni bel des demo cuin.

po tal ren te bom uil qer pisun.
e li bom la pr qil dis qei nes bon pe
e e pois li fai sofra a meuel bes
e ar dm don e es ti gn; f m liors.
e a le nochtl se tot me uir aillors.
uic ar eis be otm audar folagr.
e an poo ce ta ma morf emo diph ugr.
e i mo fol æ qe feq cur enchan tan
fo dun dgra bon costhr mo talan.
f pois mei oil emo cor tratt man.
f ma nu la done ina tona fer.
e iqe chafcuf magra morsul pognes
uimar me puec co dm ate hilh dors.
f u mon foth me fongfef tractors.

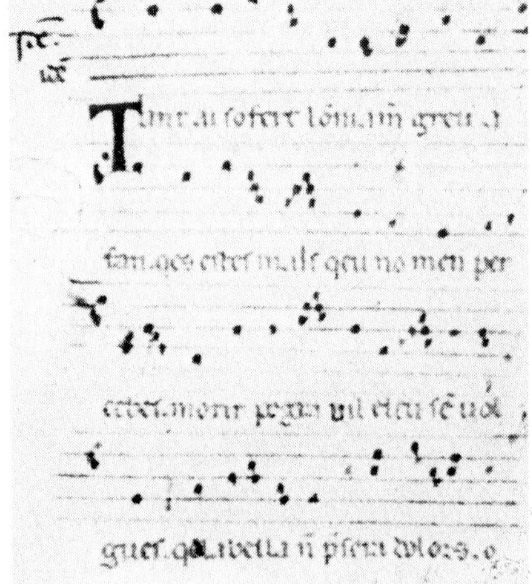

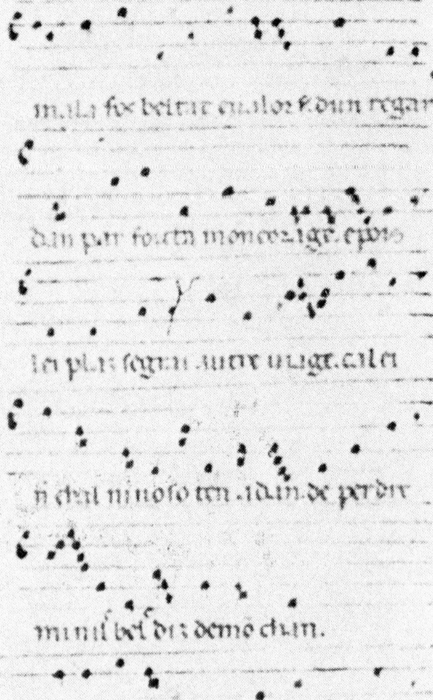

Pill. 167.59 Mss *R*, *G*

Faidit's poem "Tant ai sufert" has one of the highest syllable counts, and its melody is also the longest, not because of the melodic sections (we have already met melodies of nine or ten lines) but because all the lines are of ten syllables and so all the note groups are too. The melody itself consists here of *five sections*, in part independent of the poem and in part in irregular correspondence with the poem. In the first two bars the melody ascends (Section 1). In Lines 3 and 4 it is in the middle register around c^2 and d^2, i.e. a fifth above the keynote (Section 2). In Lines 5 and 6 it arrives at its peak of a^2 and then descends to the keynote (Section 3). This is followed by Section 4, again in the middle register, and then by the fifth and final section, which compared with the previous sections consists of only a half-line. Its cadence often uses steps of a third (b flat-d-f) (g^2-e^2-c^2-a^1) (a^1-c^2-e^2) (e^2-c^2-a^1), which are sometimes bridged by melismatic groups. Strangely enough the melodic construction of steps of a third prevails more than in any earlier Faidit piece, but in addition some definite steps of a fourth (e.g. at the end of Section 1, and in Variant *G* at the beginning of Section 3) lend the piece a most individual character. The northern Italian Manuscript *G* brings a step of an augmented fourth upwards in Section 4, which in the absence of a flat marking leaves an uncertainty about the key, but that is something which occurs several times in troubadour music. In some of the turns and line-opening notes (e.g. in Line 8 resp. Section 8) the melody is the same as the melody of the previous Faidit poem (here No. 13, Pill. 167.56): there the lower-arch formula (g^2-e^2-f^2) is a typical melodic structural element.

In its musical structure this melody belongs to the *Oda continua* type, bringing new musical matter in each line, without any repeats.

R

	1		2		3		4		5
SONG TYPE	A	B	C	D	E	F	G	H	I
METRIC FORM	10a	10b	10b	9c	10c	11d	11d	10a	10a
NOTE GROUPS	10	10	10	9	10	11	11	11	10
CADENCE	octave	fourth	key-note	fourth	sixth	key-note	sixth	key-note	key-note

G

	1		2		3		4		5
SONG TYPE	A	B	C	D	E	F	G	H	I
METRIC FORM	10a	10b	10b	10c	9c	11d	11d	10a	10a
NOTE GROUPS	10	10	10	10	9	11	11	10	10
CADENCE	seventh	third	third	seventh	fifth	lower seventh	seventh	lower seventh	key-note

The end-of-line expansions of the two d lines: *ge*, are again indicated by the song groups. Thus the so-far 10-syllable lines become 11-syllable in the two d lines (Lines 6 and 7 of the music). The cæsuras of the five-section melody always separate the identical rhymes from each other: the end and beginning, respectively, of Lines 2 and 3 of the music fall between the rhymes of the two c lines, while those of Lines 3 and 4 fall between the two d lines. The melodic notation in the two manuscripts hardly agree. Yet even though they do not tally note by note, one can still not speak of two different melodies. The northern Italian Manuscript *G* has more daring steps (instead of steps of a third often steps of a fourth, or instead of two steps of a third one of a fifth), while the Provençal Manuscript uses a larger compass. Sometimes there are differences of seconds only between the two, basically 'southern' manuscripts, sometimes a melismatic group resolves the individual note of the second one (syllables and note groups 3 and 4 in Line 2). Sometimes they agree in every note (primarily in the 'main' notes that determine the direction of the melodic line). This means that differences appear even in a melody that was noted down in two nearby areas, and neither of the manuscripts shows a consequent melodic structure or ornamental technique which would be typically determinative of a manuscript, and through it, of a geographical area.

GAUCELM FAIDIT'S MUSICAL STYLE

Faidit's musical legacy consists of 14 melodies, which have remained extant in a total of 30 variants. Faidit is the only troubadour six of whose melodies have survived in no less than three variants. By way of comparison it might be added that altogether only 17 of the 302 troubadour songs to come down to us have been preserved in three variants: after Faidit, three of these are by Floquet de

Marselha (1180–1231) and three by Vidal (see the chapter on Vidal's musical style), another three by the highly popular Bernart de Ventadorn (1150–1180) and one by Richard de Berbezil, who was active around 1200. The figures themselves are an indication that Faidit's works were known to quite a wide audience. It cannot be considered fortuitous that a number of his works were included in the most notable troubadour manuscripts. In terms of number of melodies he ranks fifth among the troubadours. Of the generation younger than Faidit, only Ventadorn has more melodies (19), while among his troubadour contemporaries he is surpassed only by Peirol (17 melodies) and Raimon de Miravel (22 melodies). In the last troubadour generation he is surpassed by Guiraut Riquier, whose 48 songs constitute the largest body of troubadour works of all. This we mention because in analysing Faidit's style one discovers a cross-section of a great period, a 'golden age' of whose works some may have been composed or at least performed in Hungary as well. From this point of view I attach particular significance to the Richard Lament (No. 4) and to the Hungarian folksong parallel discovered for the melody of the poem "Gen fora contra l'afan", No. 5. On the basis of his 14 melodies the following can be determined about Faidit's musical style:

1. Descending melodic line. Of the 14 Faidit compositions, 12 open with a descending melody. The degree and character of the descent varies, but it appears in such high proportion that it can be considered one of his major compositional features. In the northern Italian Manuscript *G*, which includes the largest number of melodies in a single codex, a third of the melodies are descending (62 out of 163). That third is remarkably distributed: a descending melodic structure appears in the work of several troubadours, but in most cases sporadically, in a haphazard manner. A larger number first appears in Vidal and then in Faidit. Finally there is an even larger number (25 melody openings) in the works of Guiraut Riquier, the last troubadour. But this phenomenon provides no real excuse for seeking out relationships or forced explanations. Certainly a descending melodic opening is not typical of troubadour music, but within melodies the broadly arched ones often show a descending melodic line at the opening of the internal lines of text. A descending tendency is all the more interesting as it is one typical trait of the early layer of Hungarian folk music, and though we do not draw a parallel between Hungarian folk music and the melody-building of the troubadours who came to Hungary, we have to recognize that a descending beginning is not unusual in 12th and 13th century European secular monody as a whole.

The descending openings of Faidit and Riquier differ from each other. Whereas Riquier begins many of his descending melodic openings by inserting an ascending incipit before the descent, Faidit opens his melody without an incipit, at the highest point in that melodic line. Although this is a question of melodic construction, the particularly beautiful pentatonic Faidit melody we have already analysed (Poem No. 5 beginning "Gen fora") is also related to descent. Some of its characteristic lines, its opening and a few other melody lines are also found in No. 13 ("S'on poguez"): the first and fourth lines of the two songs are related, while Line 5 of "Gen fora" resembles Line 3 of "S'on poguez". However, the similarity in the song *lines* does not indicate a relationship between the melodies as a whole: they belong to different types, "Gen fora" being a *canzone*, and "S'on poguez" an *Oda continua*. The example only goes to show that a troubadour can use melodic excerpts of identical character from his own repertoire and yet produce different forms from them in different poems; the melody has a clearly separate identity from the type, and furthermore, neither has any relationship with the text of the poem.

2. Keys, tonality and tonus fluctuans. As has already been mentioned, *six* of Faidit's works appear in three different manuscripts, and *four* in two different manuscripts, while the rest appear only in a single manuscript. In examining the keys account also had to be taken of the variants, since the same song was hardly ever noted down twice in the same key. In tonality they present a most varied picture, and in a way it is precisely that variety which is characteristic. We have placed the internationally recognized sign for the manuscript after the serial number in all cases where there are differences between manuscripts (thus the same serial number may feature in several groups).

Modal	Major	Fluctuating (transitional)
Dorian: 2 (*R*, *G*), 3, 5	1,4 *W*	Dorian–Mixolydian: 9 *X*.
6 (*W*, *G*), 8, 9 *R*.		Dorian–Aeolian: 2 *X*.
		4 *G*, 13 *X*.
11 *X*, 12 (*R*, *X*), 13 *G*.		Dorian–Mixolydian: 4 *X*.
Hypodorian: 11 *G*.		
Hypolydian: 10 *G*.		
Mixolydian: 9 *R*, 7 *R*, 10 *R*.		
Hypomixolydian: 7 (*G*, *R*), 11 *R*.		
Aeolian: 10 *W*.		

Of the 14 songs preserved in 30 variants, only two occur in the same key in different manuscripts (12 *R*, *X*; 14 *R*, *G*). While modal keys were rare in Vidal, they are in the majority in Faidit: of the modal keys 15 are Dorian (i.e. half of the 30 variants), followed by the Lydian-type tonalities—Hypolydian, Mixolydian, Hypomixolydian (seven altogether)—and a single Aeolian. Very few are in the major (2) and there are none in the Phrygian. The transitional type of fluctuating tonality can also be found in Faidit. *Fluctuating tonality*, which we have called *tonus fluctuans*, forms a *most important component of troubadour music*. Its basis is ti-ta fluctuation, but not in the same context as it appears in Gregorian. According to medieval theoreticians: "Una voce super La emper est canendum Fa". In the Gregorian the b flat (*rotundum*) plays a role in the ascending tritone, while in the descending melody it becomes a *quadratum*, whereas in troubadour music the fluctuation appears seemingly inconsequently within a melody, absolutely irrespective of the tritone. This can be observed particularly in cases where the same piece has been preserved in several manuscripts, and Hans Zingerle refers to it when he writes:

Da ja im (antik-) mittelalterlichen Tonsystem eine Skalenstufe eine Doppelform aufweist: 'h'-'b' ... ist für eine Tonartbestimmung außer der Finalis die Wahl der einen oder andern Stufenform maßgebend. Nun zeigt ein Vergleich zwischen verschiedenen Aufzeichnungen ein und derselben Liedweise oder zwischen melodisch gleichen Fassungen verschiedener Verse innerhalb eines Liedes, daß in der Anbringung von Akzidentien sehr willkürlich verfahren und somit vielfach mit einer Alterierung aus dem Stegreif gerechnet wurde. Daß es aber für den Tonart Character je nach Finalis in sehr verschiedenem Maß von Bedeutung ist, ob 'b' an die Stelle von 'h' tritt, dafür sprechen u.a. die (freilich wenig zahlreichen) Fälle, wo verschiedene Handschriften ein gleiches Lied in verschiedener Lage bringen.[1]

We are in the fortunate position of having *four* melodies of *fluctuating* tonality (mostly in the Lotharingian Manuscript *X*) which in the Provençal Manuscript *R* or the northern Italian Manuscript *G* are written out in the Dorian. "Chant e deport", for example, is Dorian in Manuscripts *R* and *G*, but fluctuates between the Dorian and the Aeolian in Manuscript *X*, since in Section 4 a flat sign is written before the major sixth, which determines the Dorian (e^2). No diminution appears anywhere else in Section 4 itself or in the preceding Section 3. In the following six sections we are left uncertain which alternative we should use to interpret the second half of the piece. We consider it to be in the Aeolian from the flattening onwards, but if the medieval sense of tonality was not definite, one is forced to conclude that apart from the one point where the flat sign is written in, the major sixth was sung (b with D final, and e with G final). The melody of the Richard Lament (to the poem "Fortz causa es que tot lo major dan", No. 4) raises similar questions, with still more interesting aspects. The northern French Manuscript *W* gives the melody in a pure major; the northern Italian Manuscript *G* floats between the Dorian and the Aeolian (the sixth note of the first section is flattened, but in other places no accidentals are written before the same note); the Lotharingian *X* melody floats between the major and the Dorian (and here again the first section brings an accidental—a natural sign before the major seventh). So of the three variants of the lament two are floating, but each in a different tonality. Once again we must add that the basic melody itself was the Old French secular song: "E! serventois" (a folksong or one that later became a popular song, although this cannot be proved since no early record of it is known). There are another two Faidit songs of a fluctuating tonality: one is No. 9 "Mon cor e mi", whose Lotharingian variant fluctuates between the Dorian and the Mixolydian (as against the Provençal Manuscript *R* variant in the Dorian), and the other is "S'on pogues partir" (No. 13), where Manuscript *X* is again uncertain between the Dorian and the Aeolian (as against the Dorian given in the northern Italian Manuscript *G*).

In our account we have not intended to show what keys the various manuscripts chose for melodies noted down in several codices, but confined ourselves to noting the places where the tonality changes within a song, and most cases of this have been found in the Lotharingian Manuscript *X*.

[1] Zingerle (1958), p. 5.

3. Peculiarities of melodic structure

a) Syllabic melody—melismatic melody. By the wording of the subtitle we intend to say that in Faidit's works there is no sharp dividing line between the two manners of construction. He left no purely syllabic melodies, nor even melodies which would be syllabic but for one or two inflections. Even if some of his melodies are characterized more by a song-formation of independent notes corresponding to the syllables, the ornamental group or melisma soon appears. In that sense the melodies of the poems "Jamais nuls temps" (No. 6), "Mon cor e mi" (No. 9) and "S'on pogues" (No. 13) might be considered *syllabic*. But there are not many purely *melismatic* melody either. "Lo rossignolet" (No. 8), "Si anc nuls hom" (No. 11) and "Si tot ai tardat" (No. 12), can be termed melismatic.

Most of Faidit's melodies fall into neither category, and can be considered *mixed* melodies in which both basic components are present. A fine example of the mixed group is the pentatonic Dorian melody of "Gen fora" (No. 5) where, apart from two melismatic sections, there is a syllabic character. Here one should note that the term pentatony is not used in any Hungarian folk music sense, but applied everywhere in troubadour music where the main notes of the melody avoid intervals of a semitone. Mentioning the upward steps of a fourth, Zingerle notes:

> Auch im Zusammenhang mit etlichen andern Wendungen wird sich zeigen, daß 'e' und 'h' für die Melodiebildung eine Sonderstellung einnehmen; darin ist aber offenbar eine Nachwirkung älterer halbtonlos-pentatonischer Melodik zu sehen".

Actually, another golden rule of medieval musical theory is relevant here: "Mi contra Fa diabolus in musica".[2]

The melody of "Chant e deport" (No. 2) also belongs to the mixed type, where interestingly, after three syllabic notes, the melodies of the text-lines are ornamented with at times more modest and at times richer melismatics, again in a way rather unrelated to the text (see the following section: Texts—melodies); here the consistent line-opening of three and sometimes four independent notes does not facilitate the mensural possibilities of modal notation (but rather tells against it); it lends a 'dancing' character to "Chant e deport" (of the same type we have also encountered in Vidal). A similar structure can be found in the Richard Lament ("Fortz causa", No. 4), although here the function of the poem is completely different. The question is whether this musical solution can be considered a structure or a deliberate composing principle at all. Another question which might arise, albeit one that would lead off the subject, is whether one can take the *archaic death dance* into account when studying the melody of the Richard Lament.

[2] Zingerle (1958), p. 11.

The poem "Tant ai sofert" (No. 14) belongs to the mixed group. Here we encounter for the first and last time in Faidit the structure of note repetition, the song type with a recitative bent that is so characteristic of Vidal.

b) Texts—melodies. In analysing the relationship of the lines of a poem to the note groups, the doubt repeatedly arises as to whether the melody was written to the text under which it appears in the manuscript, or whether it was merely matched with the text later.

By and large musical forms take no account of textual forms, not even of rhyme schemes, which could more easily be adhered to. On the other hand, the note groups featuring in the melody clearly indicate an attempt to keep to the *sung syllables* of the text. In contrast to this, several other possibilities were inherent in the melodies: for example the song arches, and the cadence formations of the melodic line were in different places from where the text would require them to be. That might lead to the interpretational question of whether the text was perhaps performed not according to the poem lines but freely, relying more upon the possibilities of the inner meaning division than upon the textual picture as noted down in writing. Vocal performance with instrumental accompaniment was a most suitable means of resolving these seemingly contradictory arguments. Studying the original manuscripts it appears that the first stanza, which also bears the melody, is *not* arranged *according to the lines of the text* but according to the melody, and only the subsequent stanzas, recorded without music, are shaped according to the poem's rhyme scheme.

That is why the question has arisen during the musical examination of the first Faidit poems as to whether, when the melody does not follow the structure of the text, that must mean it is a borrowed melody, originally written for another poem and noted down over the new text. Even though we initially thought that the melodies of Nos 1, 2, 3 or 4 were not composed by Faidit and are far removed from the texts, we were later convinced of the contrary on finding the identical melodic notation in several different manuscripts. The linear construction of the melody within the poem did not necessarily conform with the arrangement of the lines of the poem, and that still did not preclude the relationship between identical melodies and texts. A good example is Line 6 of the Richard Lament, where the name of the king comes at the peak. (This we have analysed in detail in the relevant place.)

A frequent occurrence (and one observable in Vidal, too) is for two lines of the poem to have a major connecting melodic arch: 2 lines of poem equal 1 melodic phrase. Sometimes the melodic phrases do not exactly correspond even with two lines; in several places they would form half-lines (according to the musical cadence-formula). Here too, as in Vidal's case, the contraction of the poem lines can transform the grand form: in the case of old numbered lines it might change into Sapphic form, and indeed, it can even influence the musical form, turning what would textually be an *Oda continua* into a *kanzone*.

c) Melodic construction—intervals. Despite the rich ornamentation, Faidit's melodic, linear construction is a modest one, employing few plagal keys, which already means a certain restriction of intervals. His songs include peaks, but they do not prevail over the whole melody. He has no line cadences of an upward fourth or fifth (apart from one or two sporadic cases, e.g. in Section 4 of No. 8), but he often uses steps of a fourth, and particularly of a fifth, within the line. It is surprising that upward sixths occur twice (in Section 7 of versions *G* and *W* of No. 4, each in a different tonality). There are frequent sequences of thirds. This is highly characteristic of medieval monody, although the tonality is not determined, for example, by whether the sequences open with a minor or a major third. It is difficult to establish how deliberately Faidit arranged that the lower third should be a *major third* in the overwhelming majority of cases, regardless of whether the sequence progresses upwards or downwards. Some *upward* tending sequences of thirds can be found in Sections 9 and 12 of "Al semblan" (No. 1): g-b-d; in Section 9 of "Chant e deport" (No. 2): b flat-d-f; in Section 6 of "Fortz causa" (No. 4); g-b-d; in Section 2 of "Jamais nuls temps" (No. 6): b flat-d-f, etc. *Downward* tending sequences of thirds are in Section 13 of "Al semblan" (No. 1): d-b-g; in Section 8 of "Cora que.m" (No. 3): f-d-b flat; in Section 4 of "Fortz causa" (No. 4): d-b-g; in Sections 1 and 3 of "Mon cor e mi" (No. 9): f-d-b flat, etc. The steps of thirds listed so far consist of two thirds, and span an interval of a *fifth*. Several times there are three thirds following one another and here the interval is a (minor or major) *seventh*: in Section 8 of "Mon cor e mi" (No. 9): f-a-c-e upwards; in Section 10 of "Cora que.m" (No. 3): f-d-b flat-g downwards. The examples generally show the same tonal relations both in the major (g-b-d), and in the Dorian (b flat-d-f). We have not selected the examples deliberately, but presented the average third relations.

The frequent use of thirds might have helped secure the movement within the melody: in certain melodic contexts it is easier to bridge a fifth with two thirds than to sing it without a third, and the role of thirds must have been particularly important in the bridging of sevenths when it came to interpretation. The compass of the songs shows that Faidit always remained within the bounds of what was singable, and so we can consider any instrumental contribution only as accompaniment.

4. Musical Types. Faidit used a mere three musical types in his 14 melodies: *Oda continua, kanzone* and one group of the *lai* fragment. In the analyses of the works we have repeatedly pointed out that the musical lines and ideas do not everywhere correspond to the text lines. In the foregoing section (3b: Texts—melodies) we have argued that in general there are two lines of text to each musical phrase. The contraction of lines has in several cases changed the type category as defined by Gennrich: "Al semblan" (No. 1) and "Chant e deport" (No. 2) cease to be the *Oda continua* he termed then and belong instead to the *2nd group of the lai fragment*; "Cora que.m" (No. 3) is turned from an *Oda continua* to a *kanzone*; "Lo gens cors" (No. 7), which Gennrich called a *kanzone,* becomes in our view of the *2nd group of the lai fragment*; "Jamais nuls temps" (No. 6), which Gennrich listed under the 3rd group of the *lai fragment*, belongs here to the *kanzone* type.

Thereby the number of pieces ranked as *Oda continua* has decreased to six: of Faidit's works "Fortz causa" (No. 4), "Lo rossignolet" (No. 8), "Nom alegra" (No. 10), "Si anc nuls hom" (No. 11), "S'on pogues" (No. 13), and "Tant ai sofert" (No. 14). We have already mentioned that from the point of view of musical structuring this is the simplest type, in which independent musical phrases follow one another. We consider the *kanzone* a more refined musical form, as here the first line is repeated and thus shows the germs of a composing technique. We have found *six* Faidit works belonging to this type: "Cora que.m" (No. 3), "Gen fora" (No. 5), "Jamais nuls temps" (No. 6), "Lo gens cors" (No. 7), "Mon cor e mi" (No. 9), and "Si tot ai tardat" (No. 12).

We consider the appearance of some of the *lai* fragments (Category 2 according to Gennrich) a higher grade in Faidit's works, because here, in addition to the first line, another line is also repeated in the song. *Three* works belong into this group: "Al semblan" (No. 1), "Chant e deport" (No. 2) and "Lo gens cors" (No. 7).

To sum up it can be established that Faidit used the same three musical types in his poems as Vidal.

5. *Contrafacta.* The borrowing, rewriting and use of a popular melody was a frequent occurrence in medieval secular monody and poetry. A troubadour's poetic personality, and composing invention, and his influence on his contemporaries, is also shown by the extent to which his works were used by others. Six of Faidit's poems appear altogether 23 times in the works of his contemporaries. When analysing some of his poems we thought that he himself was no exception in this respect and made use of works of others, but our examinations have yielded no traces of any putative sources. Faidit's poems and melodies can be found in the following works: "Chant e deport" (No. 2—Pill. 167.15) was used by Blacasset (Pill. 96.8), Cadenet (Pill. 106.13 and 24), Lanfranc Cigala (Pill. 282.23), Marques (Pill. 296.2), Peire Cardenal (Pill. 335.26), Ramonz Bistortz d'Arle (Pill. 416.3), Sordel (Pill. 437.16) and in three more works whose authors are unknown; "Cora que.m" (No. 3—Pill. 167.17) appears in Floquet de Roman (Pill. 156.9); "Fortz causa" (No. 4—Pill. 167.22) became the model for an anonymous Old French song (Pill. 461.234) mentioned before: "E! serventois, arriere t'en revas"; "Jamais nuls temps" (No. 6—Pill. 167.30) was taken over by Bernart Carbonel (Pill. 82.21) and Comtesse de Provence (Pill. 187.1); "Lo gens cors" (No. 7—Pill. 167.32) reappears with Peire Cardenal (Pill. 335.32); finally "S'on pogues" (No.13—Pill. 167.56) was used by Bertran Carbonel (Pill. 82.63 and 82), Peire Cardenal (Pill. 335.51), Uc de Saint Circ (Pill. 457.29) and three anonymous authors. Some of the authors feature repeatedly, and most of the names also appear among the troubadours who made use of Vidal's works.

FAIDIT

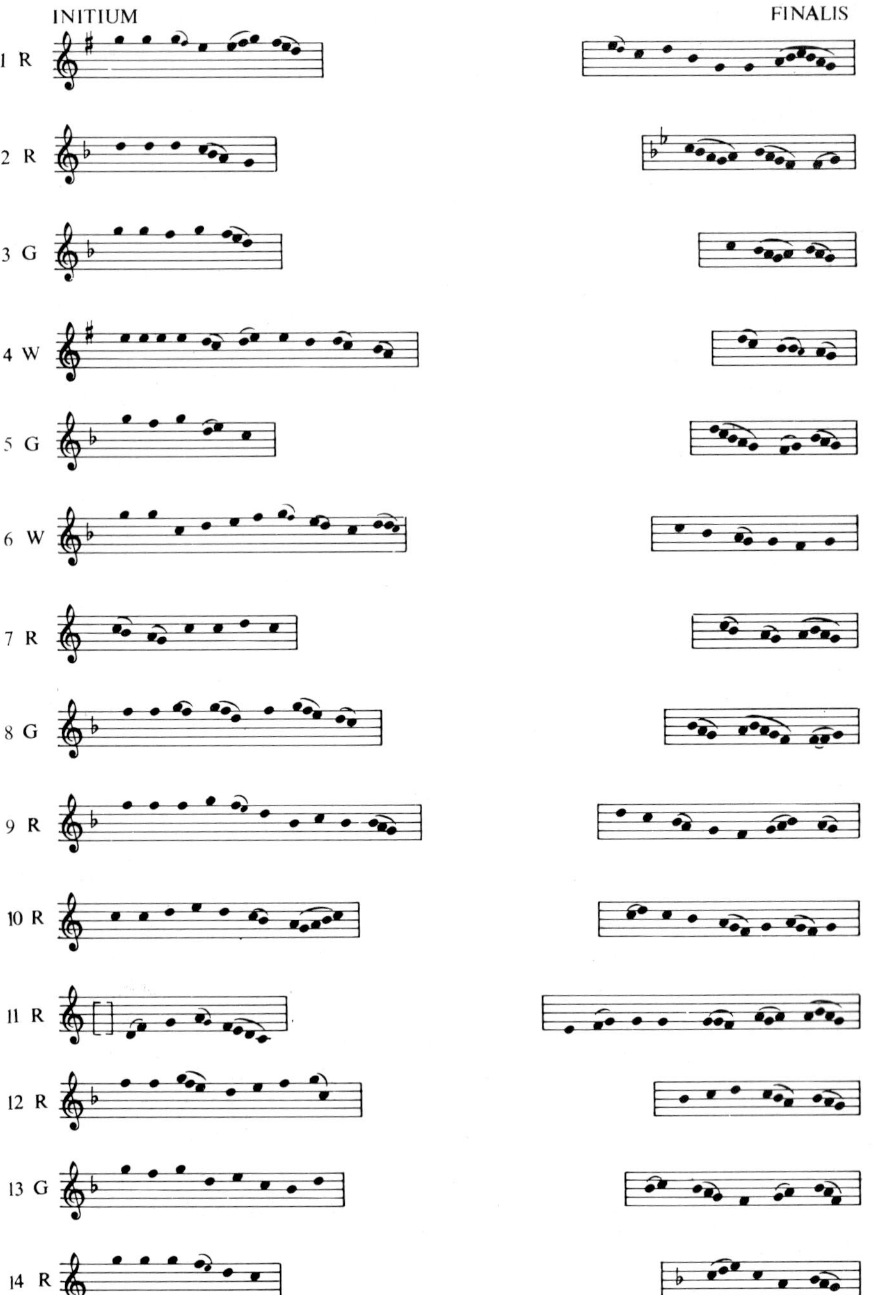

SUMMARY

Secular monody developed in Europe from the 12th century onwards in two connected and yet different geographical and political environments: in southern France and in Spain. Both areas were the scenes of changes, transformations and turbulances: from the south they were imbued with the influence of the Mediterranean and the permanent heritage of the Near Eastern cultures, while from the north came the stricter social consciousness of Europe, which was developing a bourgeois mentality, becoming settled into political formations, requiring new forms, awakening to national consciousness and unifying each of the regional, linguistic and ethnic communities by laying down state borders. In its text and with its text, monody became a basic factor in the shaping of consciousness and thus of social existence; hardly any communal manifestation was uninfluenced by it. Secular monody not only expressed the medieval world outlook in a manner completely different from church monody (Gregorian), it also expressed many elements of the life of the court, the bourgeoisie, and even the peasantry, thus initiating the development of new poetic and musical forms and containing potentially even the seeds of modern European literature and music.

The first appearances of secular monody are closely linked with the social and historical phenomena of the period. The first musical relics—the troubadour manuscripts and the Spanish cantigas—are telling witnesses of the transformation process which began at the end of the Antiquity and ended in the High Middle Ages. Scientific examination of the process, by emphasizing the Arab thesis, has concluded that Arab culture and science played a decisive role. In the first chapter we have provided an explanation of the thesis whereby Arab culture exerted its influence not directly but *indirectly*, playing a mere *mediating* role between the culture of ancient Greece and Near Eastern cultures in general on the one hand, and the cultural history of medieval Europe on the other. The various manifestations of Near Eastern culture (architecture, philosophy, poetry, musical theory, etc.) arrived in the West in the 600s with the spread of the Islamic religion (almost simultaneously with the Roman Gregorian plainsong). This westward expansion embraced not only the Arabs, but all the peoples and ethnic groups along the North African route who were pushing towards Europe and the Iberian Peninsula. Besides Arab culture, a highly significant role in the Hispanic transmitting area was played by Moorish and Jewish ethnic groups who by virtue of the development of their cultural history stood much closer in their own poetic and musical forms to the European sphere of ideas and European awareness of society.

In examining the issue we have stressed that a joint influence was felt, with several components. In a musical context one of the most important phenomena is the *refrain* form, which in its historical course reached a state of conscious formal development in the period under examination, and which henceforth became an organic part of European music.

Social and historical examinations of music and musicians, particularly the troubadours, have had the important result of showing a relationship with the heretical movements. Several biographical data led previous scholars to note the troubadours' attachment to the Albigensians as well. We have proved in this work that the setting up of the two great inquisitions coincided with the relapse into silence of some of the troubadours, while during the crusades against the Albigensians they gradually disappeared from southern France altogether.

Besides the music, the text and the poetic forms were of great significance; at the beginning of the century, scholars only analysed the music in terms of the poetry, which led to a confusion of conceptual spheres in research into troubadour music: a large proportion of the melodies were categorized according to the textual categories of the poems and the true musical forms remained unrecognized; they were even supplanted by poetic terminology and in some cases by literary analyses of the line endings of the poems. Gennrich referred to the musical parallels or musical denominations of a few expressions, but he too was greatly influenced by the method of literary analysis. In this treatise we have pointed to the difficulties of comparing prosodic and musical forms: we have shown the possibilities for comparison; and alongside the poetic forms we have listed the musical forms in which secular monody took an independent road. A survey of the whole of troubadour music has proved that the most current song form was that consisting of *independent music lines*, where the melodic cadences agree with the rhyme schemes of the text lines only rarely, and the lines of the text often do not even tally with the melodic ending, but the melody in every case takes into account the *number of syllables*, adjusting the various notes and the groups of melismas to it. The second most current type of musical construction is where the *music lines become repeated* in part or in full during the course of the melody: this repeat marks the first appearance of the refrain form. In musical terms one speaks about repeated lines, while in terms of poetic forms one speaks of terminal rhymes and their regular or irregular recurrence. This is why the literary terminology cannot be directly applied to music: *zadjal* or *mouwashshah* structures are prosodic concepts, and even if their essence includes a repeat, their effect on music was only indirectly felt through the preference they gave to the conceptual element, the regularity of the repeat and the permanent recurrence of certain lines. These are two different outward forms of the same phenomenon, but the melody uses repeats not according to the structure of the poem but according to its own internal laws.

On the basis of our research and comparisons we can state that even though text and melody affected each other reciprocally, neither ruled over the other, and each was influenced by the *instrumental* accompaniment, which served the above dialectical duality and bridged the difference between the two.

One important result of our research and the practical experience gained from our comparisons is to establish that the musical metre is based on the syllabic order of the text: the melody still conforms to the syllable count in the poem, whether there is one or even eight or nine notes to a syllable. A relationship of this kind between syllable and note group is always clear in the original manuscripts, and the puzzle and confusion over the matter has been caused only by transcriptions made in accordance with inapplicable theories.

This book is the first to present the full musical material of the two troubadours who went to Hungary: Peire Vidal and Gaucelm Faidit. Each melody is analysed separately, the musical and poetic forms of songs already published by others (primarily by Gennrich) are compared, the errors in these publications are pinpointed, and the stylistic aspects of the musical variants in different sources are compared. Here for the first time the musical style of two great troubadours is summarized, and in places (in connection with the *contrafacta*) compared with troubadour music as a whole. The stylistic examinations have led to the conclusion that in terms of *structure*, two most frequently occurring basic types are these: 1) a descending melodic opening, and 2) a terraced melodic structure in which after the first melodic section the following section repeats the incipit a fourth or a fifth higher. The descending type is characteristic not only of the two groups of melodies analysed here in detail, but of the melodic practice of the last troubadour, Guiraut Riquier, as well.

With regard to *tonalities* the analyses have shown the frequency of the major in the realm of medieval modal keys. The question is whether the troubadour songs can be classed according to our known scales. The medieval note picture (noted on lines) presents the modern scholar with a number of possibilities from which the scales of non-European music cannot be excluded in considering the melodies. In our analysis we had to give a name to a melodic structure which cannot be categorized, and found 'fluctuating tonality' as the most suitable term. Its basis is the ti-ta fluctuation known of old, but it goes further than that, partly in being inconsistent with medieval rules, and partly, according to the manuscripts note picture, consisting of many passing melodic notes which today would be called *glissando*; neither their function nor their note value agree with the structure of the relevant scale.

BIBLIOGRAPHY

Aarburg, U.: 'Muster für die Edition mittelalterlicher Liedmelodien' in *Die Musikforschung*, 10, 1957, pp. 209–17.

Abert, H.: *Musikanschauung des Mittelalters*, Tutzing, 1965.

Anglade, J.: *Les poésies de Peire Vidal*, Paris, Champion, 1923 (CFMA) pp. iv–vi.

Anglès, H.: *Les melodies del trobador Guirant Riquier*, Barcelona, 1927.

Anglès, H.: *La musica de las Cantigas de Santa María del rey Alfonso el Sabio. I. Facsímil del códice j.b.2. de el Escorial*, 1964; *II. Transcripción musical*, 1943; *III. Primera parte: Estudio crítico*, 1953; *Segunda parte: Las melodias hispanas y la monodia lírica europea de los siglos XII–XIII*, 1953, Barcelona.

Anglès, H.: 'Der Rhythmus in der Melodik mittelalterlicher Lyrik' in *Report of the 8th Congress of I.M.S.*, 1961, 3–11.

Appel, C.: *Der Trobador Cadenet*, Halle, 1920.

Arom, S.: *Nouvelles perspectives dans la description des musiques de tradition orale* in *Revue de Musicologie*. Paris 1982. pp. 205–206.

Avalle D'Arco, S.: *Peire Vidal: Poesie*, Milano–Napoli, 1960 (Documente di Filologia).

Avenary, H.: 'Formal Structure of Psalms and Canticles in Early Jewish and Christian Chant' in: *Musica Disciplina* 1953.

Barbieri, F. A.: *Cancionero de Palacio de los siglos XV y XVI*, Madrid, 1890.

Bartalus, I.: 'A troubadourok s jongleur-ök' (The Troubadours and the Jongleurs) in *Koszorú*, 1863, 2nd semester, Nos 10–12.

Bartók, B.: 'A Biskra-vidéki arabok népzenéje' (Folk Music of the Arabs of the Biskra Region); the first part appeared first in Hungarian in *Szimfónia*, 1917, pp. 308–23; the whole work appeared in German: 'Die Volksmusik der Araber von Biskra und Umgebung' in *Zeitschrift für Musikwissenschaft*, 1920, Vol. II, No. 9, pp. 489–522. The whole work appears in Hungarian in *B. B. összegyűjtött írásai* (B. B's Collected Writings) I, ed. Szöllősy, A., Budapest, 1966, pp. 518–61.

Bartsch, K.: *Chrestomathie provençale*, Elberfeld, 1880.

Bartsch, K.: *Grundriß der provenzalischen Literatur*, Elberfeld, 1872.

Bartsch, K.: *Peire Vidals Lieder*, Berlin, 1857.

Bec, P.: *Nouvelle anthologie de la lyrique occitane du moyen âge*, Avignon, 1970.

Beck, J.: *Chansonnier Cangé*, Paris Bibl. Nat. fr. 846, Vol. 2, Paris–Philadelphia, 1927, repr. 1970 (facsimile ed.)

Beck, J.: *Manuscrit du Roi*, Paris Bibl. Nat. fr. 844, London–Philadelphia, 1938 (facsimile ed.), repr. New York, 1970, I–II.

Beck, J.: *La Musique des Troubadours*, Paris, 1910; (in German: *Die Melodien der Troubadours*, Straßburg, 1908)

Beichert, E. A.: *Die Wissenschaft der Musik bei Al-Farabi*, Regensburg, 1931.

Bergert, F.: *Die von den Trobadors genannten oder gefeierten Damen*, Halle, 1913 *(Beihefte zur Zeitsch. für rom. Phil., No. XLVI)*

Berner, A.: *Studien zur arabischen Musik*, Leipzig, 1937.

Bertoni, G.: *Il canzionere provenzale della Biblioteca Ambrosiana R 71 sup.* (Gesellschaft für romanische Literatur 28), 1912.

Bittinger, W.: *Studien zur musikalischen Textkritik des mittelalterlichen Liedes*, Würzburg, 1953 *(Literaturhistorisch-musikwissenschaftliche Abhandlungen XI)*

Blumenkrantz, B.: *Juden und Judentum in der mittelalterlichen Kunst*, Stuttgart, 1965.
Borst, A.: *Die Katharer*, Stuttgart, 1953.
Boutier, J.–Schütz, A. H.: *Biographies des troubadours*, Toulouse–Paris, 1950.
Brinkmann, H.: 'Der deutsche Minnesang' in Fromm, H.: *Der deutsche Minnesang. Aufsätze zu seiner Erforschung (Wege der Forschung 15)*, Darmstadt, 1961.
Bru, Ch. I.: *Les éléments pour une interprétation sociologique de catharisme occitan*, Paris, 1952.
Burdach, K.: 'Über den Ursprung des mittelalterlichen Minnesangs' in *Deutsche Vierteljahrsschrift für Literaturwissenschaft und Geistesgeschichte*, Buchreihe Bd. I, Halle, 1925.
Chailley, J.: *L'École musicale de St. Martial de Limoges jusqu'à la fin du XIe siècle*, Paris, 1960.
Chailley, J.: *Histoire musicale du moyen âge*, Paris, 1950. 2nd ed. 1969.
Chase, G.: *The Music of Spain*, New York, 1959.
Cordes, L.: *Troubadours aujourd'hui*, Lodève, 1975.
Cornaert, E.: *Des confréries carolingiennes aux gildes marchandes*, Paris, 1942.
Cuesta, I., F.–Lafont, R.: *Las cansons dels troubadours*. Toulouse, 1979.
Dante, A.: *De Vulgari Eloquentia. II*, 1529 and 1577.
Davenson, H.: *Les troubadours (Le temps qui court)*, Paris, 1961.
Diez, Fr.: *Leben und Werke der Troubadours*, Leipzig, 1882, 2nd ed., repr. Hildesheim, 1965.
Douais, C.: *Les sources de l'histoire de l'Inquisition dans le Midi de la France au XIIIe et XIVe siècles*, Paris, 1881.
Ducamin, J.: *Juan Ruiz–Libro de buen amor*, Toulouse, 1901.
Dupuy, A.: *Petite Encyclopédie Occitane*, Montpellier, 1972.
Durliat, M.: *La construction de Saint-Sernin de Toulouse au XIe siècle. Bulletin monumental*, 1963.
Durliat, M.: 'La date des plus anciens chapiteaux de la Daurade à Toulouse' in *Cuadernos de Argueología e Historia de la Ciudad*, X, 1967.
Durliat, M.: *L'église abbatial de Moissac des origines à la fin du XIe siècle. Cahiers archéologiques*, 1965.
Duvernoy, J.: *Le Catharisme: la religion des cathares*, Toulouse, 1976.
Eckhardt, S.: 'Trubadúrok Magyarországon' (Troubadours in Hungary) in *Irodalomtörténet*, 1961, pp. 129–37.
Engelmann, E.: *Zur städtischen Volksbewegung in Südfrankreich*, Berlin, 1959.
Erckmann, R.: 'Der Einfluß der arabischen Kultur auf den Minnesang' in *Deutsche Vierteljahrsschrift für Literaturwissenschaft und Geistesgeschichte*, 1931, pp. 272–9.
d'Erlanger, R.: *La musique arabe*, 5 vols., Paris, 1930–49.
Eszmei és irodalmi találkozások. Tanulmányok a magyar–francia irodalmi kapcsolatok történetéből (Ideological and Literary Encounters. Studies from the History of Hungarian–French Literary Relation), ed. Köpeczi, B. and Sőtér, I., Budapest, 1970.
Falvy, Z.–Mezey, L. (Eds): *Codex Albensis*, Budapest–Graz, 1963.
Falvy, Z.: *La cour d'Alphonse le Sage et la musique européenne* in *Studia Musicologica*. Budapest 1983. Vol. XXV. pp. 159–170.
Falvy, Z.: *Rapporti musicali fra Ungheria ed Europa nel medioevo*, Venice, 1977.
Falvy, Z.: *Troubadourmelodien im mittelalterlichen Ungarn* in Studia Musicologica Budapest 1973. Vol. XV. pp. 79–89.
Falvy, Z.: 'Troubadour Music, as a Historical Source of European Folk Music' in: Musikethnologische Sd. Graz 1984.
Falvy, Z.: 'Zsidó muzsikusok a 13. században' (Jewish Musicians in the 13th Century) in *Magyar Izraeliták Évkönyve*, Budapest, 1978.
Faral, E.: *Les arts poétiques du XIIe et du XIIIe s.*, Paris 1958.
Farmer, H. G.: 'A Magribi Work on Musical Instruments' in *Journal of the Royal Asiatic Society*, 1925.
Farmer, H. G.: *Al-Farabi's Arabic–Latin Writings on Music*, Glasgow, 1934.
Farmer, H. G.: *Historical Facts for the Arabian Musical Influence*. London 1930.
Farmer, H. G.: *History of Arabian Music to the XIIth century*, London, 1930.
Favati, G.: *Le biografie trovadoriche*, Bologna, 1961.
Flindell, E. F.: 'Aspekte der Modalnotation' in *Die Musikforschung*, 1964, XVII, pp. 353–77.
Frank, I.: *La chanson de croisade du troubadour Gavandan*, Helsinki, 1947.

Frank, I.: *Du rôle des Troubadours dans la formation de la lyrique moderne*, Paris, 1950; (in German it appeared in the volume *Der provenzalische Minnesang: Die Rolle der Troubadours in der Entstehungsgeschichte der modernen Lyrik*, Darmstadt, 1967).

Frank, I.: *Répertoire métrique de la poésie des troubadours, Tome 1er Introduction et Répertoire*, 1953; *Tome 2d Répertoire (suite) et index bibliographique*..., Paris, 1957.

Frank, I.: *Les troubadours et le Portugal*, 1949.

Frank, I.: *Trouvères et Minnesänger*, Paris, 1952.

Fuertes, M. S.: *Historia de la música española desde la venida de los Fenicios hasta el ano 1950*, Madrid, 1885.

Gauchat, L.–Kehrli, H.: Il canzoniero provenzale H. (Cod. Vaticano 3207), in *Studi di filologia romanza*, Vol. V, Rome, 1891, pp. 341–67.

Gayangos, P.: *History of the Mohammedan Dynasties in Spain*, 1840.

Gennrich, Fr.: 'Das Formproblem des Minnesangs. Ein Beitrag zur Erforschung des Strophenbaues der mittelalterlichen Lyrik' in *DVJ*, Halle–Stuttgart 1931, p. 285 ff.

Gennrich, Fr.: *Grundriß einer Formenlehre des mittelalterlichen Liedes*, Halle, 1932.

Gennrich, Fr.: 'Grundsätzliches zu den Troubadour- und Trouvèreweisen' in *Zeitschrift für romanische Philologie*, Halle–Tübingen, 57, 1937, pp. 31–56.

Gennrich, Fr.: 'Der Sprung ins Mittelalter. Zur Musik der altfranzösischen und altprovenzalischen Lieder' in *Zeitschrift für romanische Philologie*, Halle–Tübingen, 59, 1939, pp. 207–40.

Gennrich, Fr.: 'Ist der mittelalterliche Liedvers arhythmisch?' in *Cultura Neolatina*, 15, 1955, pp. 109–31.

Gennrich, Fr.: *Die Kontrafaktur im Liedschaffen des Mittelalters*, Langen, 1962 *(Summa musicae medii aevi XII)*.

Gennrich, Fr.: *Der musikalische Nachlaß der Troubadours. I. Kritische Ausgabe der Melodien*, 1958, *III. Prolegomena*, Langen, 1965, *IV. Kommentar*, Darmstadt, 1960; in *Summa musicae Medii Aevi*, Darmstadt, 1958.

Gennrich, Fr.: 'Zur Ursprungsfrage des Minnesangs' in *Deutsche Vierteljahrsschrift für Literaturwissenschaft und Geistergeschichte* 7, 1926. Repr. as *Der provenzalische Minnesang*, Darmstadt, 1967.

Gennrich, Fr.–Fellerer, K. G.: *Troubadours, Trouvères, Minne- und Meistergesang. Das Musikwerk, eine Beispielsammlung zur Musikgeschichte*, Cologne, 1951.

Germanus, Gy.: *Az arab irodalom története* (History of Arabic Literature), Budapest, 1962.

Gerson-Kiwi, E.: 'On the Musical Sources of the Judeo-Hispanic Romance' in: *Musical Quarterly* 1964.

Golther, W.: *Tristan und Isolde in den Dichtungen des Mittelalters und der neuen Zeit*, Leipzig, 1907.

Gülke, P.: *Mönche, Bürger, Minnesänger. (Musik in der Gesellschaft des europäischen Mittelalters)*, Leipzig, 1975, pp. 1–283.

Harris, Cl.: *The Troubadour as Musician* in *Past and Present*, London, Reeves, n.d.

Hickmann, H.: *Die Musik des arabisch-islamischen Bereiches, Handbuch der Orientalistik, I. Abteilung, Ergänzungsband IV*, Leiden, 1970, p. 33.

Hoenerbach, W.: *Islamische Geschichte Spaniens*, Zurich, 1970.

Hoepffner, E.: *Les troubadours*, Paris, 1955.

Hoepffner, E.: *Le Troubadour Peire Vidal, sa vie et son œuvre*, Paris, 1961.

Husmann, H.: 'Die musikalische Behandlung der Versarten im Troubadourgesang der Notre-Dame Epoche' in *Acta musicologica 25*, 1953, pp. 1–20.

Husmann, H.: 'Das Prinzip der Silbenzählung im Lied des Zentralen Mittelalters' in *Die Musikforschung*, 6, 1953, pp. 8–33.

Husmann, H.: 'Les époques de la musique provençale au moyen-âge' in *Actes et Mémoires du Ier Congrès Internat. de Langue et Littérature du Midi de la France*, Avignon, 1958, 445.

Jahiel, E.: 'French and Provençal Poet-Musicians of the Middle Ages: A Biblio-Discography' in *Romance Philology 14*, 1960–61, pp. 200–207.

Jammers, E.: *Ausgewählte Melodien des Minnesangs*, Tübingen, 1963.

Jammers, E.: *Minnesang und Choral. Festschrift H. Besseler*, 1961, pp. 137–47.

Járdányi, P.: *Magyar népdaltípusok* (Hungarian Folksong Types) I, Budapest, 1961, p. 37.

Jeanroy, A.: *Bibliographie sommaire des chansonniers français du Moyen Age. (Manuscrits et éditions)*, Paris, 1918; *(Les classiques français du Moyen Age 2e séries: Manuels N° 18)*.

Jeanroy, A.: *Bibliographie sommaire des chansonniers provençaux. (Manuscrits et éditions)*, Paris, 1916; *(Les classiques français du Moyen Age 2e séries: Manuels N° 16)*.
Jeanroy, A.: *La Poésie lyrique des Troubadours. Tome I: Histoire externe—Diffusion à l'étranger. Liste des troubadours classés par régions. Notices bio-bibliographiques. Tome II: Histoire interne—Les genres: leur évolution et leurs plus notables représentants*, Paris, 1934–5.
Jullian, M.–Le Vot, G.: *Notes sur la cohérence formelle des miniatures à sujet musical du manuscrit j.b.2. de l'Escorial.* Madrid 1984.
Keresztury, D., Vécsey, J.,–Falvy, Z.: *A Magyar Zenetörténet Képeskönyve* (Picture Book of Hungarian Music History), Budapest, 1960.
Klosen, A.: 'Die Frau des Trobadors Gaucelm Faidit' in *Archiv für das Studium der neueren Sprachen 141*, p. 243.
Kniezsa, I.: *A magyar nyelv szláv jövevényszavai* (Slavic Loan-Words in the Hungarian Language), Budapest, 1955.
Korompay, B.: 'A jokulator kérdés...' (The Joculator Question...) in *Filológiai Közlöny*, 1956.
Köhler, E.: *Trobadorlyrik und höfischer Roman. Aufsätze zur französischen und provenzalischen Literatur des Mittelalters*, Berlin, 1962.
Kukkenheim, L.–Roussel, H.: *Guide de la Littérature Française du Moyen Age;* (in German: *Führer durch die französische Literatur des Mittelalters*, Berlin, 1969).
Lachmann, R.: *Gesänge der Juden auf der Insel Djarba. Posthumous Works II*, ed. E. Gerson-Kiwi, *Yuval Monograph Series—VII*, Jerisalem, 1978.
Lafargue, M.: 'Les sculptures du premier atelier de la Daurade et les chapiteaux du cloître de Moissac' in *Bulletin monumental*, 1938.
Lavaud, R.: *Poésies complètes du troubadour Peire Cardenal*, Toulouse, 1957.
Le Gentil, P.: 'La strophe "zadjalesque", les "khardjas" et le problème des origines du lyrisme roman' in *Romania*, LXXIV, 1963.
Le Gentil, P.: Le Virelai et le Villancico. Paris 1954.
Le Vot, G.: *Notation, mesure et rythme dans la canso troubadouresque. Cahiers de civilisation médiévale.* Poitiers 1982. pp. 205–17.
Lesure, Fr.: 'La musicologie médiévale d'après des travaux récents' in *Romania 74*, 1953, pp. 271–8.
Levy, E.: *Provenzalisches Supplement-Wörterbuch I–VIII*, Leipzig, 1899 *(Berichtungen und Ergänzungen zu Raynouards Lexique Roman)*.
Li Gotti: 'La tesi araba sulle"origini" della Lirica romanza' in: Studi medievali... Palermo 1956.
Liess, A.: *Die Musik des Abendlandes*, Vienna, 1968, p. 38.
Literaturblatt für germanische und romanische Philologie, Heilbronn, 1880.
Lommatzsch, E.: *Leben und Lieder der provenzalischen Troubadours*, Berlin, 1957.
Mahn (C.) A. (F.): *Die Biographien der Troubadours, in Provenzalischer Sprache*, Berlin, 1878.
Manik, L.: *Das arabische Tonsystem im MA*. Leiden, 1969.
Manselli, R.: *L'eresia del male*, Naples, 1963.
Manselli, R.: *Studi sulle eresie del secolo XII*, Rome, 1953.
Maróthy, J.: *Az európai népdal születése* (Birth of the European Folksong), Budapest, 1960.
Marron, H.–I.: *Les trobadours*. Paris, 1971.
Martin-Chabot, E.: *La chanson de la croisade albigeoise. Tome I.: La chanson de Guillaume de Tudèle*, Paris, 1931.
Menéndez Pidal, R.: *España, eslabon entre la cristianidad y el islam*, Madrid, 1968, 2nd ed.
Merlo, P.: 'Sull'età di Gaucelm Faidit' in *Giorn. stor. d. lett. ital. 3*, p. 386.
Meyer-Lübke: 'Zur Peire Vidal' in *Zeitschrift für romanische Philologie*, 40, 1916.
Meyer, P.–Raynaud, G.: *Le Chansonnier de Saint Germain-des-Prés. Société des anciens textes français*, Paris, 1892.
Monterosso, R.: *Musica e ritmica dei Trovatori*, Milan, 1956.
Mouzat, J.: *Les Poèmes de Gaucelm Faidit (thèse de Paris)*, 1963–4; *(Edition critique complète)*.
Nelli, R.: *Écriture cathares*, Paris, 1968.
Niel, F.: *Albigeois et Cathares*. Paris 1962.
Nykl, A. R.: *The Dove's Neckring by Ibn Hazm*, Paris, 1931.
Nykl, A. R.: *Hispano-Arabic Poetry and Its Relations with the Old Provençal Troubadours*, Baltimore, 1946, p. 380.
Nykl, A. R.: 'L'influence arabe–andalouse sur les Troubadours' in *Bulletin hispanique XLI*, Bordeaux, 1939.

Nykl, A. R.: *Hispano-arabic Poetry and Its Relations with Old Provençal Troubadours*, Baltimore, 1946.
Paganuzzi, E.: 'Sulla notazione neumatica della monodia trobadorica' in *Rivista musicale italiana*, 57, 1955, fasc. I. pp. 23–47.
Pais, D.: 'Árpád- és Anjou-kori mulattatóink' (Hungarian Entertainers of the Árpádian and Angevin Ages) in *Zenetudományi Tanulmányok*, Budapest, 1952.
Pais, D.: 'Kérdések és szempontok a szóösszetételek vizsgálatához' (Questions and Points of View for the Examination of the Compound Words) in *Magyar Nyelv*, Budapest, 1951.
Pais, D.: 'Reg' in *Magyar Nyelv*, Budapest, 1958.
Perkuhn, E.: 'Die arabische Theorie und die Ursprungsfrage der Troubadourkunst' in *Studia Musicologica*, Budapest, 1973, Vol. XV, pp. 129–39.
Petiot, A.: 'La musique chez les troubadours' in *Actes Aix*, 1958. pp. 105–12.
Pillet, A. and Carstens, H.: 'Bibliographie der Troubadours' in *Schriften der Königsberger Gelehrten Gesselschaft, Sonderreihe 3*, Halle 1933.
Popin, M.-D.: *Gaucelm Faidit. Etude stylistique des mélodies.* Strasbourg. 1974. (dactyl.)
Raynaud, G.: *Bibliographie des Chansonniers français des XIIIe et XIVe siècles*, Vol. 2, Paris, 1884.
Raynouard, M.: *Lexique roman ou Dictionnaire de la langue des troubadours*, Paris, 1838, Vols 1–6.
Réan, L.: *Histoire du vandalisme*, Paris, 1959.
Reese, G.: *Music in the Middle Ages*, New York, 1940.
Ribera, J.: *La música andaluza medieval en las canciones de los trovadores, troveros y minnesänger*, Madrid, 1923–5.
Ribera, J.: *Music in Ancient Arabia and Spain*, Stanford, 1929, repr. New York, 1970.
Riquier, M.: *Los trovadores. Historia literaria y textos.* Vol. I–III. Barcelona, 1983.
Rubens, A.: *A History of Jewish Costume*, London 1957.
Sanangelo, S.: *Dante e i trovatori provenzali*, Catania, 1959.
Schapiro, M.: 'The Romanesque Sculpture of Moissac' in *The Art Bulletin*, 1931.
Scheiber, S.: *Die Kaufmann Haggadah*, Budapest, 1959.
Schmidt, J.: *Die älteste Alba*, 1881.
Schlager, K.: *Annäherung an ein Troubadour-Lied* in: Festschrift für H. H. Eggebrecht Z. 65. Geburtstag. Archiv für MW. Bd. XXIII. SS. 1–13.
Schneider, M.: *Arabischer Einfluß in Spanien.* Kassel 1954.
Schrade, L.: 'Political Compositions in French Music of the 12th and 13th Centuries' in *Annales Musicologiques*, 1, 1953, pp. 9–63.
Schultz-Cora, O.: *Le Epistole del trovatore Rambaldo da Vaqueiras a Bonifazio I Marchese di Monferrato*, Florence, 1897; (*Biblioteca Critica della Letteratura Italiana*, Vols 23–24).
Schwan, E.: *Die altfranzösischen Liederhandschriften, ihr Verhältniss, ihre Entstehung und ihre Bestimmung*, Berlin 1886.
Scudieri, J. M.: *Per le origini dell'alba*, 1943.
Sebestyén, Gy.: 'Adalékok a középkori énekmondók történetéhez' (Contributions to the History of Medieval Minstrels) in *Egyetemes Philológiai Közlöny*, Budapest, 1891.
Sebestyén, Gy.: 'Anjoukori nyomok a nagymihályi Kaplyonok mulattatóiról' in *Egyetemes Philológiai Közlöny*, Budapest, 1891.
Sebestyén, Gy.: 'Imre király trubadour vendége' (The Troubadour Guest of King Imre) in *Egyetemes Philológiai Közlöny*, Budapest, 1891, p. 503.
Sebestyén, Gy.: *Regös-énekek* (Regös Songs), Budapest, 1902, *Magyar Népköltési Gyűjtemény IV*.
Sesini, U.: 'Le melodie trobadorische nel Canzoniere provenzale della Biblioteca Ambrosiana. R 71 sup.' in *Studi Medievali*, XII (1939), XII, XIV and XV.
Sesini, U.: *Musiche trobadoriche*, Naples, 1941.
Shephard, W. P. and Chambers, F. M.: *The Poems of Aimeric de Peguillan*, Evanston, Ill., 1950.
Sidorowa, N. A.: *Narodnye ereticheskie Dvizheniya vo Frantsy v XI:XII. vekah*, Moscow, 1953.
Smirnov: 'Contribution à l'étude de la vie provençale de Peire Vidal' in *Romania*, 54, 1928.
Spanke, H.: *Die Metrik der Cantigas*, Barcelona, 1958.
Spanke, H.: 'Die Theorie Riberas über Zusammenhänge zwischen frühromanischen Strophenformen und andalusisch–arabischer Lyrik des Mittelalters' in *Volkstum und Kultur der Romanen 3*, 1930, pp. 258–78.
Spanke, H.: 'Zur Formenkunst des ältesten Troubadours' in *Studi Medievali 7*, 1934, pp. 72–84.

Stäblein, Br.: *Schriftbild der einstimmigen Musik. Bd. III. Musik des Mittelalters und der Renaissance. Lfg. 4,* Leipzig, 1975, pp. 76–90.

Stäblein, Br.: 'Zur Stilistik der Troubadour-Melodien' in *Acta Musicologica,* 1966, Nr. 1, pp. 27–46.

Stengel, E.: *Der Entwicklungsgang der prov. Alba,* 1886.

Stern, S. M.: 'Andalusian muwashshahs in the musical repertoire of North Africa' in *Actas del Primer Congreso de Estudios Árabes e Islámicos,* Cordova, 1962, pp. 319–27.

Stern, S. M.: 'Des Chansons mozarabes: les vers finaux (kharjas) en espagnol dans les muwashshahs arabes et hébreux, édités avec introduction, annotation sommaire et glossaire' in *Università di Palermo, Istituto di Filologia Romanza: Collezione di Testi,* Palermo, 1953; repr. Oxford, 1964, XXVIII, I pp. 66.

Stern, S. M.: *Hispano–Arabic Strophic Poetry,* Oxford 1974; the work summarizes his Oxford theses. The title of the thesis is *The Old Andalusian Muwashshah'.* Bearings on music: pp. 44–5, 68–72, 171 and 208.

Stronski, S.: *La poésie et la réalité aux temps des troubadours. The Teylorian Lecture 1934,* Oxford, 1943.

Stronski, St.: 'Le nom de Gaucelm Faidit dans un acte de 1193' in *Annales du Midi,* 25, p. 273.

Szabics, I.: *Structure et sens poétiques dans les anciennes chansons d'amour occitanes,* in *Acta Litteraria Acad. Sci. Hung.* Vol. 25 (3–4). Budapest, 1983. pp. 237–247.

Szabó, K.: 'A királyi regösökről' (On the Royal Regös Singers) in *Századok,* 1881.

Szabolcsi, B.: 'A középkori magyar énekmondók kérdéséhez' (On the Question of Medieval Hungarian Minstrels) in *Irodalomtörténet,* 1928.

Szabolcsi, B.: *A melódia története* (The History of Melody), Budapest, 1957.

Szabolcsi, B.: 'A zenei földrajz alapvonalai' (Outlines of Musical Geography), an independent chapter in the work *A melódia története* (The History of Melody), Budapest, 1957, p. 333.

Szamota, I.: *A schlägli magyar szójegyzék, a XV. század első negyedéből* (The Schlägl Hungarian Vocabulary, from the First Quarter of the 15th Century), Budapest, 1894.

Szamota, I.–Zolnai, Gy.: *Magyar Oklevélszótár* (Hungarian Document Dictionary), Budapest, 1902–6.

Szövérffy, J.: Die *Annalen der Lateinischen Hymnendichtung, Ein Handbuch, I. Die lateinischen Hymnen bis zum Ende des 11. Jahrhunderts,* Berlin, 1964, p. 118.

Thouzellier, Chr.: *Catharisme et Valdéisme en Languedoc,* Paris, 1966.

Tobler, A.: *Ein Minnesänger der Provence, "Vermischte Beiträge" S. Reihe,* Leipzig, 1912, p. 125.

Torraca, F.: *Le donne italiane nella poesia provenzale,* Florence, 1901; *Bibl. critica della lett. ital.* XXXIX.

Torraca, F.: 'Pietro Vidal in Italia' in *Studi di storia lett.,* 1923, p. 65.

Ulland, W.: *Jouer d'un instrument und die altfranzösischen Beziehungen des Instrumentenspiels.* Bonn, Romanische Seminar der Univ. 1970.

Ursprung, O.: *Um die Frage nach dem arabischen bzw. maurischen Einfluss auf die abendländische Musik des Mittelalters.* ZfMw. 1934.

Van der Werf, H.: *The Chansons of the Troubadours and Trouvères. A Study of the Melodies and their Relation to the Poems,* Utracht, 1972.

Véber, Gy.: 'Überlegungen zum Ursprung der Zagal-Struktur' in *Studia Musicologica,* Budapest, 1979, Vol. XXI, pp. 267–76.

Walzer, M. R.: *Al-Farabi, the Principles of the Views of the Perfect State* (ms.).

Walzer, M. R.: *Platonism in Islamic Philosophy,* Geneva, 1957.

Wellner, F.: *Die Troubadours, Leben und Lieder,* Leipzig, 1942.

Werner, E.: *Pauperes Christi,* Leipzig, 1953.

Werner, E.: *The Sacred Bridge.* London–New York, 1959.

Wiora, W.: *Elementare Melodientypen als Abschnitte mittelalterlicher Liedweisen.* Miscelánea en Homenaje a M. Higinio Anglés. Vol. II. Barcelona 1958–1961. pp. 993–1009.

Zingarelli, N.: 'Peire Vidal e le cose d'Italia' in *Studi Medievali 1,* 1928, p. 336.

Zingarelli, N.: 'Per un "descort" di Amerigo di Pegugliano' in *Intorno a due trovatori in Italia, Biblioteca critica della letteratura italiana,* Florence, 1899, Vol. XXX.

Zingerle, H.: *Tonalität und Melodieführung in den Klauseln der Troubadours- und Trouvèreslieder,* Tutzig, Munich, 1958.